Gabe's arm, still around Lauren, urged her closer. . . .

The warmth of his body, his breath on her hair felt good. Very good. She squirmed. "Don't hold me so—"

"Shhh." He kissed the top of her head. "It's pretend, remember? We can do this."

She couldn't, at least not without feeling far more than she wanted to feel. Her only consolation was that it wouldn't last long. She'd get through tonight, and then she'd straighten everything out, or find a way to force Gabe out of town. She'd do *something* to end this as quickly as . . .

Gently, Gabe nudged her chin up with his thumb. "Ah, Laurie, don't try to be tough. I know you. I know you can be soft," he murmured. "Sweet."

"Don't you dare call me sweet," she said between clenched teeth.

Maybe Gabe pressed his lips hard against hers just to keep her quiet. It worked. By the time he gentled the kiss to featherlight, she couldn't bring herself to keep up the objections.

Praise for *Catch a Dream*

"Welcome a wonderful new voice to the world of contemporary romance. Mary Jane Meier makes a terrific debut with a book that is touching and charming."

—*Romantic Times*

"Ms. Meier has penned a tale that will live in your heart long after you turn the last page!"   —*Romance Reviews Today*

"Mary Jane Meier proves she has talent to make her writing dream happen."   —Harriet Klausner

"Charming characters and colorful scenery peppered with sassy dialogue really make [*Catch a Dream*] an entertaining tale. The characters are wonderfully defined and the story flows seamlessly to the end."   —*Heartrate Reviews*

"Mary Jane Meier's *Catch a Dream* is a delightful debut contemporary for Onyx. . . . Expect great future romance from the charming Mary Jane Meier!"

—*Belles and Beaux of Romance*

Hometown
∽◦ Girl ∽◦

Mary Jane Meier

AN ONYX BOOK

ONYX
Published by New American Library, a division of Penguin Putnam Inc.,
375 Hudson Street, New York, New York 10014, U.S.A.
Penguin Books Ltd, 80 Strand, London WC2R ORL, England
Penguin Books Australia Ltd, Ringwood, Victoria, Australia
Penguin Books Canada Ltd, 10 Alcorn Avenue, Toronto, Ontario,
Canada M4V 3B2
Penguin Books (N.Z.) Ltd, 182–190 Wairau Road, Auckland 10,
New Zealand

Penguin Books Ltd, Registered Offices: Harmondsworth, Middlesex,
England

First published by Onyx, an imprint of New American Library, a division
of Penguin Putnam Inc.

First Printing, February 2002
10 9 8 7 6 5 4 3 2 1

To my mother,
and in memory of my father.

To my wonderful clan of relatives and in-laws.
You have enriched me in countless ways.

Special thanks to my editor, Ellen Edwards, for her expert
guidance, and to my agent, Sue Yuen,
for her enduring support.

Chapter One

After two days en route from her office in Denver, stopping for meetings in Durango and Grand Junction, Lauren Van Horn emerged from her subcompact car on the main street of San Rafael, Utah. Main Street, in this case, meant the *only* street, barring a few side lanes that led to houses and cattle gates. Lauren glanced around, surveying the half dozen pickups and a single battered Jeep parked on either side of the blacktop road.

A spring wind carried the scent of sage, along with a whiff of manure. Dust particles strayed under her eyelids and grated between her teeth. Since San Rafael was her hometown, her roots, she'd always felt that she should love this place. She didn't connect, though. Not since she'd left, or even before then.

"That you, Lauren?" called a gruff, muffled voice. She looked up to see the sheriff catching his usual afternoon siesta on the bench in front of the stone edifice that housed his desk and the community jail.

Sheriff LaDell Purdy knew how to nurture a sliver of shade and a horizontal position. She hadn't seen him lift his straw hat from where it was parked over his face, but he must have peeked as she drove up. The months since her last visit didn't seem to faze him; San Rafael's lazy pace tended to distort time.

"I'm just stopping by my sister's office for a moment, Sheriff. Maybe I'll see you at the Mad House later." The Mad House was her mother's restaurant, located just up the street.

LaDell's reply was half snort, half snore. A lawman's visibility, she'd heard him allege more than once, was crime's primary deterrent. He was visible. Sometimes he was even awake.

She hoped he'd have his eyes open, should she need him. Since nearby Red Rock Canyon had become a wilderness study area the previous summer, largely due to conservationist lobbying, San Rafael wasn't the healthiest location for an environmental attorney such as herself to spend a May weekend. But Becca, her sister, had asked her to come help out with a personal problem—a fresh squabble with the exhusband, apparently. So Lauren was here, for better or worse.

Her goal was to avoid controversy on this trip. It would help if she kept her mouth shut, and she was going to try. Never again would she share her passion for wilderness in this town, not after the uproar she'd caused when she'd unofficially stated her beliefs at a town meeting last November.

San Rafael's citizens were accustomed to making their living off of surrounding federal lands through grazing, logging, oil and gas, and the occasional mining venture. Those lands were gradually being closed to commercial activities through the creation of a new national monument and additional wilderness areas.

Lauren believed threatened fauna, flora, and landscape in magnificent areas like Red Rock had to be protected. Anyone with half a brain should be able to see that. She had tried to tell the San Rafaelites that preserving the land's wild character would eventually lead to increased tourism, their best hope for prosperity. But would they listen? No. Custom and culture ruled their lives. Outsiders and new ideas were anathema.

Which was why she intended to avoid comment on the Bureau of Land Management's soon-to-be-released resource management plan. Neither her mother nor her sister would be happy if Lauren stoked up conflict, as she often tended to do.

She stretched stiff, travel-weary arms above her head, feeling a breeze on her bare midriff. While retucking her blouse into her fawn skirt, she considered wearing the matching jacket and decided against it. Since the hometown folks already thought of her as an overeducated priggish snob, dressing down was for the best.

After locking her car, lest someone nab her laptop or the purse she'd tucked under the seat, she hastened toward the detached white-brick building next to the sheriff's office, where she hoped to find Becca. She pushed open the glass door of the BLM's one-woman field office and scurried inside to escape another gust of spring wind.

Someone was leaning over the single desk, trying to catch papers whirling in the draft, and it wasn't Becca. The someone was male. When he raised his head, Lauren's whole body froze. The door sucked itself closed at her back, leaving her in what seemed like a vacuum from the past.

His face was leaner, his shoulders broader; his curly hair had sun-bleached to a burnished red-gold. His blue eyes hadn't changed, except now the corners showed tiny tracks that told her he'd kept on laughing since they had last met. She, on the other hand, had almost forgotten how.

"Can I help you?" Gabe Randolph showed no sign of recognizing her, but then he wouldn't expect her to be in town any more than she'd expected him. It had, after all, been fourteen years since he'd graduated from high school and left San Rafael.

Finding him here now caught her completely unprepared. She hesitated, thinking he'd figure out who she was any second. When he didn't, she decided to see how long it took. She moistened her chapped lips and tried for poise. "I'm looking for Rebecca Hewitt."

"She's not around, but if you ask the right questions, maybe I can answer them." He settled back in the desk's swivel chair. His slow, patronizing smile made Lauren steam. She didn't know which bothered her more, the blatant sexism or his failure to identify her.

He was bound to notice something familiar sooner or later. Pushing up her sunglasses, she stuck them on top of her head. "Would you care to explain what *you're* doing here?"

"Same as you, ma'am," he drawled with what seemed to be purposeful insolence. "Hoping to find Miz Hewitt."

"Really? I could have sworn I saw you flipping through that stack of papers in front of you."

"Nope. Not me." He propped his feet on the desk while his lazy gaze completed a tour down her ivory silk blouse to the conservative hem of her skirt. He made a quick trip up again and did a double take at her face. His cowboy boots hit the floor. "Laurie!"

"Laur*en*, if you don't mind." She enjoyed his shock in discovering that little Laurie was fully grown. Though she was only three years younger than he, the age gap had been significant during their teenage years. He had barely noticed she was female then, much less a budding woman. Come to think of it, she still resented that. "How are you, Gabe?"

"Good. Real good." Half rising, slanting forward over the desk, he offered his hand, which she gripped briefly. He must have sensed her reluctance, because he didn't push it. He motioned to a chair and sat down in his. Leaning back, he reestablished his filthy boots on the paper-strewn desk surface, his fingers interlocked behind his head. "How've you been?"

She perched on the edge of the chair he'd indicated. "Not bad. I just stopped in to— I live in Denver." She was rattled and wary, unwilling to share more until he did. After so long, she wasn't sure how to begin.

"I heard you cleared out of San Rafael as soon as you could get away," he said. "For Colorado State and then law school at Stanford. Now, I hear, you're with the Colorado Plateau Wilderness Association."

She'd had no idea he'd kept tabs on her; they'd quit corresponding after his first year at a Texas college. After Becca married, to be more precise. "I do love my work," she said, still cautious. "I amuse myself by jumping headfirst into environmental conflicts in Colorado, Arizona, sometimes Utah."

"You're good at it, I bet. You'd pour heart and soul into something like that. Which must make you real popular in this town."

"Only an IRS auditor could be more loved. What are *you* doing back in San Rafael?" she asked.

He met her gaze and held it. "I bought out Great Basin Petroleum."

She'd known that much, just as he must know, as her one-time friend, that his ownership of a company with the worst pollution record of the nineties wouldn't sit well with her. She glanced down at his blue workshirt and saw a confirming red-and-white Great Basin emblem on his left chest pocket. The buyout had happened some thirteen months ago, as she recalled. After last summer passed without his making a personal appearance, the townspeople gave up hoping that he'd come back to run the business himself.

"I thought you'd be in . . . Dallas? . . . tending your Texas drilling company," she said. "Don Ray and some of your other old friends have been bragging for years about your making it big down there."

"Randolph Drilling is based in Austin," Gabe supplied.

Lauren knew that, too, but hadn't wanted to admit she'd paid attention. "Is Mayor Hewitt planning a town party to wreathe you in laurels? Not just anybody would take on a regional company like Great Basin when it was teetering on the brink of bankruptcy. Just like the old state basketball championship days, you're San Rafael's gilded hero once again."

"I'm nobody's hero, at least not by choice." He dropped his feet to the floor and sat forward, hands gripping the desk edge. "You see, I—"

"You don't really plan to send oil rigs into Red Rock, do you?" Great Basin held leases there, acquired before the canyon's change in status. Whether oil exploration and development would be allowed to go forward was still in question.

"That depends," he said, cautious now. "First we'll have to see if the venture looks profitable, and then it'll be up to the BLM. Naturally I'm hoping they'll go my way."

"So you're not on the environmental, save-the-canyon side of this?" she asked, pouring on the sarcasm.

"I'm on the make-a-buck side, if I can manage to get there."

Great Basin's plans weren't any secret, but somehow, seeing Gabe in the flesh, Lauren had difficulty accepting that he would willingly despoil an otherwise national park–quality landscape.

"The CPWA will fight you on the canyon leases, even if the BLM bureaucrats give the go-ahead," she said.

"I figured that. I already have an attorney looking into ways to argue our case."

Her temper rose, less because of the issue than because of the man. "Extraction can't be allowed in a proposed wilderness area, or it will lose the pristine quality that qualifies it for wilderness in the first place."

"I know the reasoning, Laurie. I just don't agree."

This skunk was an impostor, not the Gabe she'd once known, she decided. Not the Gabe with whom she'd mulled over Carson's *Silent Spring* and Abbey's *Desert Solitaire* on summer evenings, all those years ago. Finding him alone in Becca's office worried her. He was up to something.

"You wouldn't be in here searching for an advance copy of the Environmental Assessment, would you?" she demanded. "Does Becca know you're here?"

"She, uh . . . not exactly. But don't kick up your temperature gauge. No way I'd steal anything from Becca. Not even if I thought it would help." He grinned, making it hard to tell whether he meant the disclaimer.

"Seeing you again, knowing who you used to be and what you plan to do now, just makes me sick. Drilling where you propose is tantamount to raping public land, and I—"

"Hold on a minute," he drawled. His slow, Texas-tinged cadence suited the way he moved, the way he smiled. "I like my sex consensual. Who's calling me a rapist?"

He'd often teased a young Lauren out of her seriousness, but it didn't work this time.

"I think you get my point," she said. "All things considered, you have no business sitting at that desk. What's your excuse?"

He leaned halfway across the surface, sleeves rolled up to his elbows, big hands rumpling stacks of paper and almost knocking over an open box of chocolates. "I don't need an excuse. Walk with me to the Mad House, and I'll explain everything on the way."

She'd forgotten how deep and seductive his voice could be, but she didn't let the intonation get to her. "I'd rather hear your fast talking at the scene of the crime."

"What crime?"

"Rooting through government documents is strictly prohibited in most social circles. Watch out, or someone might start naming statutes."

He lifted a paper from a disordered pile and invited her to take a look. She did, before glancing up to see his raised eyebrow.

"Camping permits aren't exactly top secret," he said. "And I wasn't rooting."

"Objection sustained on camping permits." She squinted to read an upside down document and tapped a bronze-painted fingernail on it. "What about this county commissioner's report on the two-tracks leading into the canyon? The county claims those are real roads that ought to be maintained—which would be bad for Red Rock's preservation as wilderness."

"But good for my oil leases," Gabe added. "That's old news. Try again."

Irritated with his nonchalance, Lauren glanced around the small room, wondering what he might find here that would aid his cause. Large, framed maps of the area's federal lands filled two walls. A third was decorated with a canyon watercolor and one of Becca's Native American–style sand paintings that always struck Lauren as simplistic, and yet very Becca. She looked back at Gabe, gauging his guilt. "Are you sure you didn't tie up my sister and lock her in a storage closet?"

He *tsk*ed. "If I wanted to get rid of someone, a storage closet wouldn't be my first choice. Get a grip, Laurie. Why wouldn't I get along with Becca? We might have some differences of opinion, but she's not a hothead like you."

"I'm not—"

He laughed.

"Okay, so I'm defensive when it comes to my sister. She's been known to trust people more than she should."

The amusement faded from his mouth and eyes. "Becca never should have married Joe Hewitt. The good news is, since I've moved back to town, we—"

"You're living in San Rafael? Since when?"

"January."

Five months. He must have arrived right after her sister's divorce went through, not long after Lauren's last visit. He and Becca were the same age, graduated from high school the same year. At one time everyone had assumed they'd get married.

Her eyes narrowed. "I'm surprised Becca didn't tell me." Maybe she shouldn't be surprised. Becca's lack of enthusiasm for keeping Red Rock Canyon untouched—which contradicted, in Lauren's opinion, a BLM employee's duty to protect the land—had strained family communications over the past few months. Knowing how Lauren felt about the canyon leases, Becca would have hesitated to mention Gabe's return.

He held up the box of candy. "Have a truffle, Little Bit. Your tongue could use some sweetening."

Why did she have the feeling he was trying to change the subject? And she didn't like what was sliding off *his* tongue. Laurie. Little Bit. She should protest, but there was something in the way Gabe said those old nicknames that she wasn't quite ready to quash.

She glanced down at the gold box in his hand. A much younger Lauren would have taken anything he offered, done anything he asked, but she'd traveled a long road since then. So had he. The owner of Great Basin could never measure up to the Gabe of old—Becca's first flame, Lauren's . . . friend.

"Where is my sister?" She let her impatience show while carefully concealing a less acceptable weakness.

"She oversees a lot of territory in this county, and that means hours of driving." He set down the candy within Lauren's reach. "Which leads us back to why I'm here, if you're still interested."

She'd lost sight of the original question, but she homed in on it again. "Please proceed."

"Missy has a piano lesson in half an hour with Mrs. Throckmorton. Remember Boom-Boom Throckmorton?"

"I remember." Lauren was bemused by the way time went into reverse whenever she came back to this town. Becca's daughter Melissa Louise—known as Missy—had existed for only seven years, but Mrs. Throckmorton would be just the same. Three hundred pounds of bosom and lungs, thundering out the count. *One*-and, *two*-and . . .

"Old lady Throckmorton gets real unhappy if a student arrives unprepared. I was about to walk Missy over for her lesson when she realized that her sheet music was locked in her house, and she didn't have a key."

"My mother must keep an extra one in the restaurant," Lauren suggested.

"She probably does, somewhere, but it's Friday afternoon. You know how busy the Mad House gets on Fridays. So while Missy was stuffing herself with cookies and milk in the restaurant kitchen, I ran over here to fetch Becca's extra." He held up a brass key, his proof of innocence. "For Missy."

"Don't call her that," Lauren said. "It's demeaning and sexist."

"Missy doesn't complain."

"She's too young to know better. One more question, while I'm thinking about it. How did you get into this building?"

"Found the door unlocked," Gabe said. "Becca's never had a knack for details. She usually doesn't lock her house, either. Not that it's all that necessary around here."

The ins and outs of small-town negligence were beyond Lauren, and always had been. Gabe's easy access to the BLM desk was just another example of San Rafael's laid-back ways.

She checked her digital Timex. "Becca said she'd meet me at four. I'm a few minutes early, but I would have thought . . ."

Gabe shrugged. "She'll show up eventually. The last couple of weeks have been hard on her. She's had a pile of rush paperwork to do, and you know Becca's allergic to deadlines." He scraped back his chair and stood. He was taller than she remembered, well over six feet.

To avoid being dwarfed, she stood too, but her five-foot-eight still seemed short.

Putting a man in his place with words usually worked for her. She'd developed the technique a long time ago, often practicing her gibes on Gabe himself. She couldn't resist sparring with him now. "I need to have a talk with Becca. She really ought to keep her house key away from rednecks in lizard-skin boots."

Gabe had always had a comeback, and he hadn't changed there. He glanced down at his feet. "Lizard skin? Can't see what's under the scuffs and dust just now, but I'd guess my boots are still plain cowhide, same as last time I checked." He smiled a slow, lazy smile and eased around the desk toward Lauren.

When he draped an arm over her shoulders, she was too surprised to evade him. "I wish you wouldn't—"

"Good to see you too, Laurie. Tell me, are you as successful as you look?"

She knew teasing when she heard it. A glance at her reflection in the glass door showed the hopelessly windblown condition of her dark, shoulder-length hair. Smudged mascara rimmed her gray eyes.

"I've had better days." She ducked free of his loose embrace and headed for the exit. Daydreaming about Gabe used to be a consuming passion for her, but she'd outgrown his jock charm a long time ago. She felt—maybe—the smallest vestige of a gut reaction, the tiniest bit of elemental lust. Whatever it was, she ignored it.

"Wait a minute." He moved faster than she did, effectively blocking the door. He turned her toward him and tipped her chin, gently brushing his thumb over the corner of her eye. "There's a speck of grit right . . . here."

She'd been about to snap at him for getting too close, but since what he'd done was so innocent, she said, "Thanks," instead.

Gabe tucked his hands into the back pockets of his jeans, reverting to big-brother mode. "I almost didn't recognize you without your Miss Professor spectacles." He gazed at her with a concentrated intensity, as if he were trying to connect the old Lauren to the new.

"I only wore them for reading," she said.

"No wonder I remember you wearing them all the time. You were always reading. Environmental essays. Theories about evolution, stars, the universe. And"—he grinned—"science fiction, wasn't it?"

He'd always teased her about the science fiction. She was glad he didn't know she was still a bit of a Trekkie.

She smothered a smile. "I should have read your favorites, the legal thrillers, considering what I ended up doing for a living."

"It really is good to see you, Laurie. I just wish Becca's troubles weren't the reason." His eyebrows converged, as if another possibility occurred to him. "You are here for her, aren't you? Because of Joe's threats?"

Threats? Becca hadn't mentioned threats from the infamous ex. Had Lauren been so critical of the way her sister handled her life that Becca had hesitated to share the worst?

"Of course that's why I'm here," she said, working around her ignorance. "Joe is an idiot with latent violent tendencies, if you ask me. Becca should have moved out of his range years ago."

"I don't trust him either. Especially not with Missy."

"So that's what this is about!" Lauren blurted. "If he's demanding more visitation, it's only to hassle Becca. In the divorce settlement, he asked for Saturdays and an overnight once a month. He got that. Why would . . ." She could guess, though. If Becca was involved with Gabe . . .

"Maybe I shouldn't have said anything." He frowned. "I thought you already knew."

Her lack of insider information made her feel foolish, so

she rushed to fill the void. "I suppose Becca wanted to break the news to me in person. When we talked, all she said was that Joe was giving her fits. I assumed he'd started drinking and calling her at odd hours again."

"That, too." Gabe hesitated before adding, "Joe wants more than visitation, Laurie. He wants full custody."

"What? That's absurd! With his irresponsible history, no judge would rule in favor of—"

"Think again. There's some choice gossip going the rounds. I'm afraid Becca's lost the sympathy card."

"It's you, isn't it?" Lauren accused. "You could have shown a little class and let the ink dry on the divorce papers before you showed up in town."

Gabe winced. "Yeah, I know how it looks. That's what Joe thinks, too, but he's all wrong. The district drilling supervisor here quit suddenly, putting the whole operation in a bind. That's why I came when I did. When I got here, I found—"

"Do me a favor and don't try to explain," she said. Gabe had set Joe off. That figured.

He shrugged. "I did offer to hire Becca a family law expert. She wouldn't accept."

"*I'll* hire her one, if need be," Lauren said. "Having you throwing your money around won't do her any good."

"Becca's worried Joe might lean on his relatives in the court system." Gabe looked grim, angrier than Lauren had ever seen him. "If I had my way, one more underhanded move out of Joe and he'd be singing soprano in the church choir for the rest of his sorry life."

"I'm not in favor of violence, but in Joe's case, I might make an exception." Lauren glanced out through the open window blinds. "Maybe I misunderstood where Becca and I were supposed to meet. I'll stop by the restaurant and check with Mom." She wanted out of the cramped office. Gabe was infringing on her personal space, and he had an effect on her that she didn't care to analyze.

Since he still stood in her path, she shouldered past him to push at the door, which didn't give. He nudged her aside.

"What do you think you're—" She ended her protest when his pull on the door handle did the trick. Ignoring his smile at her expense, she hurried outside. Her stomach felt queasy, probably because she hadn't eaten since breakfast.

She stopped on the sidewalk to breathe and take stock without Gabe in her way. Heat waves rising off the blacktop road made it seem as if she'd walked into an oven. Bright afternoon light burned her eyes until she remembered the sunglasses on top of her head and pulled them on. In the distance she could see the cool blue of the Henry Mountains. The foreground blazed in the high-altitude desert sun.

A poster in the window of the Top Chop Grocery across the street read ENVIRONMENTALISTS MAKE GREAT DOG FOOD, which didn't do much to settle her stomach.

She had to help her sister, but she didn't want to stay in San Rafael any longer than necessary—especially not with Gabe as a testament to disappointing outcomes. Great Basin Petroleum. It didn't get any more disappointing than that.

Gabe had followed her out and now stood beside her, studying her face. "You okay?"

"I seem to have . . . underestimated what I was walking into here." She felt like more of a worm than Joe Hewitt, her ex-brother-in-law. If she'd kept in better touch with Becca, she would have known about this trouble sooner and might have counseled her. Not that Becca always listened, but Lauren felt it was her duty to offer advice. Preferably *before* a crisis, not after.

Coarse mortar snagged her blouse as she leaned her back against the building's brick wall. She pressed hard enough for the sharp edges to bite into her spine.

Gabe braced a shoulder against the bricks beside her. "Don't worry. We'll help Becca work things out. You and I might be light-years apart on everything else, but we both care about your sister and Missy."

Lauren did care. In the future she intended to do a better job of showing it. How much Gabe cared, how involved he and Becca really were, remained to be seen.

As Lauren gazed across the sun-gold dusty sidewalk, she could almost imagine that nothing had changed. Time was deceptive in San Rafael.

The ambience was as dull as ever: a smattering of potted geraniums, sleepy storefronts, and a lone traffic light covered with canvas. The covering would be removed during the summer, optimistically referred to by the townspeople as the "busy" season.

A familiar snore resonated from the bench in front of the sheriff's office. Across the street and down a block, she saw the Mad House sign's shaky, crooked letters painted in multicolored hues, faded and cracked, as they had always been in Lauren's memory.

Old Ezra sat in the shade of the restaurant's wooden porch, in one of the weathered, slatted chairs that had been there since forever, as had Ezra. In her mind she could smell his pipe smoke and imagine the shine of brass buttons on his denim vest.

"Main Street looks the same," she said. "Quiet. Peaceful."

"The peace won't last," Gabe predicted. "The shit's about to hit the proverbial fan over exactly what restrictions the BLM's going to place on land use in Red Rock Canyon."

"Thanks for the warning. I'm well aware that no one wants to hear what *I* think on that subject."

He laughed. "Now, that's got to be the understatement of the century. You were always battling something, Laurie. I remember when you were in ninth grade and editor of the school paper. The article you wrote on Mayor Hewitt nighthunting deer out of season, using the high-beam spotlights he borrowed from Sheriff Purdy, sure got everyone's attention."

She allowed herself a small smile. "San Rafael politics needed a cleanup. If I'd been wiser, I would have sued for first amendment violation when the school board shut down my press."

"Maybe if you'd aimed at something less contentious to start with, you might have stayed editor for more than one issue."

"I like tilting at windmills, Gabe."

"So I've noticed." He gazed at her thoughtfully. "Little Laurie, San Rafael's own Miz Quixote. Now I guess you'll be tilting at Joe. And at oil rigs, if you get the chance. My oil rigs. Believe it or not, I admire your moxie."

"Compliments will get you nowhere." She couldn't say the same for his eyes and smile. Those might persuade her to warm up to him considerably if she didn't watch out.

She was glad she wouldn't have to represent the CPWA in any actions against Great Basin, which she knew had the town's wholehearted support. Dealing with Gabe Randolph would be even tougher. Long-term, she had a feeling his smile could melt polar ice caps.

"Walk with me, Laurie." Again the low, seductive voice.

She tried to think of an excuse, but nothing came to mind. "Um . . . sure. We're going the same way, I suppose." She peeled herself off the wall and fell right into San Rafael's time warp, forgetting she didn't want to be there, forgetting she really didn't want to walk with Gabe.

A bansheelike wail broke her trance. She turned her head to see a huge black-and-gray dog in the back of an open Jeep parked directly across the street. It pointed its nose toward the sky and emitted another wail, a hound's hunting bay.

She wasn't a canine fan. That big, noisy animal had better be tied to . . .

The sign about dog food flashed through her mind as the drooling beast leaped out of the Jeep and charged straight for her.

Chapter Two

Gabe was congratulating himself on coaxing uptight Lauren into unwinding a notch when he, too, heard and saw the dog. Bullwinkle must have just awakened from an afternoon nap and noticed a newcomer. Within milliseconds, the hound's lazy gallop had Little Bit Van Horn edging behind Gabe as if he were her personal security guard.

He grinned at becoming knight-errant material all of a sudden. Of course, Bullwinkle *was* the size of a small horse, with more forward momentum than a stampeding buffalo. The dog's wolfish howl was enough to curdle any unprepared person's blood. Gabe's amusement vanished as he recalled that Lauren was an attorney of the litigious variety. Doing something to prevent a dog–woman collision and subsequent filing of charges seemed the better part of valor.

He held out his arms in his most chivalrous stance. "Down!" he ordered the dog.

Bullwinkle's bay diminished to a whine; he slowed and collapsed at Gabe's feet. Gabe turned to see that Lauren was brandishing a lethal-looking high-heeled shoe in one hand, ready and able on the defense.

Good thing he'd stopped the dog, or Bullwinkle might have lost some teeth. Hunkering down, he scratched the hound's floppy ears. "The big fella's harmless, Laurie. The worst he'd do is lick off your makeup."

She lowered the shoe, her gaze fixed on the dog. Apparently deciding Gabe had him under control, she reached down to slip on the footwear, then thumped a hand over her chest as if trying to restore cardiac output. "Who—or what— is that . . . that . . ."

"Cute, isn't he?" Gabe said optimistically.

"Ugly as recycled sin and a hazard to humanity." She glanced toward the bench where the town's lawman snored. "I ought to rouse Sheriff Purdy. This animal's owner deserves a ticket and a hefty fine."

"What for?" Gabe was starting to wish he'd snatched the shoe and let Bullwinkle give her a good sliming.

"For scaring the wits out of pedestrians, maybe?" she suggested. "Surely San Rafael has a leash law by now, like civilized villages everywhere."

"Nope." He shook his head as if the lack grieved him, although it didn't, not a bit. "Even if there were such a law, you wouldn't turn me in, would you?"

Lauren stared down at Gabe, who was still crouched beside man's best friend. "Th-that thing belongs to . . ."

"Me. Or me to him, depending on how you look at it." Gabe put his hands on either side of the dog's damp jowls and held up the innocent snout. "Bullwinkle's part bluetick hound, part something with mammoth genes. He's my hunting dog."

"What, pray tell, does he hunt?" Lauren asked, regaining her full measure of prissiness.

"Anything that catches his fancy. He's great at finding women." As if he'd been given permission, Bullwinkle rose on all four oversize paws and approached Lauren, nudging his snout under the front of her skirt, loudly sucking in the aroma.

She gingerly shooed him away. "I can see you haven't taught him manners."

Gabe pulled a handkerchief—the pink-and-purple one Missy had given him for an Easter present—from his back pocket and knotted it around the animal's neck to serve as a collar. "We're working on smoothing the rough edges."

"I advise shock treatment." The hand she held out to shield herself from the animal was a little shaky.

"You're not still scared of dogs, are you?" he asked, incredulous that this grown-up, belligerent Lauren would be afraid of anything.

"Of course not." She straightened her spine to conform to the brick wall. "Hurtling beasts, though, I would rather avoid. And I *don't* want him slobbering on me."

"No problem. Go on, boy. Back to the Jeep."

The dog trotted across the street and hopped into the open seat of the dust-dulled red four-by-four.

Lauren looked from the Jeep to Gabe. "What, no Humvee for the head honcho of Great Basin?"

He shook his head. "Sorry not to fit the mold. I work hard and employ a few people, Laurie. Ease up and give credit where credit's due."

"You expect applause? Tears?"

"How about respect?" he said, truly irritated now. The younger Laurie had admired him. He'd kind of figured the older version would cut him some slack.

"Respect? For someone who would commercialize the untouched splendor of Red Rock Canyon for personal gain? You *are* an arrogant boor."

"Me, arrogant? What about you, all puffed up and snooty?"

"I am not snooty."

"And I'm not out to destroy anything," he said, hanging on to his cool with considerable difficulty.

She snorted.

"I'm a damn nice guy. Women love my sensitivity."

"Sensitivity? Ha!"

Gabe was getting angrier by the minute, which made him try harder not to show it. "I'm so damn sensitive, even my studly dog wears pink. Didn't you notice?"

"I assumed you were color-blind." She lifted her nose in the air and bypassed him. When she reached a shiny canary yellow bug that proudly displayed its dinky 2.0-liter engine size under its model name, she unlocked the passenger door and took out a shoulder bag. It looked like real leather, but for Lauren, the rabid conservationist, it had to be faux.

As she slammed the door shut, he glanced in and saw that she'd left several items behind. "Can you make it through dinner without the briefcase, laptop, and Palm Pilot?"

She paused, frowning. "I don't think I'll need them in the restaurant." She seemed dead serious, as if she'd actually considered lugging the stuff along.

Gabe had noticed her bumper stickers in passing. Now he backed up to read them again. TREE POWER, 4.8 MILLION ACRES OF WILDERNESS, and VOTE WILD.

"Bad idea." He shook his head as Lauren turned to see what was keeping him. "You shouldn't have parked your Tweety Bug in plain sight, not with inflammatory labels plastered all over the ass end."

She bristled. "The stickers reflect what I think. I'm not ashamed of them."

"Guess not. Anyone else would have better sense. If you drive around enough lonely dirt roads sporting that kind of message, you're liable to meet up with a truckload of certifiable rednecks eager to change more than just your mind. At the very least, you'll end up minus a bumper."

"Is that a threat?"

"Not from me, but there are a lot of people out to make statements. Do yourself a favor and hide your radical bumper stickers in Becca's garage, first chance you get."

"Gabe Randolph, I've been harassed, called every name in the book, and, yes, I've even been shot at on one occasion. So don't bother giving *me* your—"

"Shot at?" He hated to think about it. Lauren had the guts to wave a red flag at a raging bull, and if the bull were pawing a hole in one of her precious wilderness areas, she'd probably wave two flaming torches and a lawsuit. "You really ought to consider another line of work."

"I'm committed to what I do." She sent him a sideways glance. "Tell me, what does *your* bumper say? 'Drill it and spill it'? Or maybe, 'Feed the naysayers to the dogs?'"

He laughed, though he doubted Lauren was making a joke. "No need to be sacrosanct. If you're so eager to preserve the natural state, why do you own a car? You could always walk wherever you go. Ride a bicycle. Take a bus."

Hitching the purse strap over her shoulder, she kept up with him as he proceeded down the street.

"I've considered other modes of transportation," she said. "I've even used them once in a while, but they take extra time. I need every second to fight evil, rich oil barons. That's your category, in case you missed the reference."

"I like the 'rich' part, but I'm no power freak. Compared to some, I'm one of the good guys. White hat, silver bullets. Always eager to save the day. Most ladies appreciate the service I provide."

She let that pass and kept right on tooting her horn of principles. "I do accept the fact that today's world runs on petroleum, but drilling should be confined to less delicate landscapes. If everyone drove a car that gets forty-eight miles to the gallon, as I do, we wouldn't need every drop of oil we could get our hands on. We'd put barbarians like you, who would blow up the Grand Canyon to make a buck, out of business."

"You're about as subtle as a twelve-gauge shotgun, Laurie."

"Don't you appreciate having someone represent the other side? Afraid I'll find sympathizers?"

He chuckled at that absurdity. "Environmentalists? Living here? You'd more likely find double-dip ice-cream cones in hell."

She sighed. "I give. Why don't we call a truce for now? I'm in town for a family visit, not a war."

"That's why I feel obligated to keep you out of tar and feathers. For Becca's sake. She has enough complications."

"So it seems." She lowered her chin, looking genuinely upset. "Becca and I haven't talked much lately."

He raised an eyebrow.

Lauren returned a defensive scowl. "Don't look at me like that. We've traded answering machine messages. When we did connect, one or the other of us was in a hurry."

"That's one good thing about small towns. It's no problem to see each other in the flesh." He grimaced. "Come to think of it, that's one of the worst things about small towns, too. Depending on the person you're seeing, it's not always a plus."

"I know," she said. "Take running into you, for example."

That stung. He was pleased to see her. Or he had been, until she'd started acting so damn superior. "You ought to throttle back on the charm, sweetheart. A man can only take so much."

Little Bit wasn't the same. For one thing, she wasn't little anymore. She was tall, elegant, curved in all the right places. Easy on the eyes, but hard on a man's complacency. Like the old Laurie, she was up-front in expressing her opinions. Unfortunately, what she thought of him wasn't too complimentary.

They had crossed the street and reached the restaurant steps. Gabe cleared his throat. "We should get together while you're here, Laurie."

She stopped and turned to him, frowning. "I don't see why."

Maybe she was right, even if there were things left unsaid between them. But the problem with Joe was going to come up. They'd have to talk. "Well, there's Missy. Don't you think we should—"

"Gabe?" Ezra stood on the porch above them, his milk-clouded eyes aimed in their direction, his ebony face set in puzzlement. He leaned both hands on his cane and swayed his head from side to side as if to examine the view he couldn't see. "Who's that with you? Is it Laurie-girl? Sweet Laurie?"

Sweet as a cornered scorpion, Gabe thought as she ascended the steps to greet the old man. She had grace and dignity going for her, but she came up short on honey.

"I'm here." Lauren's voice was clear, vibrant, unmistakable.

"Knew it." Ezra sniffed. "My Laurie smells like wildflowers."

Gabe had noticed the perfume, too, in jarring contrast to her she-beast persona. As a kid she'd been prickly, but he'd known the soft, sensitive soul beneath. Now that old Laurie was buried deep, if she existed at all.

Her pale cheeks flushed as she clasped the blind man's gnarled hand in both of hers. "I never could hide from you, Ezra. It's good to be with someone who knows the *real* Lauren."

Gabe wondered why she slanted an accusatory glance in his direction. Was that a hint that *he* didn't know her? As outspoken as she was, he knew all he wanted to know.

The Mad House front door blasted open and a tow-headed bundle of energy burst through. It was Missy, who, after almost bowling Lauren over, promptly dove for Gabe and tackled his legs.

"Did you get the key? We've gotta go now, or Mrs.

Throckmorton'll yell real loud and make me do scales and chords till—" Missy turned her elfin face to stare at the woman she'd almost blitzed. "Aunt Lauren?"

With an uncertain smile, Lauren crouched down to kid level. "Hello, Melissa Louise."

Missy's rosebud lips took a downturn. She disliked her full name and avoided it like a double dose of chicken pox. If Lauren had any interest in winning the kid's affection, Gabe figured she'd started out all wrong.

The little girl edged close enough to endure Lauren's peck on the cheek, then quickly backed away. "Mama said you might come see us, but I thought you'd change your mind. You lied when you said you'd come to my birthday party."

Lauren flinched. "I'm sorry, Melissa. I was in the middle of a big case. Did you get the Barbie I sent?"

"Yes." She flitted away from her aunt and latched onto Gabe's hand. "Can we go now?"

"Sure," Gabe said. "See you later, Laurie." He paused long enough to watch her straighten slowly, a pained expression shadowing her features.

He felt a twinge of sympathy and even thought about scolding Missy for being rude. However, the kid could have done worse. She could have told the whole truth and said she loathed Barbie dolls and had donated the gift as a chew toy for Bullwinkle.

Missy's blunt dismissal might be good for Lauren. Maybe she'd catch on that she was not a paragon in the eyes of all. Maybe she'd learn that humility was a goddamn virtue.

Holding that thought, Gabe hurried Missy off the porch to fetch sheet music and beat the clock to Mrs. Throckmorton's piano.

Lauren stared after the departing child, her heart aching. Where had she gone wrong? Why didn't Melissa like her? She had never been prosecuted and summarily dismissed by a first grader before. And since the child was her own niece, whom Lauren wanted to love and be loved by, the rejection hurt badly.

"Missy reminds me of you," Ezra said from behind her.

Lauren turned to face him. "Is she always so tactless?"

Ezra nodded. "Smart and sassy, and too honest for her own good. That's kids for you. They call it like they see it."

Lauren sighed. "I can't seem to connect with her, not since she outgrew diapers and cuddling. Children are more complicated than I gave them credit for." She and Melissa had been pals a few years ago, before Lauren had started the demanding job with CPWA. She hadn't realized that longer intervals between visits would make so much difference.

"Missy's not an easy child," Ezra said. "She's a prideful, bossy, serious little thing. Like you were, honey, except she's got worse troubles, what with her mama and daddy not getting along."

The real tragedy was that Melissa's daddy had never taken much interest in his daughter. Until now. "What's going on with Joe?" Lauren asked.

Ezra pursed his lips. "Sit a spell with me, and I'll tell you what I can." He hobbled over to one of the weathered chairs and leaned his cane against the Mad House's outer wall. Holding his back, he lowered himself onto the hard seat. Lauren took the chair beside him.

He dug a pipe and a pouch of tobacco out of a vest pocket. "Couple of months ago, Joe starts going by the house most every day, says Missy needs checking on. Truth is, he's checking on Becca. He uses the child as an excuse. Becca tells him he hasn't got the right to be spying on her, so he says he'll go back to court. Says he'll take Missy for the summer. Says he'll take Missy all the time. Becca's worried herself plumb sick."

"You'd think Joe would let them alone," Lauren said.

Ezra gave a deep snort as he packed tobacco into his pipe

bowl. "Joe wants folks to think he's important. Wants Becca
to think so, too. Seems to me he's picked the wrong ways to
go about it, is all." Ezra shook his head. "He's sunk mighty
low, using a child. It ain't right."

"Scheming fits him," Lauren said. "Excess ego fits him,
too. But why go for custody?"

Ezra made a clicking sound with his tongue. "He wants
the say-so."

"Over his child? Or over Becca?"

"Well, now, I . . ." He lit the pipe and solemnly puffed it.
"I reckon your sister ought to tell you the rest."

"How does Gabe fit in?" Lauren persisted. "What's he
done to make Joe jealous? Because that's what's happened,
isn't it?"

Ezra's clouded eyes stared in her direction. When Lauren
was a little girl, she'd believed he saw farther and deeper
than other people. Even now that he'd gone stone blind, she
still believed he saw too much.

He took the pipe stem from his mouth. Smoke rose from
the bowl and curled in front of him. "I only know what folks
say. And you know folks. Can't b'lieve hardly a one of 'em."

Lauren knew he was holding out on her. "It would help if
you'd tell *me* what they're saying."

"Not this time it wouldn't. I don't cotton to idle gossip."
The pipe went back into his mouth for more puffing. Ever
since he'd retired as the Mad House cook fifteen years ago,
people sat on this porch and told Ezra their sins. He took his
confessor role as seriously as a priest, never repeating a confidence. However, he'd always shared idle gossip freely
enough.

"I'll find out anyway," she coaxed.

"That's right, child. You will. Talk to Becca and get the
whole truth."

Since Becca did deserve to tell her own story, Lauren gave
up. She'd learn the facts soon enough.

"How are you getting along?" she asked. *Without Chloe* was the unspoken addition. It had been nearly two years since Ezra's wife had suffered a massive stroke and died in his arms. He seemed back to his old self now, duded up in a starched shirt and bola tie, but she sensed the sadness in him.

He pulled a well-worn blue velvet pouch from the upper left pocket of his vest and handed it to her. "Open it, Laurie. I can't see for myself these days. Tell me how pretty Chloe looks."

Lauren slid out the familiar gold locket, darkened by age and handling. Inside, a dapper Ezra's photo showed clearly on one side, but Chloe's was almost worn away from the old man's fingertips caressing the image of his fair-haired, blue-eyed bride. "She's lovely, Ezra. Beautiful and strong."

"We had those pictures made on our wedding day, both of us past forty. After taking all that time to find one another, we felt mighty lucky." Ezra had loved telling about their wedding day even when his wife was by his side. Now, sadly, the telling was all he had.

"You look lucky," Lauren said. He was beaming in the photo. "And Chloe has the biggest, widest smile, as if she's about to burst with pure joy." Though that part was faded, both Lauren and Ezra still recalled Chloe's expression.

His present-day grin flashed white teeth and a gold molar. "Sure do hope my eyes cure up once I get to heaven. I have one powerful hankering to see that smile again."

"Whenever I smell cinnamon and ginger, I think of her," Lauren said. After retiring from teaching, Chloe had run the one-room county library in back of the sheriff's office. During the well-attended story hour each afternoon, she'd passed around her trademark cookies, making every child feel welcome and loved. She'd never given birth, so she'd treated all children as her own.

Ezra wasn't the only one who missed Chloe.

Lauren blinked away the moisture in her eyes. She slipped

the locket back into its pouch and tucked it into Ezra's vest. "You'll see her again. If I know Chloe, she's reading a story to heaven's kids about now. She's saving you a seat."

He nodded, closing his eyes.

Lauren leaned over to hug him hard, feeling the brass vest buttons, smelling his tobacco, and sharing a memory of cookies and spice.

When Lauren entered the restaurant, Hannah Van Horn, her mother, looked up from wiping the lunch counter. After a quick glance down the length of the oak-paneled room, she rushed around the open end of the bar. Before Lauren could get out a hello, Hannah was hissing, "Shh." As she hurried to her daughter, wisps of faded brown hair escaped a bun on the top of her head and fluttered around her heart-shaped face.

She touched Lauren on the shoulder and motioned for her to follow through an arched doorway. The offshoot room— Hannah called it the alcove—connected to the kitchen. Usually the space was reserved for private parties and favored clientele. In this case, Lauren knew her mother was using it to hide her alien offspring. The wound was an old one, but the pain was still sharp.

Hannah was short and plump, pretty in a matronly way, and a master at maintaining a careful distance—from Lauren, at least. Even when they were out of the main room's line of sight, she didn't hug, didn't kiss.

"Good to see you, baby." She gave Lauren's shoulder a slight squeeze. "Sorry to rush you into the alcove so quick, but there's loggers and roustabouts out there. It'd be best if you came in the back way next time, if you don't mind."

"All right, Mom. If that's how you feel, I'll—"

"No need to be in a huff. You know how it is. Once those boys know you're here, they'll have something to say. You'll open your mouth and heat 'em up worse. Before you know it, we'll have a repeat of last November. If there's going to be a riot, I'd just as soon it didn't happen in the Mad House."

Hannah pulled out a chair, pushed Lauren into it, and sat in the one beside her. "So tell me, are you engaged to your rich-as-sin corporate lawyer yet?"

Lauren cursed under her breath. In a moment of weakness during her last visit, she'd mentioned Tim Donovan to Hannah. *Big mistake.* "Not engaged. Not yet." Not ever, but she'd rather not explain that now.

"Good," her mother said.

Good? Lauren almost fell off her chair. Why wasn't Hannah urging marriage, the sooner the better, as she always did? What was wrong with this picture?

Hannah had begun preaching white dresses and wifely decorum when Lauren was barely past puberty. *A plain, gangly little thing can't afford to be picky. A girl without looks has to catch as catch can.* Lauren had learned all the folksy aphorisms that applied to an undesirable woman's best bets for reeling in a husband.

Though she knew her mother had only meant to be helpful, she would have taken it better if Becca had been subjected to the same lectures. Becca had been the pretty one, the congenial one. She'd had boyfriends from kindergarten on. In high school she'd been cheerleader and prom queen. She'd had Gabe. And then Joe. Emminently forgettable Joe had given her nothing but some broken bones from a motorcycle wreck, a lot of heartache, and a kid he now wanted to snatch away.

"Did you go by Becca's office?" Hannah asked.

"Yes. She wasn't there. Gabe Randolph was, which seemed curious to me."

Hannah pulled a napkin out of the holder and used it to scrub at a spot on the table. "Gabe's moved back into his daddy's old house, you know, right next door to Becca. It's good to see a Randolph living there again. Like times past,

you might say." Hannah had pushed Becca and Gabe together, years ago, in hopes that they would end up marrying.
It sounded as if she was giving it another try.

"Not quite the same," Lauren corrected. "Becca and Gabe
aren't high school kids. There's Missy to consider. I hope
Becca's using her head." By now Lauren was convinced that
Becca wasn't, but there was no point in saying anything critical about the favored daughter.

"You do plan to help, don't you?" Hannah asked.

"With the custody mess Joe's kicking up? Sure, I'll do
what I can." Technically Becca hadn't asked, but when she
did, Lauren wouldn't refuse.

"I'm glad that's settled, then." Hannah popped out of her
chair, using the napkin to swab her face. "Whew, it's hot in
here. You hungry? How about iced tea and a slice of pie?"

"Sounds terrific." Lauren would have said so even if she
weren't starving. In that one way, Hannah showed she cared,
which seemed to have a positive effect on both of them.

"I have your favorite raspberry, fresh from the oven."
Hannah had already headed through the swinging kitchen
door, where Lauren heard her telling someone to leave the
salad makings and see to the customers out front.

A moment later Trish Lomax came out, tucking her short,
strawberry-blond hair behind her ears. When she saw Lauren, she paused with a grin lighting up her freckled face. She
was a big woman, taller than Lauren. Trish's waist had en-
larged ten inches or more since she had been Lauren's school
friend, but she was as jovial as ever, still ready with her
toothy smile. She threw back her shoulders and strutted up,
delivering a robust, playful shove that nearly knocked Lauren to the floor.

"Aren't you a rare sight! Lookin' good, Laurie."

"Thanks." Lauren appreciated Trish's consistent friendli-
ness, something she had found in short supply in San Rafael.

"I was planning to stop by your house later on to say hello. What are you doing here?"

Trish tucked her wide bottom onto a seat next to Lauren and stage-whispered, "Your mama begged me to fill in. She can't get good help, paying what she pays, which isn't much, not even with the tips."

"I thought she'd hired a new girl."

"That'd be Kayleen Throckmorton." Trish leaned closer, still whispering. "She came here from Vegas to live with Granny Boom-Boom. The girl's not what you'd call reliable. She shows up maybe half the time. The other half, I help out when I can."

"What about the Hair Affair?"

Trish owned and operated the town's only beauty salon, located in a back room of her house. "Business stinks lately. Everybody's worried about jobs and hanging on to pennies. This Red Rock hoopla has us scared. It'll be the death of . . ."

Trish must have seen a reaction in Lauren's face that reminded her not to say any more about Red Rock. "You married yet?" She probably figured her old friend would shed her radical ideas once she found herself a husband.

"Not yet." To Lauren, marriage was not the prime sign of personal progress.

"What're you waiting for, girl? Time's awasting." Trish certainly hadn't waited long; she'd snagged Don Ray Lomax the same month she'd finished high school. With an admonition to stop by the beauty shop, she hefted herself to her feet and hurried away toward the main room.

Trish was a bighearted soul, but to her way of thinking, an unmarried female could never be truly happy, not even if she were winning Nobel prizes, or making millions in corporate America. Love, of course, was Trish's key, something Lauren had yet to find.

Hannah returned with iced tea and a big slice of pie, and

sat down to watch Lauren eat. Conversation was difficult to come by, as seemed to be the status quo between them.

They couldn't discuss Lauren's work. Hannah disapproved. And Lauren didn't intend to discuss marriage possibilities. Not even if Hannah brought it up, which—for once—she didn't.

"How's the food business, Mom?" Lauren improvised.

"Pretty good on weekends," she said. "With summer coming, we'll have more tourists in the place. Looks like I'll eke by another year."

"Do you still like living in the apartment upstairs? You must smell the food cooking in your sleep."

"I don't mind. I never regretted letting Becca take over the house you girls grew up in. Since your father died, the restaurant is my whole life."

Lauren knew what was coming, and she steeled herself. "I know it hasn't been easy for you."

"Might have helped if you'd stayed closer to home after you finished your schooling. Instead you went off on a crusade to save every tree and sage bush in the West. And that CPWA doesn't pay half what you could make if—"

"Mom, please." Lauren had been through the salary argument before. Working for an environmental organization was not the most lucrative job she could have found.

Hannah held up a hand. "You're right. We'd best not get into it. Every day I thank God for Becca. She's solid gold. Who else· could work for the BLM in these times and still stay on good terms with the community? She sees San Rafael's side. She sees my side. She values family."

"Yes. Thank God for Becca." In Lauren's view, Becca was so agreeable that she ended up standing for nothing at all. Nevertheless, even Becca was bound to face some complaints before Red Rock management was resolved.

Hannah brushed an imaginary crumb off the table. "I guess you'll be seeing a lot of Gabe this trip. Might as well tell you up front, he means to use those canyon oil leases. I know you won't approve, but if you're going to do Becca any good, don't start right out antagonizing him."

"I won't, Mom." She'd done her share of antagonizing already, as Hannah was likely to discover soon enough. Alas, the rebel daughter had indeed come home.

Lauren leaned back in her chair and closed her eyes, sorting the heavy aromas of roasting meats from the lighter scents of herbs and seasonings that the ceiling fan mixed together. In the kitchen Hannah banged drawers and clattered plates, preparing for the evening rush. As usual, she had declined Lauren's help. Also as usual, Lauren wasn't sorry. She'd done enough cooking and waitressing in her teenage years to last several lifetimes.

The bells on the front door jingled, and Lauren recognized voices. She peered through the alcove's arch. The man in a tan shirt with the sleeves cut out was Don Ray, Trish's husband. His hair was slicked back, as if he'd just washed up for dinner. A big man with a close-cut, sand-colored beard, Don Ray worked as a diesel mechanic, repairing logging and oil rig machinery.

His brother Chester, shorter and darker, walked in beside him. Chester, one of three Lomax boys who worked in the family business, wore a snug-fitting black T-shirt with LOMAX LOGGING emblazoned on the back. He, too, had that wet look from a quick trip by the bathroom faucet. From the rip in the shoulder of the shirt and the ragged condition of his jeans, Lauren assumed he'd had a rough day cutting trees.

Trish was taking orders at a booth. As soon as she finished, she tucked the order pad in a pocket and sailed over to her husband for a quick mouth-to-mouth. As a couple, she and Don Ray had always been public with their affection. Eleven years of marriage and five kids later, the town had gotten used to them.

"I'll have a booth for you boys in a minute," Trish said. "Two turkey specials? That'd be ready quickest."

"Sounds fine." Don Ray leaned against the lunch counter and drummed the glass top. Though his hands were red from a good scrubbing, his fingernails still had grease-darkened rims. "I have another hour's work tonight. It's not easy keeping the wife and kids in the lap of luxury."

Trish wouldn't know luxury if it poked her in the nose. She stuck out her tongue at him, and wiggled her hips as she sashayed over to a table to fill water glasses. Chester chortled. Don Ray, without rancor, told his brother to shut up and put his eyes back in his head. While they waited for a booth, Chester nabbed a toothpick out of the dispenser by the cash register and started picking.

"You're right about one thing," Don Ray said to his brother, apparently continuing an earlier discussion. "Pretty soon there won't be a spit of land left to log or drill or run cattle. If that happens, a lot of us'll be out of work. I hear Lands West has a paid organizer who knows how to get publicity and bring out the protesters. I'm thinking we ought to give them a call."

"You can bet the environmentalists'll picket the town about what we can and can't do in Red Rock." Chester had a high-pitched voice for a man, and he raised it full volume. "Them and their damn fool slogans. 'Save the spotted owl.' 'Save the black-footed ferret.' 'Save the goddamn desert tortoise.' I say we shoot all the endangered species we can find and make 'em into soup."

Several men looked up from their meals to murmur generalized approval. One with a Great Basin logo on his workshirt stood to shake a fist and yell, "Bring on the soup!"

Chester raised his arm and shot the diners a victory "V." In an aside to Don Ray, he continued, "If Lands West wants to help us fight the feds, I say more power to 'em. We can use their organizer and all the cavalry they can muster."

Trish had stopped filling glasses to rush back toward the brothers, spilling water down the front of her apron in her haste. She jerked her head in the direction of the alcove. Chester was too busy picking his teeth to notice.

Don Ray patted his little brother on the top of a head covered with a shock of dark, straight hair. "Better not speak your mind too loud, Chester. Some folks might take exception. Sheriff Purdy for one. Is he here, Trish?"

"No, but . . ." She rolled her eyes and twitched her head.

Lauren had faced the main room while eavesdropping. She was turning away when Chester swung around and saw her. His gaze widened to white rims around the blue, then narrowed in scathing outrage.

"Jesus freakin' Christ, look what we got here! Saint Lauren, out to save the world from low-down sinners who scratch a living off the public land."

Trish insinuated herself in front of Don Ray and Chester as the three of them migrated to the alcove archway. "Don't hold it against these big oafs, Lauren," she said. "They're just airing their blowholes."

"Yeah," Chester sneered. "Excuse us for breathing."

"How's it going, Lauren?" Don Ray asked. All things considered, his simple greeting seemed touchingly civil.

"Come on, boys." Trish did her best to head Chester off. "A booth's open now. Dinner'll be out in—"

"How about we eat with Lauren?" Chester proposed. "While we've got a real live environmentalist here to listen, we ought to discuss how a Red Rock Wilderness will empty this town."

"No way, bro," Don Ray said. "As I recall, I had to bail you out of jail and pay for three chairs and a window after your last 'discussion.' "

"So what? It was worth it." Chester curled a lip at Lauren. "You're here for the Tuesday meeting, aren't you, sweet thing?"

"No." Lauren hadn't known there was a Tuesday meeting. With some regret, she let the "sweet thing" insult go. "I'm just visiting the family. One memorable town gathering last November was quite enough for me."

The main room buzzed with voices, male voices, low and excited. Men and a few women craned their necks from booths and chairs. Lauren suspected the diners would be sympathetic to Chester, and she wasn't eager to find out how far that sympathy would take them.

Hannah came bustling out from the kitchen, drying her hands on her apron. "You're not out to start something, are you, Chester? I'll give LaDell a call right now, I swear I will."

Lauren heard a tinkling of bells and felt a draft as the front door opened once more. She hoped it was the sheriff, or there might well be an outbreak of furniture throwing coming her way soon.

She rose to confront the Lomaxes, at the same time motioning for her mother to stay back. "What do you boys want to talk about? I have some ideas on tourism, if you'd like to hear. That's the future of San Rafael. You may not want to face it yet, but—"

"You don't know *shit*," Chester informed her. "Not *shit* about us."

"I know you have a treasure in Red Rock Canyon. I, for one, want to keep it whole, not chop down the trees or strip-mine the minerals, or build derricks and—"

She stopped when Gabe ambled into the alcove.

"Is that you, Laurie, badmouthing my derricks again?" He said it in a teasing way that whisked the ugly tension out of the air. He came between Don Ray and Chester, slapping each of them on the back. "Talk about treasures, our Laurie sure has made good, boys. This town ought to be real proud of producing a born-and-bred attorney."

Gabe was taller than either of the Lomax brothers. He had

a presence about him, a confidence and natural leadership that took even Chester's rage down a peg. They'd played on the same teams in high school, so Gabe had male bonding going for him. Also, it didn't hurt that doing maintenance on oil company machinery was a significant part of Don Ray's business.

"Nobody in this town's happy to see her, Gabe, and you know it," Chester grumbled.

"Speak for yourself," Gabe said. "I'm willing to live and let live."

Chester barked a harsh, brief laugh. "That's a good one. As if *she's* worried about how *we're* gonna live."

"Chester," Don Ray warned.

"Go on now, out of my alcove." Hannah charged forward to shoo the Lomax boys with the swish of a dishcloth. "Trish, go in the kitchen and finish the salads, would you?"

Chester and Don Ray migrated toward the booths. Trish headed for the kitchen, the diners went back to their meals, and Lauren lingered beside her mother, wondering if she should thank Gabe. She hadn't needed his help, but he *had* defused an unpleasant scene.

He made it easy for her, addressing a serious matter with his customary teasing. "I didn't know I'd have to fend off the competition before I'd have you ladies all to myself." He mock-saluted Lauren. To Hannah, he held out his arms.

Without hesitation Hannah waltzed over to him and allowed Gabe to give her a huge bear hug and a sloppy kiss on the cheek. She giggled as if she'd shed forty years. "You are outrageous, Gabe Randolph."

When Gabe had arrived in San Rafael as a ten-year-old motherless boy, he'd promptly acquired the maternal love of every female in town, including Hannah. And now she was *flirting* with him. She turned to Lauren. "He's one fine-looking fella, wouldn't you say?"

"No, I wouldn't." She wrinkled her nose at Gabe, and he

laughed. Okay, so she lied, but she wasn't about to contribute to swelling his head any worse than it was already. She didn't take offense—at least not much—that he was welcomed as a long-lost son and Becca remained the favored daughter, while Lauren somehow didn't measure up.

"Where's Melissa Louise?" she demanded of him.

"Still at her lesson," he replied. "Boom-Boom's keeping her an extra half hour because we were late."

"Sit down, Gabe," Hannah ordered. "Sit right there with Lauren, and I'll get your favorite peach cobbler."

Gabe and Lauren sat. They both knew better than to try to thwart Hannah.

She had gathered Lauren's dishes and those from another table into a stack when the bells tinkled again. "We've been busy today. Even for a Friday, we've been busy. Never can tell how—"

The sheriff barged through the alcove archway. He stopped short when he saw the three of them. His thinning hair was mussed from his nap, but his brown eyes looked more alert than usual, more worried. He held his straw hat in hand, nervously twirling it by the brim. "Gabe. Lauren." He nodded at them, then squared his gaze on Hannah.

She paused to smile at him. "Look what the coyotes drug in. I'll fetch you a cup of black coffee, LaDell. You look like you need it." Hands full of dirty dishes, she started toward the kitchen.

LaDell grabbed her arm to stop her and then stood with jaw muscles working, as if gathering the courage to say his piece. The stillness, the tension in him reminded Lauren of the time he'd come to the door with news of her father. Blood pulsed in her neck. She shivered and hugged her arms across her roiling stomach.

When he didn't speak up, Lauren did. "What is it?" she forced herself to ask, although she wished she could block out the answer. "What's wrong?"

Gabe surged to his feet, knocking over his chair and almost upending the table. "Damn, LaDell, spit it out."

The plates and glasses in Hannah's hands started to rattle. Tea spilled all over the crumbs of raspberry pie.

The sheriff ignored Gabe and Lauren. He held Hannah by the shoulders and looked straight into her eyes. "Don't fall apart on me," he said. "The hospital over in Fairfield admitted a woman to the ER, banged up pretty bad. I wish I didn't have to tell you this, but they say it's . . ."

"Oh, God," Lauren whispered. "Becca."

Chapter Three

"**C**an you hear me?"

Becca Hewitt knew the voice, but she couldn't place it. She was locked in a dark, empty world, unable to see, unable to speak. Her tongue was thick and unresponsive. Her eyelids seemed weighted shut. Her head ached and pounded and throbbed, and the pain went deep. She didn't know where she was, or why she was there.

She was afraid. She had things she must do, if only she could remember what they were. Worst of all, her thoughts kept fogging over with the need to sleep. She fought her way toward the voice, toward the now, but she couldn't quite break through. Shadowy images played across her mind.

Last she recalled, she'd been approaching a curve in a winding canyon road while listening to advice for the lovelorn on the radio.

"Have you ever been in love?" Dr. Susan Farnsworth, psychoanalyst extraordinaire, asked her audience.

As if I have any idea what love is, Becca had scoffed to herself, changing one crackly station for another as she rounded the bend. A rock wall and a thick bank of junipers obscured her view until it was too late to put on the brakes.

Something blocked her way. She swerved, skidded. And then everything crumpled like a beer can under a boot.

The next thing she knew, she was lying right here, flat on her back, eyes locked shut, with someone leaning over her.

A hand touched her brow. "What do you remember?"

Not enough. She couldn't get past the pain. Her eye sockets hurt, and every breath brought more agony, more fear. Moaning, she turned her head, dimly aware of a pillow beneath her.

She needed to know what had happened. She'd been in a hurry to finish making rounds on the canyon perimeter and return to the office. She was meeting . . . Lauren. Lauren would be on time, tapping her foot, anxious and irritated and . . .

And Missy. Oh, dear Lord, Missy. The thought of her daughter blasted into her head and cleared away some of the numbing fog. She had to get home. Home to her little girl.

If she were disabled, or otherwise out of the picture, Joe would raise their daughter. And Joe . . . God, Joe could barely take care of himself half the time. Through three separations since they'd married close to thirteen years before, she had hung on, doing her best to keep loving him in spite of his drinking, his careless free-spending of their joint funds, and his repeated business disasters. Once they'd had Missy, Becca had believed any father was better than none. But Joe had made little effort to be there for the child. Compared to him, their seven-year-old daughter behaved like the adult.

Becca struggled to open her eyes, to lift her head, but the exertion brought a stab of pain. Her panic grew. What had happened when she rounded that bend?

She recognized the smell of antiseptic. Something pinched her hand. An IV? Her tongue moved, but no sound surfaced.

"Rest now," the voice said. "You need time to heal."

The effort to speak nauseated her. She wanted to say she should be with her daughter, but she couldn't hold on, couldn't stay alert. Her thoughts scattered and regrouped, weaving together in her subconscious until they formed a terrifying whole.

Missy needed a mother. Tears escaped Becca's eyes and dripped down to wet her hair. She had to get home. Had to get to Missy. She couldn't let Joe . . .

Please help me. Her head hurt. Her neck ached. Her collarbone felt like it had been through a paper-shredder.

Only the voice, soft and soothing, held her together. It murmured in rhythmic syllables, sounding almost like a prayer.

As Lauren hurried down the hall from the nurses' station, she saw someone in a white coat exit Becca's room and turn swiftly in the opposite direction.

"Wait!" Lauren called, hoping to find out the latest on her sister's condition.

Apparently not hearing her, the doctor neither turned nor slowed down before disappearing into the stairwell. Lauren wavered between going after the elusive medical staff or going to Becca. The need to see her sister won.

The sheriff had driven Lauren and Hannah the thirty miles to Fairfield General. While the two women had checked with Admissions, Sheriff Purdy proceeded to the ER, where he hoped to discover how and when Becca had arrived.

Hannah was right on Lauren's heels as they entered the hospital room. The window curtains were drawn. A weak light filtered from the bathroom. Lauren's eyes adjusted slowly to the dimness where Becca lay, white skin on white sheets, startlingly fragile and still. An ugly abrasion covered one cheek; her blond bangs were stiff with what Lauren feared was dried blood.

Fighting back tears, she waited at the foot of the bed while Hannah leaned over her eldest daughter and kissed the undamaged side of her face. For once, Lauren didn't begrudge

Becca receiving the extra measure of their mother's love. She'd give anything, do anything, if only her sister would be okay.

"Good Lord," Hannah fussed. "How in the world did this happen? If it was Joe, if he got you in another wreck, I'll claw his eyes out, and Sheriff Purdy won't go easy on him, either. You tell me everything, baby. I'll—"

Becca's eyes opened. She seemed disoriented as she focused blearily on Hannah. A hoarse, rusty sound came out of her mouth and formed slurred words. "I was . . . driving."

"In that beat-up old Ford the BLM stuck you with?" Hannah asked. "If something went wrong with their worthless clunker, the government's gonna hear what-for from me. What happened?"

"Can't . . . remember." Becca ran the tip of her tongue over her lower lip. "Supposed to . . . rest."

Hannah nodded. "If that's doctor's orders, then that's what you'll do. Sheriff Purdy'll get the whole story figured out, don't you worry." She began smoothing sheets and straightening the bedside table. When she went into the bathroom to fill the water pitcher, Lauren had a moment alone by the bed.

She moved forward, wondering how to offer comfort. All she knew for certain was that she wanted to help. "I'm here," she offered. "If you need me."

Becca murmured a hoarse, "Thank God."

Lauren wasn't sure whether her sister was glad to see her, or simply glad to be alive and able to see anything at all.

Before she could figure it out, Lauren found herself nudged aside as Hannah and the water pitcher took her place.

"What else can I get for you, baby?" Hannah asked. "Ice? Another blanket? A wet cloth for your head?"

Becca moaned, weakly lifting a hand in what Lauren took for a cease and desist. Hannah didn't notice. Just like when they were kids, it wasn't easy to be bedridden around Mom.

Hannah Van Horn would worry a person to health or death in an overzealous hurry.

When Lauren saw that her mother had taken over, she left the room and went directly to the nurses' station. A redhead in a white uniform looked up from a pile of charts. "You're visiting Mrs. Hewitt, aren't you? Is she all right?"

"She's awake and alert." *All right* seemed a little strong. "I saw a doctor leaving my sister's room about"—Lauren glanced at her watch—"fifteen minutes ago. Is he still around somewhere?"

"Was it Dr. Draper? Short, gray, balding?"

"No. Dark hair, medium height. Long white coat."

The nurse pinched the bridge of her nose. "Hmm. Maybe the ER doc stopped in. Or could've been a lab tech." She looked tired, as if she were at the end of a double shift, which might explain why she hadn't noticed who'd been on the floor. "Dr. Draper's called a neurologist to check on the head injury. I assume he's on his way. Meanwhile, I could beep—"

Lauren shook her head. "That's okay. I'll wait for the specialist. Can you tell me who brought my sister in? I know she was admitted through the emergency room, but is there anything more in the chart?"

The nurse glanced down at an open file. "Nothing official." She hesitated, then leaned over the stack of manilla folders in front of her and whispered, "Since you're a relative, I guess you'll find out anyway. We don't *know* who brought her in. An aide walked out of the rest room and almost tripped over a gurney with Mrs. Hewitt on it. There was a wallet tucked beside her. Good thing, or we couldn't have notified family, since she was unconscious at the time."

"My sister simply appeared? Out of nowhere?"

"That's it. Abracadabra, and there she was."

*   *   *

Lauren stayed in her sister's room through the neurologist's arrival, and long enough to get a report on her condition. Based on the exam and X rays, Becca didn't have a skull fracture or intracranial bleeding, but they'd continue to monitor her overnight to be sure. After the doctor left, Hannah took over again, generating her usual whirl of activity.

Lauren went by the ER, looking for Sheriff Purdy, but he'd left on another call. She asked a few questions of her own, discovering nothing new except that the ER doc on duty was a skinny blond woman, not the person Lauren had seen leaving by way of the back stairwell just as she'd arrived. It must have been a tech, as the nurse said.

Bumming some writing material from the nurse's station, Lauren sat in Becca's room near the window and made notes while listening to Hannah chatter and bustle around the hospital bed. She wished she had her laptop so she could do some useful work instead of worrying away her stomach lining. About nine that evening, the sheriff took Hannah home, leaving Lauren alone with her sister.

She moved close enough to hear even breathing, to see closed eyes and slack features. Since she'd first learned of the accident, she'd been haunted by the fear that Becca wouldn't get well. She'd berated herself for the wasted time, for the petty argument that had come between them. Whether or not they agreed on the canyon, or even on Joe, shouldn't have affected their love. If it were up to Becca, it wouldn't have.

Clouds of her sister's pale hair spilled over the pillowcase and reminded Lauren of how they'd taken turns brushing a hundred strokes for each other when they were small. She had always felt she had the best of the deal, because Becca's hair was soft and blond and beautiful. Lauren's hand lingered over her sister's head, but she couldn't quite bring herself to touch, caress, as she longed to do. She wasn't good at tenderness. Becca was the one who was good at that.

Her heart twisted with guilt at the thought of Melissa, who had barely spoken to her this afternoon. The child was going through a difficult time; Lauren should have thought more of her niece's hurt than of her own. Maybe then things would have gone better between them.

She took a deep breath to fend off tears building in her throat. With Becca's accident, the poor kid would have yet another burden to bear, and Lauren wouldn't be able to heal that hurt, either.

Gabe had stayed behind to pick up Melissa and explain what had happened. Lauren hoped he would know how to comfort a little girl. She thought he would. Though disenchanted with him for her own reasons, she had to admit he knew how to get along with people. He'd fit in with Hannah, Melissa, and apparently with Becca. Much better, in fact, than Lauren had.

Becca stirred restlessly. Some of the pressure in Lauren's chest eased. It was going to be okay. She'd get another chance to make everything right between them. "What can I do?" Lauren whispered, her voice rough with feeling. "Tell me how can I help."

"Laurie?" Becca moaned. "My backside's gone numb and my collarbone hurts like a bitch."

The statement was so unexpectedly normal that Lauren laughed aloud. "You don't know how good your voice sounds about now."

"Sounds like crap. Few hours ago it wouldn't work at all. I worried how I'd keep up my loudmouth ways." She croaked the words like a frog with laryngitis, but at least she hadn't lost her sense of humor.

"The queen of hearts has recovered," Lauren pronounced.

"And you're here," Becca rasped, "so all's right with the world."

Lauren wondered if her sister was being sarcastic, considering their lack of communication of late. Their eyes met through light filtering from the bathroom and the meager green glow from a detached monitor.

"I'm glad you're here." Becca weakly lifted her hand and Lauren held it, glad for the connection, needing it as much as or more than Becca did.

"You don't have to talk. Maybe you shouldn't—"

"I should. Otherwise the nurses will think I'm dead or need brain surgery," Becca said. "Help me turn on my side, would you?"

Lauren eased her over so they faced each other, and ended by gently rubbing her shoulder. "I don't want you wearing yourself out. I can do the talking for both of us."

"You wish," Becca quipped. "I . . . hope you don't mind that I asked you to come. I . . . well, I know you're busy."

"Not that busy," Lauren countered, as remorse pricked her conscience. Since November, she'd gone on an extended lobbying trip to D.C., then returned to Denver and begun work on a complicated water-pollution lawsuit. None of that served as an excuse. She should have come home before now, should have made the effort. "So tell me, why didn't you behave yourself and meet me in your office like any sensible person would?"

Becca started to smile, but quickly gave it up. "The stitches," she said.

Lauren frowned at the quarter inch of tiny crisscrosses on her sister's lower lip. High on the forehead, beneath blood-stiffened bangs, Becca had a longer line of stitches that would leave a scar.

"Looks painful." Lauren ached for her. "The sheriff has the highway patrol out searching for your truck."

"Wish I could tell them where to look. Can't remember anything but flashes before and after, until you and Mom came."

"Not a problem," Lauren soothed. "Sheriff Purdy needs something to do besides sleep."

"It scares me, having a big hole in my day." Becca shivered.

Lauren touched her sister's hand and found it cold. She pulled up a blanket from the foot of the bed, taking her time arranging it. She wished she could fill in the blanks—all of them, including the years she'd failed to sympathize over Joe and the marriage problems. For Becca's sake, Lauren could have been more understanding.

"Melissa's spending the night at Gabe's house," she said, in case Becca didn't know.

"Mom told me. I started worrying as soon as I could think, but it's okay. A girl can rely on Gabe." Becca tried to smile again. "So how's *your* love life?"

"Don't ask." Lauren grimaced, and then wished she'd been less obvious.

"Bad, huh?"

"Hey, I didn't say that," Lauren protested.

"You can't fool me," Becca replied. "You're worse off than I am, romantically speaking. Pretty darn unexciting."

Maybe. Maybe not. Something was going on with Becca's love life, if Joe's custody counterattack was any indication. "You've had way more excitement than you need," Lauren said. "As for me, I'm not complaining."

"No. You never do. Maybe you should stir up the"— Becca's voice cracked—"passion once in a while. For a man, not a cause."

Lauren offered water, and Becca sipped through a straw. "You think I'm an ice cube," Lauren said quietly. "Everyone does. If I had my wish, I'd be more like you."

Becca groaned. "Uh-uh. Bad choice."

In some ways, Lauren thought. *But not in others.* "You're friendly by nature, Becca. People are drawn to you, and you to them. While I . . . I'd rather deal in statutes and legal terms." Lauren buried her passions deep. She liked being in complete control of herself and her feelings at all times.

She'd been different once. More compassionate, less solitary, more tuned in to family. She and her mother had never gotten along that well, but she'd had strong bonds with Dad and Becca. Every year, more of her old self seemed to dissolve, and perhaps pieces of her heart along with it.

Becca's green eyes were luminescent, reflecting the monitor's glow. "While Mom was here, I kept thinking about the time you broke your foot. Did you know she was furious with me about that?"

Lauren smiled, and her muscles relaxed another degree. It was strange how sharing memories seemed easier in the darkness. "I didn't have an inkling. I thought she was angry with *me*. She said I was clumsy. She said I should have used my head and not risked my body. It was Dad who commiserated. Never Mom."

Neither spoke of walking into the bowels of this hospital with their mother when she'd come to identify their father's broken, lifeless body, but Lauren thought about it, and she knew Becca must be recalling it, too.

Lauren had just turned eighteen, almost ready to go off into the world and make her daddy proud. Eventually she'd followed in his footsteps, becoming an attorney. She hadn't wanted to practice in a small town, as he had, but she did become an environmental activist, which had been his major area of interest in those last years. He might have been proud of her. Since he hadn't lived to see it, she'd never know.

To take their minds off death, Lauren moved on to something she could act upon. "Gabe mentioned the custody battle. I wish you'd told me sooner."

Becca sent her an eloquent look.

Lauren couldn't miss the guilt-trip message. She *had* been a little hard to get hold of, and just maybe she had kept it that way on purpose. "Okay, it's my fault I didn't know, but I'm here now. Give me the facts. I'll take care of the legal end."

"Have you heard Joe's turned mean over this?" Becca asked. "He could launch a firestorm."

"Yes. That's why I'm ready and willing to lead the charge. According to the scuttlebutt my fellow attorneys circulate, I'm made of asbestos instead of flesh and blood. No worries. And if it's more than I can handle, I'll find us the best family law specialist in the state."

"I can't afford—"

"I wouldn't let you pay a cent," Lauren said. "Consider it a gift to my niece, not you."

Becca ran her tongue over the lip stitches. "Joe thinks I'm having an affair."

"Are you?" In Lauren's opinion, which she carefully did not state, Becca needed another man right now about as much as she'd needed this accident.

"No. But I've . . . spent time with Gabe. People talk."

Lauren took a deep breath. She'd guessed this was coming. She'd dreaded it. "That wasn't smart."

"Oh, Lauren, you know I don't think first. I just do."

Truer words were never spoken. "How far has it gone? In this day and age a discriminating affair shouldn't matter, but the county court will base its rulings on Utah family values, which generally run twenty years behind the rest of the world. Does anyone have evidence, photos, anything like that?"

"No," Becca said, "but the gossips are having a field day anyway. Hearing I'm with Gabe is driving Joe over the wall. The old high school rivalry is back, full force, and he won't listen to reason, not even for Missy's sake."

Lauren wanted to know the exact definition of being "with Gabe," but she didn't ask. "Joe's a moron. I never knew what you saw in him." He'd been good at sports and girls, and at bragging about his limited achievements, but he'd never taken the trouble to exercise his brain.

"I saw a party-loving, good-timing boy," Becca said. "He hasn't grown up."

"Could Joe . . . Do you think he had anything to do with this accident?"

Becca rolled her head on the pillow. "I . . . No. I can't remember, but . . ."

"Shh." Lauren stroked the rumpled flow of blond hair on the pillowcase. "Don't worry. We'll prove you're a great mother and he's a lousy father. We'll document all the times he's been late for visitation, or failed to appear entirely. We'll find every possible way to refute a charge of lewd behavior, or whatever he comes up with. If his claims are unfounded, we'll have no problem winning in court."

"It's not so simple," Becca said. "Joe's relatives will exaggerate about me and Gabe, about who's seen us doing what. I have friends who'd speak up for me, but there are a *lot* of Hewitts."

"I always thought Joe was the black sheep of the clan," Lauren said. "Why would they—"

"They might not like him, but they'll stick together. Thick blood, thick heads, thick as thieves. That's the Hewitts."

Lauren was especially leery of the county judge, who bore Joe's last name, but if the relationship was close enough, she could force Judge Hewitt off the case. She'd check the genealogy at the first opportunity. "How do you want to handle this? A final ruling will take months, as you know. Meanwhile, Joe's entitled to the usual time with Melissa, unless we can get a restraining order. For that, we'd have to claim abuse or harassment. Is there any—"

"No. I'd rather do it another way. I want you to . . ." Becca hesitated.

"To what? If you have an alternate plan, out with it."

"I . . . I need your help."

"I already said—"

"I don't mean legal help. This is more personal."

Lauren frowned. "You're my sister. I'll do anything for you."

Becca tried another smile that didn't work. "I just . . . I want you to kiss Gabe."

"What?" Lauren figured she couldn't have heard right.

"Kiss him in public. Hold hands and make moon eyes. Visit his house. Maybe even sleep in his—"

"How hard did you hit your head?" Lauren asked. "Have you lost brain function entirely?"

"I'm as functional as I ever was. Please hear me out. Please."

Lauren was afraid to listen. "This reminds me of the time you invented an entire ring of kidnappers to explain why you were two hours late coming home from a party."

"Oh, Lauren, I was thirteen then. This plan is much better. I know it'll work."

Lauren doubted it. Becca's slapdash schemes were always inventive, but not too practical. Another disastrous instance that came to mind was when she'd hastily tried to cover up a fresh cigarette burn on the rug in her room with a stack of newspapers, which resulted in burning a hole in the floor three feet in diameter.

After her marriage, Becca's imaginative cover-ups were mostly attempted on Joe's behalf, which was sad, and likewise unsuccessful. Everyone knew Joe was a screwup, though Becca wouldn't admit it until the bitter end.

Since Becca was in a hospital bed at the moment, Lauren didn't want to belabor past mistakes. "Go ahead and tell me," she said reluctantly. "I'll listen." *And then I'll say no.*

Becca lifted her IV-pierced hand. "Keep an open mind, would you? The idea is to start up fresh gossip and convince Joe—"

"That *I'm* having a fling with Gabe? No way in hell." Come to think of it, being with Gabe on an intimate basis for any length of time, for any reason, would be hell on earth, with an extra oil well or two thrown in to kick up the heat.

Becca sighed. "I was afraid you'd be stubborn about this."

Lauren made a production of adjusting the bedsheets. "Couldn't Gabe just . . . go away for a while? Or at least go live somewhere besides right next door?"

"He offered to move over to the Sandman Motel after all this started," Becca said, "but I figured that would be like admitting guilt. And he can't leave town. There's too much going on with Great Basin. Besides, he gets along so well with Missy. I can't send someone she cares about away from her now. She's had enough trouble adjusting to the divorce."

"What did Gabe say to . . . the plan with me? He hasn't *agreed*, has he?"

Becca opened her mouth too abruptly, and must have pulled her stitches. She squeezed her eyes closed for a second. "Gabe is willing. He feels real bad about my trouble with Joe."

"He should, since he's the one responsible."

"I take the rap, Lauren. I'm the one who should have foreseen Joe's reaction."

Lauren didn't quibble over blame. Either way, she was not going to get anywhere near Gabe under the circumstances Becca proposed. "I'll do what I can legally, but this . . . this I *can't* do."

A tear channeled down Becca's swollen cheek.

Lauren felt awful. What else could she say? How could she possibly go through with such a monumental farce?

She recalled how Mom had been so eager for her to "help" Becca. Mom knew. She'd been glad to hear Lauren's relationship with Tim hadn't progressed, because it would have been an impediment to Lauren's standing in for Becca with Gabe. As had usually been the case, Becca's problems were Hannah's first priority.

And Gabe was "willing." He'd said something this afternoon about working things out, about getting together. This must be what he'd meant. Lauren's mother and sister planned to shove her into his obliging arms, all to impress a gaggle of jabbering busybodies, and he was "willing" to put up with it. She would never live down the humiliation.

Nevertheless, the despair in Becca's eyes made her wish she could do something. "I want to help you, Becca, but we need to think this through." She reached out to touch her sister's gown-clad shoulder.

Becca sucked in a wheezing breath. "The collarbone. Careful of the collarbone."

Lauren withdrew her hand. She had no talent for connecting with people. She'd certainly be no good at faking an impossible romance. "It can't work. Gabe would be . . . uncomfortable. I'd be uncomfortable. Besides, he owns Great Basin Petroleum, for heaven's sake. I'm counsel for the CPWA. How would it look if I consorted right out in the open with the enemy?"

"Gabe doesn't want to be anyone's enemy, Lauren. And I'm not suggesting a *real* affair. If it gets that far, you could sleep over in his spare room. Just so word got around. In public, a little mock-kissing and harmless consorting ought to do it. No actual spit-swapping is required."

Lauren blocked out all such thoughts. She concentrated on hard, cold facts instead. "I doubt Joe would be easy to convince. And what would you do after I leave?" She hadn't planned on more than a weekend visit. Because of the accident, she'd extend her stay, but not for long enough. "Even if I take off work for a week or so, even if I play along as you ask, Joe will revert to the same old suspicions after I'm gone."

"No. I'll be careful. I should have guessed Joe couldn't accept Gabe being near me. Especially not so soon after the divorce."

"You were separated for six months before the paperwork was done. How long before he gets the idea?"

"Until it was official, I don't think he believed the divorce would happen. He kept thinking I'd give in. Even now . . ."

Lauren shook her head. "One wrong move and you'll be back where you started, with him making threats. We have to go through the legal system."

"The courts aren't worth diddly when it comes to people problems, Lauren."

"If the county judge doesn't give us the answer we want, we can appeal to a higher court. We'll win eventually," Lauren assured her.

"Yes, but at what cost to Missy? She's having trouble in school lately. She got in a hair-pulling contest with Audra Biggs last week, which isn't like her at all. I know she's worried about what's going to happen. I don't want the uncertainty going on for months and months. It'll be quicker and safer to change Joe's view of me and Gabe. Please. If you'd just do this one thing, I'd be forever grateful."

Lauren groaned. "Good grief, Becca. How did you dig us into such a hole?"

"I . . . Well, you know how appealing Gabe can be. Missy is crazy about him."

Lauren had to ask, though she thought she knew the answer. "Do *you* still love him?"

"Except for you, I'll bet every woman in this town is half in love with Gabe." Becca managed a lopsided grin. "Look at it this way. You two won't have trouble finding things to talk about, since you could debate oil wells in the canyon from now till doomsday, no problem. All you have to do is learn how to argue from real close up. It'll be good practice in control."

No kidding. Besides the likelihood that the lamebrained idea wouldn't work, there was one other hang-up.

The main reason Lauren wanted to stay away from Gabe was that with him, her control might have a tendency to slip.

Chapter Four

G abe held Missy's hand as they walked from the parking lot toward the hospital's back entrance.

"Investigate," she said in a small, sad voice, tugging on his wrist to get his attention.

Gabe looked down at her. "What's that, honey?"

"Investigate's my new word. The sheriff's gonna investigate Mama's accident. My friend Buddy Lomax says that's 'cause nobody knows how it happened and they can't find her truck. Buddy says somebody might've tried to hurt her. He says some people think my daddy's the one."

Dropping the parcel of clothes Hannah had sent for Becca, Gabe crouched down to the child's level. Missy hadn't said she was afraid in so many words, but he knew she had to be. She'd seen the conflict between her parents. She'd probably heard her father make his blowhard threats. A child ought to be able to have confidence in both her parents, but Missy had been disenchanted too many times. All Gabe could do was placate her.

"Buddy's just repeating gossip, sweet pea. I don't think your daddy had anything to do with this accident." Gabe gave Joe the benefit of the doubt, but only to shield Missy. He'd wondered, just like everyone else in town surely had, if foul play might be involved.

"What if Mama's not all right?" Missy asked, as she'd asked at least once every waking hour since she'd heard her mother was in the hospital. "Who'll take care of me? Will I live with Daddy?"

Gabe lowered one knee to the asphalt parking lot and enveloped her in a fierce hug. She was a skinny little thing, small and precious in his arms. He released her and smiled, smoothing her blond pixie hair. She had a freckled nose, and a missing front tooth that he himself had helped wiggle loose. Her unblinking hazel eyes shone with innocence and a very real concern.

"Your mom will be fine." Gabe had had a grim report from Hannah, but he'd also talked to the sheriff, who'd been more positive. "I don't want you worrying."

That didn't cut it for Missy, the world's youngest skeptic. "What if Mama can't come home soon? This was supposed to be my day with Daddy, but I called his house and he wasn't there. I watched out the window, too. He didn't come for me. He forgot again. How's he going to remember about school and piano lessons if he doesn't remember Saturdays? He doesn't care about little-girl stuff."

"He does, Missy. He just hasn't put his mind to being a good daddy yet."

"Since he's not so good at it, I shouldn't have to go live with him."

Gabe completely agreed. "Your grandma likes having you around. You could stay with her while your mom gets well."

"Grandma only wants me in the afternoons," Missy said. "She lets me have cookies in the restaurant after school, but she's too busy other times."

Gabe knew Hannah could be short on patience, so he didn't argue. "What about your aunt Lauren? She's—"

"No." Missy wrinkled her freckles. "Aunt Lauren makes mean faces. She doesn't like me."

"Sure she does," Gabe argued. "Aunt Lauren would take

good care of you." She might come across as an emotional glacier, but Lauren's concern for Becca was as real as it came. She wouldn't refuse to help her sister's child.

Missy shook her head. "If Mama's hurt so bad she can't come home, I want to live with you."

"I'd be proud to have you, ladybug." If she needed him, he'd make time, work around managing his drilling sites and the company business. He wouldn't let her down. "Like I said, I don't think we have to worry that far ahead. Your mama's going to be A-okay." He sincerely hoped that was true.

They entered the hospital room to find Becca sitting up in bed. She looked good, better than he'd expected. Well, maybe *good* was an exaggeration, considering the stitches and scrapes and facial swelling, but she was alert. The visible damage would heal.

"Hi," he said. "We missed you." He still held the child's hand, while Missy hid behind him. He glanced back to see that her eyes were squeezed shut. She was probably scared to look. "Your mom's doing great, sweet pea. Open up and . . ."

As he turned to the child, he noted a cot near the window, where brunette hair spilled out from under mummy-wrapped sheets. It had to be Lauren. The subtle curves under those sheets distracted him for a moment.

In that same fraction of a second, Missy peeked around him and apparently decided her mom looked like the mom she knew. In a flash she let go of him and leaped upon Becca's bed. "I missed you awful, terrible much," she cried, flinging both arms around the hapless patient's neck.

"Missy, stop," Becca whimpered. "You're hurting me."

Gabe rushed forward to stave off damages, cursing himself for allowing his attention to wander. Frightened, Missy released her stranglehold on Becca and cowered back against him.

Meanwhile, Lauren erupted from her sheets. She looked

around, wild-haired and rumpled, before narrowing her eyes at Missy, who scooted down onto the terrazzo floor and stood with her head bowed, rebuffed and penitent.

"Your mother has a concussion, a broken collarbone, and she's bruised all over," Lauren chided. "You have to be careful, Melissa Louise."

"It's not like the kid planned it," Gabe muttered as he delivered a careful kiss to the tip of Becca's nose. "You okay?" he asked her.

She nodded. "I'll live."

"Missy and I worried about you." He perched on the edge of the hospital bed. When he heard rustling from the cot's direction, he looked over to see a disheveled Lauren hastily rearranging her twisted blouse and tugging on her skirt. His attention once again drifted, this time to her long, firm thighs that temporarily showed before she managed to hide them under dull material again. Hot damn, Laurie had a nice pair of legs. Nice everything, when you came down to it, with the exception of her abrasive personality.

Missy clasped his hand. The kid was teary-eyed, looking anxiously from him to her mother. "I didn't mean it. I didn't mean to touch the wrong places."

Lifting the child onto the bed to sit beside him, he reassured her that everything was fine. Lauren mumbled something from the vicinity of the cot, probably an attempt to smooth over her gaffe.

"You didn't know where I was hurt, did you, sweetie?" Becca said. "How could you know until someone told you?"

Vindicated, Missy sat up straight and directed a scowl at Lauren. As Missy took a closer look, her hazel eyes widened. "Your hair's all messed up, Aunt Lauren. Did you forget to bring a brush? And your skirt's wrinkly. Were you in an accident, too?"

"More or less." Lauren hastily combed her fingers through her thick hair. The result was a long way from beauty-parlor fresh. When she caught Gabe watching, she socked him with an arched-brow challenge, as if daring him to comment.

Becca, the peacemaker, tapped a spoon on the bed rails until she had their attention. "I have a public-service announcement. The doctor came by earlier and said I can go home whenever I'm ready. Lauren doesn't have her car here and my wheels seem to be temporarily misplaced. Can you give us a lift, Gabe?"

"Anytime," he answered, relieved that she was being released from the hospital so quickly.

Missy perked up her ears and almost purred. "Mama's okay. She really is okay."

"Of course," Becca said, as if she'd never considered otherwise.

When a nurse arrived to help Becca dress, the three visitors found themselves out in the hall with the door closed firmly behind them. Seeing Missy scuffing the toes of her tennis shoes and looking downcast because she wasn't allowed to stay in the room, Gabe dug in his pocket for quarters. "Here, honey bun. There's a machine down the hall. Why don't you go buy a couple of sodas for you and your mom?"

Breaking out in a smile, Missy took the coins and shot off like a minicannonball, pounding the floor and eliciting a shout of "No running!" from the nurses' station.

"Becca looks better than I thought," Gabe said to Lauren when they were alone. "Shouldn't be long before she's back to her old—"

Without warning, Lauren lit into him. "You knew, didn't you, Gabe? You knew all along."

"Knew what?" he asked, completely at a loss. Leave it to Lauren to imagine a slight where none existed. She'd always been too complicated for her own good. He reached to smooth a strand of hair sticking up behind her ear. She pushed his hand away.

Gabe knew she was upset, and he hated that. He caught a whiff of her wildflower scent, and wondered if there could be softness and sweetness in her somewhere, even though she hid it well. Bending at the knees, he positioned himself to meet her gaze. "Tell me what to apologize for, and I'll give it a shot."

Her face pinkened. "Are you saying you really don't know? Becca didn't tell you? About the . . . kissing?"

"What kissing? You mean what me and Becca are supposed to have done?"

"No." She blushed a deep crimson. "I mean . . . you and me."

"I don't know which town gossips you've been listening in on, Laurie, but you have a wire crossed somewhere."

She took a deep breath and seemed to gather her wits together. "I don't think so. Becca wants us to get Joe off her and Melissa's case by pretending to be lovers." She spoke slowly and distinctly, emphasizing every word. "Is that plain enough for you?"

"It's plain *now*. Becca didn't let me in on it ahead of time." No wonder Lauren had her feathers ruffled, Gabe thought. Becca's idea of a quick fix was a little off the lawyerly mark. His gaze flicked down Lauren's body. A damn fine body, not that he'd ever touch it. Maybe he'd had a thought or two, back there in the hospital room, about how she'd look naked. But hell, that was testosterone talking.

"I told Becca it's out of the question." Lauren stuck her pert nose high in the air. "She implied *you* knew and had agreed, which is obviously incorrect. Not that it matters. The whole plan is insane."

"Absolutely." Loosening her straight laces might be fun, but not worth the trouble. Based on looks alone, he wouldn't mind kissing Lauren if she'd attempt to be civil, but that wasn't likely to happen. "No way I'd kiss you, Little Bit. I'd be afraid you'd bite my lips off."

"I might," she agreed. "Don't test me."

"Becca's in worse shape than I figured if she'd suggest I risk a close encounter with an environmental hellcat like you." He wished Lauren were a shade less negative. He wouldn't mind being friendly, if she'd give him half a chance. "When did I become repulsive to you, if you don't mind my asking?"

"I . . . I didn't say you're repulsive."

"Not in so many words," he said. "Is it because I didn't keep writing? Didn't stay in touch?"

"You didn't come to Dad's funeral." She leaned against the hall's flowered wallpaper as if she needed the support.

For the first time since he'd become reacquainted with her, he saw vulnerability in her silvery eyes. He began to realize that he'd sorely disappointed her years ago.

"Ah, Laurie, I'm sorry. I wanted to, for you and Becca, even for Hannah, but I was in the middle of finals and . . . Damn, that's not the real reason. After Becca married Joe, I felt like I'd lost my place in your family. I wasn't sure my being there would help, but I guess I was wrong." He gazed intently at Lauren, seeing beneath her passionless mask to someone far more sensitive. Someone he knew, and might even like.

"My father drove over from Texas," Gabe reminded her. "He came for both of us. And I did write after that, remember? It was you who didn't write back."

"I . . . couldn't say how I felt in a letter. Not at first. And then it seemed too late."

"Is it too late now?" he asked.

Lauren straightened her spine. "I think so. Unless you want to change the direction of Great Basin Petroleum. Because otherwise, talking about Dad to you would be . . ."

He braced the flat of his hand against the flowered wallpaper on the side of her head. "Don't you think you should know more about me before you pass judgment? I thought lawyers were supposed to be logical."

"I *am* logical." She glared at him. "It's logical that we're on opposite ends of the spectrum. And Becca's idea is beyond good sense. Touching you, or letting you touch me, is certainly not a fate either of us would *choose*."

"No, I don't suppose it is." He wondered, though, if her apparent distaste for him could be defensive. Under all that protest, maybe some nostalgic sentiment remained. Probably not. "You're turning into a dried-up old maid, Laurie. You need to let *someone* touch you before it's too late."

Her mouth formed an "O" for a full three seconds before she managed a comeback. "Really! What makes you think I haven't been touched? Even if I were as desiccated as the Mojave desert, you're the last man I'd—"

The door opened, and Becca stood there in a loose sundress Hannah had sent. She leaned against the door frame, pressing her fingers to her temples. "I have a monster headache. Could you two quit arguing long enough to get me out of this place?"

The nurse stood at her elbow, mouth pursed in disapproval. "I wish you'd wait in a chair, Mrs. Hewitt. Or better yet, in bed."

"I'm holding my ground," Becca said stubbornly. "Gabe, lend me a supporting arm while the nurse fetches a wheelchair, would you?"

Missy arrived with the sodas in time to hear the word *wheelchair*. "Can I push it?" she asked the nurse. An affirmative reply had the child plunking the drinks onto a nearby table and accompanying the nurse down the hall.

"I'll . . . go by the pharmacy and pick up Becca's prescriptions," Lauren offered. She avoided direct eye contact with both Gabe and Becca. Gabe suspected she was embarrassed by what she'd said, and by what Becca might have

overheard. She left them in a hurry, following close after
Missy and the nurse, leaving Gabe to attend the patient.

He noticed Becca's white face about the time she started
swaying on her feet. Before her knees crumpled, he swept
her into his arms, careful of bandages he could feel on her
shoulder and rib cage. He carried her back into the room and
laid her gently on the bed.

"Forgive me for being a wimp," she said, clinging to his
shirt. "It's one of my worst faults."

"Is that right, darlin'? I'd say your plan for me and Laurie
rates way higher on the Richter scale."

"I thought I'd have a chance to talk to you before she
brought it up, Gabe."

When he frowned, she turned her head into the pillow. "I
thought you wouldn't mind. Lauren would have said no out-
right unless I convinced her that it would be fine with you."

Gabe took her hand and felt tremors. Exhaustion, he figured. Weakness induced by narcotics and pain. "Easy now."
He leaned down to her, kissing her forehead in a place that
looked free of stitches and cuts. "I'm not going to leave you
to deal with this alone."

She met his gaze then, and her big green eyes delivered a
heartfelt plea. "I know you're not in love with me, Gabe.
You've been honest about that. But you're still my good
friend and favorite neighbor, and you love Missy, I know you
do. I'm counting on you to get me out of this mess."

She didn't add that he'd helped to get her into it in the first
place, but he knew the facts. He couldn't turn down her plan
unless he came up with something better. So far, he hadn't.

"I don't want Missy to be bounced around according to
Joe's whims any more than you do," he admitted.

"Then you'll help?"

He thought it over for a couple of seconds before offering
a wry grin. "For a limited trial period, if it'll make you feel
better. I'll even do my best to convince Laurie to cooperate."

Becca hiccuped and mumbled, "Thanks."

"You're welcome."

The bad news was, Lauren had one hell-bent prickly attitude. A few hours or days in her pithy company, and *he* might be the one in need of a wheelchair.

"More potato salad, Lauren?" Hannah asked.

"No, thanks, Mom." Lauren watched her mother finish mounding Gabe's plate and pass it on to him. No sooner had they arrived home and settled Becca in a living room La-Z-Boy than Hannah had shown up with food. Lots and lots of food.

Much to Hannah's disappointment, Becca had declined lunch. That left only Melissa, Gabe, and Lauren to gather around the table. Hannah wasn't going to let any of them starve to death, that was for certain.

"Tell us about the plastic surgeon who took such a shine to you summer before last, Lauren." She was back to her old tricks, rehashing her daughter's life crises as she passed a platter of roasted chicken.

Lauren looked up, met Gabe's eyes, and glanced away. She dreaded his hearing the particulars her mother undoubtedly had wormed out of Becca. "Nothing to tell."

"Why, sure there is. What about how he said he'd do you a nose and boob job for free, and give discounts to everyone in the family?" Hannah sighed dramatically. "Wish you hadn't ditched him before we could take him up on it."

Lauren knew Hannah was of the opinion that her younger daughter's bosom could use improvement. Lauren, however, had never indulged in so much as a padded bra. "Let me set the record straight. He ditched *me,* Mom, because I refused to be remade according to his idea of beauty." Actually, their relationship had gone into a nosedive after she'd discovered that his big donation to the CPWA had been for Denver newspaper publicity, not out of any real commitment to the beliefs she found important.

Hannah sniffed. "Shows what he knows. Just because a person could benefit from reconstruction doesn't mean she's ready for the wrecking ball. I know it's Becca's figure that catches your eye, Gabe, but our Lauren's going to latch onto a fine man one day, wait and see."

"Mom, don't do this." Lauren slid lower in her chair.

Gabe scrubbed his mouth with a napkin, but he wasn't able to wipe off the smile. "No need to convince me, Hannah. You know how highly I rate both your daughters."

Lauren's skin warmed as Gabe surveyed her. At least Mom hadn't specified the need for renovation in any particular place, an omission for which Lauren was truly thankful.

"Her latest boyfriend is a corporate attorney who knows a good thing when he sees it," Hannah persisted. "What's his name, Lauren? Tom, isn't it? The boy's eager to marry her, Gabe. Good thing she's making him wait awhile. Whets the appetite, I always say."

"It's Tim, not Tom," Lauren said wryly. "You can scratch him off the list. He moved on, and so did I." While she and Tim had collaborated on a case, they'd gotten along well. Again, she'd mistaken their mutual interests for something that might last. It hadn't. She'd been sorry, but Hannah was sure to make her sorrier. She took a bite of chicken, waiting for the inevitable reaction.

Hannah threw up her hands. "Rain, sleet, and hail above. He got clean away? How did that happen? Why didn't you tell me before?"

"Can we talk about something else?" Lauren felt like crawling out of the room. Hannah's effort to make her appear almost, but not quite, as desirable as her sister appalled her. She would not be hawked like discount merchandise. Her mother *did* know about the performance Gabe and Lauren were supposed to give for Joe's benefit. Becca had admitted as much on the ride home. This was Hannah's way of encouraging Lauren to play, while making it clear she wasn't supposed to win.

A brief, tense silence followed. Young Melissa fractured it with, "Hoity-toity."

Gabe put down his fork and looked interested. "That's the best word you've come up with all week. Use it in a sentence for me, Missy."

" 'If she wasn't so doggone hoity-toity, maybe she could catch herself a man.' Grandma said that when she was putting rolls in the oven. I helped," Melissa added, her pixie cheeks aglow with pride.

Lauren almost choked on a mouthful of bread. To her ears, the child's sweet voice hinted of the diabolical.

Hannah leaned both elbows on the table and buried her reddened face in her hands.

Gabe had the ever-loving gall to laugh.

After lunch, Lauren stayed in the living room, where Becca rested, and watched through the window as Gabe and Melissa engaged in a game of one-on-one under the backyard basketball hoop.

As a child, Lauren had not been big on team sports, maybe because she'd never been good at them. When Becca and her friends had invited her to play, she'd always hung back, afraid she'd fail to perform as well as she should. Afraid she'd be scorned.

The only time Lauren had joined them, she'd ended up with a broken foot, for goodness' sake. The doctor bound it in a cast that made her leg look like an out-of-proportion golf club, which incited more ridicule than sympathy from the kids at school.

Later, when Lauren was out of the cast, Gabe showed up at the house and offered to shoot hoops with her. She was thrilled, thinking he had finally noticed she was nearly twelve and growing up fast. He'd meant only to give her a confidence boost, but she hadn't realized that then. Her usual self-consciousness had melted away; she'd enjoyed each moment of his attention, every drop of sweat, each innocent touch of their hands.

Now, as she watched through the window, Gabe lifted Melissa onto his shoulders so the child could slam-dunk. Both of them cheered, and even Lauren smiled at the kid's enthusiasm. The one time she'd played ball with Gabe, he'd done that with her. It had been the thrill of her young life.

"Lauren?" Becca said from the nearby recliner. "Why don't you go out and have some fun? Gabe won't mind if you can't shoot like Michael Jordan."

"How decent of him." Lauren turned toward her sister, glad to see she was awake and alert. "But as you know, basketball and I don't go together. I'd probably break something."

"Bad luck won't strike twice on the same court."

Lauren wasn't sure that was true. "I don't want to take the risk."

"No, I guess not," Becca said. "You like to have your strategy carefully worked out before you do anything, but sometimes it's more fun to just go for it. Remember when I took a spontaneous dive off a cheerleader pyramid and managed a double flip?"

"I closed my eyes, Becca. All I remember are the X rays."

"Yeah, well, maybe it was stupid, but it was a thrill, too. My point is, masterminding your entire existence in advance hasn't made you happy."

"It keeps me out of trouble." Which was more than Lauren could say for Becca. Lack of any real strategy had been the one consistent element in Becca's life. Fortunately, her good-natured personality had landed her a BLM job, because finishing college had never made it to the top of her list after she'd married Joe.

Instead she spent her spare time on beautiful but impractical art projects. The walls were covered with Becca's forays into oil, pen and ink, watercolor, and sand paintings. "The single-minded, measured approach has its virtues," Lauren said. "You should try it sometime."

Becca waved off that idea. "What can a few rounds of basketball hurt? Maybe you'd find that Gabe *hasn't* turned into the bogeyman, which ought to make helping me out a little easier."

"I still don't think it's a good idea," Lauren protested. And that went for both of the games Becca had in mind. "Besides, I'm wearing a skirt and heels."

"I have a whole drawerful of shorts, and tennis shoes that should fit you. Don't worry, I won't watch you play," Becca promised, apparently guessing Lauren wouldn't tolerate an audience. "In fact, I'm going to crawl between the sheets right now and get some shut-eye."

As Lauren helped Becca to bed, she thought about it. In a way, she'd like to show Gabe she'd improved. Playing an assortment of sports at a Denver health club, plus lifting weights over the past several years, had toned her muscles. She wasn't as inept as she used to be.

And she did need to talk to him. She'd convince him once and for all that she couldn't go along with Becca's plan. With a little brainstorming, maybe they'd think of something else. Better yet, maybe he'd agree to leave town, which really would solve their main problem. Melissa couldn't be all *that* attached to him, could she?

Since Lauren saw no advantage in putting off the confrontation, she emerged from her sister's room in baggy gym shorts and marched out the door toward the backyard hoop.

Gabe and Melissa both stopped what they were doing and stared at her. He held the ball. He'd changed into ragged cut-off jeans and tennis shoes. A faded navy T-shirt, darkened with sweat, stuck to his chest.

Lauren hiked her shorts, bent her knees, and waved her widespread arms in front of him. "Try to dribble past me," she dared him.

He raised an eyebrow. "Sure you want to play games with a lowly redneck?"

"It is against my better judgment, but I'm making an effort here, Gabe Randolph. Give me a break, would you?"

"Don't count on it." He easily dribbled around her, made his shot, and then threw the ball inbounds, straight at her. It was a good pass, but her reflexes needed tuning.

"Oof!" The ball hit her soundly in the stomach. She recovered and took two long strides in for a hook shot, which swooshed through the net.

"Look out, she's on a roll!" Gabe called. "Bold move, Laurie."

The compliment washed over her like a wave of pure sunshine. To her great surprise, she was enjoying herself. She knocked the ball out of Gabe's hands and passed to Melissa, who looked pleased to be included. Lauren hurt for the kid, for her youth and uncertainty and awkward efforts. Like Laurie at the same age, this child could barely maintain a dribble.

Gabe stopped the play to coach Melissa on technique. Lauren noted his patience and enthusiastic praise of the slightest improvement. The child was giggling within minutes, and making moves with more confidence, too. Lauren wished she had Gabe's talent for setting her niece at ease.

When they began another three-way round, Gabe faked playing badly, missing easy shots so his competition would look good. The game ended when he lunged sideways, feinting to the left to cut off Lauren's drive for a lay-up. Something happened on that last play. When he straightened, he winced.

"What's wrong?" Lauren asked.

"Nothing much. Old injury." He bent down to rub his ankle.

It was enough to put him out of commission. Lauren was left holding the ball, literally, while Gabe suggested Melissa go inside to see how her mother was doing. When the child was gone, he limped up to Lauren.

"Did you have fun?" he asked.

"More than I expected. You're still good. Seems like a redneck never forgets his game."

He grinned. "Seems like Miss Hoity-toity's been practicing."

Without warning, he grabbed her around the waist, spun her so her back was to him, and lifted her up for a slam-dunk. She squealed in surprise but regained her poise in time to send the ball swishing through the hoop. It bounced high on the blacktop and kept going downhill toward a back fence lined with a weedy vegetable garden and peach trees. She laughed, caught up in the moment, in triumph, in fresh air and elation.

He lowered her feet to the ground, letting her slide along the length of his body. She savored his damp heat and hard muscles. She opened her senses to sweat and male musk, to the touch and scent and breath that were Gabe. The Gabe she'd wanted to love, way back when.

His hands settled just below her breasts. She stopped breathing and closed her eyes as his deep voice whispered in her ear.

"No reconstruction necessary, Laurie. You've filled out just exactly right."

Chapter Five

"I'm fine," Gabe insisted when Lauren asked about his limp again. It almost made him think she cared, though she'd elbowed her way out of his arms a few moments earlier and told him to keep his paws and his anatomical opinions to himself. Her seeming concern for him was an aberration, a brief respite from their ongoing power play. Probably she was hoping his bad ankle would send him into a coma, or cause a permanent handicap.

"I'll walk you down to the BLM office to get your car," he offered. "Just to make sure nobody bothers you when you climb into the Tweety Bug."

He knew Lauren hadn't had a chance to retrieve her vehicle since she'd first arrived in town. Because Little Bit Van Horn's friendship had meant a lot to him once, he wanted to show his goodwill. He didn't like losing her respect, no matter how different they were now, no matter how opposed their views.

"I suspect that ridiculous nickname is an insult to my car." She still sounded breathless from their scrimmage, and her skin glowed from exercise and sun.

He held up his hands. "Hey, I don't give a flying flip what you drive. But with those pizza-cutter tires and left-wing stickers, somebody's liable to think you're a 'goddamn out-

sider.' You might as well hold up a sign that says, 'I hate locals. Go ahead and kick my butt.' "

She glared at him. "Please don't be vulgar. You can walk
with me if you like, but only because we need to talk." She
stepped inside the house to get her purse and keys and came
out combing her tangled hair.

He placed a hand on the back of her blouse, which was
warm and damp, and escorted her around the house toward
the street. He smiled when he felt the broad elastic of a sports
bra. In the old days, Lauren had been snooty about her intel-
lectualism, looking down on jocks and sports in general.

"If you're fine, why are you still limping?" She crammed
the comb into the leather-look shoulder bag she carried.

Encircling her ribs, he pulled her close enough for their
hips to bump. "Because I thought if I looked pitiful enough,
maybe you'd lend some support."

She wrenched his hand off her body and dropped it as if he
were diseased. "Go home and prop your foot on a cushion.
I'm not supporting any part of you."

"No need to stress yourself. The pain is bearable." He grimaced, exaggerating the limp, expecting her to call him on his
bad acting.

Instead her expression hinted of sympathy. "I saw your last
game on television, when you tore your ankle ligament."

Not exactly his suavest hour. "You, the hater of sports,
tuned in to basketball?" Too bad she hadn't seen a better
game, one where he'd done something more than get himself
trashed.

"I walked into a crowded freshman dorm room at Colorado State, and there you were on the screen. Seeing you reminded me I was homesick, I guess, so I stayed to watch. I
saw the huge black dude fall on you. Your leg twisted and it
looked . . . really bad. The fans wailed." She sniffed, more for
emphasis than out of any emotion he could tell. "Even I shed
a tear."

He didn't think she'd exaggerate about crying. "For me?" Maybe she did care, just a little.

"*One* tear," she stressed. "And it was probably from smoke and beer fumes."

He toughened up and disguised the limp as best he could. Damned if he'd give her anything to pity him for.

"Your dad must have been disappointed," she said. "He'd transferred to that new coaching job in Texas just so he could see all your games. From the day you got your scholarship, he told everyone you were sure to go pro."

"That was his dream, Laurie, not mine. I knew what I wanted from Geology 101 on."

She frowned. "*Oil* excites you?"

"The *discovery* of oil," he corrected. "Mapping layers of time and rock, tapping into a new field, then finally seeing raw energy come gushing out. The whole package is an adrenaline shot like . . . nothing else." He'd been about to say it was like sex, but he didn't think Lauren would appreciate the comparison.

She tilted her head. "I guess the discovery would be interesting. Still, I wish you'd gone in for solar power, or thermal energy. Something more environmentally correct."

"If I'd started there, I might have stayed with it, but after four college summers roughnecking on West Texas rigs, I knew the oil trade. Three years later, I wildcatted my first well and hit black gold."

"Congratulations," she said. "You're now a major contributor to the greenhouse effect."

He wished she hadn't put it that way. "Civilization needs fuel. Somebody has to provide it. Why not me?"

"Shock waves roll over me when you say things like that, Gabe, with no regard for what you destroy along the way. You used to be a concerned citizen. In fact, it was you who organized the first-ever recycling campaign in San Rafael."

"That was a long time ago. And unsuccessful, I might

add." Nowadays, he worked hard to run clean drilling operations, not that Lauren would believe him if he told her. "I'm not oblivious to the environment, just practical. On the plus side, oil burns with a lot less pollution than coal."

"It's still a problem," she said. "I have an immediate and serious problem with your leases in Red Rock Canyon. You used to love that area. I'd never have thought you'd personally inflict damage."

"Drilling in the canyon isn't something I planned from the get-go. It wasn't like that at all."

"So why did you buy into a Utah company? You could have stayed where you were and expanded Randolph Drilling. Why take on Great Basin when it was about to go bankrupt?"

"I got involved when Don Ray called me and asked if I'd consider taking it on. I wasn't too keen on the idea at first, but I looked over the possibilities and decided to go for it. The town really needs the employment, Laurie."

"How altruistic of you." She placed a hand over her breast. "I'll bet you were pretty darn sure you'd make a profit."

He shrugged. "I don't like to lose. Especially when I've put up my own savings to make the deal and staked my reputation to round up investors."

"From what I've heard, Great Basin's track record has been less than stellar, even since you've owned the company. I'd hate to see our canyon become one big, eroded ruin."

"Me, too, believe me. And that won't happen. I can't deny the EPA violations, even the recent ones, but that was before—"

"Please, Gabe. I can't take anything you say about those violations at face value. Remember, I'm on the other side."

"How could I forget?" He wanted her to understand, and even though he doubted she would, he gave it a shot. "If we strike oil with our wells on the rim, I'll push the BLM hard to let us go into the canyon. It's not just my personal profits on the line here. I'm saddled with savvy investors who'll want my neck in a noose if I don't follow up to their best advantage."

"But going in, drilling in the canyon, is ultimately your call, isn't it?"

"Well, yes. It's a business decision."

"I see it as a moral decision," she said. "If you bring oil rig equipment into the canyon, the necessary road building will ruin Red Rock's chance for permanent wilderness protection. Any future development will be on your head."

"Yeah." He couldn't say he felt good about it.

"What if the courts close you down and the BLM refuses to compensate you for the leases? That could happen, you know."

He looked over at her. "It could. I'm gambling it won't. I figure keeping San Rafael's economy going is worth some risk."

"You're playing Robin Hood, is that the idea?"

"You want to be Maid Marion?" He hoped a little teasing would lighten Lauren up.

She rolled her eyes. "Forget that. I'm the much-despised Sheriff of Nottingham, more like."

They'd walked across Becca's two-acre lot and traversed most of his when Bullwinkle, who kept watch from under the porch swing, spotted them. The dog bounded down the steps. Lauren stopped, turning pale. "Oh, no, not the dog again."

Gabe moved behind her and grasped her upper arms to keep her steady as the dog loped their way. He could deal with a vulnerable Lauren. "Bullwinkle won't hurt you, darlin'."

"If he touches me, I'm using Mace," she said between clenched teeth. Holding her purse against her stomach, she scrambled through the contents.

Her hands were trembling. She really was afraid, though Gabe couldn't see why she'd think Bullwinkle was dangerous.

"Whoa, boy. Down," Gabe called, more to save his dog from Lauren than the other way around.

Bullwinkle halted just short of them. Gabe was amused by the animal's appearance in the pink-and-purple kerchief. He'd been meaning to buy a real collar, maybe one with spikes to improve the beastly image.

When the hound took one small sniff at Lauren's crotch, she screeched and slapped at him, missing by six inches or more. Bullwinkle sat and yawned. His long tongue stretched as he emitted a mournful whine.

"Now you've gone and scared him, Laurie. You shouldn't have done that. He's a sensitive guy."

"Takes after you?" She wrinkled her nose, which still had a tilt at the end, and a freckle or two. The cute nose belied her stubborn, semiobnoxious nature.

"Us guys have to stick together. With women, we go for the basics first. If that doesn't work, we try charm."

"If 'the basics' refers to where that beast put his snout . . . You really are disgusting."

"Are you talking to the dog?"

"No. To you." Lauren started walking again, hitching her purse strap over her shoulder while giving Bullwinkle a wide berth.

Gabe grinned as he caught up. He was getting a charge out of being with Lauren and matching quips with her. Maybe playing out Becca's scheme wasn't going to be so bad after all. In fact, it might be the only way, considering their differences, that Lauren would give him a chance to know her better. And he wanted that. All of a sudden he knew he wanted that a whole hell of a lot. "I've been thinking. Maybe the town should have a preview of our relationship."

"We have no relationship," she stated.

"Exactly. That's why, for Becca and Missy's sake, we need to develop one."

Lauren glanced his way, challenging him with sparks in her eyes. "What kind?"

"Fake," he assured her, careful to be the soul of nonchalance about it. "Public, chaste kisses. Otherwise, platonic all the way. You can handle that, can't you?"

"I can handle anything you dish out," she said with lawyerly overconfidence. "The question is whether I choose to do so."

She kept walking, looking straight ahead now, avoiding eye contact. As Gabe watched her profile and the swing of her glossy mahogany hair, he wondered what it would take to persuade her. "Afraid you'll fall head over heels in love with me?"

"Holy purgatory," she huffed. "No, I'm afraid I'll faint from horror." But there was an upward curve to her lips, so he knew she didn't mean it. She liked their verbal tussle as much as he did, even if she'd undergo torture before she'd let on.

"If you're that scared of being close to a man, I'd be doing you a favor," he teased. "You need the practice."

"I've *had* practice. My mother wasn't making up *everything* she told you at lunch." She sucked in a breath, then glared over her shoulder at the hound, who must have touched her with his nose or tongue. Bullwinkle sat back on his haunches and appeared about as angelic and brainless as a hundred-pound dog could possibly look.

Gabe took her hand, pulling her along. "What kind of practice? Don't tell me you slept with Dr. Frankenstein, the plastic surgeon. Or with the big-shot attorney. Tom?" He'd have thought Lauren would be more discriminating.

"His name is Tim." She nailed him with eye darts. "I'm not fifteen anymore, Gabe. Fortunately for me, I haven't lived as sterile a life as you and Becca seem to think."

"Maybe you should have held out. Doesn't sound like either of those guys is worthy of you." Gabe's stomach churned as he pictured her with some jerk-off who didn't care.

"Don't tell me *you're* the worthy one." She yanked her hand out of his. "Butt out. I'm capable of deciding who's worthy and who's not."

"Yeah? I think you could use some help."

"Not your help, Gabe Randolph."

"Maybe you ought to give me a try before you rule me out."

"Dream on."

He wasn't discouraged. He enjoyed a challenge, and Lauren was a formidable one. She'd gotten better at sparring since she'd grown up. Much better. He was looking forward to more of the game.

Gabe glanced up at the two-story house they were strolling past. A window curtain moved slightly. The old lady who resided there watched the streets of San Rafael like a housebound soap fan might glue herself to *Days of Our Lives*. "Mrs. Marley's panning for nuggets," he said. "Bingo, she's found one. Probably she's on the phone with one of her granddaughters right now, speculating on why we're walking down the street together in the heat of the afternoon. She has telescopic eyes, they say." He leaned toward Lauren and whispered, "She claims she was abducted by aliens in 1998."

Lauren laughed.

"I thought that would get your attention." He liked her husky laugh. Always had. "I'll bet you still read sci-fi books. Me, I limit myself to *X-Files* reruns."

"Was it Mrs. Marley who came up with the initial eyewitness report on you and Becca?" she asked. "Where were you two acting out your daydreams, anyway? On the sidewalk?"

Damn. He really didn't want to talk about it, but he'd figured Lauren would ask. "Since I've been back in town, the sum total of our 'dating' was a couple of evenings on my porch swing."

Lauren's eyebrows rose. "So the gossip is *all* lies?"

Double damn. Did she expect a blow-by-blow? Becca

could fill her in if so inclined, but not him. "My guess is, one of our small-town busybodies looked into shadows and let her imagination run amok."

"Okay," Lauren said. "If you say it's pure slander, that's fine with me. All I want is a plan of defense, in case Joe takes the custody battle to court. And, should you and I attempt to convey an illusion, we need to know our target audience. In other words, who told the tale on you in the first place?"

"I've heard old lady Marley uses binoculars. If we were to go up on my porch and start smooching, she'd see plenty, don't you worry. Want to give it a try?"

Lauren scowled her disapproval. Of him, it seemed, not Mrs. Marley. "Why would anyone believe the old lady? She's been senile for years. If she's added a tale about alien abduction, then—"

"I made that up. It was a joke."

"Oh." Lauren's fair skin flushed. "Nevertheless, maybe we should expand our horizons." She glanced around for inspiration, fixing her gaze on a small, bespectacled boy riding a red bike.

"Yo, Mr. Randolph!" The sandy-haired boy lifted both hands off the handlebars. The bike swayed precariously.

"Hey, Buddy." Gabe turned to watch bike and rider swoop into Becca's driveway. "That's Buddy Lomax, Don Ray's son," he explained, smiling as the kid came to an impressive sliding stop. "I coached a Short Stuff basketball team this spring, and he was my star player."

"Could he be our gossip source?" she asked. "He's too young to be credible in court, but Joe and Don Ray are still friends, I assume. Little Buddy might—"

"The kid is eight years old and completely benign. He and Missy hang out together. No need to worry over Buddy."

Not to be deterred in her hunt for suspects, Lauren pointed out a green-and-white Dodge truck rumbling toward them. "Is that Al Hewitt?"

Gabe looked at the driver and saw Al's white hair contrasting with a well-aged cowboy tan. When Al wasn't herding his cows, he tried his best to herd the town and everyone in it. He was the more-or-less self-appointed mayor. No one had bothered to oppose him in an election for the last twenty years.

Al pulled across the deserted street and stopped in the wrong-way lane beside them. His powerful engine rocked the cab as it idled. "What's the word, Gabe? I've been waiting to hear from you on leasing my two hundred acres. It's still up for grabs."

"I appreciate your letting me know," Gabe replied. "I'll get back to you in a couple of weeks." He watched Bullwinkle trot to the curb, sniff the mayor's left rear tire, and raise a leg to wet down the hubcap.

Al had his mind on money, not hubcaps. "Fact is, Olympus Petroleum's been after me to sign mineral rights over to them. I said I'd rather work with a local boy and keep the gold in the family."

Like hell, Gabe thought. Olympus just hadn't offered enough. He reached behind him where Laurie had lingered, doing her best, he suspected, to avoid renewing her acquaintance with the mayor. Pulling her up beside him, he said, "You remember Laurie Van Horn, don't you, Al?"

The mayor raised his wraparound sunglasses above his eyes so he could look Lauren over. Lowering the glasses again, he spat sunflower-seed husks at her feet. "Yeah, I know her." He didn't sound friendly. Probably Al had never forgiven her for the school newspaper debacle. Factor in Lauren's environmental affiliation, and she was doomed to be on his permanent shit list. "Headed back to Colorado soon, Miss Van Horn?"

"Not as soon as some people would like, Mayor Hewitt," Lauren said in syrupy tones. "I'm extending my stay indefinitely, due to Becca's accident."

To Gabe's surprise, she clapped an arm around his back and snuggled against him. "Thank goodness Gabe's here. He's been a godsend, helping me bear up under the strain."

Doing what came naturally, he draped an arm over her shoulders. He couldn't help wincing when she pinched the skin of his flank with her rapier fingernails. Damn, this wasn't going at all as he'd planned.

He locked his grip on her shoulder. Her body stiffened until she felt about as inviting as a prickly pear, complete with thorns. Gabe gazed into her warrior eyes and tried to look besotted, hoping their battle over control was invisible to Al.

The mayor lifted his sunglasses and stared. He sprayed the curb with more tiny husks. "She's with the CPWA, son. Better watch your step."

Gabe nodded. "Yes, sir, I know."

Compressing his fleshy lips, Al positioned the sunglasses back over his eyes and roared away.

Lauren dropped her pose and twitched out of Gabe's grasp. Bullwinkle had gone from hubcap wetting to attempting to stick his nose under the wide hem of her shorts. She swatted at him and missed. The hound retreated, shaking his head and flopping his long ears. He collapsed on the pavement to rest his muzzle on his front paws.

"Can't blame a dog for trying." Gabe grinned in response to Lauren's glare. "I liked how you cuddled so close and friendly to me for Al's benefit, but you were supposed to swoon when I put my arm around you, not tighten up like a wrestler trying to break a stranglehold."

She shrugged. "I doubt our venerable mayor noticed. He was too worried about whether I'd do something to ruin his land-lease deal with the big cheese from Great Basin. He'll spread the story that I was all over you, just to flatter your ego."

"You might be right. Assuming he thinks I'd want anyone to know Laurie Van Horn's trying to get into my jeans."

Her brows drew together. "I hope you haven't forgotten this is all a hoax."

"Would I be here otherwise?" Since he didn't need his foot stomped or his testicles crunched, he knew better than to admit that he actually enjoyed her company.

She swept a length of windblown hair from her face. "Fortunately, Al doesn't think in circles, as you do. He'll tell what he saw, which should be good enough. He is Joe's uncle, after all, and surely Al's relatives will be the first to hear we're cooing like a couple of turtledoves. That ought to wrap up our act. We can go back to snarling at each other."

"Hold on now, Laurie. I don't think we've been nice—if you want to call it that—long enough. We need a lasting relationship. To convince Joe." And Gabe wasn't about to give up the foreplay, either, not when it had turned out to be so downright entertaining.

"How lasting?" she demanded.

"Hmm. Couple of weeks would be best."

"Weeks! No way I'm staying here that long," she said. "I couldn't possibly pretend that long, either. I have work to do in Denver."

"Doesn't the CPWA allow for time off? There's such a thing as a family emergency. That's what this is, wouldn't you say?"

She drew a deep breath. "Becca's gotten herself in a bind, all right, thanks to you."

He didn't deserve one hundred percent of the blame, but he decided not to protest when he knew it would do no good.

"Wouldn't this all be solved if *you* left town?" Lauren proposed.

"You'd like that, wouldn't you, Laurie? You'd like it even better if Great Basin left town along with me. But you lose this time, because my oil rigs are staying. So am I. Becca and I discussed it and she's already said—"

"I know what she said," Lauren snapped. "Melissa's little heart would be broken. Well, *I* don't believe it."

But he did. Not broken, maybe, but bruised some, and the kid didn't need that. Besides, they hadn't given a fair run to what was looking more and more like a perfectly good alternative. "Why not stay with the fake-lovers scheme? For a few days, anyway. If it doesn't work, and if, by chance, you can convince me that my leaving town *will* work, I'll go."

Lauren opened her mouth to protest, but since she'd pretty much gotten what she'd asked for, she had to shift gears. "What else did you have in mind for this afternoon, Gabe? We started with the mayor—at the top, so to speak. Want to stroll by the sheriff as he sleeps on his bench? We could clang an alarm bell in his ear and start doing the wild thing the instant he looks up."

He chuckled. "Not bad, but maybe we should go with something a little more subtle." He moved in on her, hoping to receive a better reception than he'd had when Al was looking.

She stepped back, right into Bullwinkle. "Wretched beast," she muttered, looking behind her as the dog scuttled out of her way. "You'd think he'd have more dignity than to wallow at my feet. He knows I don't like him."

Gabe stalked closer.

"Keep your oil-slick hands to yourself, Gabe Randolph." She sidestepped to avoid contact. "If we do any further acting, *I'll* take the initiative. Meanwhile, keep in mind that I take karate lessons. I'm prepared to inflict damage."

He laughed, but did maintain a distance. "Fair warning. No physical contact until you say it's okay."

They'd reached a side street with a view of Don Ray Lomax's white frame house. The front yard looked like a used-car lot with two rusted pickups framing the drive. The truck corpses had been there so long that Trish—the epitome of go-with-the-flow—had filled the beds with dirt and planted a flower garden in them.

"Joe's visiting Don Ray," Gabe noted. "See the Harley parked in front of Trish's tailgate geraniums? How would you like it if you knew Missy was going to ride home with him tonight on that big ugly murdercycle?"

Lauren shuddered. "You've heard about—"

"Yes. Becca told me. Joe was a reckless bastard in high school. Sounds like he got worse. Zooming around curves at sixty-five on a dirtbike with his wife riding double was the height of stupidity, even for Joe. It's a wonder either of them survived wheeling off a twenty-foot cliff."

"She almost died," Lauren said. "Joe wasn't even badly hurt."

"She should have quit him then." Gabe suspected Becca had loved Joe's wildness once, but the lapses in judgment must have worn on her.

"Becca was too softhearted to treat him like he deserved. He shed a few tears, then swore he'd shape up, stop drinking, and fix the leak in the roof. Good old Joe," Lauren sneered. "He might have been sincere at the time. Sad to say, he has a short memory. It's been nine years now. As far as I know, he still drinks plenty, the roof leaks worse than a colander, and he's been in at least one other wreck, fortunately without Becca."

"Can you figure it?" Gabe shook his head. "Those two do something dumb like stay together, and the result is Missy, who's smarter than both of them."

"Mmm," Lauren said noncommittally.

"What? You don't like me criticizing Becca? Hell, she did marry someone else less than a year after I left town. She would've saved herself a lot of trouble if she'd had the good sense to pine over me." At the time, he'd thought he wanted her to wait for him to finish college, which showed how little he'd known back then. He and Becca were too different. They'd never have lasted.

"I think . . . she made a mistake," Lauren offered. Whether the mistake was in choosing Joe or in failing to choose Gabe, she didn't specify.

They had passed plumber Bill Whalen's house, the side yard adorned with eight toilet bowls Bill had tiered on every other step of an old, salvaged staircase. He'd rigged a pump to keep water overflowing through the toilets in a continuous cycle to form a one-of-a-kind cascade. Gabe had never figured out whether the display was meant as a decoration, or as an advertisement of Bill's trade.

Molly Dockins's plastic pink flamingos decked out the next yard. At least their purpose was clear, even if Gabe had doubts about their beautifying effect.

Looking ahead to the following block, he noted a CLOSED sign in the bay window of the Top Chop Grocery. Across from the store, the sheriff's bench was empty.

"Damn shame," he said with a sly glance at Lauren. "Too late to catch LaDell napping. I've always wanted to wake him up with a fire alarm and a sex orgy."

Lauren blushed at the reminder of her flippant proposal, but she didn't comment. As they approached her bright yellow car, still parked in front of Becca's office, she fumbled through her purse for keys. "I've been wondering. Does Melissa realize Joe's using her as a battleground?"

"She knows more than you'd think," Gabe said. "Christ, she's only a little kid. I don't want her hurt any worse, Laurie, not if there's something we can do."

Lauren sighed. "We should go through the court system, but Becca doesn't trust it. All things considered, she might be right."

"Maybe our faking a relationship won't help," Gabe said. "No one can predict how Joe will react. From our standpoint, though, what do we have to lose?"

"I . . . suppose we could give it a try. Let me take my car back to the house and check on Becca. Tonight, after dark, I'll come over to your place. We'll talk."

"We'll have to do more than talk. Why wait until after dark, when being seen is the whole point?"

"Don't we need to discuss strategy?" Lauren asked.

He laughed. "There's no strategy to making out in a porch swing. Next you'll want a practice session. I thought you said you were experienced."

She squared her shoulders. "I just thought, since we don't really know each other anymore . . ."

"I'll be gentle. I'm not *that* bad, am I?"

Her eyes softened ever so slightly, and for a minute he thought she might smile. He wished she'd drop the holier-than-thou halo. She could be warm and womanly; he was sure of it. He wanted to see her smile, hear her beguiling, husky laugh.

"You ought to leave town," she grumbled, fidgeting with the strap of her purse. "*I* ought to leave town."

"But neither of us can do that right now, so we'll go for the next-best thing. It's Saturday night. People will be out walking, driving around, which makes the timing perfect. We'll put on a great show. Meet me on my porch at seven. Winky and I will be waiting."

"Winky?" She glanced from him to the dog, who had followed at close range and now angled his head under her hand in shameless pursuit of affection. Rolling her eyes, she gingerly patted the animal. One pat. "I'll make my next appearance with Mace and a karate handbook. You and 'Winky' had better be on good behavior." She climbed into her car, plugged in the key, and ignited the four measly cylinders.

"Careful," he told her. "No drag racing."

She nodded, probably thinking he meant it as a real warning instead of a joke. As she did her best to accelerate, the little yellow car squealed and tweeted into full song.

Chapter Six

Becca hung up the bedside phone and cautiously swung her legs over the side of the bed, inching her feet toward the floor. Her head hurt, but she thought being vertical for a while would do her good.

Lauren had just called to say she'd retrieved her car and was on her way to Fairfield to buy a fax machine so she could keep track of business. Lauren could not relax, and that was a fact. Hannah had left after lunch for "a quick trip to the restaurant," which probably meant several hours. Trish had invited Missy over for the afternoon to play with Buddy. At the moment Becca was alone, with no one to fuss at her for leaving the bed.

After making her way into the kitchen, she sat on a stool by the counter while she decided if she felt up to eating anything.

She heard a knock at the back door. So much for solitude. She hoped it wasn't a well-meaning neighbor bringing chicken-noodle casserole dotted with green peas, or, heaven forbid, fruit salad encased in lime Jell-O. Right then, the thought of facing one of San Rafael's traditional sympathy dishes made her nauseous. Thank goodness Gabe had had the good sense to send mint truffles, her all-time favorite health food.

Even as she turned to see who was there, the door opened and a voice called out, "Becca!"

"Joe!" She stared at him standing in the door frame. He looked like he'd cleaned up for her. His dark hair, trimmed since she'd last seen him, was brushed back from his forehead. He had on the jade-colored shirt she'd bought him a few years ago—she'd always liked how it brought out the green in his eyes. His long, sooty lashes, high cheekbones, and Elvis Presley mouth reminded her of why local girls had once thought him the best catch in the West.

Now his good looks just made her sad. He held out his hand to show her a copper bracelet in his palm. "I . . . thought you might like this." He paused, as if trying to think what else to say. "It's supposed to take away the . . . pain."

Becca knew Kayleen Throckmorton had been peddling metal jewelry around town. She had no doubt that the little slut's sales techniques catered to males under forty. Too abruptly, Becca looked up from the bracelet to Joe. The room seemed to sway as she held on to the counter's edge. "Thanks, but you shouldn't have bothered."

He set his offering on the countertop, in the middle of a sand painting she'd been working on the night before the accident. As usual, he didn't notice her work, or much of anything else that wasn't directly related to fulfilling his needs or stoking his self-image, which she suspected was what this visit was about. "Why are you here, Joe?"

"I wanted to see you. I . . . heard, and I worried. I couldn't stop thinking. . . ."

She started to smile, to be pleased that he was concerned, but then she remembered that Joe acted out of need, not love. She shook her head. "No reason to give yourself an ulcer. I'm perfectly fine." My God, she sounded as bitchy as Lauren. And she was enjoying it, too.

"I heard thirdhand from Don Ray that you were in the hospital. That hurt me, Becca. You should have called."

"I was unconscious for the first several hours." If she'd really hurt his feelings by not calling, she was sorry for it, but Joe had taught her to be wary. "The hospital contacted family. As you should know, a woman's ex-husband isn't considered next of kin."

"I'm Missy's next of kin. Somebody should have called me to look after her," he said.

"Take your complaints to someone else. You won't squeeze a drop of sympathy out of me, not after the way you've treated me lately."

"As soon as I found out, I went by the hospital. You were gone. It's all over town that Gabe drove you home."

Now she was catching on. Her choice of travel companion had bruised Joe's delicate ego. When Gabe had helped her into the Jeep, he'd suggested that maybe Lauren should drive her home and he'd hitch a ride. He'd been thinking ahead, but it had seemed ridiculous to her that Joe would make an issue of something so innocent.

She should have known. He still hated Gabe for winning the high school basketball accolades that Joe had coveted. And now Gabe had come back to recapture the town's—and Becca's—respect. Joe had always craved a cheering section, and she'd been willing to be that for him for a long while. He certainly hadn't gotten much praise from his parents, or from his uncle Al. She did understand Joe, but that sort of thing ought to go both ways. It was *his* turn.

"Should I have made a secret of how I got home? Lauren and Missy were with me, and we all needed a ride."

Joe's lanky frame stiffened. His hazel eyes with their bright green highlights blazed at her. "Someone should have called me, damn it. I should have been the first to know."

She shook her head slowly, so as not to make the room spin. "Please don't lay this on me now." At least he didn't smell like alcohol. From what she'd heard, he was cutting back on the binge drinking. She hoped he'd decided to change for his own good, not just to up his chances of taking Missy from her.

"I felt bad for you, Becca. I wanted to be with you and . . . I wanted to do right by you, but then you went off with *him* again."

"I'm free to make that choice," she reminded Joe.

"You're making it hard for me to show my face in town. It's like we were never married. Like I'm a nothing. I thought maybe you'd wise up and stay away from him so you could keep Missy, but no, he's even more important to you than our kid. You'll be sorry when I take her. I'll show everybody— you, him, and this town—that she's *my* kid, not his."

Joe's selfish, macho possessiveness made her want to strangle him. "Since I hadn't seen Gabe in six years when she was conceived, I guess she'd have to be yours. But she's mine, too," Becca said. "I don't know why you came here bearing gifts when you were going to ruin it with more insults and threats."

"If you'd just kiss off Gabe and let me try again . . ."

She'd already told him, numerous times, that Gabe was only a friend. "If Missy is so important to you, why weren't you at the house this morning to pick her up for your regular Saturday? She told me she looked for you."

"I . . . forgot. I'm having problems with my rental business."

So what else was new. "I'm sorry. I'm especially sorry because I'm sure it means no child support again this week."

"The fact is, I can't—"

"You can buy beer when you want it. You bought a fancy new motorcycle. But you can't do your share for Missy?"

"I'll pay two hundred next week, I promise."

Sure, sure. "I won't hold my breath."

"Slipped my mind that this was our Saturday. I overslept, then the phone started ringing, then I had customers wanting to rent wheels. The Biggs boy, the one I hired to do the rentals on weekends, didn't show until noon. I had to fire him. Can't afford to pay him anyway."

"Did you call and leave Missy a message?" She already knew he hadn't.

"I'll make it up to her." He put on a crooked, charming smile. "Wilt Moseley opened his new snow-cone stand over by the Sandman Motel. How about I take Missy there right after dinner on Monday? She'll like that."

Becca put her hands to her temples. Their daughter would be as pleased as a kitten with a new ball of yarn. In the same pathetic way that Becca had put up with him for so long, Missy took whatever offhand affection Joe remembered to give. Sadly, there'd been very little of it.

"You don't deserve our daughter," she said.

He kept smiling. He didn't even flinch. "I'll call her this time; wait and see."

"Just don't make Missy wait too long. Now go away, Joe. Please."

At dusk that evening, Lauren found herself sitting next to Gabe on his freshly painted dark green porch swing. Bullwinkle slept with his head on her sandals, soaking her ankle with his slobbery gums. Being around Gabe must have inured her to the dog's grossness, because she really didn't mind.

To her surprise, the hound had turned out to be harmless. He'd done nothing more menacing than grovel, sleep, and drool. She was beginning to think of the beast as cute, which made her wonder if she was losing her mind completely.

Gabe slid his arm from the backrest onto her shoulders.

She looked pointedly at his offending hand. "I didn't ask you to do that." His touch burned through her blouse, which was bad. Very bad. She was all too aware that he was one hundred percent mature male, not the boy she'd once known. And her woman's needs cried out for attention whenever she was near him. Like it or not, she was attracted to him, a full-fledged sexual attraction.

Only sexual, she told herself. Shouldn't she be able to rise above mere hormones?

"Someone's driving by." He waved at a passing dusty pickup. "Jimbo Johnson and his son Artie. We don't want them to see us sitting here like a couple of seventh graders on a blind date, do we? A little hugging is good for getting us in the mood."

"Why do we want to be in the mood? Better if we keep this as emotionless as possible." She certainly wasn't going to do anything to let on that she wasn't as immune to Gabe as she wanted to be. If he found out, he'd tease her about it, and she'd end up having to whip up some karate moves and practice them on him.

He toyed with her short sleeve. "Maybe you'd rather not feel anything, but I need inspiration if I'm going to be convincing. Don't take it seriously. Remember, this isn't for pleasure."

"Of course not."

He moved his thumb up under her hair and feathered across the bare skin above her collar. "If we should happen to reap some fringe benefits, I don't see the harm."

She shivered. "Well, I do. I prefer to stay as far as possible from the nearest hypocrite. Such as you. If there's anything I can't stand . . ." She wanted to scoot out of his range, but his hand caressed her neck, urging her nearer. She stayed stiff, her spine perfectly straight, and concentrated on emulating a frozen corpse.

Gabe frowned. "You mean I'm a hypocrite tonight? Or in general?"

"Both. Remember when the big coal company first talked about putting a power plant on the Kaiparowits Plateau? Whose side were you on then?"

"I was against it, just like you and your dad were, Laurie. You know that."

"Well, then. I rest my case."

"Yeah, but that was different. Drilling a couple of oil wells in the canyon's not going to pour out pollution and acid rain and destroy air quality like—"

"Oh, no? Maybe not in the same volume, maybe not in the same way, but your oil wells aren't doing the earth any good," Lauren argued. "So why have your basic beliefs changed so much? How? What made it happen?"

"My vision widened, that's all I can say. Energy is a need the world wants filled. There's oil in the canyon, and I'm going after it. Do you know how many good-paying jobs Great Basin brings to this area?"

"I can guess. I can even agree that we need the industry. Just not there. Not in the canyon."

"You are hardheaded, woman. Like I've tried to tell you, Great Basin may not be able to stay afloat without going for those canyon wells. I'll do what I have to do."

She was quiet, contemplating that.

"Maybe you're a hypocrite, too," he said. "If you're going to shut down one industry, there has to be something to take up the slack. You can talk till your jaw falls off, but this community needs viable alternatives. What are they?"

"Well, tourism, for one, is—"

"It's a possibility, but not enough, not by itself."

She drew a deep breath. "I admit I don't have all the answers. I just know protecting the canyon is right. If you go in there with oil rigs, if we lose wilderness protection, then it'll be open to mining and any other development the BLM decides to allow. And they've been shockingly liberal in the . . ."

Another truck went by. Lauren looked up and noticed an older couple on the sidewalk gazing back at her.

Gabe waved. "Evenin', Mrs. Dockins. Evenin' Bob." Out

of the side of his mouth, he added, "Could you reverse the rigor mortis, darlin'? Because the way you're sitting there, you look like a ghoul in one of those sixties horror flicks, about to pull a hatchet from behind your back and start chopping off my extremities."

She tried to relax. She waved to the Dockinses, too. The couple appeared puzzled, but they nodded and continued on their way.

Gabe's arm, still around Lauren, urged her closer. The warmth of his body, his breath on her hair, felt good. Very good. She squirmed. "Don't hold me so—"

"Shhh." He kissed the top of her head. "It's pretend, remember? We can do this."

She couldn't, at least not without feeling far more than she wanted to feel. Her only consolation was that it wouldn't last long. She'd get through tonight, and then she'd straighten everything out by legal means, or find a way to force Gabe out of town. She'd do *something* to end this as quickly as . . .

Gently, Gabe nudged her chin up with his thumb. "Come on now, before Molly and Bob get clean out of sight. And I just saw a curtain move on Mrs. Marley's second floor. It's showtime." For a long moment she felt only his gaze on her. Then he brushed his lips over her cheek.

"Ah, Laurie, don't try to be tough. I know you. I know you can be soft," he murmured. "Sweet."

"Don't you dare call me sweet," she said between clenched teeth. No one ever called her sweet, except Ezra, and she didn't even know why she let *him* get by with it. "And remember what I said about the hazards of kissing me. 'Pretend' doesn't mean actual contact. Don't—"

Maybe Gabe pressed his lips hard against hers just to keep her quiet. It worked. By the time he gentled the kiss to featherlight, she couldn't bring herself to keep up the objections.

His lips were mostly closed, though she could feel his breath, feel it quicken, as hers did. He cupped the back of her head, fingers threading in her hair. His mouth opened a fraction more.

She was curious, that was all. She wanted to know what it would be like to really kiss him. Her hands gripped his hard-muscled shoulders. Her lips moved under his. He seemed startled by that, but she clung for a second. One second too many.

His tongue touched the seam of her lips.

"N—" She tried to get out a no, but he persisted, and she failed to resist. He moved inside her mouth, and she responded there, too, following his lead.

When he came up for air, he looked surprised. She felt shell-shocked and shaken. She searched for a way to save face. The game. She recalled the game, and played it by squinting over her shoulder. "Are you sure Mrs. Marley's looking?"

Gabe grasped Lauren's chin and made her meet his gaze. "Why did you let me do that?"

"It was . . . part of the act." It *had* started out that way.

"You forget one detail. No one can see where our tongues are, darlin'." Gabe was nobody's fool.

"I was getting into the spirit of—"

"Yeah, babe, you were." His gaze moved to her lips, and he lowered his mouth to hers again. Why couldn't she think of something to argue about? She pulled away and again pivoted to regard the street. "It's getting dark. No one can see us here."

"We can fix that." He reached inside the door to switch on the porch light and then drew her out of the swing. Bullwinkle slept on when they stepped over him and across the wooden planks to one of the square columns near the front steps.

Gabe moved up close, backing her against the post. "You're warming up real fine. Quicker than I figured you would."

"Is that supposed to be a compliment?" Heaven help her, warming up to him was the last thing she'd intended.

"No. I'm just glad you don't need the practice."

"I don't, but maybe you do. I didn't know you'd find my response offensive."

"Believe me, sweetheart, I am not offended." In fact, Gabe was turned on.

On the surface, Lauren was like spiked rawhide. He'd sensed the softness in her, and he'd started out kissing her with the restraint he'd figured she deserved and would demand. Calling her "sweet," tasting her lips, had been an experiment as much as anything else, an attempt to rile her. Damned if it hadn't backfired on him. Damned if he didn't want more.

There was something incredibly appealing about coaxing a controlled and controlling woman like Lauren into letting go. He'd awakened a feminist Sleeping Beauty. She tantalized him by giving, tantalized even more when she tried to hold back.

He leaned down until their mouths nearly touched.

"Do we have an audience?" She sounded as breathless as he felt. "I think we should—"

"Don't think." He ran his thumb over her lips, and ended by tickling the corner of her mouth. Her head fell back; her lips parted. She made a sound in her throat that he could have sworn was a moan.

He covered her mouth with his, angling for the right depth, the maximum contact. He'd never have guessed that prickly Laurie would respond so readily, and with so much . . .

"Want to see the rocks we found, Mr. Randolph?"

Gabe barely heard the voice over the rushing of blood through his veins. He shifted his position to shield Lauren from the street, even though it occurred to him that the whole idea was for both of them to be seen. He turned his head to

take in little Buddy Lomax, who'd stopped his bike in front
of Gabe's house.

"Can me and Missy bring them by tomorrow?" the boy
asked, pushing his glasses up with one finger. "We found an
awesome arrowhead, and a shiny red rock, and another one
with black crystals that Missy named Starlight."

"She means staurolite." Gabe tried to keep the frustration
out of his voice. "Bring the whole collection over tomorrow
evening and we'll have a look."

"Okay. See ya, Mr. Randolph."

"See ya." Gabe took a breath and blew it out slowly.
"You'd think the kid would've noticed I'm busy here. Now,
where were we?"

She licked her lips, moist and full. "Exactly where I never
thought I'd be."

"Kissing me?"

That was what she'd meant. Every night when she was
fifteen, Lauren had dreamed of kissing him, with no hope of
it happening. The reality was . . . amazing, incredible . . . and
she had to put it right out of her head. "The kissing is unim-
portant. It's corrupting San Rafael's youth that concerns me."

"Corrupting? Young Buddy's seen more R-rated movies
than I have. He knows about more than kissing."

"That doesn't excuse our behavior. I can't do this. I should
have known better." She shoved at his chest, though not hard
enough to move him.

He took her hand and caressed the back of it with his
thumb. "Knowing better and doing better are two different
things."

She had a hollow feeling in the pit of her stomach when
he looked into her eyes. He knew she'd been out of control.
He knew.

"I'm quite capable of determining that difference for myself," she said, "and I intend to live up to—"

"We're doing this for a cause, remember? I won't hurt

you, Laurie. You can't think I would ever hurt you." His mouth lowered slowly toward hers.

"Mr. Randolph?"

"Jesus," Gabe said under his breath. "Why won't the kid go away?"

His gaze remained locked with Lauren's. The spark of desire in his eyes warred with a glint of amusement. She smiled. He smiled back.

"What is it, son?" he asked.

The light from the porch shone on Buddy, who had stopped just a few yards up the street. "I won't tell I saw you with Missy's aunt, Mr. Randolph. Just like I didn't tell nobody last time, when I saw you with Missy's—"

"Uh, sure, Buddy," Gabe said. "Thanks a lot."

His hands rested on Lauren's shoulders and her palms lay flat on his chest. She felt the tenseness in him. For a moment she wondered why. Did it matter that Buddy had seen them? Wasn't that what Gabe wanted? What she wanted?

As understanding dawned, their moment of harmony exploded in her face. Buddy must have seen Gabe with Becca. Kissing Becca. Loving Becca.

Of course. That had to have been what went on, even if Gabe had toned down his version of it. She should have been thinking of Becca the whole time she'd been with him. She hadn't wanted to think about it, but she'd known from the start that Becca wanted him for herself. Otherwise why would they be in this situation to begin with? Somewhere along the line, she'd completely lost sight of that.

"Aren't you gonna give me a dollar like you did before?" Buddy was a persistent little weasel. Greedy, too. Lauren wished the child would shut up and leave.

Gabe reached for the wallet in his back pocket.

Lauren sent him her steeliest glare. "You don't need to pay Buddy off. We want the word spread, don't we?"

Gabe drew out the wallet anyway. "I'll pay him to spread it then."

She stood by while Gabe forked over the cash and crouched down to talk to the boy. When he straightened and came back to her, she asked, "Am I wrong, or did you downplay what happened between you and my sister? Not that I care from my own viewpoint, you understand, but if the custody issue goes to court . . ." Lauren couldn't keep a tremor from her voice. "You should have told me the whole truth. I needed to know."

He gazed at her steadily, and she had a feeling her glare of steel hadn't fooled him one bit. "You're adding this up all cockeyed, Laurie. Okay, sure, Buddy saw something. Becca and I did kiss, once or twice, but it was no big deal."

"If that's so, what's with the gossip?"

"Someone—I don't think it was Buddy—spread the rumor that Becca and I were taking up where we left off. You know how it is here; everyone believes what they want to believe. All it took was one report, and pretty soon the news was bouncing around town like a pogo stick. I should have told you more, sooner, but I figured that this, what we did tonight, would be easier for you if . . ."

Feeling too tawdry for words for having responded to him as she had, she tuned out his explanation. She watched a grinning, wealthier Buddy ding his handlebar bell a couple of times and ride away, patting the hip pocket where he'd securely stowed his ill-gotten gain.

Chapter Seven

As Lauren headed back to Becca's house a few minutes later, she wondered exactly what she should tell her sister. Not the whole truth and nothing but, not this time. If she said that she'd kissed Gabe and *enjoyed* it, Becca would never believe her anyhow.

Thank God young Buddy had come along to show Lauren how far she'd pushed the lunacy index. She'd betrayed Becca; she'd betrayed herself. Lauren Van Horn sued people like Gabe. She did not kiss them.

Any more pretense was out of the question. If Becca insisted, she'd simply say she found Gabe revolting and couldn't possibly be near him anymore.

With that plan in mind, she pushed open the kitchen door. Or tried to. A lumpy pillowcase that clunked and seemed as heavy as an andiron lay on the floor, partially blocking the door's inward arc.

Melissa sat at the kitchen table, looking displeased. "Those are my rocks," she said, pointing possessively at the pillowcase. "You're not supposed to touch 'em." A dozen or more specimens of her collection, some light, some shiny, some dark, were spread across the oak surface in front of her.

"You'll scratch the varnish," Lauren warned.

"Mama says it's okay. She says I can look at my rocks

wherever I want. *You* can't say what to do. You're grouchy and mean and I don't want you here."

"Touché," Lauren murmured. "You're right, Melissa, I—"

"I don't like that name. Missy's my real name."

Lauren sighed. "Okay, Missy. I'm not going to do anything with your rocks, and I'll try my best to be . . . cheerful." She forced her mouth into a phony smile for half a second before she realized how insecure the kid must feel after her mother's accident. This child, like Lauren, tended to hide her true emotions. Lauren had to find a way to get past that if she hoped to become close to her niece.

"I know it's hard to take, having your mom hurt, and then having me barge into your house and get in the way. But Missy, I'm only trying to help. Will you be patient with me?"

Melissa, alias Missy, narrowed her big hazel eyes. "Mama *says* you came here to help us. She says you promised to make everything better, but you promised to come to my birthday, too, and that was a lie. Buddy says lawyers tell whoppers all the time."

Lauren did not let the lawyer-bashing get to her. "I said I was sorry about your party. I wanted to be there. If you'd give me the chance, I'd like to do what I can now, for you and your mom."

Missy stared down at her rock display. "Mama doesn't want me to go live with my daddy. She'll cry if I go."

Lauren wished she knew more about kids, especially this kid. She wanted the child's trust, wanted it so much, but she didn't have a clue how to earn it. "How do you feel about living with your daddy, Mel— I mean, Missy? Don't you like him anymore?"

The child pooched her rosebud lips and frowned at the rocks. "I like doing things with Daddy. We had fun when we went to the rodeo at Easter time. I like when he visits here or takes me places. But I don't like his house."

"Why not?" Lauren didn't relish the idea of using a kid against her father. However, as Becca's legal counsel, it was her job to ask.

"He lives in a trailer, way far out of town, far away from Mama and school and my friend Buddy. We have to eat peanut butter 'cause Daddy doesn't cook."

"You used to like peanut butter," Lauren coaxed.

"Only with jelly. Did you know lots of people come to Daddy's house? They rent his ATVs. That's what he calls dirtbikes and four-wheelers."

Lauren nodded, well aware of Joe's all-terrain vehicle rental agency, his latest moneymaking strategy in a long line of unsuccessful ones. He'd tried ranching, running a used-car lot, and operating a video store. His plans invariably grew too grandiose, and the overhead ate him alive. Recalling the Harley Gabe had pointed out as Joe's newest toy, she asked, "Have you ridden your daddy's motorcycle? Or any of his ATVs?"

"No. He wants me to, but loud engines make my stomach hurt. Then at night, sometimes he drinks beer. Mama says that's bad, and he says he's trying to quit, but he still drinks it. Once, he made me . . ."

Lauren's heart almost stopped as the child's pause lengthened. She was afraid she might be digging deeper than she wanted to go, but someone had to find out if the child had reason to fear her father. Lauren doubted Becca would think to ask. Her sister had trusted Joe too much for too long. "What did he make you do?"

Missy rearranged the rocks. "Some of his friends came over. Chester, and . . . somebody else. They had to talk about important business, Daddy said, so he made me go to bed early."

Lauren started breathing again. "What business?" Maybe there was something illegal going on, something that might be of use in custody negotiations.

Melissa chewed her lower lip. After a few seconds, she shook her head. "Good girls don't tattle on their daddy."

Lauren saw Missy's point of view. The child had loyalties, too, and was struggling to deal with them. The push and pull of her parents must leave her feeling traumatized, and Lauren felt torn right along with her. The poor kid had gotten a bum rap.

"You're a good girl, Missy." Lauren touched the top of the child's head and felt warmth through the thick tousle of baby-soft hair. "I'm proud of you for thinking for yourself and trying to decide what's fair. That's not easy. Not even for people as big as I am."

The child glanced up, smiling now. Under the kitchen lights, she looked like a gold-and-cream little angel about to sprout wings, yearning for approval, for love. She was so dear, so very innocent, and much too young to have to wonder where she'd live and who would take care of her.

Lauren's heartstrings pulled tight as she bent down to plant a kiss on Missy's blond hair. "Just so you know, I don't make a habit of telling lies. I promise I'll do everything I can to make sure you and your mother stay together."

She meant she'd do everything, legally speaking. She didn't know what she'd do if helping Missy meant spending more evenings on Gabe Randolph's front porch.

"Where did you and Gabe go? What were you doing all this time?"

Lauren stood in the doorway of Becca's room, her face growing hot as she tried to formulate an answer for her sister. "I, um . . . We—"

"Sorry. I guess I asked the wrong question." Becca was sitting in bed, propped up by pillows. She laughed. "From your giveaway blush, I know *something* happened. And it's okay, really. You don't have to worry about offending me,

Lauren. I asked both of you to do this, and I know I can trust you."

Lauren's face felt even hotter, and she was still having trouble forming words.

Becca seemed undaunted. "Start with when you went out to play basketball. I don't want to miss anything."

That afternoon, Lauren had returned to Becca's house with her car and her new fax machine to find that Joe had come and gone, causing his usual upheaval. Becca had been distressed, Hannah had returned from the restaurant to cluck over her, and then Becca had taken a nap, partially, Lauren suspected, to escape their mother's suffocating care.

Only now, after Missy had kissed her mother and aunt good night and gone to her room, did they have a chance to discuss the rendevous with Gabe.

Lauren pulled a chair up to the beside, sank into it, and began. When she came to the tryst on the porch, she simply said, "Everything went as planned." Well, almost as planned, except for her knee-jerk lust. She regretted that and could never admit it to her sister.

"We can only hope someone saw the two of you," Becca said.

"Not a problem." Lauren described the various witnesses of the afternoon and evening, ending with Buddy. "He wanted money to keep his mouth shut."

"Welcome to Buddy's standard ploy. How did Gabe handle him this time?"

"I— Becca, I wish you'd tell me more about what's been going on between you and Gabe. I'm feeling my way in the dark here."

"I told you, what really happened doesn't matter. It's what people think that counts. Buddy'll be a big help. Gabe gave him some money and told him what rumor to spread, right?"

"I guess so. I didn't listen in on the exchange."

"Buddy's a sweet kid." Becca attempted a smile. "And

Gabe won't let him get away without doing some work for the money. Last time, Buddy painted Gabe's porch swing."

Lauren felt like wiping the seat of her shorts to see if the fresh green had come off. "Couldn't you and Gabe have found someplace private for your little tryst? It would have saved all of us grief."

"Call me stupid if it makes you feel better," Becca said.

Lauren bit her tongue and didn't. "Anyway, assuming Buddy received a large enough bribe, our newest news ought to be out in force tomorrow." She brushed her hands together. "So that's that. I'm finished with 'Gabe and Lauren's Sordid Affair' by Rebecca Hewitt."

Becca tilted her head. "What do you mean?"

"I think—in fact, I *know* I'm not going to do a repeat performance." Lauren could still feel the tingling from Gabe's kisses clear to her toes.

"Why not? I hope he didn't tease you mercilessly, the way he did in the old days."

"No, not too much." Teasing wasn't the problem.

"Well, then, being with him couldn't be that awful. Can't you bear up a little longer? I wouldn't ask if I weren't in a mess and feeling desperate."

Lauren was also feeling desperate. She only wished she could convey that to her sister without exposing how susceptible she was to Gabe. Since she couldn't, she acted as if she were impervious. "Can I help it if I'm the only woman in the world who can look into Gabe's blue eyes without the pheromones fluttering like confetti at a New Year's party?" She hoped Becca saw no telltale signs of confetti floating around her head. "As you know, my heart is an ice sculpture."

"Get over yourself," Becca said. "You'll have to stay frozen awhile longer, because one night won't be enough."

Lauren imagined spending an entire night with Gabe. In his arms, in his bed, limbs twining, skin slick with his heat mingled with hers. "I told you, no more. No more nights, days, or any other times."

"This evening's show might start tongues wagging, but we need to keep up the gossip," Becca said. "Since Joe's not the steadfast type himself, he doesn't expect anyone else to be. He'll assume you were a one-night stand. The only way to convince him that you and Gabe are the real thing is to expand on the relationship. Go through the usual courting rituals. Movies. Picnics. Public displays of affection. That sort of thing."

After tonight, even hand-holding with Gabe wouldn't be easy. The worst was that she'd responded to his mouth on hers. "Honest to God, Becca, I don't think I can go through with it."

"Why not?"

"We have a . . . conflict of interest. A huge one. We're incompatible. We just don't jibe, not in the least, not enough to convince anybody of anything."

Becca shook her head. "I'm afraid people are going to keep speculating about me and Gabe unless you provide a more definite change of subject." She reached over to the bedside table, picked up Joe's copper bracelet gift, and let it fall with a discordant metallic jangle. "And unless we change Joe's mind, he'll come after Missy."

Lauren wondered about Joe, about where he'd been at the time of the accident. Everyone knew Becca couldn't remember the actual event. Today's visit, with him pretending he hadn't known she was in the hospital, might have been a smoke screen. Of course, that assumed Joe was capable of thinking ahead and plotting his own alibi, which didn't seem likely.

Still, his threats about custody seemed real enough. Lauren had to take him seriously. She drummed her fingers on the mattress, working out her strategy. "First thing tomorrow I'll call some people who specialize in family law. I'll explore every option. Never fear—if Joe takes us to court, we'll be ready."

"That's all to the good," Becca said, "but wouldn't it be better to change Joe's mind before we get to court? Because what if we lose, even temporarily? I can't—*can't*—let him have Missy. Please, Lauren. Won't you reconsider this thing with Gabe? I know he won't back out. Can't you—"

"We'll see." Going along might be, for now, the safest course, everything considered. However, when Lauren recalled the startling intensity of what she'd experienced with Gabe, she felt as if she, too, had been in a car wreck. "Try not to worry, Becca. We won't let Joe win."

Becca rubbed her temples. "Lauren . . ."

"I told you not to worry." Lauren removed the extra pillow and settled Becca flat on the bed with covers to the chin. She kissed the patient's damp forehead. "I'm here for you."

"I know," Becca said.

Lauren inwardly cringed.

When she next talked to Gabe, or did whatever she ended up doing with him, she had to keep her sister foremost in her mind.

The next morning at nine-fifteen, Lauren was pouring her second cup of coffee when the doorbell rang. Her first thought was that Gabe had come over to see Becca. With Lauren there, surely gossip wouldn't be a problem, and seeing him ought to make Becca happy.

Moreover, Lauren needed to see her sister and Gabe together, placing their joint image firmly in her mind. She had to start thinking of him as Becca's Gabe again, because she'd already forgotten it once. If he was outside waiting, she meant to reverse any impression he might have that she actually liked him. Barefoot, wearing an oversize T-shirt, faded Levi's, and her sourest expression, she yanked open the front door.

"Morning, Laurie," greeted Sheriff LaDell Purdy. He was in full uniform, complete with gun. "Is your sister up yet?"

Lauren was too surprised to be disappointed that the sheriff wasn't Gabe. "No. She went to bed late, and she's still having headaches. I'd rather not disturb her. Do you have some follow-up on the accident?"

He shifted his weight and took off his straw hat. "Got an extra cup of coffee in there?"

She took the hint and invited him in. He settled at the kitchen table to sip coffee and describe the previous day's fruitless search. "Wasn't until an anonymous phone tip at four A.M. today that we knew where to look. Found Becca's BLM pickup nose-down in a ravine out in canyon country, just like the caller said. An old winch truck was decorating the same ditch. Looks like the two trucks ran into each other. I've already brought in the Highway Patrol to check it out."

Lauren leaned forward in her seat, her heart beating faster. At last they would unravel the mystery. "Have you traced ownership of the winch truck? You didn't find the other driver, did you?"

"Now, Lauren, don't get your panties in a twist."

She folded her hands on the table, clasping her fingers so tightly they hurt. "Tell me."

He traced the lines on the table where Missy's rocks had scraped crevices. "No driver, but we do know who owns the truck. Great Basin Petroleum."

"Great Basin!" Her hands unclasped and slapped the table. She jumped out of her chair. Gabe would feel awful about this. He'd feel responsible. He'd . . .

Lauren had a flashback of him rummaging in Becca's office on the afternoon of the accident. She couldn't come up with a connection, but that didn't mean there wasn't one. She began to pace the kitchen, back and forth.

The sheriff finished the story. "Gabe didn't drive out that way yesterday, what with Missy and the accident and all. He didn't know anything was wrong with his company truck until this morning when it wasn't where it was supposed to be, and patrol cars were there instead."

"Who had access to the winch truck? Who drives it?"

"Seems like the day crew for the nearest rig uses the truck to get to and from the job. They leave it parked right where the road starts to get rough, keys in the ignition, so it's available for whoever's working the next day to drive. Saves 'em ruined tires and busted axles."

"Did you question the men?"

"Some of 'em. Gabe'll send the rest by my office today or tomorrow. He's out at that nearby drilling rig right now, and he promised to let me know if he learns anything new. Best we can tell, the day shift drove out together on Friday, parked the winch truck, and left in their own vehicles. Nobody saw hide nor hair of Becca. All I can come up with was that the Great Basin truck was old and parked on an incline. Let's just say the parking brake failed. Why then, that truck could've slid down into the road, to where Becca ran smack into it as she came around a curve."

Brake failure? Lauren's stomach churned. Her father had died on a mountain road when his brakes had failed. She wasn't the only one who believed his death had been no accident. "You forgot something. Somebody brought Becca to the hospital."

"Well . . . yeah," the sheriff said, scratching under his collar. "I don't know who it could've been. Do you?"

"No, and that's why I wouldn't be too quick to find Great Basin employees innocent of wrongdoing."

"I, uh, I'm considering that, Lauren. Meanwhile, a Highway Patrol officer took photos at the scene, and a county detective arrived about the time I left. We'll have Becca's pickup hauled in to Herb's Junkyard over in Fairfield. I imagine the BLM'll send an insurance man."

Insurance man. That struck a chord, too. "You'd better make sure neither of those vehicles disappears, Sheriff."

"Now, why would—" He sent her a startled look. "This isn't like your daddy's accident. Nobody's out to get Becca."

Lauren wasn't so sure.

Sheriff Purdy's directions were nothing to brag about, but Lauren's area map filled in the blanks. She drove along the dirt road as fast as she dared, hoping to reach the accident site before Becca's vehicle was disturbed.

When she saw a tow truck hauling a smashed green pickup, its roof caved flat, the front wheels askew, she almost lost her breakfast. She couldn't believe her sister had come out of the wreck alive. After seeing the condition of the vehicle, she didn't have the heart to explore the accident site. She had to see Gabe.

The sheriff had asked her not to stir up trouble, but that was exactly what she intended to do. Unless she found evidence to the contrary, she had to assume a Great Basin employee was at fault, and Gabe was the only source she had. Surely he'd want to get to the bottom of it as much as she did.

Continuing along the road Purdy had indicated as the way to the drilling rig, she avoided numerous huge rocks that could easily have trashed her low-slung undercarriage. She had to admit a gas-guzzling SUV would be useful for the occasional trip afield. Her principles, however, would not bend far enough to allow her to own one.

She kept driving around sharp turns and steep, rocky ridges until she reached a plateau where the tall metal skeleton of a rig was visible from several miles distant. A surrounding view of twisted junipers and red sandstone rising to cliffs on the west and dropping off into the canyon a hundred yards eastward would have been hauntingly beautiful, if the sight weren't defaced by manmade greed.

The drilling made her so angry her teeth clenched. Great

Basin had finagled a lease from the BLM on the very rim of the proposed Red Rock wilderness area. Here, free enterprise ruled, but she'd be damned if that would extend into the canyon itself.

Thinking about huge trucks driving daily over a delicate desert landscape made her blood steam. Full restoration of soil and plant life could take years. Then there were the drill pads, storage tanks, waste pits, nighttime lights, and constant racket. The noise slammed through her brain even now. She had a hard time understanding how Gabe could do this. How did his conscience allow him to run an oil operation roughshod over a land that had once been almost sacred to him?

She spotted Gabe's Jeep right away. As she parked near it, she saw one man high on the rig, and three others grouped under the derrick, all looking down to where a length of pipe disappeared into the bore hole. Maybe they were reading depth, or monitoring drill rate or pressure. She didn't see Gabe. Since no one was paying any attention to her, she'd look around on her own, seeking a possible connection between this rig's operation and Becca's accident.

If Great Basin, or one of the men, had something to hide, if they'd been subverting some regulation that Becca might have recognized and reported, there could have been a motive for causing an accident that prevented her from reaching the rig. Gabe couldn't have been present—Lauren herself was his alibi. Whether he might have known, before or after . . . well, the thought was disturbing, at best.

Lauren decided to start with the mud pit. Drilling mud wasn't really mud, but a specialized substance used to lubricate the drill bit. After circulating down through the bore hole, the leftover "mud" went into a shaker pit, located on the platform itself, where a screen filtered out the largest of the rock fragments cut by the drill. The remains were pumped back into a pit situated some twenty yards away.

Federal regulations required lining the pit with plastic, to prevent the caustic mud from seeping into the earth. Lauren wanted to be sure the liner was in place, since any leak was a serious infraction of the Environmental Protection Agency's rules. If an EPA inspector found such a thing, the entire rig site might be shut down. And Great Basin *had* broken rules in the past.

She fumbled under her seat and came up with one of the sample containers she kept on hand for gathering pollution evidence. While she was at it, she might as well learn what she could about the drilling operation itself. The viscosity, salinity, and small rock fragments in the mud might yield information on the formations being drilled through. It wouldn't hurt for the CPWA to have insider knowledge about the rim well's level of descent and likelihood of success.

Sample container in hand, Lauren left her car and headed surreptitiously for the mud pit. A berm of dirt had been pushed up around a depression, where the murky waste substance was stored in what looked like a scummy pond and smelled like a combination of clay and salt and . . . something similar to olive oil. Residue around the edges might be hiding the liner, but she couldn't tell for certain. As soon as she obtained her sample, she'd do some excavation to check the setup further.

She was crouching down, opening the sample container, when her feet began to slip out from under her. It all happened too quickly for her to save herself. Her tennis shoes lost purchase, her butt hit the ground, and then she slid the rest of the way off the berm rim, letting out a yelp of surprise and fear somewhere along the way. She flailed, but there was nothing to grab. She felt weightless as she pitched through several feet of air, down to the scum—and then right on through into viscous muck.

She didn't know how deep it went, and her heart seemed to rise to her throat as she sank in past her ankles, calves, knees. She came to a stop, her feet squishing in the thick gunk at the bottom. Sludge oozed to her thighs. She struggled to maintain her footing on the slippery base while she groped back toward the shoulder-high berm.

Panting from the effort to keep her balance, she grabbed onto the side of the pit, only to find that there was, indeed, a plastic liner, covered with a thin layer of mud. That was what her feet had slipped on, and now she found that the blasted liner was too slick to hang on to. She nearly panicked as she realized getting out wasn't going to be easy. The hole was just deep enough that she couldn't hang a leg over the edge. And she couldn't pull herself up by the arms without anything to grip.

The drilling rig pounded, metal on metal, sending vibrations through her skull, shaking the semisolid scummy substance around her. She peered at the rig platform, thinking someone might have noticed her little problem. The men seemed preoccupied, which was just as well, she told herself.

She intended to get out of the pit without anyone's help, but she needed to do it quickly. Her skin itched. She was probably dissolving layer by layer in the corrosive gunk. And she was developing a serious case of claustrophobia. Not to mention the smell of raw, salty clay that seemed to grow stronger and sharper the longer she was immersed in it.

Noting a heavy black hose, eight or ten inches in diameter, through which recirculated mud was returned to the pit, she decided that was her way out. The hose was only a few yards from where she stood. All she had to do was inch over, grab on, and do a simple pull-up.

It was trickier than it looked. Mud dribbling out of the open end of the hose coated her below the waist, weighing her down. Her hands were so slippery that she felt like she was losing ground as quickly as she gained it. Fortunately, though, the hose was stable enough to hold her weight. Inch by inch she made progress. She had finally managed to heft her upper body onto the top of the berm when she heard a shout.

One of the men had spotted her. At the same time that the crew started yelling, she saw Gabe emerge from a travel trailer parked next to the rig. He wore his usual jeans and workshirt, plus a hard hat, and was frowning at a long strip of paper in his hand.

He must have heard the commotion, because he looked up toward the rig. A helpful worker pointed right toward Lauren, and Gabe glanced her way.

At first he seemed astonished, then, damn him, amused. "Laurie?" She saw the word on his lips, though she couldn't hear. He rushed across the open ground, past the men, past the rig. She had gotten to her feet by the time he reached her, but she was still dripping muck. Her face heated with embarrassment, even though the wet mud was cold enough to make her shiver. Good grief, of all the times to be caught in a mess like this. She'd never felt at a worse disadvantage. And it had to happen now, with Gabe.

"Morning, Laurie." He kept a straight face, though it was obvious he was fighting a grin. "You're looking . . . good."

"Thanks." She felt like a fish, all wet and slimy. An ungainly, finless fish. Wiping her hands on her hips, she tried to pretend wallowing in drilling mud was normal behavior. If only he'd laugh out loud and get it over with, maybe she wouldn't feel so foolish. "I'm here about Becca's accident."

"Right. I was hoping this isn't your usual method of touring a well site." Again he tamped down a smile. "Did you find any clues in the mud pit?"

Her face felt so hot she thought it might have caught fire. "I wasn't . . . Never mind." She'd lost her sample container, but she could hardly dive back in to get it with Gabe watching, even if she were willing to go to such an extreme. With no alternative in sight, she launched what she hoped would come across as a serious interrogation. "Tell me, how often does Becca drive out here? Because if she found a problem, she'd have to report it, wouldn't she?"

Gabe must have caught on that the time for being amused at her expense was over. His gaze hardened, and his mouth went flatline. "Come in the trailer to wash up. That mud'll sting if you leave it on too long." He began walking away.

Moving awkwardly with her heavy mud overlay, she followed. "You didn't answer my questions."

"I could ask why you decided to take a bath in sludge, but I don't think I want to know." He ushered her to the trailer's tiny bathroom. "When you come out, we'll talk."

There was not much she could do about her jeans, or about the raw-pottery smell that clung to her, but she cleaned up as best she could. She found Gabe outside, studying the log reports that he'd spread over the hood of his Jeep. When he looked up and saw her emerging from the trailer, he pulled off the hard hat, dropped it on the papers, and ran a hand through his curly hair.

As he started toward her, his easy gait made her impatient and reminded her that he still hadn't given her the answers she needed. She hurried to meet him halfway. "Well, Gabe? Are you going to tell me what you know?"

"Sure, Laurie, for whatever it's worth. Becca's been out here only once since we started drilling. At least only once when I was here," he said. "Yes, I suppose she'd report a problem, but there hasn't been one. No infraction of the rules, nothing Great Basin could be fined for. That's your real question, if I'm reading you right. As far as what happened on Friday, I don't know any more than you do."

"A vehicle you own knocked my sister off the road. You're accountable, like it or not."

"I feel like hell about Becca's injuries, Laurie. I'll take care of any hospital bills the BLM or the insurance company won't pay. I'll help out however I can."

"That's not good enough."

"What do you want? I'm sorry. I apologize. To you and Becca both. But as you know, fault isn't determined just yet. We don't even have another driver."

She glanced toward the well. The men didn't seem to be loitering anymore. They were clanging long lengths of pipe, perhaps preparing to replace a drill bit. "I want to talk to your employees," she said.

"Go ahead, but these men aren't the same crew that worked Friday. They can't tell you anything. Besides, Sheriff Purdy's already spoken to them."

"Fine, then. I'll question you instead." She tossed her head, clearing her eyes of her windblown hair. "Why would the other party have failed to come forward unless he's guilty of *something*? Maybe he was driving without company permission, or carelessly. Or maybe it wasn't an accident. Maybe it was to one of your men's advantage to prevent Becca from coming this way. To Great Basin's advantage. To *your* advantage."

Gabe took a step closer. "I know you're angry, and I understand why, but stop right there. I wouldn't hurt Becca."

"When I saw you in her office on Friday, what were you *really* doing?" Lauren asked, backing up to keep her distance. She didn't want him too close. She couldn't think when he was close.

"Fetching a key, damn it," he said. "And yeah, I sneaked a peak at the canyon Environmental Assessment I saw on Becca's desk. No crime in that. A copy'll be in my post office box by the time I get around to checking."

"Why didn't you suggest the sheriff look down this road, if you had nothing to hide?" she demanded.

"I didn't know where Becca was. She could have been anywhere within a hundred-mile radius." He met Lauren's gaze, seeming to mask nothing of his thoughts or feelings. He looked . . . hurt. Deeply hurt. "I've known your sister since I was ten years old. Hannah was a substitute mom for me. Your family's practically my family. You can't believe I'd harm any one of you."

The deep blue of the sky matched his eyes. The reddish tint in his hair was almost the same color as the red rock cliffs of canyon country. Lauren turned her head so she wouldn't have to see the candor and reproach in his gaze. She wanted to believe in him. She wanted to trust him.

"It's your dad, isn't it?" he said. "Becca says you've been carrying a chip on your shoulder ever since he died, and not just against me for missing the funeral. Your paranoia's running pretty high about now, don't you think?"

She locked gazes with him again. "It's more than paranoia. My father is dead. Becca could have died."

"True, but that doesn't mean I had any part in it. I'm willing to take responsibility for my truck, or even for my men, should it turn one out of them was involved. Just don't get crazy on me and suggest I ordered someone to do her in. I'm not the Mafia. I don't hire hit men. You know me too well to think that."

"I—" She shrugged, because she wasn't sure how well she knew him, wasn't sure what she knew and what she only wished was true. "We've both changed. Maybe you think last night meant something, but—"

"Oh, I'm getting it now," he said. "You're upset about more than the accident, more than Great Basin Petroleum. You're mad that I came back to San Rafael, annoyed that I moved in next to Becca, angry that I kissed her, pissed off that I've been an inconvenience to you and your kin."

"At least you admit you've caused trouble," she said evenly, though it took some effort to steady her voice. He was right; she was angry about all those things. "Actually, I'm more disgusted with myself than I am with you. For . . . for allowing you to—"

"Allowing! Hell, I had to fight you off. You sure weren't complaining, that I could tell."

"Never mind," she snapped. "I'm through with that, and I'm through with you. No more. In fact, as soon as Becca's head stops hurting, I'm going to suggest she sue the socks off you and Great Basin. You own the truck. We'll win the case."

She sidestepped him and charged toward her car, where she slipped into the driver's seat and slammed the door closed behind her. Her blue jeans and tennis shoes made squishing sounds, but she was too incensed to care.

For him to spell out the response she'd had to him last night, at a time like this, was the height of insensitivity. She *would* sue him, if she could get Becca to agree. She started the engine and shifted into first, flooring it, only to crunch along the rutted road at an abnormal tilt. She braked, lowered the window, and stuck out her head. The left rear tire was a rubber pancake under a wheel rim.

Her dramatic exit was shot all to hell. Through the rear-view mirror, she saw Gabe approach.

He leaned on the door frame of her open window, bending low to look in. "Maybe you're not quite through with me? Ready to kiss and beg pardon?"

She felt like banging her head on the steering wheel. She needed to get away from him now. Otherwise he might find a way to charm her into believing not just that Great Basin employees were blameless, but that the company produced petunias instead of petroleum. Gabe had a powerful personality when he decided to bring it to bear.

"Go . . . stick your head in the mud pit," she muttered.

"Pardon me?" Gabe asked, feigning deafness or stupidity. Either one was equally irritating

"Tweety is incapacitated." Lauren realized, too late, that she'd called the car by Gabe's pet name. "I'd like to be alone with my grief."

"Why not try an SOS?" He raised an eyebrow. "Ask nice, Laurie, and the rescue squad'll go right to work."

Gabe's smug superiority was more than she could stand.

Besides, she should not—make that *would* not—rely on him in any way, shape, or form.

"*I'll* change the tire." She was already reaching into the glove compartment for the manual. She didn't know a single thing about tires. Under normal circumstances, she'd call AAA. But not here. No phone lines, and cellular wouldn't work so far out, even if she'd brought hers, which she hadn't.

Holding his hands up to let her know she was on her own, Gabe backed away.

She wanted to reconsider. Maybe she was being stubborn, or just plain boneheaded. But how could she accept his help when she'd just promised him a lawsuit? Besides, his physical proximity had a way of destroying her resolve, ruining her objectivity, melting her mind.

Trusting her own skills, however nonexistent, was a whole lot safer than trusting Gabe's.

Chapter Eight

Nearly an hour later, Lauren had added a layer of grease and dirt to the muck on her T-shirt and Levi's. Her skin felt as if she'd spent a couple of days in a dehydrator. She wiped a forearm over her face. It was hot—almost unbearably hot in the noon sun. She notched the jack down and stowed it, along with the ruined tire.

Gabe had traversed between her car and the rig a half dozen times, shouting directives to his men, and then returning to assess her progress. The entire time she'd slaved over the tire, she'd noticed the men on the drilling platform eyeing her. Even over the pounding and screeching of pipe metal and torque, she'd heard an occasional bark of laughter. Sweating in ninety-degree-plus heat did not seem funny to her. At least she was dry now, and the odor of salted clay had evaporated with the moisture. The downside was that the sun had baked the drilling mud onto her jeans like stucco on a wall. She felt like a walking brick.

As she slammed the trunk shut, Gabe approached yet again. "I'll follow you out. I insist," he shouted over the clang and grind of drill pipe being craned and twisted into position.

"Don't bother," she yelled back. Covered with dust and filth, her head pounding from the noise, she was in no mood to be patronized. She tossed the worse-for-wear instruction manual into the front seat. The book hadn't been much help. The jack was small and hard to crank, the lug bolts had seemed to be glued in place, and the spare was low on air. Trial and error had gotten her through, along with a teeth-gritting determination that she would not require Gabe's help.

"Fine with me," he shouted. "If you break down, you can swelter until I find you on my way home. Even then, maybe I'll drive on by. I wouldn't want to impose myself on an overheated woman. I'm tired of getting burned."

She thought she was rid of him when he stalked away. Before she could dig keys out of her pocket, he'd reached into his Jeep and started back. "Here, take a water bottle," he offered.

She glared at the vessel in his hand as if it were poisonous.

"Okay, so you don't trust me," he said. "I understand. I'm sorry about me and Becca, sorry the whole town got wind of it, sorry Buddy had to come along and blab what he knew in front of you. Maybe I should have explained more ahead of time, but you were already leery about being anywhere near me. I figured telling you I'd kissed your sister on that same front porch would sure as hell make it worse."

"Oh, it's worse now, believe me," she yelled over a new, louder, metallic screech that had just begun. "Also, you'd better believe I'm going to look into this accident. I'm going to look into Great Basin, too, and find all the dirt I can on you, especially on a personal level."

He glanced down at her filthy jeans. His lips twitched. "Take the water."

She snatched the full bottle out of his hand as she climbed into the car and slammed the door. Good thing he hadn't smiled, or she'd have killed him bare-handed.

"Since I'm the shadiest character you've ever come across, better keep the locks locked and the alarms on when

I'm in the same county," he said. "Who knows what I'll do, maniacal sociopath that I am."

She narrowed her eyes. "You're suggesting something, I can tell."

"Jesus H. Christ, I've never met a more tunnel-vision woman." He clenched the door frame of Tweety's open window and peered inside again. "I'm suggesting you get your head straight."

His low drawl cut through the oil rig noise and skittered inside her. "Call a time out from your vendetta against me, Laurie. Much as you'd like to simplify things by speculating I'd do anything, cross any boundary, stomp on any friend, if it would somehow benefit Great Basin Petroleum, that's not the case. I do have scruples. I care about people. I even give a thought to the environment once in a while. You could relate to me if you gave it a try."

"Is that right?" Of course, she knew he was right. She'd related plenty last night—to the man he had become, not the boy she remembered. When he stood close, like now, when she smelled his warm skin and felt his body stealing her space, she related all over again. "Anything else?"

"I suggest you hold off on suing me over the accident. You can always do it later, but if we're going to keep up the love game—"

"Don't be absurd," she said. "If Becca's hitting you with a negligence suit, Joe will have ample reason to believe you two are no longer together."

"Wrong. Because he won't believe Becca would sue me or anyone else on her own. He'll figure you're behind it, and he'll be correct. He might see the lawsuit as a ruse, but he wouldn't see you and me courting that way, because that's *not* what he'd expect from you. That, he'd figure, would have to be real."

Lauren puffed out her cheeks and exhaled a tired breath.

"You might be right about how Joe would look at it. But I still don't think—"

"Now, Laurie, if we can do some good for Becca and Missy, does it matter what *we* want, or think, or understand?"

Lauren's palm itched to slap him. "How dare you insinuate that you are the only one interested in Becca's welfare?"

"I'm not insinuating anything except that playing out our bogus relationship doesn't bother me, but it sure seems to put a burr under your saddle. The way I see it, our game could suit your purposes better than you think."

"How?" She was suspicious. Curious, too.

"You can learn a lot about my employees and company operations if we're spending time together. You can investigate the accident *and* spy for the CPWA in one swoop."

"Hmm," she said thoughtfully, not quite buying the line. "What's in it for you?"

His blue eyes bored into her. "I'm as innocent as a Red Rock Canyon sunrise, at least when it comes to this accident of Becca's. I want you to know that for a fact."

She tapped her fingers on the steering wheel. "I . . . know you didn't do anything directly. I shouldn't have suggested that you did. Still, that does *not* rule out negligence."

"We could look into it together. Like I said, if my company's responsible—or even if it's not—I'll take care of Becca's expenses. Can't we make an effort to get along, for your sister's sake?"

"Maybe you just want to keep me in sight so you'll know what I know. That'd give you advance notice to think up a counterattack."

"Only one way to find out." He smiled with a confidence custom-made to provoke her. "You call the distance, sweetheart. I'm looking forward to your next move."

"If you're worried you'll have to 'fight me off' again, you need a brain transplant," Lauren said sourly.

He backed away, still smiling. The gall of him, implying

she was a featherbrained sex object he could condescend to at will. She started the engine and ground into gear. This time she and Tweety made a respectable, if somewhat sputtering, exit.

Driving more slowly on the way back to town, she avoided the worst of the sharp rocks and major dips. She didn't have another spare, and she sure didn't want to be on the side of the road begging a ride when Gabe left his oil rig and headed home.

She stopped at the site of the accident, marked by crushed sagebrush and juniper. Climbing out of her car, she looked around and speculated on what might have happened. If Becca was traveling uphill, she would have been unable to see an obstruction around the bend.

From above, someone wishing to do Becca harm could have seen her approach along the road below. The truck, a significant barricade, could have been placed in her way.

Disturbed by how simple it would have been, and by the fact that the crash could easily have been fatal, Lauren descended the hundred feet from the side of the road to where the careening vehicles had come to a crushing halt. Pieces of amber brakelight were scattered over what appeared to be a dry creek bed. The winch truck was still there, overturned and battered, but she couldn't determine the area of impact. Since she had no choice but to leave that to the experts, she returned to her car and continued toward San Rafael.

As she parked in Becca's driveway, she noticed a nondescript black sedan that had come to a stop on the other side of the street.

For a moment she thought FBI. As confusing as events seemed at the moment, she'd welcome an unbiased investigation by federal agents.

When a man stepped out of the vehicle carrying flowers, she discarded the optimistic notion that the government had taken note of Becca's accident. Not FBI. FBI did not come bearing gifts of any sort.

She crossed stepping stones leading from the drive to the front door of Becca's white frame house, while the man approached along the sidewalk. His black hair was combed back to reveal a high forehead and widow's peak. He had olive skin, dark eyes.

"Looking for someone?" Lauren asked when they were within a few feet of each other.

He nodded. "For Rebecca Hewitt. Is this the right place?"

"Yes." Lauren frowned at his fistful of red and yellow roses. Becca's love life was getting more complicated all the time. "I suppose you've heard about the accident. She's not feeling strong enough for visitors."

Lauren wasn't about to let a stranger in the house. Not that this guy inspired fear. On the contrary, he looked like the quiet, sensitive type. He wore slacks and a sports coat, for heaven's sake. He seemed quite civilized. All of which, in Lauren's cynical frame of mind, added up to a possible serial killer. Besides, given Becca's ex-husband's jealousy, they didn't need male visitors. Lauren had to consider the repercussions if her sister were forced to go to court against Joe over custody. Becca's relationship with Gabe, whatever it involved, had already done enough damage.

The stranger eyed the caked mud on Lauren's once-blue jeans, but quickly altered his gaze when she caught him at it. "Let me see her," he insisted. "Just for a moment or two."

"Sorry, I don't think that's a good idea. Not right now, anyway. Maybe in a few days . . ." By that time Becca would be making her own decisions. Lauren only hoped they would be wise ones, for a change.

His grip must have loosened. The flowers listed downward. "Will you at least *ask* her if she'll see me?"

"She's sleeping." Lauren didn't know if Becca was sleeping or not, but her level of consciousness was immaterial.

"I'd be happy to deliver the flowers and any message you'd like to leave."

He muttered something under his breath. Something rude, Lauren guessed.

"Tell Rebecca I'll see her soon." After thrusting the bouquet at Lauren's chest, he retreated to his car.

The roses had a tiny sealed envelope stuck amidst the thorns. Good thing there was a card, because she'd completely forgotten to ask the man's name. What other suitors for Becca's hand might pop out of the sage? In a town as small as this, she'd have thought strangers and secrets would be hard to come by, but apparently that wasn't the case.

Entering through the front door, Lauren slipped down the hall to her room for a quick shower and change of clothes. She felt more civilized once she was clean. Retrieving the roses she'd thrown on the bed, she went to the kitchen to find a vase.

Two noodle casseroles lay on the table. Offerings from neighbors, she assumed. A sack of rocks blocked the back door again. Missy had hauled the collection with her when she'd left for a visit to Buddy's house first thing that morning, but she must have returned. Though the child wasn't immediately visible, Lauren detected an overturned Froot Loops box with colorful rings spilled all over the counter. She jumped when she heard a low-pitched voice droning in the living room.

She found Missy stretched out on the floor in front of the TV, a bowl of cereal under her chin. Missy craned her neck to watch the screen as she slurped and crunched. The announcer oozed a description of rocks and formations and eons worth of time, while the camera panned the layers, textures, and colors of the Grand Canyon.

What kind of kid watched documentaries to the accompaniment of Froot Loops? It occurred to Lauren that at about the same age, she had preferred documentaries to cartoons,

too. As she'd grown older, she'd favored perusing encyclo-
pedias or, on the lighter side, devouring an Isaac Asimov
novel or a *Star Trek* sequel. No wonder Hannah had considered her younger daughter abnormal.

Missy had the same oddities, ones not readily accepted in
a town like San Rafael. Again Lauren felt the ache in her
heart, the need to connect, to touch, to love and be loved.
Missy paused with a spoon in the air. Her eyes widened at the
screening of canyon wildlife—scorpions, huge lizards, a
peregrine falcon swooping down from a cliff. She sat up
slowly, gaze glued to the television, one hand still clutching
the forgotten spoon.

Lauren longed to reach out and hug the child, to tell her
that she knew how it was to be enchanted by knowledge for
its own sake, how it was to be different from the other kids.
They'd been drawn to each other instinctively once. She
could remember a time when Missy was about three and had
clung to her neck, and then cried long and loud when Lauren
tried to explain why she had to go away.

But months and years had passed, and that special feeling
between them was no longer there. Lauren hoped that they
would grow into the hugging stage again. She hadn't realized
how precious the love of a child could be—until she'd lost
that love. No other pleasure, no other magic, could quite
compare. She took one last, lingering look at the little girl's
blond pixie hair, at the profile view of a pink cherub cheek,
and sighed.

Still wondering what she should do about the custody battle, especially with her suspicions of Gabe further complicat-
ing the dilemma, Lauren turned down the hall to Becca's
room, vase and roses in hand.

At a tap on the door, Becca lowered Garth Brooks's voice
booming "Friends in Low Places" on the radio.

Lauren entered, looking flushed, as if she'd spent the

morning in the sun. Becca had found Lauren's note saying she'd gone out on a business errand and was happy to see the business had involved being outside. In her opinion, Lauren worked too hard. She needed to relax more.

"Flower delivery." Lauren produced a bouquet from behind her back.

Now that was a surprise. "Roses? Lauren, you shouldn't have."

"I wish I could take credit, but I can't. Someone came by and left these for you." Lauren set the vase on the nightstand, pushing aside the copper bangle Joe had brought.

Becca had thought about throwing the bracelet out, but hadn't quite been able to carry through. She'd loved Joe best on those rare occasions when he'd offered her gifts, when he'd tried to show he cared. Even now, giving her copper because it was supposed to take away pain was sweet. If only he hadn't followed it up with selfish demands . . .

She was grateful for the fresh blooms, which reminded her that she was making a fresh start, or trying to. "With all the complaints I've heard in the office lately, I've wondered how many friends I had left in San Rafael. Everyone's been great, though. I've had cards, phone calls, food—even if it is that awful potluck stuff—and now, flowers."

"Yeah, right." Lauren was skeptical, as always. "The town is behind you one hundred percent. Today. Maybe even tomorrow."

"I'll take the sympathy while it lasts," Becca said. "I like being liked much better than the alternative."

"You might want to check the card." Lauren plucked a square white envelope from the blossoms and presented it.

Becca read the inner note aloud. "A secret admirer."

"What?"

"That's all it says." Becca dropped the card in her lap. A secret anything was not what she needed right now. She wrinkled her forehead. Big mistake, she thought, on a painful intake of breath. Drat, she couldn't even worry without her face hurting. She finger-tested the cut under her bangs. "It wasn't Joe, was it? Because I don't want anything else from him."

"Not Joe. Not Gabe." Lauren, always diligent, leaned over to examine the suture line and reported there wasn't any blood. "The secret admirer was well dressed, mid-thirties, nobody I've ever seen. He had a faint accent and looked Hispanic."

"Rio. He must have heard about the accident from the radio news report this morning. You should have asked him in."

"Who is he?"

"A . . . friend." Becca rubbed the unstitched part of her forehead, wishing the ache would go away. "We met maybe three or four months ago. He came by the office to ask directions to a canyon overlook. He noticed my paintings; we started talking art, and ended up having coffee at the Mad House."

"Just how friendly are you?" Lauren perched on the foot of the mattress, arms crossed over her ribs.

"Not very," Becca said. "He bought that old Victorian place on the Fairfield highway, and he's turning it into an antiques shop. We met by chance in the restaurant a few times. We ate lunch together once, but I've made it clear I'm not interested in a relationship."

"Then why did you have lunch with him?" Lauren scolded. "Don't you have enough trouble with men in your life?"

Becca picked up the vase and buried her nose in the blossoms, inhaling the scent. She found Lauren's logical approach exhausting on the best of days, and this was a long way from the best. "Just let me enjoy the attention. It doesn't mean anything."

"He seems concerned about you," Lauren admitted. "And the flowers are pretty."

Becca took another whiff of the roses. "I like Rio. Last week he called to ask if I'd come out to have a look at his shop, which just opened, but I haven't had a chance yet. He sells art in addition to antiques; he says he'd like to display my work."

"Sounds like a come-on line to me."

Becca shrugged her good shoulder. "Maybe. I think he's sincere. He has a gentle way about him. He's not bad-looking, either."

"I didn't notice," Lauren said, standing again, restless.

"No, I guess you wouldn't. If Gabe's heart-stopping smile doesn't drop you to your knees, nothing will."

"Just call me the Snow Queen." Lauren wandered over to the dresser, where she picked up a brush and went to work on her hair with short, quick strokes.

Becca realized, too late, that she'd hurt her sister's feelings. "I don't think you're cold, Lauren. You've never been cold to me." *At least not very often, and not intentionally.* "You will stay, won't you? Just for a week or two." Besides needing help throwing Joe off the scent, she wanted the closeness she'd once had with Lauren.

All through her rocky marriage, Becca had had to avoid certain subjects with her sister, because Lauren had openly disapproved of Joe. Becca wanted to put all that behind them. With some concentrated time together, they could heal old wounds and put salve on new ones; she knew they could.

Lauren sighed as she set the brush down. "If you need me, I'll stay." She met Becca's reflected gaze in the mirror over the dresser. "The sheriff found your smashed pickup this morning."

Becca shuddered. "Could he tell what happened?"

"You were driving out toward the canyon rim and smacked into a truck that belongs to Great Basin." Lauren gave the news as though she were exploding an atom bomb, but Becca felt relieved. A piece of the puzzle had fallen into place.

"I remember the road now! I can see the curve, right before . . ." She paused, waiting for the next scene to appear in her mind, but nothing came. "Good Lord, Lauren, could it have been my fault? Was the other driver hurt?"

Lauren turned slowly and rested her back against the dresser. "Since no other driver has shown his face, apparently not. I don't suppose you've had any other memories? Anything at all?"

Becca remembered a dream. A dreamlike, soothing voice, but no face. Nothing worth mentioning. "I know you've been wondering if Joe could have—"

"No," Lauren said. "The possibility did occur to me, but that was when I thought he might have been drinking and driving with you on board. After learning where it happened, and something about the circumstances, I think the whole incident is related to the drilling operation. Frankly, I blame Gabe."

"But why? He was in town that afternoon, so how—"

"In my opinion, the buck stops with the truck owner who carelessly leaves the keys in his vehicle, no matter who was actually driving. We ought to slap Gabe and his company with a lawsuit."

"Don't be ridiculous. I'd never sue Gabe. He's having enough problems trying to keep Great Basin going. And even if I wanted to sue, you couldn't be involved, not while you're pretending to have an affair with him," Becca pointed out.

Lauren didn't protest the logic. Instead she gazed across the room toward a framed photograph on the wall of the three of them, Lauren, Becca, and Gabe, taken up on the canyon rim. Becca had found it in the garage after the divorce and decided to hang it again. She remembered the day, even the moment, the photo was taken, and she knew her sister did, too.

"You don't really want me to go on pretending with him, do you?" Lauren asked. "Not now that you know it was Gabe's truck that hit you."

"Forget the stupid truck," Becca said. "Joe's still my main worry. He needs to see you with Gabe."

"As if that will make any difference."

"It will. Once Joe's jealousy is under control, I can talk to him. He'll be more reasonable."

"Joe? Reasonable?"

"Sometimes," Becca said. "Right now he's still agitated over the divorce. He's hurt and angry, and he wants to make me hurt along with him, especially since it's Gabe who's stolen his thunder, so to speak. I think he's lost sight of what he's doing to Missy. I keep hoping he'll calm down and see that we need to be fair about our custody deal, for her sake."

"That'll be the day."

"All I ask is that you keep up appearances with Gabe while you're in town," Becca pleaded. "Is that so difficult?"

"Yes, it is. You see, I . . . said some things, made some accusations about the accident."

"Oh, is that all?" Becca felt better, now that she understood what was bothering Lauren. "He doesn't hold grudges. If you were a little tactless, I'm sure he'll overlook it."

"Think so?" Lauren sounded the teensiest bit caustic. "If you'd heard what I said you wouldn't be so sure."

"Just talk to him. It'll be okay."

Lauren hesitated, and finally shrugged her resignation. "If you really want me to, I'll see what I can do." She brought the brush to the bed and began working through the tangles in Becca's long hair. "If we ever clear up this mess, do you think you'll get back together with Gabe?"

"I . . . don't know. But he is great with Missy, isn't he?" Becca knew Gabe would be the perfect father. He was strong, steady, trustworthy, salt of the earth. Unfortunately, he didn't seem to be interested in her. Yet. But maybe when the situation with Joe was resolved . . .

"Yes, he's good with Missy." Lauren yanked at a knot in Becca's hair a bit too vigorously. "So I guess that means you do want him."

"Ouch. Don't get mad. You think I'm fickle, don't you, Lauren? Well, I'm not. I've just taken an extra long time to figure out what I need in a man." She reached up to halt the brush in her sister's hand. "I like Gabe, and I can't see why you don't. When we were kids, you used to tolerate him just fine. So what if he owns Great Basin now instead of a recycling plant? If you'd let up about his oil leases, he'd fit right into our family."

Lauren started brushing again. "Maybe so, Becca," she said, sounding sad and a little subdued. "In a lot of ways, I guess he would."

The next morning Lauren answered the phone on the first ring, at just past ten.

To her "Hello," the reply was, "*Gloria in excelsis Deo!* Lauren Van Horn really is in San Rafael!"

Lauren recognized the Latin trademark of Eve Worthy, Colorado Plateau Wilderness Association's fearless leader. "How did you know where to—"

"We keep family addresses and phone numbers on file in case of emergency," Eve said. "This is an emergency."

"Yes, that's what I said in the e-mail I sent you on Saturday. My family needs me here."

"If you'd stated your location, I could have saved hours of assignment juggling, since you're also right where *I* need you."

"I asked for time off," Lauren contended. "I'm not available."

"You happen to be in San Rafael, dearie, where the

wilderness movement has a major crisis. You mentioned an accident, but nobody's dead, right?"

"No, but—"

"If you have a conscience and any loyalty to the CPWA, you'll attend the town meeting Tuesday night. Tomorrow."

Oh, no. San Rafael town meetings were the worst kind of curse. "Send someone else, Eve. You don't need an attorney. A representative would serve just as well. Before you hunted me down, I know you had other arrangements."

"I did, but the man I thought was on the docket bugged out. It's too late to fully inform someone else and have him or her on the scene in time. We're swamped over here with us versus the mine owners from the Silverton area. Just in the few days you've been gone, everything has escalated. Their lawyers have moved up the next hearing to June tenth. Unless we can get the court to uphold the preliminary injunction issued last month, the mines will be back to business as usual, dumping arsenic-laced waste in the Animas River, by the end of the summer."

Lauren's frustration grew; her grip on the phone tightened. The Animas River case was the biggest she'd worked on thus far in her career, and she didn't want anything happening without her. "My sister needs me with her for another week or two. Can't we delay—"

"I made some calls Friday night and it's not looking good." Eve sighed heavily. "We'll have a difficult time pulling together our stats and developing a quality case against the mines in three weeks, but with our summer law students and Dave Ingles, we'll manage."

"What about the brief I'm working on? I've done the research on case law, and I have most of it with me. I thought I'd finish it this past weekend, but—"

"Just send the brief as soon as possible. Ingles can take care of this end. No need to worry."

Lauren had known Ingles, a more experienced CPWA attorney, was likely to handle the case if it went to court. However, she had counted on at least being there, assisting with the major aspects.

In fact, Ingles did worry Lauren. He was borderline lazy, in her opinion, and would be likely to settle. He would never stand as tough on water quality as she would.

"Meanwhile," Eve continued, "the least you can do, since you're there and not here, is to handle our Utah crisis. Come on, Lauren, you aren't going to let us down, are you?"

"I can't. . . ." She could. She didn't want to, but the main excuse was cowardice. As much as she wished she could cringe out of this one, she plunged into Eve's expectant silence. "What do you want me to do?"

"Deo gratias." Eve had done a brief stint in a convent before giving up Catholicism for pantheism. In emotional moments, she often reverted to Latin. "First, state our position at the meeting. Our active supporters are pretty strung out, but I'll get the telephone committee to make some calls. We'll try to have some of our people in San Rafael on Tuesday, just to provide moral support. Afterward, for as long as you're there, you can feel the local pulse, speak to the media, arrange rallies, et cetera, et cetera."

"Eve, over and above my family emergency, getting involved in wilderness issues here is sure to cause personal problems for me. My sister runs the local BLM field office; my mother owns a restaurant on Main Street. Neither of them will welcome my butting into this, or any other town meeting, much less taking further action."

"They'll get over it. You can't let familial friction keep you out of the crusade. Think what a time in history this is! We're embarking on a landmark battle. If we win, we'll have a road-free corridor extending all the way from central Utah to the south rim of the Grand Canyon. The fact that you have connections in the San Rafael vicinity should be an advantage, not a hindrance."

"I made a single comment during last November's meeting and almost started a riot. And that was just a scoping hearing."

"Tuesday is important," Eve said. "Essential. The more I think about it, the more convinced I am that you're ideal. You know the town, so the BLM district people will pay attention to you. Unlike the actual residents, however, you have no stake in oil leases, no logging or mining affairs."

"I do have a stake in my family." She had a feigned affair with Gabe, too, which she didn't care to explain. "Openly stating my opinions won't be easy. Because I represent the other side, because the locals figure I ought to understand their side, they'll be all over my back. Literally, I would guess. With tar, feathers, and lighter fluid."

"Fighting for the right isn't supposed to be easy," Eve insisted. "Our main contention is that neither Great Basin nor any other petroleum company should be allowed to drill in Red Rock Canyon."

"I agree. Surely the BLM won't let those leases stand."

"I've seen the BLM's Environmental Assessment," Eve replied. "As I thought might be the case, it blatantly kowtows to the oil industry. That's why we need you at the meeting."

"You want me to voice CPWA's stand," Lauren said tonelessly, feeling more doomed by the moment. "I can do that. What else?"

"Start thoroughly investigating Great Basin. Come up with every mistake, every tax evasion, every polluting event in their despicable history. When the newspapers get hold of that, we'll make hay on the negative publicity. As soon as you have the EA—I'll send you a copy—start work on an appeal. Oh, and prepare a motion for a preliminary injunction, in case big oil tries to maneuver past us. No rush on getting back to Denver, since one of us would have to be traveling to meetings over there anyway. You can do the CPWA a favor while sorting out your 'family emergency.' *Mea culpa* for any inconvenience."

The phone clicked in Lauren's ear.

As she hung up, she rolled her head from side to side to rid herself of a crick in her neck. Good grief, her family problems had just increased a hundredfold. She could imagine Hannah's outcry. Becca would be less than appreciative when Lauren put heat on the BLM, adding to the agency's problems. And Lauren already knew that Great Basin provided jobs in this town. Taking a chance of driving the company away by limiting their leases would not find favor with a single soul in San Rafael. Then, of course, there was Gabe himself.

She groaned. Until this morning she'd had hopes of resolving the custody issue in a hurry, propping Becca back on her feet, and scampering the hell out of Dodge. If Becca didn't want to blame Great Basin for the accident, so be it. Let the police figure out what had happened. Lauren would escape the Red Rock furor, and the feigned affair with Gabe would be as much in the past as her youthful infatuation with him.

No such luck.

She had hoped to find a means of keeping Judge Hewitt off the custody case because he was kin to Joe. Late last night, she'd searched the shelves in the junk-packed garage surrounding Becca's rusty Nova, and had finally located a Hewitt family tree. To her dismay, Joe and the judge were a couple of degrees shy of the disqualification guidelines.

And this morning, before Eve's call, she'd made a cursory phone call to the county court in Fairfield. Old Judge Hewitt did still handle the bulk of family law cases. He was due to retire in September, but that was an eternity away. Meanwhile, the ancient judge would have heard every scrap of gossip about Becca, and would almost certainly hold it against her.

In truth, the judge wouldn't incline toward Joe because of kinship as much as because of the old man's antiquated, patriarchal attitude toward a woman's sexual activity—or even the suspicion of it—outside of matrimony.

Becca and Missy were in trouble, should they come before Judge Hewitt's court. So Lauren had to make sure they didn't.

She and Gabe would somehow have to stay on speaking terms long enough to alter the course of gossip. If that weren't tricky enough, Lauren would simultaneously be engaging in a legal standoff that would make her, hands down, San Rafael's least popular native daughter.

Chapter Nine

On Tuesday evening, Lauren arrived at the high school gymnasium fifteen minutes before the meeting, in plenty of time to set up a table near the door and arrange stacks of the wilderness pamphlets Eve Worthy had sent special delivery. As she finished her preparations, the regional BLM staff from Cedar City filed in.

Arch McFarlane, assistant director, remembered Lauren from the scoping meeting she had attended months before. He knew all about the accident.

"How is Becca?" he asked. "I surely do think a lot of her. I've been meaning to send something out to her house. Would she like a fruit basket? Flowers? Candy?"

"Anything you send would be fine," Lauren said.

"I could drive back over tomorrow and pay her a call." Arch was an average-looking man, dark hair, light brown eyes, an uneven complexion marked by acne scars. He seemed to have a greater-than-passing interest in Becca.

"Maybe you should wait. She's not strong enough for visitors yet." Lauren was starting to think her sister needed a full-time chaperon. They did *not* need more men around to provide fuel for Joe's custody case.

As Arch moved on to the front podium, Lauren watched the doors. Bill Whalen, plumber, and Fred Biggs, taxidermist, sauntered in. They saw her and waved, but looked askance at the table spread with CPWA pamphlets.

Old Mrs. Marley hustled in next. Her osteoporotic spine arched so severely that she walked bent over, her head at waist level. The awkward posture didn't slow her pace, although she had to cock her head and peer sideways to see. Thick glasses magnified her faded blue eyes to twice their normal size, making the theory that she'd been abducted by aliens and morphed into one seem almost believable.

Boom-Boom Throckmorton, piano teacher, followed Mrs. Marley. Boom-Boom had to be at least sixty, but her hair was still a vibrant puff of honey-gold—due to frequent trips to Trish's Hair Affair, no doubt. Her weight seemed to be about the same as it had been for the last twenty years; she barely managed to squeeze her bulk through the door. In her characteristically loud voice, Boom-Boom chatted with her older companion about snapdragons wilting in the heat.

Mrs. Marley changed course and headed for Lauren's table, presumably less interested in snapdragons than in seeing what freebies might be available. The woman carried something under the hunch of her withered body. As Lauren took a closer look, she couldn't believe what she saw. Fur. Dog fur. The indestructible, loathsome little Taz had risen from the dead.

Lauren's heart started beating again when she realized the animal was stuffed. A Biggs Taxidermy special. Taz —Lauren had always assumed the name was short for Tasmanian Devil—lived in effigy, same pointy fangs exposed beneath curled lip.

A six-year-old Lauren had made the mistake of running from the beast, and he'd become the terror of her entire first-grade year. He'd given chase on a routine basis. Once when she'd fallen, Taz had bitten her viciously enough to require stitches. Her lingering fear of dogs—something she'd exerted considerable effort to disguise over the years—was Taz's legacy. To her surprise, the stuffed version appeared quite small.

"It's the hussy," Mrs. Marley hissed, referring to Lauren, but speaking to no one in particular. "I saw her parading around with that young oil man on Saturday night, rubbing up against him in plain sight of God and everybody. A tramp, she is, just like her sister."

"Hush." Boom-Boom Throckmorton had followed Mrs. Marley to the table. Boom-Boom's voice carried throughout the room and silenced most everyone. "She's a lawyer, not a hussy."

Mrs. Marley looked scandalized, her eyes enlarging behind the glasses. "Hear that, Taz? A lawyer!" She hugged the dog as she reversed direction and shuffled away.

The gym was filling rapidly. Trish stopped by the table to say hi and take a wilderness pamphlet. Though she quickly stuffed it in her purse and probably wouldn't read a word, at least she'd made the gesture. She joined Don Ray near the front, along with his brother Chester and three other Lomax loggers. Joe Hewitt was in the same row, sitting beside his uncle, the mayor.

Lauren was surprised to spot Rio in one of the back seats. She wondered if he had come hoping to see Becca.

Also near the back were the owners of the Sandman Motel and a gas station, businesses on the main highway that passed near town. According to Becca, both men were less hostile to wilderness than most. If they hadn't been ridiculously outnumbered, their presence might have been a comfort.

Sheriff Purdy and Hannah walked in with Ezra between them. The old man raised his head and flared his nostrils before turning squarely toward Lauren, bringing his guides along with him.

"There's my wildflower girl," he said. "Why don't you come sit by me?"

Lauren had to decline, since she was manning the largely

ignored information table, but she did appreciate the offer. Good old Ezra didn't care whether or not she was popular with the masses.

"You shouldn't be here, baby," Hannah said. "I thought you learned from the last time."

"I'm representing the CPWA, Mother. I don't have a choice."

Hannah clucked her disapproval. "Watch what you say then. No point in making the whole town crazy."

Lauren had known what to expect, but that didn't make her mother's lack of support any less painful. "Here, have a pamphlet."

Hannah waved the offending paper away. "I don't want that propaganda."

Lauren froze, hand extended. The brusqueness hurt. It always had.

Ezra spoke up. "Shame on you, Hannah." He took his hand off her arm. With his uncanny inner sight, he reached within an inch of Lauren's hand. "I'll take one."

Lauren gently transferred the paper to him.

"Don't reckon they come in Braille." Ezra chuckled, testing the paper between his fingers. "Don't you fret, child, I'll find out what it says." He tucked it into his vest, flashed his gold-molar smile in Lauren's vicinity, and took Hannah's arm again.

For consistency's sake, Lauren offered a pamphlet to the sheriff. LaDell Purdy coughed. "Don't have my glasses on me," he muttered before scuttling away, taking Ezra and Hannah with him.

The crowd numbered perhaps three hundred, a large turnout for a town of eleven hundred souls. No CPWA minions had showed; Lauren hadn't really expected them.

Gabe hadn't arrived, either, though she'd been watching for him with both anticipation and dread. She hadn't seen him since she'd gone to his oil well, and they hadn't parted on the best of terms.

He finally ambled through the open double doors just as Arch McFarlane was testing the microphone.

Tall and lean, Gabe looked terrific in his worn jeans and work shirt, if a person went for the strong, virile, outdoorsy type. As Lauren did, she admitted to herself wryly. Her breath quickened at the sight of him, even with dust in his hair and mud caked on his boots. He must have come straight from a rig site.

When he walked in, several people called out greetings to him, and a number of women, young and old, rose from their chairs to make sure he noticed them. It wasn't just his broad shoulders and too-blue eyes that captured female attention. His easy moves and down-to-earth smile were enough to accelerate every opposite-sex pulse in the room, hers included. She was absolutely disgusted with herself for admiring, for caring, for wanting him to notice her.

After a quick scan of the room, his gaze came to rest on Lauren, and he started toward her.

Hot blood heated her face—more from embarrassment and uncertainty than from any sensual response. She didn't know what to expect from him after the ugly accusations she'd hurled his way. Her presence at tonight's meeting, for the sole purpose of promoting wilderness and demoting Great Basin's leases, wouldn't endear her to him, either.

Would he give her a public dressing-down? Yell at her? Shake her until her teeth rattled? Though she'd never known him to be violent, she was still tense.

When he reached her table, his eyes searched hers for a moment. Apparently what he saw satisfied him, because he smiled—a slow, sure, confident smile. That was one reaction for which she *hadn't* prepared.

"Can you spare a little reading material for a semiliterate redneck?" His low, intimate tone shivered right down her spine. He placed his hand over hers, where it lay on top of a big stack of pamphlets. As she slipped her hand free, his blue eyes sparkled. He must not be holding a grudge, she thought, because it was obvious he was willing to continue their game.

He helped himself to a pamphlet. "Thanks, ma'am. I like to stay informed."

Up front, Arch McFarlane started telling a preparatory bad joke. Gabe moved twenty feet across the room, where he braced one scuffed cowboy boot against the back wall. He glanced toward her once more, his gaze lingering, before turning his attention to the man at the mike.

Lauren felt flushed and flustered, which she guessed was his intention. Whenever he smiled at her, touched her, even looked at her, she had one heck of a time recalling he was the enemy.

Gabe wished Lauren would quit thinking of him as the enemy. He'd seen her sigh, probably with relief to have him at a safe distance. But she'd relaxed her guard too soon. She had real enemies in the room, no doubt about it.

Arch was reviewing the BLM's latest study of Red Rock Canyon. "Now folks, the idea is to apply this Environmental Assessment"—he waved a sheaf of papers—"and come up with a land-use plan. The sad truth is that it's going to take a few tries, probably, to get it right, because everybody won't agree the first time around. First off, though, I might as well warn you that a proposed wilderness area—officially called a W.S.A., or Wilderness Study Area—deserves extra protection. With that in mind, we're going to have to consider some management changes in Red Rock."

He put on a pair of black-framed reading glasses and cleared his throat. "One. We need to cut way back on running off-highway vehicles in the canyon."

As Gabe and everyone else could have predicted, Joe jumped out of his chair. "You'd limit access for four-wheelers and motorcycles? What're we hurting, riding the two-tracks out there? You'll ruin my business! If you take away Red Rock, there aren't enough trails left to spit on."

"I didn't say we'd close *all* trails in Red Rock," Arch said, trying to regain control of the meeting.

Since riding various all-terrain vehicles in the backcountry was a popular sport, others spoke out, too. Gabe, however, sided with the environmentalists on that matter. He had nothing against ATVs running in nonsensitive areas, but the burgeoning use of them any- and everywhere caused erosion, muddied the streams, and terrorized wildlife.

When the locals had vented their dissent, Arch eased into the next point. "Two. Looks like alteration of waterways in the Red Rock drainage would severely impact stream ecology, so we'll probably need to ban the construction of any new dams."

"Bullshit! You can't keep us from holding on to water," Mayor Al Hewitt bellowed. "You're taking away what's ours."

Shouts of agreement backed him up. "The government's stealing every dang right we've got!" "How're we gonna irrigate our fields and pastures when the Rafael Dam silts up and goes dry?" "We need water!"

Arch listened patiently until the uproar died down. He pulled off his glasses and glanced around the room. "Three. Logging's a problem. I know there're some fine ponderosa pines at the high end of the canyon, but cutting down trees doesn't go with wilderness."

"The hell with wilderness." Chester Lomax screeched his chair on the polished floor as he leaped to his feet. "That land's ours, not the federal government's."

"The land was never yours," Arch McFarlane stated calmly, apparently accustomed to such complaints. "The government has just allowed you to use it as your own all these years."

"Yeah? I say it's ours by right of use. Not the government's. Ours." Chester pointed to his chest. "And we know how to take care of it better than the BLM or the goddamn environmentalists."

Approving calls and whistles sounded throughout the crowd. Chester remained standing, growing red in the face as if he were on the verge of volcanic eruption. Don Ray pulled his brother back down onto a chair.

Gabe glanced at Lauren and found her looking his way. They both knew what was coming next.

"Lastly," Arch said into the microphone, "oil and gas. We won't be allowing any new leases, but we still have to decide what to do with the old ones. This assessment"—he raised the papers again—"finds that drilling down there won't cause excessive damage."

An Olympus Petroleum representative—Olympus also held leases in the proposed wilderness—applauded loudly, along with several men who had worked the oil fields for years. Gabe didn't move or say anything. He didn't want to rile the crowd worse than it was already riled. He just leaned against the back wall, stone-faced.

"The BLM will turn out a land-management draft within a couple of weeks," Arch said. "But since the CPWA has already complained that our EA is incomplete, looks like we'll be doing some more studying. Could be our decision on the drilling will have to change."

Boos, curses, and uncomplimentary references to environmentalist scum rumbled and resonated. Many faces turned to glare in Lauren's direction. A child molester would have been held in higher regard than she was at that moment.

Arch pointed to her and announced that she'd asked to comment in the name of the CPWA. Gabe had expected her to speak, but he kept hoping she'd have the good sense to duck out to the ladies' room and hide.

She stepped right on up to the microphone, poised and

conservatively dressed in a navy skirt, plain white blouse, and high heels that clicked briskly on the gymnasium floor. She paid no attention to the mumbling and rude comments aimed her way.

Gabe watched her with a certain pride, even though her formal objections to oil drilling might well mean he'd go broke on his Utah foray. For her to address this angry crowd wasn't the smartest move she'd ever made, but it was courageous. He admired her for doing what she thought was right.

She stood tall and confident at the podium until the contending voices gradually died down. "As most of you know," she began, "I've spent the last four years working for the CPWA because I believe in saving our country's wild lands. There's not much of it left. More roads are built on federal lands every day, cutting into the few remaining pristine areas. We're losing biological diversity at an alarming rate, because species don't have the space to survive. The Wilderness Act of 1964 recognized the need for preservation, but change is a slow process."

Lauren glanced around the room, seeking to hold her audience, although she must have known most of them would never embrace her beliefs. "I don't have to tell you, the people of San Rafael, about the beauty and wild character of Red Rock Canyon. You know its virtues better than anyone, and that's why I hope you'll join with me in protecting it from human impact. Wilderness means no roads. The old two-track remnants in the canyon must go back to nature."

"Those are our roads. County maintained!" Al Hewitt shouted.

Lauren ignored him. "And we must not allow new roads to be built for commercial purposes such as oil wells, logging, and so on. I know this will hit some of you in the pocketbook, and I know that hurts."

"What do you know about us?" someone shouted. "You don't have to worry about your next paycheck like we do."

"I know the statistics," she responded. "Extractive activity is no longer the core of Utah economy. It doesn't have to be the core of San Rafael's economy, either."

"You can twist statistics any which way," the mayor shouted. "We need to grow! We need new residents and new jobs to keep us alive."

"Red Rock Canyon's unique appeal will draw new residents, once the area becomes better known. There are many retirees who want to live near a wilderness area, land that is guaranteed to remain beautiful and undeveloped. And you're right, new residents mean new jobs, but in this case the employment will be service-oriented."

The audience buzzed, but no one spoke up. Lauren went on to give facts and figures of success stories in similar communities. "Other towns have adapted to changes in federal land use. San Rafael can, too. It might take some time for tourism to develop, for new businesses to prosper, but—"

"We don't *have* time," someone protested.

"I realize that's a concern," she said, "but there are interim jobs you could—"

"We don't want any interims. Can't afford 'em." "We want everything to stay the way it is." "Don't try to tell us what to do, lady."

Gabe knew a few of those in the audience basically agreed with Lauren, but they weren't going to speak out in this climate.

Lauren moved on to her summation. "My organization commends the BLM's proposal to ban logging and waterway obstruction. We differ over their tolerance of off-highway and all-terrain vehicle use, and their complacency over the development of oil leases in the canyon. However, I believe further assessments will consider these issues more carefully. *All* motorized vehicles must be kept out of Red Rock if we hope to protect the wildlife and landscape. *All* extraction of oil and minerals, now and in the future, must be blocked."

The waves of discontent in the gym were palpable. Gabe wished she'd quit there, but she took a deep breath and went on. "That's the CPWA stand. And my stand. I know most of you don't agree, but because you love Red Rock Canyon as much as I do, I hope you'll take one of the pamphlets from the table in back and try to see where I'm coming from. Thanks."

Lauren seemed relieved to leave the microphone. As she walked down the aisle all alone, Gabe wanted to go to her, to shield her from the malevolent glares. Instead he flexed his jaw muscles and bided his time. She glanced his way, as if concerned about what he'd do or say.

Gabe knew the real threat lay elsewhere.

He scanned the rows of folding chairs, expecting someone to jump out of one and grab her by the throat. He tensed for whatever trouble would come. She'd had enemies in town before. After tonight, he doubted that many of these folks would offer her the frayed end of a rope if she were drowning.

"Remember, I need all comments in writing," Arch McFarlane said, as Lauren reached her pamphlets and turned to the front again, leaning her hips against the table edge to wait for the meeting's close. "We'll do our best to respond personally to every concern. If there's nothing else . . ."

Chester popped out of his chair. "Damn right there's nothing else. You're leaving us with Jack-squat. I don't like having my rights jerked out from under me. Nobody's taking my rights to the land."

He charged past Don Ray and Trish, and stomped down the empty aisle toward the back of the room. Gabe thought at first that Chester would continue right on out the door.

Instead the man swerved toward Lauren, pulled a long, glistening blade from a leather belt scabbard, and raised the knife high in the air.

Chapter Ten

A collective gasp arose from the audience as Chester ad-
vanced on Lauren's table. Gabe was already in full
sprint, afraid he might be seconds too late.

Fortunately Chester wasn't going for Lauren. He whipped
the knife in a downward arc, impaling a stack of wilderness
pamphlets. He withdrew the knife and came down again, ripping chunks out of the stack of papers.

Instead of running to save herself, which would have been
the commonsense thing to do, Lauren leaped forward to latch
on to Chester's arm. "Stop that! What's wrong with you?"
she scolded. It didn't seem to occur to her that he might turn
the blade on her. Because she'd known Chester Lomax all
her life, she assumed she was safe.

Gabe wasn't so sure. He slung a forearm around the man's
neck from behind, but caught a glimpse of Lauren karate-
chopping Chester's wrist at the same time. The weapon clattered to the floor.

Chester clutched his arm to his chest. His yowl was cut
short by Gabe's choke hold. He flailed for a few seconds before his body went slack, all the frenzy draining out of him.

Lauren was rubbing her own hand, glaring at Chester.

"Get away," Gabe yelled. She was too close. He didn't
want her anywhere near a man who'd pull a knife.

She stumbled backward, out of range, as if the possibility that she could have been stabbed had just gotten through to her. Gabe let up on Chester's neck after kicking the knife toward the door.

Don Ray, who'd come running from the front seats, recovered the weapon and stuck it through his belt. "Whoa, Chester," he said, approaching his brother cautiously. "You lost it for a minute, bro."

The sheriff arrived on the scene and took charge of Chester.

Gabe and Lauren looked at each other, both a little shaken, until he broke the tension with, "Remind me to keep your self-defense techniques in mind next time I'm putting the moves on you. What belt are you, anyway?"

She smiled. "Yellow."

"Could've fooled me. I would've thought black, darlin', at least."

She glanced down at her hand. "I . . ." Her voice quavered. "I never hit anybody before. Only in karate practice, and that wasn't . . ."

"Ah, Laurie." Gabe covered the few feet that separated them. With tender care, with feeling, he embraced her, hugging her close. His heart was still pounding, he'd been so damn scared for her. "You shouldn't have tried to stop him," he murmured into her hair. "Didn't you know you were supposed to wait for me to rescue you?"

She pushed away, smoothing her skirt, regaining her dignity. "You have to be quick if you want to be in the rescue business. My pamphlets would have *all* been destroyed if I'd waited for you." As it was, not many of them were in one piece.

Gabe was glad pamphlets were the only casualty. Together he and Lauren watched while the sheriff and Chester progressed slowly toward the door. The curious crowd parted like the sea before Moses. Chester bowed his head and emitted what sounded like a sob. His broad shoulders shook.

"Is he . . . crying?" Lauren asked Gabe as the townspeople around them began to mill again. She seemed more horrified by the man's loss of emotional control than by the violence.

Gabe peered down at her pale face, nose peeling and freckly with sunburn, eyes shadowed with an uncertainty that surprised him. He knew she had compassion for family; he hoped her soft spot might extend past that, to embrace the townspeople and their needs.

"One by one, all the big government tracts are being closed to logging," he said quietly. "Chester doesn't know how to do anything but cut trees. You see that, don't you? You have to see, unless you're blinder than old Ezra."

"Nothing wrong with her eyesight."

Lauren whirled to find that Joe had spoken from right behind her. She'd expected trouble from him, and now it looked as if she'd have it. "Why, Joe, what a disagreeable surprise! I'd know your ugly mug and macho swagger anywhere."

"I see you're the same old self-centered, tight-assed bitch, Lauren." Joe had been vain about his looks in his younger days. Tonight his clothes were rumpled and stained, his jaw unshaven, his thick brown hair borderline greasy.

Though her sister would never believe it, Lauren had felt sorry for him at times. But not now. "You, Joe, are a heartless rat. Why don't you let up on Becca and Missy?"

"Why don't you mind your own business?" he snarled. "Everybody says you're smart, but you're dumber than a blond on a billboard when it comes to what's going on under your nose. And I'm not talking about just my wife and kid. I'm talking about *this*." He swept a hand through the mutilated pamphlets, knocking most of them onto the floor. "We don't want your kind here. We don't want your useless, high-minded ideals."

Gabe loomed beside her like a guardian angel, protective and deadly calm. "Leave her alone, Joe."

"I can handle this," Lauren insisted, though she did appreciate Gabe's support. However, it became apparent that she was no longer the focal point. The two men ignored her and glared at each other. Some of the people streaming out the doors paused, curiously eyeing Lauren and the pair that had squared off on either side of her.

"I don't get it, Randolph," Joe said to Gabe. "Why are you defending her when I just heard you telling her how it is? Whose side are you on, anyway?"

"Maybe I'm not on a side."

"Maybe not. The whole town's flapping their lips about you and Lauren being strange bedfellows. First you're playing around with my wife, then you're after my wife's sister."

"Becca is not your wife," Gabe pointed out.

"Ex-wife. Not that I'm crying in my beer over you switching fillies, if that's what you've got in mind. I'm just confused. Why in hell would you go for a meddling tree-hugger like Lauren? What's the payoff? Did she promise to cut you environmental slack on the oil leases?"

"I'm not cutting anyone slack," Lauren said, outraged. "I've done nothing—"

Gabe squeezed her hand and broke in with, "If we spend time together, that's our business, Joe. Nothing in our personal lives will affect her job or my company. You ought to know Laurie Van Horn better than that."

Joe snorted. "Why else would you want her? She's skinny and bitchy, and most likely a lesbian, come right down to it. Nobody's gonna believe you'd waste your time on the ugly sister unless you had a damn good reason."

"Ugly?" Gabe said. "If you think that, Joe, you're the one who has eye trouble."

"Oh, for heaven's sake," Lauren blurted. "What is this, a beauty pageant?"

"If it is, you lose." Hostility gleamed in Joe's hazel eyes. "I know what Gabe's up to. He's bought you out, and I'll bet it didn't cost him a dime. He always did have a way with the ladies."

She couldn't believe he'd said that. Couldn't believe he'd thought it. "You . . . you lying bastard!"

With a smirk, Joe began strolling away.

Lauren's muscles bunched to lunge after him, but Gabe gripped her shoulders from behind. "No," he said. "Joe's spoiling for a fight. Don't give him the satisfaction."

She wrenched free. She'd known Joe resented her for helping Becca with the divorce, for making no secret of her disapproval of him. Still, she hadn't foreseen this particular blow. "Did you hear what he said? He thinks you're buying my influence with sex."

Gabe shrugged. "Sorry. How was I to know he'd jump to that conclusion?"

"I should have guessed Joe would come up with something like that." She knelt to pick up the pamphlets, slamming them into the cardboard box she'd brought them in. "This 'affair' of ours is—"

The Olympus Petroleum man came up and slapped Gabe on the back, which cut Lauren's comment short. As if nothing unusual had happened, Gabe shook his competitor's hand and introduced Lauren. Still shaking with rage and embarrassment, she rose with her pamphlets and lightly grasped the Olympus rep's damp palm, offering him a tepid smile. She excused herself to fold up the table. As soon as possible, she snatched her box of papers and escaped into the cool night air. The crowd had dispersed. Of those who were left, a few nodded. Most just moved out of her way.

Trish was waiting for her on the sidewalk. "Oh my heck, Laurie, I'm *so* sorry for what Chester did. Don Ray's with him over at the jailhouse. Don't worry, now; if the sheriff lets him go, Don Ray'll make sure he behaves."

"What got into him, Trish? I don't understand why he'd go berserk like that. I know he doesn't want change, but this was *hate*. He hates me."

Trish shook her head. "It's hard on him, seeing the family business fall apart. Kenny, the oldest Lomax, is moving away. Says he can't support a family on small-time logging anymore. The other brothers might be next."

Lauren shifted the box of pamphlets from one hip to the other. "I didn't know it was that bad for them."

"Well, it is. We all love the canyon, Laurie. We do. It's just that locking up what's in it might not be the best way."

Lauren believed it was the only way. History had proved that unless land was protected by law, the temptation to deface it and develop it for profit was too great. But she'd said enough for one night. She thanked Trish for her concern and moved on down the sidewalk.

She had often been shunned for her ideals, but the chill factor seemed especially high in San Rafael. Because this was the town that had raised her, the people's reactions made her feel forlorn. She'd acted upon the highest principles and stated the absolute truth, but what good had she done?

Walking home on the quiet street, she looked up at the star-kissed velvet sky and tried to absorb the balm of its serenity. She'd always loved the desert night, the rich beauty after the daytime glare, the coolness after the heat. The vast, open space and all-encompassing sky called to the passion in her soul.

She could commune with the desert sky, but not with the San Rafaelites who lived under it. They had problems and concerns. She knew that. But they didn't see anything the way she did. She doubted any of them had been on her wavelength in the gym. She'd been as incomprehensible as Eve Worthy's Latin would have been. She spoke the language of wilderness versus their vernacular of custom and culture.

To Lauren's regret, it seemed the two would never meet.

*   *   *

The next afternoon, Becca was alone in her house when the doorbell rang. Missy was in school, and Lauren had walked to the Top Chop for groceries.

"Hold on to your horses," Becca sang to the tune of "She's Single Again" on the CD player. She turned down the volume and Texas two-stepped out of the kitchen, where she'd been making tea, toward the front door.

Her head felt much clearer now, on the fifth day after she'd had her bell rung in the crash. The doctor had removed the external stitches, and her face looked almost normal. She was in a great mood, relaxing in the green satin pajamas and robe she'd bought for herself the day the divorce went through. It had taken months to get over the melancholy. Surviving the accident had made her realize she was lucky to be alive, and maybe even luckier to be free.

She paused near the door as the chimes rang a second time. She hoped Joe hadn't come back for another visit. More likely her drop-in guest would be one of the town busybodies making certain she knew every detail of last night's meeting, the most exciting event to happen in San Rafael this year. Lauren had added spice. Too bad the seasoning wasn't appreciated in a more positive way. The whole thing would be almost funny if it weren't for Chester's knife and the phone calls they'd gotten in the middle of last night.

Lauren had worried about the calls, but Becca shrugged them off. She knew the people here. They might kick up a fuss, but she didn't believe anyone would hurt her or Lauren on purpose. Even the accident, she was sure, would have a reasonable explanation. She just didn't know what it was yet.

Flinging open the door, she was startled to find Rio framed there. He smiled when he saw her and gushed something in Spanish, of which she understood not a word. His eyes translated for him, caressing her face, and then a bit lower, with undisguised admiration. She looked down at herself, long blond hair falling forward like a veil. Her lounging outfit gaped a little at the neckline, showing a section of her considerable cleavage.

Self-consciously, she drew the robe closer around herself and tightened the sash.

"I am glad to see you are well, Rebecca," he said. "Your pale cheeks bloom like roses at dawn."

She'd just bet they did. When a man's gaze took in a woman the way he'd taken her in, a blush was the natural reaction. So was a sense of illicit excitement. She peeked past Rio into the street. No one seemed to be around, and he'd parked in front of a neighbor's house, not hers. Maybe she could let him inside without anyone knowing.

Lauren would be outraged if Becca admitted a male visitor with the nasty custody accusations on her heels, but as long as she was careful, as long as Joe didn't find out and raise a ruckus about loose morals and such, what could it hurt? Besides, she was an invalid, so no one was going to think anything out of order was going on. And Rio might just counterbalance what everyone was saying about her "affair" with Gabe.

"Come in," she said to Rio. "Come right on in. You can wait in the living room, and I'll change into . . ."

"Something more comfortable?" Mischief glinted in his dark eyes.

My, my. She'd thought Rio too reserved to make a suggestion like that. But then, she didn't know him, not really. She wanted to, though, she had to admit.

He bowed his head, as if he thought he might have offended her. "Please don't change. You look very beautiful."

"I . . . guess I'm decent enough," she said, unsure how to react to the compliment. "I'm heating water for tea. I'd love to make you a cup."

"Ah, but you are the patient, are you not?" His slight Spanish accent seemed both formal and romantic. "Let me make the tea and bring it to you in the living room, dear one."

Dear one. How absolutely quaint. "Why, thank you, Rio. I do believe I'll accept."

He offered an arm and she took it. He had a muscular arm. She supposed it took strength, moving all those antiques around. However, it wasn't the muscle that impressed her most. Never had any man treated her like a goddess on a pedestal, as Rio was doing now. She had to remind herself he was an ordinary guy, albeit with a whopping dose of old-fashioned charm. He'd been the same way when they'd met in her office, and in the restaurant. Letting him into her house might have been a serious wrong move. The attraction was stronger when they were alone.

He insisted on arranging the couch pillows, setting one behind her back and one beneath her feet, which he propped on the coffee table. Her feet were bare, with chipped purple paint on the toenails and probably dirt on the soles. If Rio noticed, he didn't comment.

He left her lounging in style while he prepared the tea. Rattling around in the kitchen, he called to her several times, praising the sand painting laid out on the counter, admiring the watercolor landscape hanging above the microwave, even noticing a couple of painted flowerpots decorating the windowsill. Since they were all Becca's creations, she basked in a warm glow. So few people in San Rafael knew that she painted, or cared.

Soon Rio brought out two china cups on a black lacquer tray she'd forgotten she owned, complete with herbal tea bags, cream, and sugar.

"You must be heaven-sent," she said, when both of them had settled back with their hot brew. "Thanks for this, and for the roses. My sister Lauren told me you came by on Sunday. I'm sorry she didn't ask you in. She thought I'd be too tired."

"She loves you," Rio said. "That is something I can easily understand."

"I suppose she thought I wasn't ready for the stress."

Becca decided Lauren might have been correct. Her heart was pumping double-time just from the tender look in his chocolate brown eyes.

"If you allow me to call on you again, I will bring more roses," he said.

"Oh, I wasn't hinting. You really shouldn't—"

He reached over and pressed his index finger to her lips. "A beautiful woman deserves beautiful gifts."

Oh, God. She was going to swoon.

He sat back after that one simple, eloquent touch. Such a gentleman. A dark, mysterious, foreign gentleman, she reminded herself, dangerous by definition. She hadn't known that men like him existed except in fairy tales. Even then, Becca theorized the handsome prince would be nice only until the princess delivered the key to her chastity belt.

Rio couldn't possibly be for real. And she wasn't tempted by him, because safe and sure were what she needed in a man. She'd had the mindless passion and wild sex, and look where that had gotten her.

"After your sister sent me away, I returned the next afternoon," he said. "A little girl answered the door."

"That must have been my daughter. She didn't tell me you'd come."

"You were in the bathtub soaking, so the child said. I had more flowers—lilies, not roses—but she wouldn't take them. She said I was a stranger. Wise of her, I thought."

"They're teaching safety in school now, although Missy has never trusted strangers. Especially men strangers. She's not very social."

He smiled and shook his head. "You should review the safety rules with your daughter. She wouldn't take the flowers, but she did invite me in to watch a documentary with her. On rock crabs, I believe. Fascinating as it sounded, I could not accept."

Becca frowned. "I thought she knew better." But then,

Missy often astonished her mother, one way or the other. The little girl was surprisingly adult in some respects, which made it easier to forget how young and innocent she was. Becca recovered from her shock and chuckled softly. "Missy's an unusual kid."

"I would like to spend time with her. I would have stayed, but I thought your lioness sister must be lurking nearby. Since I learned at Tuesday's meeting that she is an attorney, I feared she'd take legal action the moment I entered the house."

"Lauren just might. She's protective."

"I think you would be equally fearsome if you saw the need," he said. "How are you feeling? Am I tiring you by staying too long?"

"No, not at all." She wanted him to stay, just this one time. "I'm much better already. Another week, at most, and I'll be back to work."

"I heard you have a concussion."

"Yes, but the headaches are lessening."

He set down his teacup. "You've been through a trauma, and you mustn't allow anyone to pressure you. Relax, Rebecca. Let your body renew itself." He had the most delicious voice. The faint accent mesmerized her.

"I'm trying," she said.

"I took a course in massage therapy once." He lifted her feet onto his lap. "Massage is good for muscles and good for the soul." He was already kneading the top of one arch, moving down to the pads of her feet, to her toes. She almost groaned, it felt so good, but she wasn't going to be taken in that easily.

She pulled back her feet, which he reluctantly released. Becca didn't want body manipulation from him or any man. She'd been bruised and abraded in more ways than one during her tumultuous years of marriage. If she was going to have another man, she wanted someone she could rely upon, who wouldn't let her down.

Someone like Gabe. She knew him, had known him forever.

She could fit what she knew about Rio into one of the teacups on the coffee table. One thing she could tell right up front; he was way too . . . accommodating.

She reached behind her back to rearrange the pillow. Her inner alarm clamored when he moved to help. She must have jumped, because he took her hand and held it very gently.

"I will not harm you." His gaze caressed her face. He didn't try to disguise his desire, but his respect for her was also clear.

She wasn't afraid, though probably she should have been.

He lifted her hand to his mouth, raising her heart rate yet again. He delivered a light kiss to the back of her hand. She felt the hair at her nape curl, and a tingle went down her spine.

She pulled free, tucking the hand under her thigh, out of sight. Much more temptation and she just might strip off her robe and let him manipulate whatever he pleased. She did *not* need that kind of excitement.

"So how's the antique store?" she asked casually. "How long has it been open now?"

"Through the Ages has been open two weeks. The location on the highway seems good. Tourists come through on their way to Cedar Breaks or Bryce Canyon. Many have stopped. If the sales keep up as they've been, I'll make money. When you are well, you must come by. I hope you will allow me to sell some of your art on consignment, as I suggested before."

"I'll think about it." She was warm from his touch, and flattered that he was still interested in her work. "How long did the shop's renovation take?" She didn't recall his telling her exactly when he'd moved to the area.

"I bought the house four months ago, right after I met you. There's still much more to do, but now that I've opened, I can finish one room at a time."

"And you moved here from . . . California, right?"

"Yes. In San Diego, I also sold antiques. When I was young, when my father first came to this country from Mexico, he found work as a janitor in a museum. I would help him dust the old and precious objects. We lived in poverty, but there I saw beauty. For me, trading in antiques and art has been a way to touch those things, to have them for my own, at least for a time." He paused, gazing into her eyes. "Any more questions?"

"Can't think of any," Becca said. His forthrightness disarmed her, swept away her misgivings.

"I am no longer a stranger. Your daughter would approve. But perhaps not your sister."

"Not yet. We'll work on her." Becca wasn't sure she'd make any progress, but Rio might be worth the effort. Since he had an interest in her art, she had a business reason for seeing him. And that was the only reason, she told herself. Absolutely the only one. Of course, she might have a difficult time convincing Lauren and Joe of that. But *she* knew the truth. Didn't she?

"May I visit again?" Rio asked.

She smiled, her mouth still a little stiff. "I'll give Lauren the high sign, now that you've passed the history test."

He reached forward, brushing her bangs from her forehead and outlining the healing ridge. "I am so sorry, *querida*. For this I am sorry."

His touch on her skin radiated heat. When he sat back, separating them again, the warmth in his dark eyes made her feel happy, appreciated, confident in herself and her womanly powers.

Lounging on pillows like the Queen of Sheba, Becca

pointed to a box of mint truffles on the coffee table. "Would you like some candy? Help yourself."

He opened the box and offered it to her. "Please, you must join me."

She was hungry, but she declined, lest Rio notice that she was a teensy bit overweight. She'd been meaning to go on a diet.

"You're too thin," he said.

She wasn't thin. Nevertheless, when he chose one of the mints and held it to her lips, she nibbled it right from his hand.

Never take candy from strangers. Becca didn't know Rio at all. A big no-no.

Yet she doted on the romanticism. Joe had never fed her anything directly from his hands except a slice of their wedding cake. If Gabe ever hand-fed truffles to her, he'd make a joke out of it. With Gabe, she'd be laughing too hard to feel the quivers in her spine that she was feeling now.

"I like a woman who eats with passion," Rio said, as he watched her swallow the last of the morsel.

Becca grinned. Even if it was all a lie, even if he thought she was as fat as a corn-fed pig, she enjoyed the blatant flattery. "I could grow attached to you, Rio. Truly, I believe I could."

"Yoo-hoo! Laur*en*!" The voice started low, but the last syllable hit a high note and hung there for long seconds.

Lauren was returning from the grocery store carrying a bulging paper bag, enjoying the afternoon sun. At the sound of her name, she almost dropped the groceries. She glanced around, saw Mrs. Throckmorton's red brick house, and knew the voice. Boom-Boom at her genteel best.

The imposing woman's torso protruded from the front window. She waved a hankie like a peace flag, and her puff of honey-gold hair bobbed in the same rhythm. Piano scales pounded in the background.

"Yoo-hoo! Laur*en*! I have something for you to take to your sister!"

Lauren sighed. Her memories of Boom-Boom and the Throckmorton house were less than fond. She'd hated piano lessons. Considering the volume of the call, however, she could hardly pretend not to hear. The yard had a neat white picket fence. She opened the gate and walked through, but a rustle behind a leafy shrub warned her she wasn't alone.

She glanced to the side and saw a goat with head and horns poised only inches from her hip. The smooth arc of the horns gave her a nudge.

Lauren sucked in her breath. She'd forgotten how blasted rural San Rafael really was. Okay, maybe it was contradictory thinking, but couldn't a person dedicate herself to preserving the great outdoors without an abundance of obnoxious species, human and otherwise, butting in? Literally butting, in this instance.

Mrs. Throckmorton leaned farther out the window, waving the hankie vigorously. "Shoo, Myrtle. Go eat paper and tin cans like a good goat."

Myrtle nuzzled Lauren's hip, a "maaa" vibrating deep in the animal's throat. Lauren scratched the top of the goat's head, telling it to get lost out of the side of her mouth. She didn't dislike the goat; she just didn't trust it. For all she knew, it might decide to eat her clothes and leave her naked, holding an assortment of equally naked canned goods in her hands.

Mrs. Throckmorton waddled outside to shove a bulging plastic Ziploc into the top of Lauren's grocery sack. "Strawberries from my garden," she said.

The goat was investigating the sack, using teeth to test it, or maybe following Boom-Boom's directive to eat paper. In any case, Myrtle ripped a hole that sent a can of tomato soup tumbling out. Lauren caught it in midair and managed to stopper the gap in the poor-quality bag with her other hand, wishing she'd asked for plastic instead.

"Poor Becca. Such a shame about the accident. And about her and Joe." Mrs. Throckmorton seemed oblivious to the havoc her goat was wreaking. She tilted her head to listen to the stumble of ongoing piano notes. "Yoo-hoo! Start over, Elizabeth. Hands separately this time. And slow it down, please."

Turning her attention back to Lauren, she added, "Becca had no aptitude for music whatever, just like Lizzy in there. Lizzy's Bill Whalen's only girl. Heaven help her, she does want to learn, but it's a good thing her daddy's paying for the lessons by fixing my plumbing. At least it's not costing him cash money. Now Missy's another story. She's got a real talen—"

The front door opened again, and someone, or something, came bolting out. "Owwww," the creature screeched, holding its ears. "I can't listen to any more scales. Freakin' A, Grans, how do you stand it!"

As soon as Lauren had a moment to adjust her vision, she knew it was a woman, of sorts. Short black hair stuck up in spikes. A gold chain circled her neck and torso, round and round, all the way to her hips. Thick metal bands bound her upper arms and wrists. She wore rings in her eyebrows, nose, lower lip, and exposed belly button. Beneath her tight black wraparound shirt, which covered her breasts but not much else, Lauren even spied a telltale hint of nipple rings. The only incongruity was a distinct milk mustache.

"Kayleen, don't cuss in front of the neighbors," Mrs. Throckmorton said sharply. "Lauren, I don't think you've met my granddaughter, Kayleen. She's my son Doug's oldest. She's going through a stage with the hair."

The hair wasn't the girl's only problem, Lauren thought as she offered a wary hello and some small talk. Besides everything else, Kayleen had a tattoo of a trumpet-shaped flower on one bare shoulder, and something that very much resembled an erect male body part on the other. Lauren tried not to stare. If this girl waitressed in the Mad House, as Trish Lomax had claimed, Hannah must be either desperate for help or she figured Kayleen's outlandishness would draw customers better than free doughnuts and coffee.

Kayleen shifted her slight weight from one foot to the other. "I'm meeting someone over in Fairfield, Grans. I'll call."

She extracted keys out of her cleavage, clinked her chains past Lauren, and hurried across the street, where she opened the left front door of a rusted ice-cream truck. The brand name had been obliterated—probably a wise move, considering Kayleen did not qualify as a poster child for the moral majority. She climbed behind the wheel, her ultrashort shorts riding up to show the curve of both hind cheeks, revealing the beginnings of more tattoos.

Lauren closed her gaping mouth as the truck rattled down Main Street.

"Elizabeth!" Mrs. Throckmorton yelled. "I want to hear scales."

Lauren caught sight of a face disappearing from the window. Apparently Elizabeth was as fascinated by Kayleen as Lauren was, but she also had a healthy fear of Mrs. Throckmorton. Within seconds the stumbling notes started up again.

Boom-Boom hefted her massive breasts with a forearm and absently fondled Myrtle's horns as the goat rubbed against the woman's bulky hips. "If Doug had raised Kayleen here instead of in Las Vegas, she wouldn't be having an identity crisis. But then she's only twenty-one. I think she'll grow out of it, don't you?"

"I'm, uh, sure you're right." In Las Vegas, being different might require such excess. In San Rafael, Kayleen could have skipped the tattoos, chains, and facial hardware. A belly-button ring was considered radical around here.

"Kayleen spends a lot of time in Red Rock Canyon. Could be she has environmental leanings," Boom-Boom announced, presumably to make Lauren feel more loved.

God forbid, Lauren thought. She had enough problems without Kayleen coming over to her side.

"Could be it's catching," Boom-Boom said. "My stars and hot pink garters, I'm not sure this wilderness thing's as bad for the community as folks say. There could be some good in it. Take my son Doug. He runs a camping supply store in Vegas. With more hikers and river runners coming to this area, he could start up a San Rafael shop and raise his five younger kids right here. Then there's Jack Hartman. He's planning a horseback guide service into the canyons, and he says wilderness would do his business good."

"I'm glad someone recognizes the benefits besides me." Lauren saw a glimmer of hope. It would be so much better if she didn't enter a war zone every time she left the sanctuary of Becca's house.

"Don't know about Chester," Boom-Boom said. "I can see he's afraid the logging's playing out, but that's no reason to start pulling knives. Makes us all look bad." Boom-Boom cocked her honey-puffed head of hair. "I'm glad you weren't hurt, Laurie. You're one brave girl, coming here, saying what you think is what. Just look out for yourself now. And tell Becca to call me sometime, you hear?"

Boom-Boom lumbered back to her student. Lauren shooed the pesky goat into the shrubbery, rearranged the groceries in what was left of the paper sack, and let herself out through the gate. She had forgotten that the piano teacher's loud voice hid a softer heart than one would expect. Boom-Boom was a nice lady, in a lot of ways.

As Lauren walked on, her spirits rose to meet the wispy clouds in the bright blue sky. The sun was warm, not hot. The

fecund smell of horses and cows, and the sharper scent of al-
falfa, drifted to her from the pastures that started right off
Main Street. Beyond stretcched acres and acres of sage, in-
terspersed with irrigated fields along the creek that ran south
of town. The distant dark blue mountains were clearly visible, with closer multihued ridges rising from the clefts and
crevices of canyon country.

San Rafael did have its own special beauty. Since she'd
moved away, she'd rarely been home long enough to become
acclimated to it again, but this time it was sneaking up on her,
taking hold.

Continuing toward home, she passed Bill Whalen with his
head in the lowest of the eight stair-stepped toilet bowls. The
cascade of water had stopped, and it looked as if Bill was
doing maintenance, with a stereotypical plumber's crack
plainly visible above the rear waistband of his loose trousers.

He lifted his head and caught sight of Lauren. "Last year's
leaves plugged it," he explained, gesturing at the bowl. "Waterfall won't work right, but I'll run a Roto-Rooter in there
and fix it right up. I'm thinking I have an old bathtub going
to waste, too. Maybe I'll make a fountain out of it. That
ought to spruce up the place."

Lauren nodded, both appalled and amused.

As Bill Whalen stood, he stuck his pipe wrench in his
back pocket, which weighed down his trousers almost to the
point of falling off.

Lauren waited on the sidewalk, since he seemed to have
something more to say.

He sidled up, a little shyly. "You know, Laurie, my son
Jake wants to stay in town and work with me, but business
has been real slow. You really think that dang wilderness
thing in the Red Rock will bring more folks here to live? Retirees and that?" His brow furrowed, as if she were his one
hope for a straight answer.

Lauren gave him the best she had. "We can't know for

certain, but it's happened in other communities. Take Spring-
dale, down near Zion National Park. People come from all
over to live there. Why not here? We'd have to get the word
out, but the current media blitz is helping. We could do more,
I think. We could—" We? What did she mean by that? She
started over. "There are ways, Mr. Whalen. The town could
make this work in its favor."

After she'd answered a couple of questions about Spring-
dale's growth, she wished Mr. Whalen good afternoon and
happy rooting before hurrying on, smiling. If the city fathers
ever put out tourist fliers, Lauren was certain Bill Whalen's
flushing cascade would be featured prominently. A photo of
Trish's tailgate geraniums would surely be included, as well.

The town was . . . quaint. Colorful, some might say. *Tacky*
or *bizarre* were other ways to phrase it. Maybe Kayleen
wasn't so far from the norm after all. If there was room for
toilet waterfalls, why not chains and tattoos? Heck, maybe
there was even a place for environmentalists.

As she neared Gabe's house, she glanced down his driveway and noticed his parked Jeep. She was still confused as to
why he'd taken up for her with Chester, or even with Joe. She
wanted to discuss Becca's accident with him again, this time
with a cooler head. She needed to apologize for jumping to
conclusions. Maybe this evening . . .

A black sedan pulled away from the curb across the street
and sped past her. She knew the car. She knew the driver.

Rio. She hoped Becca hadn't let the man inside while she
was all alone, but Lauren feared she had. The way her sister
was going, Joe would think his ex had multiple lovers. Unless Becca started turning them away at the door, Lauren
could spend the next ten years simulating affairs with
Becca's alleged sexual partners, all in what was probably a
futile attempt to keep her sister and Missy out of a custody
battle.

She rushed past Gabe's house and into Becca's driveway,

meaning to reproach her sister and lay down some ground rules. With her view partially blocked by the grocery sack she held, she was dodging around Tweety, which she'd left parked in the driveway, when she caught a glimpse of a bright, glistening color that didn't belong on a yellow car. Backing up for a better view, she stopped and stared. Her bumper and associated bumper stickers were spray-painted red. A red-lettered sign on poster board had been wedged above the bumper. The message it bore wasn't what she'd call neighborly.

She shouldn't be surprised. Those phone calls last night had been a preview, though she'd tried to convince herself that the caller was just one malcontent. Maybe this was just one, too, but the incidents were piling on top of each other.

The optimism she'd felt while walking down the street today was rare for her. She'd thought, briefly, that consensus and eventual harmony between her and the town were possible. Now her hope of peace plummeted. The war continued.

She glanced at Becca's house. She didn't want to burden her sister, but she had to talk to someone, and there was no one else she could . . .

Except Gabe. He'd stood with her against Chester, against Joe. She knew he had nothing to do with this, but maybe he'd be willing to help her figure out who did. She'd be free to vent with Gabe, to let out her frustrations, because . . . well, in spite of their differences, she knew he'd listen to her and at least try to understand. What that said about him, about who he was, she wasn't quite ready to scrutinize.

Yes, it was Gabe she wanted to see. She dropped the grocery bag beside her car and marched across a ragged lawn toward Gabe's house.

Chapter Eleven

Bullwinkle was on Gabe's front porch, hackles up, and a huge bluetick hound in a bad mood was no one Lauren wanted to mess with. He growled, sniffing the air, the incongruous pink-and-purple neckerchief vibrating with the sound. The dimwit dog seemed to have forgotten he'd been slavering at her feet only a few nights past.

She avoided the porch and went around back instead. Bullwinkle followed at a stiff-legged, wary distance. Before Lauren made it to the deck at the rear of the house, she heard voices in the garage. Gabe's and Melissa's.

"Hello," she called. At the sound of her voice, Bullwinkle emitted one of his ear-piercing bays and promptly began wagging his tail. At last the mentally challenged animal had recognized her.

She walked in an open side door to the garage and saw several tables set up under the fluorescent lights. Missy, with a monocle device pressed to one eye, was sitting on a stool and staring down at a small purple rock crowned with protruding crystals. Gabe stood beside her, leaning over to offer advice about what she should look for. He glanced up, saw Lauren, and straightened to his full six-feet-plus of exceptional male physique. Her breath caught. She really couldn't help herself. Every time she saw him she was impressed by

how ruggedly handsome he was. How strong and compelling
and—

"You sure you're in the right place, ma'am?" he asked.
"Get too close and I might try to buy some more of those favors you're supposed to be selling." He was teasing, of
course. She could tell from the way his mouth quirked up at
one corner.

Lauren should have known he wouldn't let Joe's inappro-
priate comments go without a follow-up. "You can't afford
my favors, buster." She wanted to say more, but she bit her
tongue because of Missy, who had unglued her eye from the
monocle and was all ears. She also held back the bad news
about the bumper. She'd wait and raise the issue with Gabe
in private.

"Hi, Missy." Lauren walked around Gabe to come up on
the child's opposite side, where she noted an array of rocks,
presumably from the pillowcase hoard, spread out on the
table. "I thought you'd be out playing with your friend
Buddy."

"He has baseball practice. Did Mama send you to find
me?" Missy pointed to a clock on the wall. "It's only quarter
past five o'clock, so it's not time for dinner yet. I want to stay
here longer." She seemed happy and relaxed, which was a
significant improvement over the last time they'd talked.

"Nice rocks," Lauren commented, seeking common
ground with her niece. "We don't have to go yet, Missy. Why
don't you tell me about your collection?"

The child's expression grew serious as she explained that
the purple crystals were amethysts, a gift from Gabe. Next,
she picked up a chunky white rock. "Figuring out what
they're made of is the fun part. First we study the color and
shine and crystals and stuff. We smell it and taste it." She
lifted the white chunk to Lauren, who reluctantly sniffed and
even touched her tongue to the rock.

Missy seemed pleased. "We can scrape for a hardness test, or put on a drop of hi-bro-doric—"

"Hydrochloric." Gabe had come up behind Lauren. His voice, so close, made her jump.

"Hydrochloric acid," Missy said. "This one made bubbles, so that's how we know it's calcite." She picked up another rock. "Now this one . . ."

Lauren had difficulty paying attention to the mineral ID with Gabe at her back, once again stealing her space.

"Good job, Missy," Gabe put in after the child had covered the details on five or six specimens. "You're one heck of a professor, honey. You remind me of somebody else I once knew."

"Who?" Missy asked.

"Your aunt Lauren." Gabe inclined his head toward Lauren's ear as he said it. The heat of his breath touched her skin as a reminder of the many times he'd teased her over acting the expert. For instance, there was the occasion when she'd read an article in *Scientific American* and thought he hadn't, but he'd known all the facts even better than she had, to her ultimate chagrin.

A phone rang inside the house. He went to answer it while she remained with Missy, watching the little girl at work. Lauren knew one thing for certain: Gabe did provide a guiding light for the child, and Missy would lose that if he left town.

Lauren could hear his voice from a room just out of her view. Snippets of conversation caught her attention.

"We'll get another loan," he said. "Yeah, I'm worried about the BLM's final decision, too, but the well on the rim is . . . Give me three more weeks, and we'll know more. No one can guarantee—"

After a lengthy pause, he said heatedly, "Core samples are expensive. We don't need . . ."

Gabe moved farther into the house, putting an end to her

eavesdropping, but she'd heard enough to guess that all was not smooth sailing—or drilling—with Great Basin. And cutting costs could result in regulatory lapses, which in turn could make visits by government employees, even Becca, unwelcome.

Lauren thought she could trust Gabe, wanted to trust him, but she fully intended to follow up on his company. Before she was finished, she'd know whether anyone in Great Basin had a motive for causing Becca's accident.

Missy held the monocle to her eye again to study the amethyst crystals. Lauren roamed around the far end of the table, inspecting a diverse collection that she presumed belonged to Gabe. When she righted an overturned shoe box that had been used to cover something, she let out an "eek" of surprise at what she found. Underneath were two small creatures in a clear plastic bag. "What in the world are these?" she asked.

Missy popped off the monocle and looked at her as if she were daft. "Mice, Aunt Lauren." Any idiot could see they were mice. Dead ones.

"Yes, but why are they here?"

"For Harriet," she said. "Gabe keeps her in the mews."

Lauren opened her mouth to ask more, but she was afraid of what she might hear.

Missy apparently thought Lauren needed an explanation. "When somebody in town catches a mouse in a trap, they call me or Buddy or Gabe. Then we put it in the freezer for when Harriet gets hungry. Harriet's an eagle."

"Oh," Lauren said. "A real eagle?"

Missy nodded with undaunted vigor. "In the mews. That's a place to keep birds." She pointed through the open garage door, which faced away from the street.

Lauren saw an outbuilding about a hundred feet down a weedy path. Could Gabe be hiding an eagle out there? As a boy he'd nursed an injured goshawk back to health, later setting it free while she and Becca watched. Becca had a photo on her wall taken that day, of the three of them together, the bird soaring over the canyon in the background.

Lauren had admired Gabe's sensitivity then, his love of all things wild and beautiful. She'd like to believe he was still exactly the same way. But then she reminded herself that keeping an eagle as a backyard pet was against all sorts of federal regulations. She'd have to inquire further.

Wandering past the other tables, she surveyed rocks and fossils until Gabe appeared at the kitchen door. His hair was curlier than before, a sign he'd been raking his fingers through it during his conversation.

He clicked off the portable phone and tossed it on a chair. "No need to call the cops, Laurie. Everything in my collection is from private lands, nothing whipped out from under the auspices of BLM, state, or forest service."

She had wondered, though she didn't say so out loud.

He looked down at Missy, who turned her small face up to him. "Auspices. That's a good word for the day, munchkin. It means control, Aunt Lauren's favorite activity."

"Can we show Harriet to Aunt Lauren, Gabe?" Missy asked. "Is she hungry yet?"

Lauren raised her eyebrows at Gabe. "Tell me about this alleged eagle."

"I have a license to rehabilitate wild birds, in case you're wondering," he said. Amazing how he'd guessed exactly how her mind worked. "I've been doing it for years, completely legal and aboveboard. Harriet was hit by a van, but she's mending well. Why don't we go out back and have a look?"

Missy jumped up with a cheer. "You'll like her, Aunt Lauren. Harriet is *way* cool!" She took Lauren's hand and practically dragged her outside and down the path.

Lauren went along willingly enough. Tending an eagle's wounds was like the old Gabe, and the old Gabe was a powerful draw. Likewise, seeing Harriet up close was an experience she didn't want to miss.

They stopped at the dark green outbuilding with white-painted bars over glassless windows. Inside, a big golden eagle with bright topaz eyes perched on a rope-wrapped board in a far corner.

"It's best if you two wait here," Gabe said as he unlatched the door. "The goal is to keep her wild so we can eventually set her free."

As Lauren and Missy watched through the bars, Gabe entered slowly, set the mice on a platform near the perch, and just as slowly withdrew.

The eagle fixed her golden eyes on the tiny rodents but didn't make a dive for them. "She feels vulnerable when she eats," Gabe said. "She likes privacy."

Harriet fluttered. Downy feathers rose in the dust-sparkled air. "Look, Gabe," Missy said. "She must be feeling better."

"Keep your voice low," he warned. "We don't want to scare her."

With a hand on Lauren's waist, he drew her nearer the door. She resisted for a second, but he urged her with gentle pressure, and she went along. Missy leaned against his other side, Gabe's hand on her blond head.

Warmth coursed through Lauren as he pulled her nearer. She knew he wasn't making a move on her, and that made it okay. His touch was inclusive, and because of it she felt less a bystander, more involved. Gabe was considerate that way. He'd done the same for her in the past. This time she became temporarily one with him and Missy and the eagle. Sunlight spilled past them, directly onto the bird, giving them a better view.

"Why's Harriet holding her wings out?" Missy asked in a stage whisper. "Does she want to fly away?"

"She spreads her wings to catch more sun rays," Gabe explained. "It's a good sign, but it doesn't mean she's ready to leave us. She has some healing to do first."

"When will we let her go?" Missy asked. "I can watch, can't I?"

"I already promised you, sweet pea. It'll be a few months before she's strong enough. You'll have to be patient."

Seeing this side of him, the soft-spoken, tender side, the Gabe who loved wild birds and was so gentle with Missy, smashed the last layer of the villainous plaster Lauren had attempted to cast him in. He wasn't a dastardly blackguard with a handlebar mustache. Far from it.

He made being in San Rafael an interesting experience. And right now he was encouraging her to spread her wings like Harriet and catch the sunshine. She smiled.

Gabe had been hoping to coax a smile out of Lauren, and seeing her relaxed and receptive was his reward. Having her close felt good. She could be a warm, sensuous woman, if she'd only shed the cactus spines and let herself feel. When he caught her gazing up at him, the silvery light in her eyes was so damn beautiful he didn't want to look anywhere else.

He'd surprised her with the eagle. He'd pleased her, and that thrilled the hell out of him.

"We should go," she said, glancing back to the bird. "If Harriet needs isolation to eat, then we . . ."

He didn't want to go yet. Once they left this spot, the moment of intimacy would be over. Lauren would freeze behind her emotional shields again, just when he'd finally started to bypass the barriers. He slid his fingers down from her waist to her hipbone. That got her attention. She stopped talking and stood absolutely still, as if focused on his touch, on how his touch made her feel. Her gaze locked with his once more. Neither of them moved.

"What time is it?" Missy asked.

Reluctantly Gabe took his hand off Lauren to check his watch, then crouched down beside Missy to show her.

Lauren escaped him and moved to the mews window, where she could concentrate on the eagle instead of the man. She didn't want to like Gabe, but it was getting harder to deny that she did. He was generous and gentle. He was good with Missy. He was good with Lauren—better than she should allow him to be.

After a few moments, Missy skipped across the lawn toward home, yelling a quick "See you later, Aunt Lauren," as she went.

Lauren glanced at her own watch. Six o'clock. "I should leave, too," she told Gabe as he approached her again. "Becca's not in any shape to fix dinner."

"I wouldn't worry about that." He walked with her, back up the weedy path. "Missy told me the house is overloaded with food. Trish brought over a turkey roast today, and Hannah sent an apple pie from the restaurant. That's not counting all the casseroles."

Though Lauren never wanted to eat chicken and noodles again, she had to admit the community had rallied around Becca, which was heartwarming.

But then she recalled the vandalism to her bumper.

"I have something to show you," she said.

Before they reached her car, she spotted Bullwinkle with his nose in the paper grocery sack she had left on the ground earlier. She started running. "Shoo!" She yelled and waved her arms, making no apparent impression on the beast.

When Gabe reached the dog, he separated the sack from Bullwinkle's teeth. Meanwhile Lauren knelt on the ground to inspect the spilled groceries. "He ate my tofu!"

"Damn. If he'd stoop to eating vegetarian crap, he must be sick. I'm worried about him."

"Shoo!" Lauren shouted again, swatting at Bullwinkle as he tried to get his snout back in the bag. With a hurt look in his soulful eyes—soulful? When had she started thinking of a dumb dog as soulful?—he trotted away to sulk on the porch.

"Why are you worried about *him*?" she demanded. "*I'm* the one who's minus my dinner!"

"I'll buy you more tofu." Gabe circled the vehicle and ended up behind it, frowning at the sheen of red. "What the hell! Didn't I tell you to put Tweety in Becca's garage? Don't you ever listen?"

"My listening ability's not the subject here. Painting bumpers is only petty vandalism, but what's next? What's going to keep someone who's trying to scare me out of town from creeping into the garage to do damage, or into the house, for that matter?"

" 'Take our land, and we'll take blood,' " Gabe read from the red-painted sign. Lowering one knee to the blacktop drive, he took a closer look at the printed letters.

"Who did it?" she asked. "Who do you think?"

"You want a list of possibilities? It'd be too long to do any good. I'm sorry to see things get uglier than they already were, but I have to say you asked for it." He stood, shaking his head.

"What!" *Of all the unadulterated nerve.* "I didn't—"

"Hell, yes, you did. You flaunted the bumper stickers and your principles right under the natives' noses. You don't seem to understand. They're fighting for a way of life, and they'll do just about anything to keep it from dying."

"I'm beginning to see that." She'd underestimated how angry, defensive, and nasty this town could get. "After what happened with Chester . . ." She slumped against the car and closed her eyes. "Haven't San Rafael citizens heard of free speech?"

"They've heard. That doesn't make them like it." He moved in front of her and rubbed his big hands up and down her arms. "You okay, Laurie? You should have expected something like this out of the good old boys."

"I would have expected it elsewhere. I've *seen* it elsewhere. But here, I really didn't think . . ." She opened her eyes to glower at him. "You're defending them."

"No, I'm saying this was predictable. I'm not saying it's right." His hands stilled on her upper arms, his thumbs gently caressing from the bottom of her capped sleeve to the inner crease of her elbow. "If you want, I'll help you clean off the paint."

"I don't need help. Not for that." She'd needed Gabe to sympathize and commiserate; instead, he'd given her the unvarnished truth. She wanted him to believe wholeheartedly in her cause, though she knew that would never happen. And at this moment, she just plain wanted him, which muddled her mind, randomized her molecular structure, fried whole nerve bundles. She pushed him away. "Please stop touching me."

He released her. "What's wrong? I'm not trying to molest you. I'm trying to be your friend."

The wind picked up, stirring the grass, mixing the scent of sage with the perfume of poppies from the yard across the street. She glanced uneasily at her bumper. "Excuse me if I'm a little jumpy. I guess you know that Chester's out on bail."

He nodded. "I'm worried about you, Laurie. It scared the hell out of me when Chester came at you in the gym. I wanted to protect you from him and any other sorry son of a bitch who—"

"Why? You don't owe me anything. You're not my big brother." She certainly didn't think of him that way. The tenderness in his voice had warmed her until the blood was whooshing through her veins. She could feel the surges, hear them.

"I don't want to be your big brother." He seemed closer now, though he hadn't moved. He was taking up all of her space. "I want us to get to know each other and find out what kind of relationship we *do* want."

She could barely breathe with him so near, much less think rational thoughts. His body heat, his strength, engulfed her. "What about you and Becca?" Thank God she'd remembered Becca this time. At least she hadn't lost it completely.

"We gave getting back together a shot," he said. "It didn't work out. We're old friends now, that's all."

"I'm not sure that's clear to Becca," Lauren protested. "She acts like she still has hope for you two."

He groaned. "I thought she understood. She said she did when I talked to her a few weeks back, before you came home. I explained exactly how I feel, that we can't ever be—"

"At least you've spoken to her," Lauren said. "That's good, I guess."

"I don't want to hurt her any more than you do, but she's a grown woman. She can accept reality." He touched the side of Lauren's face, his warm hand covering her cheek. "And the reality is, it's you I want to know more about. You, Laurie."

"I—I made some wild accusations the other day, about Becca's accident, and . . . I'm sorry." She turned her head to evade him.

He took the hint and let his hand fall to his side. "I don't blame you for what you thought. The way it happened made me look bad, I admit. But the sheriff's cleared my crew. They all had alibis."

"Not great ones," Lauren replied. "Any third-class detective could drive a winch truck through the holes in them."

"That may be, but I believe my men. I've known them a long time. They're mostly local, all good people. They wouldn't run a woman off the road and drop her in a hospital ER any more than I would."

Lauren was convinced now that Gabe wasn't capable of such a thing. "If not you or your men, who else is on the short list?"

"I hate to bring this to your attention," he said, "but not all environmentalists are candidates for sainthood. We had some Earth First-ers through here last week, the same day you showed up. They almost got in a brawl with the attendant at Rigsby's gas station."

"Over what?"

"Wilderness, land use, bumper stickers. Who knows? The enmity is on so many levels, it's hard to say. Then there were some kids from California who picketed the road to my canyon rim site about ten days ago. They could have still been in the area when Becca had her accident. The Red Rock's had plenty of state and national attention. Outsiders, other than you and the CPWA, might try to interfere."

"How does that relate to Great Basin's guilt or innocence?"

"Let's say someone wanted to turn the tide against my drilling in the canyon by setting me up as the criminal element. Planting a roadblock using my truck, with the intention of causing an accident, would make me look bad. People would figure I was involved. You, for one, were easy to convince."

Lauren frowned at him. "I can't rule out a rogue conservationist, but—"

"Just like you can't rule out my employees' involvement. See any parallels, darlin'?"

She rolled her eyes. "I don't want to argue either case right now. Without proof, there's no point."

"I don't know if you'd call it proof, but there is something else. Someone's been tampering with my equipment for weeks. Sand in a gas tank. A stolen generator. A fire under a travel trailer on one of my sites."

"You've reported these incidents to the sheriff?"

"Sure. Becca knows, and a BLM ranger from the district office is supposed to be investigating. Even with men on the rigs most of the time, whoever it is still manages to sneak in and out without being seen."

"Becca mentioned something about Great Basin troubles. I didn't realize . . . It does make me wonder. However, I still plan to check out your company," she warned. "In fact, I've already sent off for EPA reports and so on. Not just because of the accident. It's my job to—"

"Sure, I understand. You do your job, but if you find something that gets you agitated, come talk to me about it. Give me a chance to defend myself. And if there's any way I can help, if you want anything, need anything . . . If you're scared or lonely or—"

"I haven't slept well lately," she whispered, suddenly needing to share her fears with someone. "I keep seeing Becca's smashed truck, and . . . Chester's knife."

"Hey, it's okay," he soothed, as he pulled her into his arms. "You don't have to be the toughest woman in canyon country all the time. It's okay."

Her cheek rested on his broad chest, and she found that being there felt . . . natural. Right. The chambray of his well-worn shirt was smooth against her skin, but the muscle beneath was as hard as granite, as steady as the earth. The scent of him was earthy, too. She heard and felt his heartbeat, resonant and sure, and the strength of his arms lent her his courage, his comfort.

Gabe leaned back, lifted her chin with one finger, and studied her. "Want me to stake Bullwinkle outside your window tonight? Or I could stay in the room with you myself."

She laughed a little shakily. "No, thanks."

"I love to hear you laugh." His thumb moved over her lips in a soft caress. One side of his mouth quirked up. "You don't want me for a bodyguard? You don't want the big badass oil baron looking out for you?"

She shook her head, a smile lingering. "Sorry, but having you guard my body doesn't seem like a good idea at all."

He smoothed the hair from her forehead, warm hand against cool skin. "Hey, sweetheart, you're killing me with rejection. I'm sensitive, remember? And I'm supposed to be your lover, after all." His hands migrated to her shoulders, applying a light, sensual pressure.

Lauren struggled to keep her mind on logic instead of heat and desire, as Gabe's touch drifted down her back. "We need to talk about Joe."

"What about him?" His hands stopped at the middle of her spine and rested there.

She told what she'd learned of Judge Hewitt, and of his impending retirement. "I can't believe I'm saying this, but if we could stall a custody hearing, even for a few weeks, it might make a difference."

"You're not going to ask me to leave town, are you?" His eyebrow rose, questioning.

She thought he already knew the answer. "I . . . I saw how you were with Missy today. I saw how . . . No. I don't want you to go."

"Good. Real good. Because, for a lot of reasons, I've set my mind on staying."

She exaggerated a sigh. "I guess we're back to Becca's plan, then."

He nodded. "Fine with me. You say the word, and we'll give the neighborhood biddies enough fire to smoke their glasses for a year."

Creating the smoke would be easy. Lauren just worried about dousing the subsequent inferno. As if by unspoken mutual consent, the distance between their bodies shrank again, millimeter by millimeter.

"I think we've done a better-than-average job so far, don't you?" His hands were at her hips now, pulling her closer. "Lighten up a little, and you might even enjoy it."

"I am lightened up." And she was enjoying it. The truth was, she always enjoyed being with Gabe.

He kissed her forehead, sending heat to her lips, making them tingle, making her want his mouth on hers.

Lauren's heart hammered beneath her breasts. She thought surely he must be able to tell, to feel, to see for himself. "But who'll take us seriously? What about our professional differences? And our lack of physical attraction?"

"What lack?" His voice was hoarse. His hips moved right up against hers, making it evident that the physical attraction *was* there, for him as well as for her.

Her whole body caught fire. God help her, she wanted him. Wanted him so much, with such a bewildering rush of heat and feeling, that she was terrified. She pushed against his chest to gain a few inches of distance. "Maybe not precisely a lack."

He smiled down at her. "Joe might be right that you're bitchy sometimes. Skinny, maybe. Definitely *not* a lesbian." His fingers circled the bumps on her spine, going lower, ever lower.

Another rush of heat mellowed her further. She gave up resistance and molded her body to his. "Mmm. Clearly heterosexual," she said.

"Thank you, Jesus."

Finally he kissed her, a full-fledged mouth-to-mouth unlike anything she'd ever experienced before. Like mercury in a thermometer, she was rising, reaching. She longed to touch all of him with all of her, to imprint his hard ridges on her softness. She stood on her toes, her hands locked at the back of his neck, her mouth hungry for his.

He ended by brushing his lips across hers, ever so gently. "And that's not all Joe's confused about," he said. "I like intellectual women. Don't even mind tree-huggers most of the time."

She wished he hadn't said that, because the words jolted her, reminded her of why this was not supposed to be real. She wasn't in love with him, couldn't possibly . . . She disentangled herself and stood flat on her own two feet. "Don't get ideas, Gabe. Don't think . . . that this is going anywhere. We have nothing in common besides a little lust."

"What!" Mock horror spread over his face. *"Little!* Don't use the word 'little' when you refer to *this* man's lust."

"Okay," she said, holding his gaze and struggling not to smile at his male arrogance. "Not little. I could have said *fake* lust, but some things"—she nodded downward—"are hard to fake."

"Thanks for the vote of confidence. What do you mean by nothing in common? We grew up next door to each other. I can remember you running across my front yard in your Smurf underpants."

She took a step back and leaned against her car. "You must be where Buddy gets his ideas for blackmail. Keep in mind that I dressed more appropriately after age six."

"You were seven the year I moved in. For the record, I thought you looked cute in your Smurfies."

"Please." She groaned. "How long until your memory fades?"

"A long, long time. I recall your first bike, the pink one with streamers on the handlebars."

"And I remember the first time you invited me and Becca into your garage to play Monopoly and view your rock collection," she said.

"Our fathers were good friends," he added. "Your mother and Chloe and a half dozen others mothered me, the little boy without a mom."

"You had no lack of female attention."

"From all the ladies, young and old." He leaned over her, arms braced on the car frame on either side of her body. "If you'd dare to admit it, you liked me then. And we don't make bad company for each other now. You think my eagle's 'way cool,' to quote Missy, don't you? Who knows what else we might find to—"

"Let's not pretend so hard that we fool ourselves." She pushed on his chest until both of them were standing straight again. "There can't be anything real between us. I wish I could head home to my desk in Denver right now and forget I ever saw you here." That wasn't exactly accurate. She didn't want to forget him. At this moment she didn't want to be anywhere but with him.

He ran a thumb down her cheek. "I'd miss you if you left me. What would I do to keep up my stress level without you around to threaten lawsuits?"

"Never fear. Whether I'm in town or not, I'll sic the CPWA on any attempt you make to drill in Red Rock Canyon. Legal papers will follow." As they both knew, in that she'd have no choice. But she felt certain she'd be safely back in Denver long before then. Far away from Gabe and the temptations he presented by just being here, by just being himself.

"Ah, Laurie." His voice had lowered to a seductive pitch that heated her senses like summer sun on sandstone. "You can hit me with those papers anytime, as long as your hands deliver them. And your mouth," he said, touching her lips. "I want your mouth . . . to clarify all the fine print."

Leave it to Gabe to make even dry legal maneuvers sound hot and shivery and breathless.

Lauren broke out in goose bumps. She turned her head, half afraid that if she spoke, her mouth would clarify her own feelings, her own hidden needs.

Chapter Twelve

When school let out on Thursday afternoon, Audra Biggs's chant rang across the schoolyard. "Missy never heard of the Dixie Chicks. Missy doesn't know the Backstreet Boys. Missy is a big fat ner-rd. Missy is stupider than dir-rt." The singsong went on and on, with a few of the other girls chiming in.

Missy slipped her arms into her backpack straps and started running with hands over her ears. What were Dixie Chickens, and why didn't she know about them? She'd have to ask Buddy. Buddy never made fun of her, even when she didn't know things everyone else knew. Maybe she really was stupid.

She hurried through the open schoolyard gate and stopped at the street corner. Buddy wasn't anywhere, but she did see her aunt walking up to her.

Missy thought about running the other way. She felt like crying, and if she didn't find Buddy soon, she almost surely would. Aunt Lauren wouldn't be any help. No help at all. She'd been living at their house nearly a whole week, and Missy was starting to like her better, but Aunt Lauren still didn't know much about little girls.

Her aunt was waving and hollering, "Missy!" At least she wasn't calling her Melissa Louise anymore.

"Why are you here?" Missy asked as soon as Aunt Lauren reached her.

"I wanted to see you. I thought we might walk home together."

Missy frowned. "What about Buddy? I always go home with him. His cousin Sal baby-sits me when my mama and his mama are at work. Did Mama go to work today?"

"No, she's not quite ready for the office yet. She knows I'm here, and everyone's agreed it's okay for you to go home with me. I saw Buddy a moment ago. He said to tell you he has baseball practice."

"Oh." Missy felt sad that Buddy would desert her for baseball again.

"What's wrong, Missy? Did you have a bad day?"

She nodded. "Daddy stopped by at lunchtime and said he'd be too busy for me again this Saturday. He promised he'd take me for a snow cone on Monday, but he forgot. Then he said he'd take me to the movies on the weekend, but I should have known he wouldn't. He *says* he has to work, because business is bad and he can't pay a helper, but I think maybe he wants to be with . . . his other friends instead of me." Missy wanted her daddy to love her best, but he didn't, no matter how hard she tried to be good.

"Like who?" Aunt Lauren asked.

Missy didn't say. She wasn't supposed to tattle, Daddy said. And he'd probably never love her if she made him mad.

Aunt Lauren launched into the "How's school?" routine. Missy pretended nothing had happened. She didn't like grown-ups trying to make everything better. No grown-up would understand how ashamed she'd been when she was picked last for Four Square in PE. Or how rotten she'd felt when Kelly Henley tripped her as she'd walked up the aisle to hand in a spelling paper. Missy had fallen to her knees, and everyone laughed.

The whole day had sucked.

After a pause, Aunt Lauren tried again. "I, um, ordered you a special book on rocks and minerals today. I thought you'd like it better than the Barbie I sent for your birthday. You didn't like the Barbie, did you?"

"I'm not supposed to say anything not nice about a present, Aunt Lauren. I might hurt someone's feelings."

"I won't be hurt. You can tell me the truth."

Missy shrugged, skipping over a crack in the sidewalk. "I don't play with dolls. I like teddy bears that are soft to sleep with, but not dolls, especially ones with too-big boobs and dumb clothes. If I played with them, Buddy would think I'm a wimp."

"We wouldn't want that," Aunt Lauren agreed. "I'll remember for your next birthday."

Missy was surprised her aunt would understand. Maybe she wasn't so bad after all. Missy came closer and took her hand. "Did you play with dolls when you were seven?"

"No. Your mother had a huge collection, but I thought dolls were boring." She smiled, squeezing Missy's hand. "Maybe you're more like me, at least in that one way."

Missy nodded cautiously.

Cars whizzed past, followed by a long yellow bus that took home the kids who lived too far away to walk. Audra rode the bus. So did Kelly. Missy looked up in time to see both girls' faces in the rear window. Audra stuck out her tongue.

Missy looked down at the sidewalk. "Did you have a rock collection when you were a kid?"

"I enjoyed nature shows on TV, but I never paid a lot of attention to rocks," Aunt Lauren said. "Maybe if I'd had Buddy for a friend, I would have played outside more and become a better observer." She cleared her throat, like she was nervous or something. But that couldn't be right, because grown-ups didn't get nervous talking to little kids. "I was interested in Gabe's birds. He once had a goshawk, the most beautiful creature I'd ever seen."

"I think Harriet's prettiest." Missy skipped over another crack. She recognized an uneven break in the sidewalk and looked up to see they were right in front of Grandma's restaurant. "Can we go in the Mad House? I forgot a book there yesterday."

Lauren glanced at the restaurant sign and sighed. She and Missy had been getting along quite well, and she didn't want to spoil it by refusing a simple request. However, Hannah wouldn't be happy to see Lauren in the Mad House, not while the meeting fiasco was still the talk of the town.

She considered waiting outside. Chatting with Ezra might have been an excuse, but he wasn't on the porch. She glanced at her watch and guessed he'd retreated to the alcove for a midafternoon cup of coffee.

Lauren wondered who else she'd find in the restaurant. The tables visible through the plate-glass window were empty, but she was still wary. Sneaking through the back door might bypass the patrons and avoid raising her mother's ire, but how would she explain such roundabout behavior to Missy?

She did not relish making excuses. In fact, she refused to do so. With Missy's hand grasped firmly in hers, she marched up the steps and through the front door. The first thing she smelled was fried onions. She could almost hear the grease popping, the odor was so strong. In her mind, because of long association with Mad House cooking, the odor translated to the nitty-gritty of a working-class crowd.

She spotted Don Ray in a booth, nodding as he listened to someone across from him. Chester sat on the same side as Don Ray. A smaller person with spiked hair sat between them. Lauren identified Kayleen from the nose and eyebrow rings, though she wore enough clothes, thank God, to cover the shoulder tattoos. Across from the trio, Lauren saw the back of a head as bald as a California condor.

She heard the whispery voice of Hyrum Dupont—everyone in the CPWA called him Riot-for-Hire—and knew more trouble was brewing. The man was an organizer for Lands West, a supposedly grass-roots organization that was, in fact, financed by the mining, timber, and oil industries. She'd met him during a previous run-in over Colorado land use. His modus operandi was to keep a low profile while staging protests and, it was rumored, the occasional act of anarchy.

"We'll call in the TV crews," Riot-for-Hire rasped. "When that new management plan comes out, we'll hold a demonstration in front of the BLM office. We'll send protesters out to where the highway meets the canyon turnoff. We'll use signs like, 'The feds are stealing my livelihood.' Or maybe, 'Save families, not trees.' It'd be good to have little kids carrying homemade posters about going hungry because Daddy's getting screwed by tree-huggers and the government."

"Do we need a license to demonstrate?" Chester seemed to have developed a law-abiding streak after a night in jail.

"Good point," Riot-for-Hire replied. "We don't want anyone herding us into a paddy wagon. I'll make sure all's in order."

The three men nodded, unified in macho enlightenment, until Don Ray looked up. "We have company, boys." He untangled his long legs and stood. His sleeveless gray sweatshirt and jeans were stained and worn. "Hello, Missy. Lauren."

Kayleen slithered out of the booth and wiggled her hips to slide her short skirt low enough to cover her panties. She didn't meet Lauren's eyes, but just fetched a coffeepot and sashayed toward the kitchen. Some environmentalist Kayleen was, Lauren thought. She'd been sitting practically in Chester's lap while they planned an antiwilderness demonstration.

Lauren offered a general greeting. Chester's response was to glare at her as if she were a bad smell. The bald head of Riot-for-Hire did not move so much as an invisible hair follicle.

Missy let go of Lauren's hand and went right up to Don Ray. "Have you seen my *Tell Me Why* book? I left it here yesterday."

Don Ray reached over his seat to the table behind him and snagged the book from between the ketchup and steak sauce bottles. He handed it over.

"Thanks. Do you have any dead mice or rats for me, Mr. Lomax?" Missy asked. "Gabe's eagle needs 'em bad."

"Not yet." Don Ray ruffled the little girl's short blond hair. "Buddy's been asking, and I'm keeping you and the eagle in mind. Could be I'll have something when I check the traps out in my shed."

It seemed a strange partnership to Lauren—Don Ray providing food for a protected raptor species, when he was seemingly against protecting that raptor's habitat. Also, Lauren was surprised Missy wasn't concerned about one animal dying to feed another. Was the child unusually gruesome, or simply compassionate in an unusually broad-minded way? Or was she a realist, accepting the give and take of life better than many adults could manage?

Lauren, on the other hand, tended to put things in categories, black or white, gruesome or compassionate, human or alien. Maybe she should take a hint from her niece. Maybe she needed to view life as a whole spectrum of possibilities, without automatically interjecting her own sharp divisions.

While Don Ray talked mousetraps, Lauren heard a "Psst," from behind her. She turned to see her mother peeking from behind the cash register. Lauren had no choice but to saunter over. As soon as she was close enough, Hannah latched on to her arm and drew her to the far side of the lunch counter.

"You'll run off my customers," Hannah hissed, pushing down on Lauren's shoulders until both of them had crouched low enough to be hidden from the patrons. "I told you to stay away."

"I was walking Missy home, Mother. She wanted to stop in."

Lauren lifted her head above counter level to glance at the child. The discussion still focused on eagle food; Riot-for-Hire was chipping in with advice. No one seemed to have noticed Lauren's disappearance.

Hannah pulled Lauren's sleeve until she'd ducked out of sight again. "Don't you dare start spouting environmental crappola in here, or this place'll go empty for sure." Hannah wrung her hands in her white apron. "I know how it'll be. You're too much like your daddy, always touting causes. When he was alive and here to help me, I could tolerate the conflict. But you . . . you'll whip folks into a frenzy and then run off to Colorado, leaving me to live with the mess."

Lauren couldn't deny it, since she'd never planned to stay. She was saved from further reproach when Missy romped across the room, skidded, and banged into the metal stools fronting the lunch counter. Hannah grimaced at the noise.

The little girl peeked around the side and spotted them. "What are you doing down there? Did you drop something?"

Lauren stood, adjusting her shorts and her spine. She caught Don Ray's steady gaze and nodded, as if hiding out behind the lunch counter were the most natural behavior in the world. Chester was watching, too, and even Riot-for-Hire turned his head.

The bald man looked like a comic-strip Charlie Brown, with a broad face, big head, and vacuous smile. In his case, looks were indeed deceptive.

"We were cleaning," Hannah lied, as she, too, revealed herself to the curious clientele. "Go to the kitchen and have some cookies and milk, Missy Lou, while I talk to your aunt."

Missy looked from one to the other, her eyebrows drawn together as if she didn't quite buy the cleaning story. Reluctantly, she left them.

Hannah scuttled to the alcove.

Lauren followed. "If I've caused you trouble, Mom, I'm sorry, but I won't take the blame. You and Becca wanted me here. You both wanted me to stay and play two-faced games with Gabe."

Hannah threw up her hands. "We did not ask you to participate in the town meetings."

"As I've already explained, my boss insisted I attend. I didn't have a choice."

"There's always a choice. Your daddy had choices. Looking back, it's obvious he made the wrong ones."

Lauren was shocked. Hannah had never said anything so blatant against her husband since the tragedy. He'd been on his way home from a meeting to protest the building of a huge strip-mine and coal power plant on land that had since become part of the Grand Staircase National Monument.

His vehicle had gone over a cliff, with brake failure as the alleged cause. The wrecked vehicle vanished before an investigation was complete, and environmentalists had called foul play. Daniel Van Horn became a cult hero.

"I don't think he was wrong," Lauren said softly. "What he did, what he believed, shaped my life." His death had forged her mistrust of the community, her disgust with corporate greed, and her absolute commitment to protecting the land.

"Well," Hannah said, taking a lighter tack, "you're doing good with Gabe. The gossip gets juicier every go-round. Pretty soon they'll be saying you're pregnant with his baby."

"Um . . . thanks, I guess." Lauren thought that a mother welcoming gossip about her unwed daughter's pregnancy was probably a first in the annals of mankind.

Hannah made a dismissive noise. "Just watch that *you* don't go falling for him. Once Joe quits trying for custody, it's up to us to make sure Becca gets the man she really loves, the man God intended her to have."

Ah, so that was how her mother saw it. Divine intervention was Lauren's role here. How could she have failed to recognize what God and Mom had decreed? Tears built behind her eyelids. She blinked and held them back.

No point in Lauren trying to tell her mother that Gabe might not love Becca. Hannah wouldn't believe her. Lauren wasn't sure she believed it herself.

As Hannah dictated, so it must be. She was a woman who loved to run things, and she usually got her way. Lauren had been drawn into a cruel hoax. All her feelings for Gabe, the good and the bad, bunched up inside her like a condemnation.

When the door jingled, Hannah brightened and called out a greeting to Sheriff LaDell Purdy. To Lauren, she murmured, "Good thing LaDell kept the lid on Chester at that meeting, or you might've been hurt."

LaDell hadn't done one thing to save her—hadn't even been close—but Lauren withheld a correction. Might as well let him bask in the praise while it lasted.

Hannah picked up a coffeepot from the electric burner in the corner. "Behave yourself," she warned as she started for the main part of the restaurant. "Stay as long as you like, but please, leave by the back door."

"Nothing like being wanted," Lauren muttered.

"Laurie?" Ezra came strolling out of the kitchen, a coffee mug in one hand and his cane in the other. He was sniffing, tracking her scent, separating her out from the onions and roasting meat and a hint of baked apples. Before he could locate her, she went to him and enveloped him in a silent hug.

He felt good. Familiar. Best of all, she had no doubt that he accepted and loved her exactly as she was. Even if her beliefs were radical. Even if she dared show her face in the Mad House main dining room. She could kiss trees and shout "Wilderness rules!" to the sagebrush, and Ezra wouldn't think any less of her. She guided him to an alcove table, where they sat side by side.

He patted her hand. "I heard what Hannah said. She doesn't mean to put you off."

Lauren brushed a hand over her damp cheeks. "My mother wishes I hadn't come home. I'm too much trouble for her. Sometimes I think she's sorry I was ever born."

"That's not so. It's just that you scare the stuffing out of her, what with your way of rattling the windows and rearranging the order of things. She's worried for more than herself and her business. She mourned your daddy. She knows what can happen." He shook his grizzled head. "Like that damn fool Chester letting his knife do his talking. Some of the others are verging on violence, too, best I can tell."

"What a surprise," she said glumly.

"There is some good, child. They listened to you at the meeting. They didn't like what you said about times a-changing, but they heard. Before folks can start thinking fresh, somebody has to open some ears."

"I know. I yell to the deaf for a living, but it's . . . personalized here in San Rafael. I've gone to towns to speak on issues before. I didn't always feel loved, but I didn't know anyone, so I didn't care. I've fought most of my battles on paper, not with people slashing knives at my face. Add my own mother's resentment, and this situation's a whole lot more than I bargained for."

Ezra's clouded eyes stared in her direction. "You giving up?"

"No, of course not." Lauren had never been a quitter.

"I didn't reckon you would." He slouched forward in his chair again, relaxing. "It's funny how folks get ideas in their heads, sometimes almighty strange ones. Makes a body wonder, do we always know which are right and which are wrong?"

"I thought I knew, Ezra, but lately I'm not as sure."

"Let yourself hear and see both ways, child. Know what you're thinking *and* what they're thinking. When you can do that, you have the best chance of finding what's clear and true."

"I'll hope for improvement, because at the moment my thinking is muddier than it's ever been."

"You keep thinking, and it'll come clear. You're a whole lot like your daddy." He patted the denim vest pocket where he kept his locket. "Me and Chloe count that as a fine way to be."

"My father was a good man," Lauren agreed. Alas, one aspect of his example troubled her considerably. She wanted to save wild lands for posterity, but martyrdom wasn't in her game plan.

"A long time before he started worrying over the environment, your daddy was already worrying over folks' rights. When me and Chloe hitched up, she lost her teaching job in Georgia because our skin color didn't match. Same thing almost happened when we came here. Your daddy, he stood up for us. Your mama offered me a job at the Mad House. LaDell's daddy was sheriff then, and a different Hewitt was mayor. They helped keep the peace, and they were fair. Hadn't been for all of them, me and Chloe would have had to move on. We found a home, and we were grateful."

"I can't imagine this town without you, Ezra. And I understand what you're saying. We have some good people here. I know that. I don't expect any of them to be in favor of a Red Rock Wilderness, necessarily. I do wish my own mother wouldn't try to hide me like I'm some sort of malignant tumor."

"Hannah's a fine woman, but she's a mite too cautious sometimes. She'll come round."

"I hope so." Lauren hoped the whole town would come around, but she knew it wouldn't happen. She heard Missy's voice in the kitchen, which reminded her of custody, of Joe. And of her dilemma with Gabe.

"I wish I wasn't always the one going against the grain, making the speeches, insisting on change. Even with Gabe, I—" Lauren stopped, afraid her emotions were going to tangle her tongue and show just how muddled her thinking had become. "I know you've heard things, Ezra. Tell me . . . what you think."

The old man clicked his tongue. "Don't matter what I think, honey. You're the one who needs to sort out the truth."

Lauren was trying. She kept telling herself that her earthy attraction for Gabe meant nothing. So what if he made her head spin and her blood heat. Spontaneity was fleeting, and so were out-of-control emotions.

Reason would prevail. Surely it would.

A lump built in her throat. She wanted to cry, because the sad truth was too plain to ignore. Reason said she and Gabe were not meant to be.

She looked out through the archway to where the sheriff sat in his chair, straw hat on the table. Hannah had set down her coffeepot and taken a seat, leaning forward on her elbow, chin in hand.

" 'Oh, learn to read what silent love has writ. To hear with eyes belongs to love's fine wit,' " was what Lauren thought she heard coming out of LaDell Purdy's mouth.

She gaped. "Are you hearing what I'm hearing, Ezra?"

"I reckon so. The sheriff's been going on like that ever since somebody called in to the Love Doc show on the radio and asked how to woo a woman's heart. Doc Susan said a woman would go plumb crazy-wild over a poetic man. Right then, the sheriff got himself a book and set to spouting Shakespeare."

LaDell glanced up from his sonnet and sent Hannah a crooked, sleepy smile. He reached across the table to put his hand over hers, saying something in a low voice. Hannah stood abruptly, snatched the coffeepot, and moved on to the booths.

"Sheriff Purdy's putting in the effort, but it doesn't look like he's getting anywhere. I guess Mom's not bowled over by poetry."

"Hannah's so dad-blamed afraid to care about a man again, she's not listening hard enough. She keeps putting him off. Thinks it's safer that way." He shook his head. "It might be safe, but it's not good. Your mama's getting more bitter and set in her ways every year. Pretty soon even the sheriff's gonna give up on her."

Lauren, too, felt safer when she kept up her guard. She knew her efforts to shield herself were no secret when Ezra's cloudy gaze moved from Hannah to fix directly, unfalteringly, on her.

Gabe was on the phone all Friday morning, the same as every other morning that week. His next month's long-distance bill would most likely rival the national debt.

He'd finally gotten the last of his Great Basin investors on the line. "I know you're concerned about the wilderness uproar," he said. "Yes, I know it's been on all the networks."

The investor, a budding politician, was extra worried about the networks.

"This isn't going to be a PR disaster," Gabe assured him. "Your constituents are poor working folks, more interested in jobs than wilderness. If you play it right, supporting the common man's need for energy and progress ought to convince the voters that you're on their side."

The politician wanted a guarantee of quick returns so he could sell his shares soon, at a profit.

"I'm still confident the rim well will hit oil," Gabe told him. "I can't say how much, or how expensive it'll be to get it out. We'd need a crystal ball to know that."

By the time the conversation ended, Gabe figured he'd assured the man that Great Basin was competent, if not the get-richer-quicker scheme the man seemed to expect.

Next, Gabe called the Austin offices of Randolph Drilling, his first company, based on his first wildcat well. From there it had expanded to cover the field around the well, and then developed interests in two other major fields. Overall, Randolph Drilling was doing fine without his immediate supervision. Gabe had hired good people to handle the day-to-day headaches, and they had, in general, made good decisions. Several gas wells had begun producing since Gabe's last trip to Texas. His head geologist came on the line and delivered a lengthy report on the pressure, quality, and duration of each source.

In a way, success took the fun out of the oil business for Gabe. He'd rather be out on the job working his arm muscles with his men than working his jaw on the telephone. He liked being an innovator, not an administrator. That was why coming to Great Basin and running a small company again was appealing to him. First chance he got, he wanted to develop a new idea he had for reducing carbon dioxide emissions from producing gas wells, thereby doing his thing to prevent global warming.

Hanging up the phone, he thought of Lauren and smiled. In his own way, he was as committed and as idealistic as she was. However, considering that his idealism had a practical bent, which mostly applied to oil wells, he doubted she'd see his commitment as anything to brag on.

Hearing her, seeing her, learning about her, was like rain on desert soil. He soaked her up. She made him feel alive, clean, refreshed.

Maybe Lauren still thought they were role-playing, but he'd known for a while now that he wanted more. More every time he saw her. He wanted to explore the possibilities, to make her believe they could have fun together, enjoy each other even if they didn't always agree.

He'd been looking forward to the weekend, because one way or another he intended to spend time with her. He intended to convince her that she wanted to spend time with him.

* * *

Late that afternoon, Lauren lingered outside Becca's house, pulling weeds from the flower garden. Every couple of minutes she scanned the street for signs of traffic. For Jeep traffic, to be precise.

Gabe wasn't home. He'd probably gone out to eyeball one of his wells, but she hoped he'd be back soon.

She'd last seen him when she'd discovered the red-painted bumper, two days before. Since then, for most of her waking hours, she'd been on the telephone or the computer, burning her candle at both ends. That morning she'd completed a preliminary Animas River brief, with the help of faxes and another Internet search through every related legal case she could find over the last ten years. She'd fired off the finished product to the Denver office.

Having met that first priority, Lauren felt herself sinking deeper and deeper into the mire of Red Rock Canyon affairs. She'd begun a study of Great Basin. What she'd found so far was going to be very hard on her dealings with Gabe.

Although she didn't have much hope that he could whitewash what she'd learned, she was going to listen to his defenses. She'd promised to do that, and she meant to confront him the instant he came home. But her outrage was already building. She'd started to trust him, wanted to trust him, only to discover he'd failed to be up-front with her.

She yanked at a bit of green and ended up with a geranium plant in her hand. Cursing, she tossed it onto the wilted pile of weeds she was accumulating. She stood, straightened her back, and mused over the white clapboards and green shutters of the house she'd grown up in. Peeling paint and curled roof shingles were a testament to the financial struggle Becca had had with Joe, both before and after they'd parted ways.

Gabe's house, on the other hand, was in perfect repair, courtesy of all the money he'd made while blithely contributing to the world's pollution problems. Little Buddy had applied fresh paint to the front porch on one of the afternoons he hadn't had baseball practice. As Lauren surveyed it, she thought of the evening she'd spent with Gabe on that porch. The same feelings she'd had then, traitorous as they now seemed, invaded her, skulking from her brain to her chest to her lower abdomen. She couldn't seem to rid herself of—

Bullwinkle jumped out from under the porch swing and barked loudly, an ear-piercing hound's "ba-oooh." The dusty Jeep rumbled up the street and turned into the drive. As Gabe climbed out of the seat, Lauren allowed herself a moment to admire him. His wind-ruffled, curly hair. His long, muscular body, wide at the shoulders, narrow at the hips. The lithe, athletic way he moved. And his eyes, so blue and . . .

Oh, no. He'd looked up and caught her staring.

She steeled her resolve, squaring her shoulders and traversing the yard toward him. She wasn't going to let her attraction for him weaken her. She'd demand that he explain himself. And when he couldn't, when he wallowed in guilt, she'd make sure he knew exactly how upset and disgusted she was.

"Hey, Laurie." Raccoon-eyed from sunglasses, he squinted at her for a moment as she drew near. "If you're about to start an argument, I wish you wouldn't. When I'm in an optimistic mood, I like to hang on to it as long as possible."

"What happened to make you optimistic?" she asked suspiciously.

"I hesitate to tell you, but I had a look at the wireline logs we did on the rim well. The formations look real promising. We're getting close. With luck, we'll be down to caprock soon."

"How nice." Her fingernails dug into her palms. Good news for Great Basin was bad news for her. If he struck oil, not only would he push for approval to drill on the canyon leases, but he'd be likely to get the okay. The BLM wouldn't want to give up their percentage of potential profits. Short of a legal battle initiated by the CPWA, Red Rock's chance to become a permanent wilderness would be doomed.

Gabe peered at her, probably wondering why her reaction was so mild. "You okay? Aren't you going to yell at me?"

"No need for yelling when an injunction will work just as well. And, Gabe, with what I have on you so far, an injunction ought to be a piece of cake."

"What do you have on me?" He leaned back against the car, not looking overly concerned.

"The mother lode," she said. "The worst case was that dry hole your company drilled on the Grand Staircase National Monument boundary, leaving behind a big diesel spill, toxic substances leaking into the groundwater, and a huge pile of rusty metal. An inspector filed reports, the EPA started slapping fines, and still, Great Basin did nothing for months. Not even for a good six months after you, Gabe Randolph, had bought out the business."

Her voice rose, along with her dismay that he hadn't stopped her, hadn't objected or explained. "I called the area EPA office, and a clerk told me there's a letter in the file with your signature, accepting full responsibility." She paused, smiting him with her most scornful glare. "It's true, isn't it?"

He hitched his thumbs in his front jeans pockets, head back, eyes closed. "Yes, Laurie, as far as it goes." He brought his head up and met her gaze. "Great Basin's previous owners left a hell of a mess. I put my district supervisor to work on it, but he wasn't as diligent as I expected him to be. That's why, when I came out here in January, I ended up staying. There was plenty to do, and limited resources for cleanup."

"Am I supposed to believe you've done something about it since then? Have you even tried?"

He shifted, straightened. "Well, darlin', if you'd finished your research before you started hammering on me, you'd know you've missed one important fact. The EPA reversed the fines they imposed last August. Even they had to acknowledge that I was making every effort. I don't have any-thing to hide."

Her face heated, and she knew she was turning red. She had requested additional reports on both Great Basin and Randolph Drilling, and she should have waited until she'd read them all. With any other person, on any other charge, she would have.

"I guess I was a little hasty. Believe me, if what you're say-ing is accurate, I'm relieved. Because I want to think well of you, Gabe. I really do."

"As long as you don't jump the gun and send misinforma-tion to the newspapers, I can handle it. I told you to ask me if you found something that looked bad." He shrugged. "You did, so I guess I can't blame you for that."

She gnawed her lower lip, recalling the e-mail she'd sent to her boss that afternoon. If everything Gabe said was true, what she'd told Eve in that missive was misleading, to say the least. Of course, it was meant only for Eve's eyes, and Lauren could correct it later, but she still wished she hadn't sent it.

Bullwinkle whined. Gabe reached down to knee-level to scratch the dog's ears just as Lauren, too, reached down to pat the beast.

Her hand touched Gabe's. He clasped her fingers and held on. With their gazes locked, both of them straightened, leav-ing the dog to wriggle and sniff between them. Lauren tingled at his touch. Time seemed to stop, the earth to stand still. She heard a breeze rustle through the elm trees in Gabe's back-yard, felt the rush of cool air and the sun on her face. Yet all she really knew, or cared to know, was Gabe. His warmth, his scent. Him.

Shaken, she glanced away, pulling her hand out of his. She cleared her throat, trying to regain her self-control, trying to seem composed. "I, um, was thinking." *Yeah, right.* "I won-der if you'd give me a well tour. Just to show me how you do things. That way I'll have more to go on next time I try making . . . assumptions." Letting him defend his operation on the actual sites seemed only fair, given the way she'd rushed to condemn him. Besides, she wanted more time to . . . evaluate who he was and— Oh, good grief, she might as well be honest with herself. He made her feel alive with a capital A. Who wouldn't want more of that?

He grinned. "Why, sure, Laurie. We have four wells in the drilling stage, and six others pumping oil. Since they're spread all over a couple of hundred miles of bad roads, the tour would take most of a day. Not tomorrow, okay? I need a break." He rubbed his unshaven jaw, where a wealth of red-gold stubble glinted in the sun.

"Maybe next week then." She tried not to show her disappointment. "I should work tomorrow anyway."

"Why don't we go on a picnic?" he suggested. "We'll pack the Jeep and peel out together. That ought to impress the gossips."

Lauren feared the joy showed on her face. She was probably glowing like one of those phosphorescent fish she'd seen in a documentary last night with Missy. To disguise her pleasure, she hedged. "We'd be wasting our time once we'd left town. No one would see."

The intensity of his blue eyes made her knees quake.

"I have it all arranged, darlin'. It's Saturday. Missy's free—Joe's bailing out on her again, I hear, which is a shame, but at least we can give her an alternative. Buddy can come, too. As you know, Buddy makes a great snoop. What do you say?"

She glanced toward Becca's house. Just last night Becca had asked when Lauren and Gabe were going to go back to work on keeping up appearances. Of course, Becca had no idea how much they'd already embellished the original plan.

Gabe bent at the knees to meet her gaze. "Come on, Laurie. A picnic is conventional, safe, and even functional, since we'll get a meal out of the way. Besides, it'll be fun."

"I . . ." She faltered and risked a smile. Going on an all-day outing with Gabe *would* be fun, for now, but how much pain would it cause in the long run? "There are pros and cons."

"Always. But, hey, look at me." He assumed a classic biceps-flexing pose. "I'm a hunk, right? That's got to put me heavy on the pro side."

Her smile broadened as his bulging arm muscles filled the rolled-up sleeves of his workshirt. "Not bad, but if you win the pleasure of *my* company, it's not because you're a hunk. I like my men not only good-looking, but intelligent and congenial at all times."

He laughed, dropping his show-off stance. "So tell me, am I making progress?"

More than you know, Lauren thought. "A picnic sounds great, Gabe. I need a break from tilting at windmills."

"Tired of tilting? That doesn't sound like my Laurie." He leaned inches closer.

Her nostrils picked up the manly scent of sweat on his skin. She longed to be closer, and closer still. She might have moved right up against him, except the dog was between them, canine haunches planted on top of her tennis shoes like a concrete block.

Gabe touched the side of her face, tracing her cheekbone ever so gently. "Don't let the bad stuff get you down. You're doomed to tilt with the best of us." His hands came to rest on her nape, lightly kneading the muscles on either side of her spine.

She rotated her shoulders. "That does feel better."

He pulled her nearer, their bodies forming a triangle over the dog. "Stick with me, and I'll make everything as better as I know how. Have you been out in the canyon country since you've been here?"

"No." She leaned her head back to look at him, one hand on his chest for balance. "When have I had the chance?"

"I'll give you the chance. You need a renewal. You need to see the land you've been fighting for."

She felt his strong heartbeat under her palm. His warmth seemed to transfer to her own heart, making it beat faster. "Isn't that counterproductive for you, Gabe?"

He grinned. "Call me contrary, a rebel, or maybe just a damn fool. I don't want my favorite adversary to give up the fight. What fun would that be? We both need a time-out. Come with me tomorrow, and we'll make a day of it."

"A day of what?"

"Renewal, like I said. A picnic, a hike, maybe even a swim in the creek."

She took her hand from his chest and straightened, the dog still resting on her foot. She was glad for the ballast, because Gabe had a way of destroying her equilibrium. "I shouldn't leave Becca."

"Sure you should. She's fine. She'll want you to get out. Hell, she asked us to spend time together." He paused, his smile fading. "You worry too much. You'd think we were planning a felony instead of a picnic."

"*Us* planning? Wait one minute. I didn't plan this. You did. And without my consent, I might add. I would never have suggested—"

She stopped when she noticed his raised eyebrow, an indulgent tilt to his mouth. He was on to her.

And he was right. She already knew she'd go.

Lauren couldn't imagine any more perfect pleasure than spending one whole day with Gabe Randolph.

Chapter Thirteen

Gabe lay on a blanket and looked up at the sky. The early afternoon sun felt good on his skin. The fellowship felt good, too. Missy was sandwiched between him and Lauren. Being close, sharing food and space, made them seem almost like a family, and he liked that.

After lunch, with Hannah's excellent fruit tarts for dessert, the three of them had collapsed for a nap. Buddy and Bull-winkle, still full of energy, were splashing in Red Rock Creek, probably freezing their collective behinds off.

They'd walked a couple of miles into the canyon to reach this spot. Vertical sandstone walls hundreds of feet high flanked their haven, and ancient cottonwoods grew tall along the creek. They'd chosen to take a break in an open area with a clear view of the sky. Even Lauren had seemed relaxed and content for once, which made him think that she was starting to enjoy being with him as much as he liked being with her.

Gabe closed his eyes and listened to the wind in the leaves, the murmur of water over cobblestones in the shallow stream bed. The dog barked. A squirrel chattered.

"If I see something in the clouds and make a wish to have it, do you think the wish will come true?"

Gabe must have dozed for a moment, because Missy's voice startled him. "Hmm," he said, blinking up at the sky and wondering what a little girl would imagine in the white puffs that moved slowly across their frame of reference. He wondered if Lauren was listening, and what she'd say if she had to give an answer.

"I've never wished upon a cloud, sweet pea," he said, "but why not? I'll bet you can find whatever you want up there, if you look really hard."

After a moment's pause, Missy confided, "I see a shiny silver bike." She pointed to a nebulous form. It bore no resemblance to a bike that Gabe could tell. The child had either a great imagination or a powerful desire for better transportation.

"Is that what you want most in the world?" he asked.

She shook her head. "I can't see what I want most. I'm afraid it can't come true."

"Give it a try," he urged. Little Missy didn't dream enough, in his opinion. In that way, she was a whole lot like her aunt Lauren.

The child searched the sky as if determined to find a cloud shape that would serve her purpose. Finally she pointed at a thin wisp that stretched above the fluffier plumes. "It's a trapeze," she announced.

Gabe frowned. "You want a trapeze?"

"No, silly. I want Daddy to take me to the circus. He promised a long time ago that we could go, but the circus comes in June, Mama says. I asked Daddy again this week, and he said he might be busy. He's busy a lot with his business, and with . . . things he says are important. I don't think he remembers what he promised."

Gabe's heart lurched for her. Knowing Joe, good old irresponsible Joe, Gabe had serious doubts that Missy's wish had a chance in hell of coming true. "What if I took you to the circus? Would that count?"

She was still looking straight up at the thin wisp. Her

lower lip trembled. "If Daddy forgets, I guess it'd be okay to go with you."

Gabe understood it wouldn't be the same. Joe had left his child with a void in her life, and the attempt to take her away from her mother didn't help. Missy felt deserted and lonely, and she needed her daddy to care about what she wanted and needed. Gabe could attempt to heal the hurt, but he could never make it go away.

Missy's joy had gone out of the wishing game. She stared solemnly at the sky. A tear rolled from the corner of her eye and plopped onto the blanket.

Gabe hated seeing her sad. He found a fat round cloud above him and pointed it out. "That one has just the right shape for a geode, ladybug. And see those shadows? I swear there's a big 'M' written across it."

"For Missy?" She sat up, a hand shading her eyes to better study the signs above. She had coveted her very own geode ever since she'd first seen Gabe's collection. He would have given her one of his, but she didn't want that. She'd insisted she had to find one herself and cleave it open to discover the distinctive colored crystals inside. So far, even with his help, she hadn't found the right rock.

"You really think it's for me, Gabe?"

"I really think so," he said.

Her grin showed a gap from the missing front tooth. Lifting her face to the sun, she searched for more wishes. Soon she'd located a cowboy-boot shape. "I want boots just like yours. Do you think they come in my size?"

"Guaranteed, sugarfoot. If they don't come from the factory that way, we'll have some made just for you."

Missy threw her small body across his chest and wrapped her arms around his neck while she delivered a big smack to his cheek. "I love you."

"Ditto. Who wouldn't love you, the best kid on the

planet?" He stroked her hair, stringy and sweaty from the sun and a morning's play.

"Missy!" Buddy called from the direction of the creek. "C'mere. I found us some skipping stones!"

She bounced off Gabe like a jack-in-the-box with super-charged springs. "Is it okay if I play with Buddy now? I'm all rested up."

"Sure, kid. Go."

When the child had raced out of sight, Gabe inched his hand over to cover Lauren's, where it lay on the vacated blanket space between them. Her eyes were still closed. Her fingers twitched as he touched them, but she didn't move her hand away. In fact, after a moment, she turned it over, palm up, and laced her fingers through his.

"That was nice, Gabe. What you did for Missy was nice."

He grinned, realizing Lauren had been awake all along. "Don't tell anybody. If word gets out, no one in this town'll believe I'm a badass anymore."

She scratched a fingernail along the back of his hand. "I know you're bad to the bone. Except with Missy, of course."

"Are you crazy about me because I'm bad, or in spite of it?"

Lauren turned to him, sleepy eyes growing wide as she took in what he'd said. "I am *not* crazy about you."

"Anything I can do to change your mind?"

She pulled her hand out of his. "Please don't try."

The wistfulness in her voice convinced him that she didn't mean it, but he was willing to wait. She was opening up to him, slowly but surely, and he was satisfied, for now. He settled back to look at the sky.

"Find yourself a wish, Laurie. I don't suppose you see a shiny new sports car with a gas-guzzling V-8 up there, do you?"

She snorted. "No way."

Gabe didn't say anything else, waiting to see if she'd take

the bait and reveal something personal. He wanted to know all about the woman, as he'd once known the girl.

She surprised him with, "I see a spaceship." She pointed to a sprawling cloud that vaguely resembled the starship *Enterprise.* So Lauren was still a Trekkie. Some things never changed.

"How's it powered?" he asked.

"Hydrogen, I would imagine. Definitely *not* by petroleum products."

He laughed. "A spaceship doesn't count as a wish. Not unless you're secretly training to be Captain Kirk."

"Okay, how about if I wish that a Vulcan, Spock-like life-form would appear and give us a mind-altering solution to Earth's environmental problems? The Vulcan will arrive in a spaceship, so that makes my cloud count."

"A little farfetched, but I'm not going to knock it." He propped himself up on an elbow and studied her face, her sun-sparkled silvery eyes, high forehead, chin with a tiny dimple in the center. "Whose mind would be altered?"

"Yours," she said promptly. "Certainly not mine."

"Certainly not," he said. "You're getting the idea, but it's time to move beyond do-gooder bullshit and on to selfish brass tacks. Close your eyes."

"Why?"

"Just close them," he ordered.

When she did, he waited for her features to grow peaceful. "I want you to clear your mind of the Earth's, and everyone else's, problems. Open up, Laurie, and look for your own dreams."

She smiled when she found him leaning over her, and he saw what he'd hoped to see in her eyes. He was right in there with her top-of-the-list wishes. Damn, she made his heart ache when she looked at him like that. He wanted to tell her, but he knew she wasn't ready to hear. She'd only bury her own feelings deeper if he came on too strong, too soon. What he really wanted to do was kiss her until her toes curled.

Good plan. He was working in that direction, and he meant to get there soon.

He doubted Lauren had ever experienced a no-holds-barred relationship. Neither had he, not on the level he thought he could have with her. He wanted to share everyday thoughts and faraway dreams, his and hers. If she'd just open up a little, stop judging him by where he had drilling rights, they might understand each other a whole lot better than she realized.

He moved out of her viewing space. "Look up," he said. "Really look."

She furrowed her brow as she searched the sky. "I don't believe in wishes. Even the spaceship is gone now."

"Come on, darlin'. Look with your whole heart, feelings bared, and tell me what you find."

She glanced over at him wistfully. "First, tell me what Gabe Randolph finds, feelings bared."

"Good thing I'm not as chicken as you are." He rolled to his back and scanned the sky, finding two wispy clouds, one sidling against the other. "Lovers. See? Their lips are touching. If the wind keeps blowing just right, they'll get closer and closer, touching chest and hips and—"

"What if the wind blows just wrong?"

"It'll be over. Short but sweet." He turned to her, propped on an elbow again. "The only way they'll know how close they can get is if they give themselves time and opportunity, which won't happen if one of them's fighting the wind. Why can't you relax, Laurie? Why can't you just enjoy the kiss? The touch. The soul mingling that goes on up there in the clouds."

Lauren wasn't at all sure he was talking about cloud lovers any longer. She saw the same clouds and imagined much the same scenario, but she didn't allow herself to add names.

She sighed. "I thought stars were what people wished upon. If clouds are wishes, what are stars?"

He was silent a moment. "We discussed this once, remember? A long, long time ago. I stuck to science—gases and molecules and chemical explosions. But you, for once, waxed whimsical. You insisted stars are the souls of those who came before us. I still think about it sometimes—that the night sky is man's legacy from one civilization to the next."

Lauren pictured them stretched out in lawn chairs in Gabe's or her backyard, as they'd often done in their youth. Gabe had invariably been in the middle, between Becca and Lauren. He'd held Becca's hand, though it was Gabe and Lauren who'd shared ideas.

"What if it's true?" he asked. "What if we all end up as stars?"

"Hmm," she mused. "Think who's already up there. Your mother, my dad, Ezra's Chloe. They've been looking out for us all this time. And when it's our turn, we can send parcels of light and insight down to Missy and anyone else we leave behind."

"To our offspring, you mean?"

"Well, yes." The *our* jolted her. "I mean . . . not ours together, but . . ."

"I know what you mean," he said softly.

Lauren frowned, wondering if he'd guessed that she *had* been thinking of their possible offspring. "What do you want your legacy to be, Gabe?"

He was quiet for a moment, taking her hand, caressing it with his. "I'd like to leave my kids lots of love that they can pass along in their turn. I'd like to pioneer for them. Create possibilities. Hold together a community. Leave them a better Earth." He squeezed her hand. "What's your version?"

"I'm astonished to say it's quite similar." Except, up to now, her emphasis had been on the Earth rather than on community. She was starting to wonder if one meant anything without the other.

"Didn't you expect we'd think alike? We always used to," he reminded her. "So what about kids? How many would you have?"

"Two. I might *want* more, but I've been advocating zero population growth for so long, I'd have to live up to it. And if I could choose a child, the first one would be just like Missy."

He chuckled. "Me, too. But then, I wouldn't mind Buddy, either. He's a hell of a kid."

"A hell of an extortionist, if you ask me." Lauren smiled. "I do like him. Very much. But about me and children. I don't know if I'd be a good mother. Maybe I'd be good with one child and not . . . another."

He squeezed her hand again. "You're thinking of Hannah. I don't know why she's been that way, except maybe she's just as prickly as you are. The two of you are like a couple of porcupines. The only safe way to do any loving is from a distance."

"I always wanted to be close to her, Gabe."

"I know, and I'm sorry, but I don't think you'd make her mistakes. You'd do fine with kids of your own. You're good at everything you do."

When she turned her head toward him, he was looking straight up at the sky, not at her. Did he mean what he'd said? Did he truly respect her work and the person she had become?

"All you need are the right genes," he added, his mouth taking on the one-sided rise that meant he was teasing. "To make the right baby."

"Oh, sure, Gabe." She almost wished he had been serious, which only went to prove that being with him addled her to the point of mental disability. "And I guess you're the correct sperm donor?"

"You could do worse," he said. "Dr. Frankenstein, the plastic surgeon, or that Tim-Tom guy would be a whole lot worse. There's always the artificial insemination route, but, personally, I'm not in favor of it. I'm your physical contact kind of redneck."

Her skin tingled just thinking of Gabe and physical contact. "I suppose you've had more women than you can count."

"No. I'm discriminating. I have to like and trust her first. The liking's easier than the trust."

She wanted him to like her, trust her. "If I *should* require a sperm donor, I promise I'll consider all options."

He grinned. "That's real wise of you, darlin'." Plucking a blade of grass, he stuck the succulent end in his mouth. "I like being with you, Laurie. I like talking to you."

And she liked arguing with him, smiling with him, pitting her wit against his.

He leaned on an elbow, taking the grass stem from the corner of his mouth. "Remember when I was maybe fifteen and came running over to your house to tell you all about plate tectonics? I'd just read a book on it, and I knew you'd be as fascinated as I was, unlike every other kid I knew."

"But . . . I assumed you were only talking to me because Becca was at cheerleader practice," Lauren said.

"Didn't you wonder why I timed my visits that way so often? Becca wasn't interested in reading anything heavier than *Seventeen*. She didn't have a burning need to know."

Lauren started to speak, to defend her sister, but Gabe beat her to it.

"I'm not taking anything away from Becca. She's a terrific person, a real survivor. Lately, though, since I've met you again, I've thought back and realized that I always went looking for you when I had something important to share.

Because we had a bond between us, an understanding that went a lot deeper than what we'd read, or what we could say to each other in words. I think you knew that then, but I was a little slower. I'm only now beginning to see."

"What do you mean?" She was startled by where he seemed to be going with this. His perceptiveness scared her. She didn't want him to know how she felt. How she'd always felt.

He held her gaze, dead serious for once. "I mean there's something extraordinary between you and me. I'm saying we ought to give it a chance. We owe it to ourselves to see what happens, which way the wind blows."

"We're in an unnatural situation here; keep that in mind," she said. "We're enemies forced to be friends."

"Or maybe we're friends forced to be temporary foes. Isn't that another way of looking at it? We're a lot alike, you have to admit. From the time we were kids, you and I had mental wrestling matches—and, hell, we both got a charge out of it. We'd argue anything from how the earth formed to the pollution that's taking over the—"

"Wait. Did you say pollution?" she asked. "Let me get this straight. You like *discussing* pollution, but you're not willing to do your part to end it? What about Gabe's Earth legacy? What about—"

He shook his head, one eyebrow raised. "See what I mean? By now I'd have any other woman agreeing with everything I said. Not you. You proceed to jump down my throat with both feet. I love it."

She laughed. "That's the first time I've heard a man say he enjoys being criticized."

"I love the challenge. You always had a good mind, Laurie. Now you've grown beautiful, and you're real hard to resist."

"I'm not beautiful." She was strong-featured and strong-minded, not soft and pretty.

A smile tugged at his mouth. "I beg to differ."

She looked up into his sky blue eyes and saw that her childhood fantasy had become a charismatic, virile, irresistible man. He made her ache to be with him, and such wholehearted longing for togetherness was not like her at all. She craved independence, not soul-deep companionship.

And yet she couldn't help sharing a little of what she felt. "I do enjoy talking to you, Gabe. Being with you is always interesting, never the least bit dull."

"I'm more than just entertaining. If you give me a chance, I'll show you I'm not so despicable after all."

She didn't think him despicable any longer, but she wasn't ready to tell him so, even though she was half-certain he already knew. "With your oil leases in all the wrong places, my opinion's necessarily on the low side."

"Maybe it's time to raise that opinion to another level." He tickled her nose with the soft, seeded end of the grass stem he held. When he dropped it, he leaned down to kiss her mouth. She turned her head to avoid him. He kissed her ear instead. He breathed into it, licked it, and grazed his lips along the angle of her jaw.

She shivered. "Gabe . . ."

"Hmm?"

"I don't . . . want . . ." Oh, yes, she did want this. She'd wanted it forever. The heat in her breasts spread to her lower abdomen, to her womb, and settled at the juncture of her thighs. She wanted with all her passion, all her hope, all her heart. The scent of him, the gentleness of his hand that now eased over her breast, made her long for more. So much more.

"Kiss me, Laurie."

Slowly she turned her face toward him. For long seconds they stared at each other, registering their mutual need, acknowledging it. She lowered her lashes and he carefully touched his lips to hers.

She put her hands on his shoulders; he laced his fingers through her hair, slanted his mouth, slid his tongue over her lips. She opened eagerly and savored the taste of him, dancing to his lead, adding a few moves of her own. Lauren had never felt more female, more spontaneous, more indescribably buoyant.

When at last he paused to smile at her, she grasped at the edge of reason, feeling light-headed, lighthearted. "So . . . you actually do like me?"

Gabe figured out right away that she was doing her own teasing now, because what he liked sure wasn't any secret. "Don't pretend I'm the Lone Ranger here. That was one fiery kiss from a woman who prides herself on being as cold as a polar bear's belly button."

"I think I could use more practice," she said slyly.

"Oh, yeah? Not till you admit you're goddamn hot and bothered."

She shook her head, pursing her lips. "Sorry. No can do."

"How about saying you're crazy for me and can't wait to peel off my jeans?"

She smiled, started to say something, then pressed her lips together firmly. Again she shook her head.

He narrowed his eyes a fraction. "Are you still ticklish?" He started inching his fingers up under her arm. "Because if you are, I'll bet I can make you . . ."

She giggled. "All right, I give. I like you. I do."

Good, but not good enough. "How about trust, darlin'? Can you give me that, too?"

Her eyes regained some of their usual sharp, uncompromising focus. "I've been working on it, Gabe. Believe me, I have."

He'd prodded too deep, and he wished he hadn't. He didn't want her focused. He wanted her misty and dreamy-eyed again. "Don't work on it right now, okay? Just let yourself feel."

"Too late. I keep hearing voices saying, 'Run,' and 'Beam me up, Scotty,' and 'Do not let this outrageous oil man make you feel anything at all.' "

Gabe suspected that she felt way too much, and it scared the bejesus out of her. She had doubts, a lot of doubts. So did he, but . . .

"I think I'm falling for you, Laurie. Bad idea, I know."

"Wait." She pushed at his chest, forcing him to halt the inexorable path of his mouth dipping toward hers. "We both have to stop this nonsense right now. It *is* a bad idea. Don't go there, Gabe."

"Ah, darlin', it's too late. All this week I saw your face in unexpected places. In the windshield of my Jeep, in the canyon walls near the oil rig, in the limbs of a pinyon pine, in the lines of a log chart. This isn't about what we're doing for Becca, or about old friendships coming back to haunt us. I see you as a woman. A beautiful, desirable woman. I think things about you that I'd never think about Little Bit Van Horn."

She laughed. "Since I'd love to ditch that nickname, thank God for small favors."

"Right this minute I'm more inclined to thank God for the bigger ones." He brushed his fingertips from her shoulder downward, along the outer edge of her breast. Her soft, husky laugh made him feel a little out of control.

Lauren didn't want to respond to him, but with pleasure rippling through her body in waves, she couldn't seem to help it. His slightest touch made her surrender the inhibitions and restraints she'd worked so hard to maintain. She ached with a hunger only he could satisfy. She'd been with other men, she'd enjoyed being with them, but true intimacy had escaped her. It was the laughing with Gabe, the teasing, even the tickling, that made her feel free and wild and willing.

She could see now that she'd chosen unemotional lovers

who had kept her at a distance, just as she'd kept her deeper needs apart from them.

With Gabe she had nowhere to hide. He knew her. He'd known her as a girl, when she'd giggled and cried and dreamed without trying to pretend otherwise. Now he effortlessly tempted and tantalized her strongest passions as no other man ever could. She was already opening up to him, but she feared he'd demand more of her, perhaps more than she was able to give.

And Gabe did want more. His hand trembled as he touched her soft belly and traced along the top of her jeans. His fingertips itched to move lower. He held off and studied her face instead. She was as alluring as any woman he'd ever met, and she wasn't even trying—in fact, maybe that was part of what made her so damn sexy. She was thoroughly interesting, a challenge in more ways than one. Her features fascinated him. Her cheeks were pink, eyes closed, lips parted, reddened, and wet.

He wanted her. Badly. "You don't even know, do you? You don't know how beautiful you are."

Lauren opened her eyes and saw only his dear face, his true-blue gaze. She reached up to touch him, to trace the outline of his firm lips. "Beauty comes from the heart, Gabe. Or maybe from the soul. I've always thought you were beautiful." She knew that sounded foolish.

Gabe didn't seem to mind. He smiled tenderly. "Just when I'd gotten used to your tough act, you go and say something nice. I like it, honey. I like you."

With him, Lauren felt free to be herself, as he urged her to be. With him, she became a passionate woman, filled with need and want and . . . perhaps even love.

A gust of wind whisked down the canyon, rustling cottonwood leaves and whining along the rock cliffs. She glanced up at the sky, but she couldn't find lovers, or any clouds at all. They'd blown away, leaving only the deep blue that matched Gabe's eyes.

"Give us a try," he whispered. "I want to get to know you as you are now. What can it hurt?"

She wanted to say it might hurt her sister, but with Gabe above her, touching her, Becca slipped out of her thoughts like sand through a misted hourglass.

Lauren knew that caring too much for him might affect her work. She should say so, but she couldn't, not with his mouth hovering over hers. She wanted him too badly. She wanted this moment, this closeness. This Gabe.

She drew him down until their lips joined.

And she let herself feel the passion, the sharp, fiery point of Cupid's dart as it spread its rich nectar through her blood and heated her with permeating, mind-numbing pleasure.

Chapter Fourteen

Lauren ran a hand over sandstone whorls and hollows deep in the heart of a narrow passage. Children and dog bounded ahead of her, following Gabe's lead. Shouts and a howl echoed off the walls of the slot canyon.

Lagging behind, Lauren savored the scenery. Though she'd explored some parts of Red Rock Canyon years ago, with her father and Becca, and sometimes Gabe, she'd never been here. The sandstone walls looked perfectly smooth, but she found them as rough as sandpaper to her touch.

She felt sensitized all over, newly aware of her environment, of herself, of even the air that touched her skin and moved in and out of her lungs. Gabe had done that to her. He'd given her a whole new understanding of passion. And the strange thing was, her passion wasn't just for him, but had expanded into a heightened awareness and appreciation of everything around her.

She caressed the rock. The flow of water over centuries had shaped it, but had not taken away its texture. It occurred to her that the people who lived in canyon country likewise had been shaped by the elements, by circumstance and need, while maintaining an essential grit. She and those who shared the scenery were equally hardheaded, equally convinced they knew what was best. As Ezra had said, sometimes it was hard to tell who was right and who was wrong.

Missy called from up ahead, and Lauren hurried to catch up. The farther they ventured, the more the sandstone closed in around them, until Lauren could reach out with her arms and touch both walls at once. In places, the rock surface met over their heads and formed a sloped ceiling.

The water that had once run through here—and probably still did, in times of spring flood—had created a magical maze that could only have been designed by the most whimsical of gods. As she came around a bend in the passage, she saw rays of light filtering down from above, illuminating Gabe, turning both him and the sandstone a fiery red-gold. The color of hearthfire. It seemed right, thinking of him with her, sharing a home, a hearth, a family. . . .

What in the world was she thinking? When had she become so hideously domestic? She didn't even like to cook, for heaven's sake. She didn't crave children. She didn't particularly want to stay in one place for the rest of her life. And she didn't want a man for the long haul, unless that man could be . . . *No.* She refused to take that thought any further.

She rounded one of the many twists and turns of the slot canyon. Gabe and the kids had stopped at the apparent end of the line, where the two walls met in a vertical cleft that extended higher than even Gabe could reach.

Lauren looked up at a crack through which the sun entered and fanned out in rays. "This is it, huh? No way out?"

"There's a way," Gabe said. "We follow the light." He was already hefting Buddy onto his shoulders. The boy scrambled through a small opening above.

"Are you sure it's safe? How will we find our way back?" she asked.

He insisted everything was fine as he lifted Missy next. The dog howled, the sound reverberating along the rock. "Quiet, Winky," Gabe ordered. He hoisted the dog and pushed him up after Missy until the animal's front paws found solid ground.

Gabe looked back for Lauren. "Come on, darlin'. I'm taking you to the most interesting spot in all the canyon country. You'll like it, I promise."

He held her by the waist and was about to give her a boost when she said, "Wait. I took rock-climbing lessons. I can do this."

Gabe stood out of her way. "Hell, Laurie, I should have guessed. What *haven't* you had lessons in?"

"Scuba diving," she said. "That's my next project." Though she'd never climbed an actual wall, she used the chimney technique, bracing feet and hands on either side of the triangular convergence of sandstone walls, and inched her way up. It wasn't far, and accomplishing the climb was invigorating.

As she reached the sunlight and pulled herself out of the slot, she emerged on a valley floor a hundred yards wide. Her breath caught at the beauty of an oasis surrounded by red-gold cliffs. The huge cottonwoods meant there must be a perennial water source, a spring flowing out from the layers of rock. She smelled the sweet blossoms of the cliff rose, heard the hum of honeybees gathering pollen.

Gabe climbed up to join her. "It's amazing, isn't it?"

She had to agree.

They weren't the first to find this beautiful Garden of Eden. The children had already discovered the stone-piled-upon-stone of an Anasazi ruin. Not a single shelter, but an apartment complex, multistoried, each connected to the next, an entire community from the past.

The cliff dwellings lured Lauren. She began snapping pictures with the camera she'd brought. "My God, what a find! Ruins are a boon to wilderness designation. I'll send copies of these photos to the BLM and—" She was on the verge of adding "the CPWA," but she stopped herself in time. "I'm sorry, Gabe. If you'd rather I didn't use the film for that, I won't, since you brought me here. It's just that road building, development, and other hazards might damage an ancient ruin."

"You're right," he said.

Lauren hoped his environmental conscience was showing, but expected the punch line to be coming any second.

"I want you to use the photos. Feel free." He seemed dead serious. "I want this site protected. I want the canyon protected. If you'd ever bothered to ask, I'd have told you I'm in favor of most aspects of wilderness."

"What? This makes no sense coming from the man who owns Great Basin."

He shrugged. "You've got me all wrong, Laurie. I didn't create the mechanized world. I just happen to be good at finding oil, a commodity people want. I'm making money and providing jobs. That's how our economy works. You wouldn't have a job either if it weren't for people like me."

She found a disturbing truth in what he said. The concept of wilderness had always seemed simple and obvious to Lauren, but she was beginning to see that land use and land need had as many facets as a prism. She'd heard the arguments against it, but now she saw personalities, emotions, faces.

Chester's rage. Hannah's worry. Gabe's financial concerns. Don Ray's quiet deference laced with mistrust. Trish, wondering if she'd end up raising her kids in a ghost town, or worse, having to move somewhere else.

They walked on, while Gabe pointed out a granary, a kiva-shaped structure nearly buried in dirt, and the sandstone above the highest dwelling that seemed to have served as an art gallery for the community. He explained to the children that painted images were called pictographs, while those carved into the rock were petroglyphs. Both forms were represented in this canyon art. There were pictures of men, weapons, and animals, assorted handprints, and a spiral of dots, which was a common symbol found in ancient ruins.

"What does that mean?" Missy asked, pointing to the spiral.

Lauren glanced at Gabe, but he waited for her answer.

"No one knows for sure. I've always thought it represented stars," she said. "A galaxy of stars. Maybe the symbol was part of the Anasazi religion and their belief in an afterlife. Maybe they thought stars were the sky trails of people who'd lived before."

Gabe seemed pleased with the explanation. He'd awakened the fanciful, dreamy Lauren, brought her imagination out of deep hibernation and started it breathing again. She felt renewed in a deeper sense than she would have thought possible.

"Is 'afterlife' like heaven?" Missy asked.

"Yes, it's—" Before Lauren could finish, the buzz of two-cycle engines on the canyon rim distracted her. Though she couldn't see the ATVs, engine noise in a location that spoke of ancient secrets, haunting beauty, and natural gods seemed obscene to her.

Gabe followed her gaze as she searched the top of the cliffs. "This isn't our private domain, Laurie, much as we might like it to be." The intimacy in his voice almost made her forget the ATVs. Almost.

"If Red Rock survives the proposal stage and becomes a designated wilderness, as it should, we won't have to listen to machines," she said. "Of course, in that case, we won't have oil wells down here, either. Where's your nearest rig?"

"A couple of miles that way." He pointed in the direction of the sun. "It's the one you visited when you took your mud bath."

She grimaced. Gabe smiled benignly, as if he had no idea that he'd just reminded her of one of her all-time most mortifying moments.

"Can I keep these?" Buddy asked, holding up a two-inch corncob and a triangular pottery shard. "I found 'em over there, in one of the little houses."

"Afraid not," Gabe said. "Put them back where you found them, and don't collect anything else." He explained to Buddy that collecting artifacts on federal land was illegal.

"I saw a show on the Disney Channel about artifacts. That's my new word for the day," Missy announced. "I'm going to be an archeologist when I get big. They're allowed to dig up artifacts."

"Me, too," Buddy said. "It'll be fun, digging up stuff."

Lauren shared a rueful glance with Gabe. If Buddy had his way this minute, the dirt would be flying. But at least the kid was temporarily restraining himself.

After snapping more pictures, an entire roll of film, Lauren sat beside the ancient kiva and soaked in the mystique of the pueblo-style ruins. The late-afternoon sun touched a protected alcove on the cliffside, glowing golden with the warm tones of Navaho sandstone, and she could almost imagine . . .

"Is this place secret?" Buddy asked.

Lauren wished it could be. Secret forever so that no one would ever disturb the haunting beauty.

"No, it's—" Gabe began.

"Yes," she said. "It's a big secret. I'll pay you . . . two dollars not to tell a single soul."

A few moments later, after she'd paid Buddy and the kids had moved away, Gabe leaned down to whisper, "Buddy's cousins have all been here before, and he knows it. Don Ray brought *me* here the first time. You wasted your money on that secret."

Lauren laughed. "I should have guessed. The boy is a con artist." She vowed she'd get some work out of the little swindler, just as Gabe had.

Unfortunately she didn't have enough money, not nearly

enough, to protect the land by buying off mankind. And it wasn't even right to do that, because everyone had an equal stake in it, perhaps an equal need for it.

But she wasn't going to start thinking of controversy, not now. The day was too beautiful, the sun too bright, her eyes and heart newly sensitized to life, to love, to joy.

Gabe took her hand, and they walked together through the ancient valley, exploring with as much enthusiasm as the children.

"Why are you making me and Mama sad, Daddy?"

Joe almost dropped his cherry almond surprise with extra cream. It was Sunday afternoon. He and Missy were sitting on a park bench in front of the snow-cone stand.

He was nearly a week late in taking her there, but Missy hadn't seemed to mind the delay. He'd thought things were going fine. "What are you talking about, pumpkin? I'm not doing anything to make either of you sad. Is that what *she* told you?" He knew Becca was down on him, but he wouldn't have thought she'd try to turn his own kid against him.

Missy shook her head, bending down to take of bite of bubble gum-flavored ice. "You're scaring Mama," she said with her mouth full. "She needs me."

"So what? I need you, too."

"No, you don't. You forget me lots of times. Mama never does." A dribble of blue syrup was going down her chin, and Joe reached over to wipe it with a napkin just before it hit her white shirt.

"I always know you're safe, pumpkin, and that's what's important. What's the big deal if we miss a couple of Saturdays? You know we'll make up for it."

Missy frowned at him.

"If I'm a little late once in a while, you're not worried, are you?" He thought hard, wondering where he'd gone wrong.

"Have I forgotten something special we were supposed to do? Is that why you're mad at me?"

Missy took another bite of ice and chewed it noisily. "I'm not mad."

"I thought the two of us made a team. It's not fair that your mother wants you all the time."

"It's not fair for you to make the judge say where I have to be," Missy countered.

"Don't you *want* to move in with me?"

Missy looked up from her blue ice. "What about Miss Kayleen, Daddy? When she came over to your house, I had to go to sleep early. I thought you wanted to be with *her*."

Had he ever said anything like that to Missy? He didn't think so. "I'm not seeing too much of Miss Kayleen these days."

He'd been careful not to let on to his little girl, but for a few weeks there, he had been working on wholesale removal of Kayleen's chains, bracelets, and other coverings. He'd gone along with what she wanted for a while, and he'd been living with regrets ever since.

The traitorous bitch had quit him now that she'd found out he wasn't interested in being her puppy dog. She'd taken up with poor, dumb Chester, who was probably going to end up with third-degree heartburn, if he didn't end up in jail. The woman was trouble. Like most women, come to think of it.

He and Missy both chomped snow cones for a silent minute.

Joe had an inspiration. "Tell you what, pumpkin. I'll arrange with your mom so we can go out to my place tomorrow night. We'll buy some cookies and milk, and jelly to go with the peanut butter, just the way you like it. We'll rent Disney flicks or nature videos, whatever you want, and we can watch them all night long."

Missy observed him with wary, intelligent eyes that were too grown-up for a kid. He wondered what she was thinking.

He talked faster, trying to fill up the quiet. "You could spend a couple of days with me, maybe, and we'd ride out into the canyon country on one of my dirtbikes or four-wheelers. You can pick what we ride and where we go. You'd like that, wouldn't you?"

Missy shook her head, her mouth firmly set. "ATVs are too noisy."

"Okay," he said, starting over. "What if I take you down in the canyon? You seemed to like that hike you had yesterday. I've been thinking that you and I should do some exploring together. Tomorrow. Is it a deal?"

"Tomorrow's Monday, Daddy. I have school."

Shit, why hadn't he thought of that? His own kid was too smart for him. "We can do something after school, then."

"I have homework," she accused, making it obvious that he should have realized.

"If you lived with me all the time, I'd know about your school and homework, pumpkin. Right now I just don't see you enough. If we were together more, you'd remind me."

Missy stuck the plastic spoon she'd been using straight up in the cup of crushed ice. "You need to practice first, Daddy. You don't know how to take care of little girls."

Joe felt way too sober all of a sudden. He wondered if a swig of the nearest bottle of beer would make Missy's truths any easier to take.

"Can we go home now?" she asked. "Mama worries about me. She doesn't want me riding on your ATVs, because someone could get hurt. I know you're trying not to drink beer anymore, but Mama worries about that, too. Sometimes you make her scared."

Joe wrinkled his brow. He guessed that Missy was the one who was scared. And what else could he expect?

The kid wanted to be with a parent she could depend on.

If he'd thought a little about *his* childhood, he'd have understood.

His own daddy had run off with a hot little belly dancer from Reno, leaving him and his mom to make do as best they could. The whole town had felt sorry for them. He'd hated it. He'd even hated Uncle Al, who had taken them in out of Christian charity. When his mother remarried, he'd thought everything would be okay, but then his stepfather had kicked him out, and he was back to Uncle Al's place for the duration. Al had loved his own kids, all ten of them. He'd tolerated his nephew.

Joe hated pity, which was one reason he'd gone apeshit over Becca divorcing him and then going for Gabe, who'd always had life easy. No wonder Gabe Randolph had been so damn successful.

Joe looked down at Missy. Stability. If that was what a kid needed, she wasn't going to get it from him.

He knew Becca wouldn't ever love him again, not after all the ways he'd let her down. Sooner or later she'd find herself another man. Maybe not Gabe, since he seemed to be chasing Lauren these days, but Becca would find someone. Joe had to accept the divorce as final and get on with his own life.

What had he been thinking? He'd made a fool of himself, trying to show Becca and everybody else in town that he had the power. He hadn't proved anything. Worse, he'd made his Missy unhappy. He didn't want to end up with her despising him, the way he'd despised his own derelict dad.

The kid was right. Joe didn't know how to be a daddy, but he was going to work on it. He really was.

ver right now. The wilderness issue in Utah is too hot. We need you to stay right there until the BLM management problems are solved one way or the other. You can work out of Cedar City, if that's better for you. I'll assign you a secretary, and our summer intern can do research and fax case reports as needed."

Lauren couldn't believe Eve was dealing her such a below-the-belt blow. "I worked hard on the mining case. If it goes to trial, I want to be in the courtroom."

Eve's answer was a firm no, followed by a quick *"mea culpa"* and a dial tone.

Lauren was angry and upset and . . . confused. She didn't want to stay in San Rafael and oppose the town, much less be around long enough to file the papers that would shut down Great Basin's canyon drilling. Of course, she'd known her relationship with Gabe had no future, but she'd thought there wasn't much harm in spending an hour with him here and there. She'd never believed she'd have to stay and face the consequences of developing a passion for the CPWA's clear and present adversary.

Heartsick, she doggedly continued her duties. She went to the Salt Lake EPA office, where she rounded up all the facts on Gabe and his companies. Not only did what he'd told her about his management of Great Basin pan out, but she discovered that his Austin-based drilling operation had received many commendations over the past five years. He himself had been responsible for several Earth-friendly innovations.

He'd implemented computer software to convert seismic data into models of subterranean formations, thus reducing the number of dry wells drilled, and the subsequent waste. He'd also been a leader in introducing new drilling-mud additives to replace those that were most toxic.

She was happy to find that Gabe was a good guy by EPA standards. She was, personally, proud of him, but that wouldn't change the CPWA's stance, or the actions she would take if and when they became necessary.

On the several-hour drive back to San Rafael, she tried to focus on her work, but she kept thinking of Gabe.

The pretend affair gave her a reason for continuing to see him. Just for a week or so longer, until the new BLM management plan came out and enviros began showing up in town to carry signs and demonstrate their protests. After that, Becca would have to find some other way of dealing with Joe's jealousy.

Lauren would have that week or so to satisfy her curiosity about Gabe, to get over this infatuation she'd developed. By then she'd be ready to give him up. What she felt for him *seemed* strong and overwhelming and delicious, but it wouldn't last. It wasn't love. The entire notion was absurd.

She repeated that to herself over and over.

By the time she reached Becca's house, late Tuesday night, she'd *almost* convinced herself.

Lauren emerged from her room at nine forty-five on Wednesday morning to find her sister singing and dancing down the hall, swinging her hips to a hokey country tune.

Becca was out of her lounge wear, which seemed a good sign. She wore a tight knit top that showed off her cleavage, and snug Wrangler jeans. She appeared fully recovered, except for the side of her face that still had black-and-blue bruises fading to yellows and greens.

She looked good in spite of it. With her generous curves and sunny disposition, she was about as close as anyone could come to a thirty-something all-American cheerleader.

"It's about time you woke up," Becca said, as Lauren followed her to the kitchen, toward the aroma of fresh coffee and warm cinnamon rolls.

Lauren rasped out a "morning," without a "good" to go with it, while Becca poured for both of them. She set two cups, cream, sugar, and rolls on a black tray, and brought the whole of it into the living room.

"What's with the fancy china?" Lauren asked.

"It's a celebration." Becca looked entirely too chipper for precoffee viewing as she handed Lauren, still bleary-eyed, a cup of steaming brew.

"Celebration of what?" Lauren sat back in the recliner, across from her sister, who took the couch.

"Be patient, and I'll tell you. Joe came by to talk to me Sunday night." Becca grinned out of the side of her bruised mouth.

"That's a reason to celebrate?"

Becca nodded. "Yep. You won't believe it, but he's given up. We're off the hook."

"What do you mean? No custody battle? He changed his mind?"

"He isn't going to take us to court." Becca gyrated both hands in the air and exclaimed, "Hallelujah!"

"What happened?" Lauren demanded, leaning forward in her chair.

Becca popped a cinnamon roll onto a napkin and passed it to Lauren. "He took Missy out on Sunday afternoon—you remember, she was all hyper about it, even before you left. She must have said something that made him reconsider what he was doing. When he brought her home, he told me he'd been wrong. He even choked up a little and swore he's going to quit listening to gossips. He said he wants me and Missy to be happy. I think he meant it." She glanced over at Lauren. "Actually, I'm still in shock."

Lauren was in shock, too, but for a different reason. "Do you think he'll stay with this change of heart?" She sipped her coffee, mulling over the news and its implications, trying not to show how shaken she was.

Becca tilted her head, blond hair falling to one side. "With Joe, it's hard to be sure. He said he wants Missy to respect him. He even said he's going to do better with child support, just as soon as he gets his business straightened out."

Lauren almost sprayed a mouthful of coffee. "I hope you don't believe *that*."

"No," Becca said cheerfully. "But I do think he'll try. I've told you for years that Joe's not *all* bad."

Lauren wished he'd shown his good points sooner. Thirteen years sooner would have been ideal. "Have you told Gabe?"

Stretching out full-length on the couch, Becca held up one of her feet and admired the shiny red polish on her toenails. "You tell him, Lauren. It should be a great relief for both of you, and I'd just hate to spoil that special moment."

"Yes, a . . . relief." The relief had to be there somewhere, but Lauren didn't feel it. Her chest ached with regret, mostly. Disappointment. A penetrating sense of loss.

She made herself think. Think logically. Ending it now was for the best, after all. She was becoming too involved. She felt too much for him. She showed too much of what she felt.

"Gabe mentioned something about setting up his telescope tonight, if I made it back and wasn't too tired." Lauren had been looking forward to it. "We were going to create a big scene for Mrs. Marley, or whomever might have spyglasses at the ready. Thank goodness that won't be necessary." She didn't feel happy or thankful; she felt empty, lonely, and inexpressibly sad. "I guess I could call and tell him over the phone."

"No, no. Go on over," Becca insisted. "You can celebrate with a couple of bottles of that fancy sparkly water you're stockpiling in my refrigerator. Lord knows, you won't get me to drink the stuff. If you stay here you'll spend the evening pounding on your laptop, and you could use a diversion. That is, if . . . Are you and Gabe on reasonable speaking terms? Not that it'll matter one way or the other after tonight."

True, it wouldn't matter. The fun would end, along with the game. "Let's just say that we no longer spit in each other's eyes regularly."

"Hmm," Becca said, as if she didn't quite believe they'd progressed that far. "I guess now you'll be free to leave town."

Lauren shook her head. "As it happens, no." She explained the extension of her Utah job assignment. Unfortunately Joe's threats had ended too late to give her a shot at a once-in-a-career court case that she'd hoped might change the laws governing mining on federal land for all time. And too late to allow her to escape a burgeoning desire for Gabe. "I'll do some traveling—to Cedar City, Moab, and Salt Lake—but I may as well keep my base of operations here. It makes sense, location-wise."

"I'm sorry, Lauren. I've really screwed things up for you, haven't I?"

"It's okay." Lauren was surprised to realize that missing out on a career high was not the end of her world. Getting to know her family again, or perhaps getting to know them as she hadn't before, would be more than adequate compensation. She didn't think about putting an end to knowing Gabe better. She wasn't ready to think about that.

As she glanced around the room, she noted the homey atmosphere, much more comfortable than she remembered this house during her childhood. It must have something to do with Becca's decorating. A new framed painting dominated one wall. The glistening oil made powerful use of light and shadow, depicting two children playing beneath a huge tree. The kids could be Missy and Buddy, or the Lauren and Becca of twenty or more years ago.

"Your painting has improved," Lauren said. "Maybe that Rio fellow is right. Maybe the artsy crowd will go for it."

"Why, thank you, Lauren." Becca's eyes actually grew teary, which made Lauren wonder if she'd failed to compliment her sister's work before.

She vowed to do better in that regard. In the past she'd criticized Becca without the accompanying praise she might give an associate, or a friend. She'd taken her sister's tolerance and forgiveness for granted. She'd considered Becca immune to hurt feelings, which was completely wrong and unfair.

With her niece, Lauren hoped she was learning faster. "Since I'll be hanging around here for a while, I'd like to teach Missy to play chess. She'll be great at it."

"I'm sure she will. She and I usually play Scrabble. I confess, I haven't been able to beat her at the junior version since she started first grade," Becca said. "She'll be glad you're staying, you know. Me, too."

Lauren smiled. "Me three." She was making progress in understanding Becca, and she looked forward to seeing Missy capture bishops and checkmate kings. Maybe they could have a chess lesson soon, right after school was out this afternoon. "Your daughter's curiosity is great to see, Becca. When we were in the canyon, she . . . Oh, you won't forget to report that archeological site we visited, will you? It's a big one, and if it's not on the official list, it should be."

"I'll take care of it when I go back to work tomorrow. I already called Arch McFarlane, and he's sending forms."

"I don't suppose Arch minded hearing from you." Lauren pointed at a daisy plant on a table next to her chair. Arch's name was scrawled across the card in letters big enough for the legally blind to read. "The man obviously wants you to notice him."

The whole room smelled of flowers and candy. Daisies from Arch, roses from Rio. Chocolates from Gabe.

Becca should have been glowing with contentment, but instead she looked vexed. "Missy asked if I was supposed to know about all the ruins in the canyon already. I feel incompetent for not knowing."

"Don't. I doubt anyone's covered every square inch of the area. That's the beauty of it. I was surprised to learn from Gabe that plenty of people have been to those ruins, yet they're as intact as any I've seen. The locals, bless them, have looked after the remains of Anasazi culture fairly well."

"Am I hearing right?" Becca asked. "Are you praising this town?"

"I'm just thinking out loud, wondering . . . How bad is the economic picture around here?"

"It's never been all that good," Becca said. "The main problem, right now, is fear of change. People are afraid more wilderness means they'll be the next endangered species."

"I do see their concerns. However, we can't make decisions about federal land based on—"

"Don't waste your breath lecturing me." Becca laughed. "I'm just a BLM peon, remember? Save the details for Gabe. He'll love arguing over them. And since you've already planned a point of contention, how about some war paint? I've wanted to do your toenails for absolutely *years*."

Lauren thought about hiding her feet, but it was too late for that. She raised a leg and studied her au naturel toes critically. She had never gone in for life's hidden pleasures. Fingernail polish, she could see, because outward appearance was part of self-projection. Painted toenails, though, had always seemed a little frivolous to her. But she might as well make Becca's day. "I *could* use a pedicure, I suppose. Any earth-tone polish around here?"

"Stay right where you are." Becca scooted off the couch and peered underneath it, drawing out a cardboard box that contained at least a decade's worth of nail polish. "I have every shade under the sun, as you know, but I never thought I'd talk you into primping your feet. I'm delighted and amazed. I thought only spineless wimps—such as *moi*—would indulge in mundane vanity."

Lauren recognized one of her own ill-considered quips. "I never should have called you a wimp. Nor should you have called me arrogant, or a self-appointed world savior, or . . ."

Becca giggled.

Lauren laughed along with her. "I'm the world's worst stuck-up bitch sometimes. Why do you put up with me?"

"Maybe because you're my only sibling *and* the smartest person I know," Becca said with a one-shouldered shrug.

Lauren scoffed. "If I were really smart, I'd be nicer. I'd take a lesson from you."

Becca waved off the compliment and kept digging through the bottles of polish until, with a flourish, she produced a shade of deep bronze. "Perfect! I can touch up your fingernails, too. You just lie back in that chair, little Laurie, and let me at you."

At dusk Lauren climbed the steps onto the redwood deck that Gabe had added to the back of his house. She wore leather sandals to show off her newly painted toenails, sported a sassy haircut from the Hair Affair, and bore gifts in the form of a six-pack of Perrier and a six-pack of Pepsi.

She knew it was the wrong approach. All wrong. The pretense was supposed to end tonight, and she was flashing signals of a beginning.

Since she'd now be stuck in San Rafael for the duration, continuing her association with Gabe would be ignoring her own basic concept of legal ethics. She might soon be opposing him in court, and if she had any sort of relationship with him at that time, she could be charged with conflict of interest and might even lose her job. Certainly she'd lose all credibility in environmental circles.

But she couldn't just ignore what she felt for him, and what she thought he felt for her. She owed him an explanation. That was why she was here, in person. She'd explain and then leave. Obviously that was the only rational way to handle it.

He wasn't outside, but he'd already set up the telescope and a couple of lawn chairs on the deck. Lauren noticed an open book lying facedown on the chair webbing. She paused to read the title. *Southwest Canyon Ecology*. The title served to remind her of how wrong she'd been about him. She'd been wrong about a lot of things.

"Where are the kids?" he asked, sliding open the glass door and coming out of the house. "I figured you'd bring them to report on our bad behavior. We can't count on Mrs. Marley to stay up past eight-thirty."

"I don't know about Buddy, but Missy's busy perusing an encyclopedia disk on my laptop. She wants to tell her class all about Anasazi ruins, and I want to encourage her interest."

"Good for her. Missy's one smart little munchkin. And I'll let you in on a secret. I don't give a damn about witnesses if you don't." His heart-melting smile made Lauren want to cry.

"That's what I came to tell you, Gabe. We don't . . . need witnesses anymore." In other words, she had no excuse, absolutely none, for being here with him, and that made her throat close and her entire chest ache.

Gabe paused, his smile fading, while she blundered on. "Joe's called off all custody threats, I hope permanently."

"Becca must be relieved." Gabe stood in front of Lauren, searching her gaze, his brows coming together in a frown. "So I guess the question is, do you want to stay for the star party?" He'd caught the essence of the problem and addressed it directly, as Lauren had been reluctant to do.

"Are you taking back the invitation?" She felt awkward, wondering if he wanted her to leave. This had all started for show, and maybe that was all it was, even now. She hadn't thought so, but . . .

"No. Please stay." He took the drinks from her and set them on a wrought-iron table near the door. "I'm just worried about your motives, pretty lady. I was hoping you lusted after my body, but I'm thinking it's the telescope you want. You're using me to search for your great spaceship in the night sky."

Lauren smiled, relaxed by his teasing. "Yes, that's it." She told herself spending a few more hours with him wouldn't matter. A night of stargazing didn't violate any laws.

He stared down at the toenails peeking out from under her jeans. And then he tilted his head, studying her shorter hair. "You've been to Trish's beauty shop?"

"Yes. Mrs. Whalen was there to enthrall me with the story of her second son, Jake, who finally got his plumber's license and is now in the market for a wife. I believe she's eyeing me as a prospect. Poor Jake must be a sad catch if his mother would stoop to checking out an environmental attorney."

"Jake could use the matchmaking help," Gabe said. "He's about the shyest man I've ever met. Maybe Mrs. Whalen and Hannah are cooking something up between them."

Lauren laughed. "Don't feel left out. The oldest Biggs daughter works in Salt Lake—I think she's younger than I am by at least four years, but most important, she's on the make. With the gossips reporting that Gabe Randolph may be up for grabs, Cindy Biggs is arranging a nice long vacation right here in San Rafael."

With both hands, Gabe smoothed Lauren's hair away from her face, taking his time framing her features. "Cindy might as well stay home, darlin'. She can't compete with you."

Lauren should have said something then, explained about her change in job focus, but her tongue seemed stuck to the roof of her mouth. She had to tell him, and she would, eventually. All she wanted was a little more time. A few more hours. Was that so wrong?

He led her to the deck railing, where they watched the

shadows grow deeper on the distant mountains, watched the brightening of the first stars.

With no clouds and no moon, the night was perfect for amateur astronomy. Through the telescope they viewed Jupiter and its four largest moons, Mars, the Andromeda Galaxy, and a tiny, cloudy complex in Sagittarius that was either a smudge on the lens or a nebula, as Gabe claimed.

When they'd tired of squinting at the heavens through a lens, they sprawled in the lawn chairs, aligned within inches of each other. Gabe popped open a Pepsi; Lauren had her Perrier. She was surprisingly relaxed in his company. She found it easy to forget all the outside forces that would come back to haunt her soon enough.

"I built this deck myself," he said. "Finished it the week before you came home. What do you think?"

"Nice work. Your dad would approve. I always wondered why he kept this house for so long. Every time a renter moved and it sat vacant for months at a time, I thought he'd sell out."

"He kept it at first because he wasn't sure how he'd like living in Texas again," Gabe said. "Later I think he kept it for me. He worried that I didn't have roots. This was his way of giving me some. And, too, he liked keeping up with his old friends and finding out what his former students were up to. He'd call Hannah a few times a year and ask about the tenants, which gave him an excuse to find out the rest of the news."

"He was an excellent biology teacher, but I didn't mourn the loss of his coaching skills, as some around here did." Lauren stole a glance at Gabe to see if the old sports dig got to him, but he didn't seem to notice. "Where is your father now?"

"In Florida. He retired from teaching and coaching last year, and he's found himself a nice lady friend. I think he might marry her eventually."

"He's waited a long time." San Rafael women had whispered that he'd been devastated by the death of Gabe's mother from cancer the year before he'd moved to San Rafael. He'd never lacked for female sympathizers. Yet, as far as Lauren knew, he'd remained faithful to his wife's memory the whole time he'd lived in town. "Are you two still as close as ever?"

Gabe nodded. "We've had our differences. Sometimes I thought he pushed me too hard in basketball, but I never doubted that he loved me. After my mother died, it took us both some time to get used to having only each other, but we did okay. I appreciate him more every year."

He looked up at the stars for a while, and she followed suit. Now that she was older and had suffered the death of a parent herself, she could sympathize more with the younger Gabe, with his loss.

She missed her father, but she was grateful for the new ease she had developed with Becca and Missy. To some degree, she was even getting along with Hannah better than before. She wondered if somehow Gabe, who understood people so well, was responsible. Maybe it was her time with him that had cracked her icy, prickly shell, allowing warmth to trickle in.

She looked up at the Milky Way and let her mind expand along with the universe. With the nearest big-city lights hundreds of miles away, the stars were incredible. A meteor streaked across the sky, leaving an ephemeral trail of white.

"Did you see that?" she asked. "Our future is falling out of the heavens. Our legacy is vanishing before our eyes."

Gabe found her hand and caressed the underside from wrist to fingertip in long, slow strokes. "We haven't made our legacy yet. And we won't have one if we keep repressing what we feel."

Lauren's palm tingled. Her chest felt tight. Her lower abdomen fluttered with anxiety and emptiness and need. "I'm afraid, Gabe. Afraid that our legacy . . . is not meant to be."

"You never know about legacies, because they're not over until we die." He squeezed her hand in his. "Tell me about your life. What do you do in Denver besides work?"

"I have friends at my office, and a couple of girlfriends from college who live in the area. We go to movies, the occasional concert. Then there's Moody," she said. "I called him just before I came over here."

Gabe raised an eyebrow. "Who's he?"

"A history professor and fellow tree-hugger. He lives in the condo next to mine."

"And to you, he is . . . ?"

Lauren smiled, noting that Gabe sounded almost jealous. "He's gay."

"You had me worried for a minute there." He continued stroking her hand. It felt so good, she let him.

"Moody's probably my closest friend. We share meals and work out at a health club twice a week."

"I'd like to see you in a skimpy spandex outfit," Gabe confided. "Chances are, I'd appreciate it more than your friend does."

"No doubt. Anyway, he takes care of my condo when I'm not there. I was a little worried about my goldfish, until I finally got Moody on the phone. I should have known he'd look after everything no matter how long I was gone. He's been feeding the fish every day; he even remembered to water my cactus."

"Cactus?" Gabe sounded like he was about to laugh.

Lauren beat him to it. She laughed aloud. "Us prickly-skins like to stick together."

With the softest caress imaginable, he traced a path along her inner forearm. "No prickles here. Maybe I've gotten underneath them."

"Gabe, don't." She pulled away, because it was clear that

her defenses against him were woefully ineffective. "The need to pretend is over, and there's no other reason to—"

"Were we pretending?"

Lauren hadn't been, not by the time they'd gone to the canyon. Probably not before then, either.

"If you want an excuse," he offered, "maybe you should consider spying on me some more."

She shook her head. "If you're referring to my investigation of Becca's accident, I've ruled out Great Basin."

He looked surprised, but all he said was, "It's about time. I hoped you'd trust me eventually. I was starting to wonder if—"

"This has nothing to do with trust. I couldn't rely on my judgment for something so important. I needed facts, so I checked with the EPA man who goes out and inspects in this area. It took me awhile to locate him, but he had visited the rim well on the morning of the accident. Everything was hunky-dory. So, unless you paid the guy off, you and your company are in the clear, motive-wise."

"To tell you the truth, I wasn't worried," he said. "Innocence breeds complacency, I guess. Did Becca get an insurance report in the mail today?"

"No. Did you?"

He nodded. "Becca's pickup broadsided my winch truck on the passenger side. The only scenario I can see is that someone had backed the truck out from its parking spot and left it blocking the entire road. But since we don't have a clue about who might have been around to do that, it looks like the why and wherefore of the accident are going to stay a mystery."

She sighed. "At least Becca's okay."

"Yeah." He took her hand again. "So that leaves you and me, sweetheart. Got any ideas on how you're going to make it up to me for holding me under suspicion for so long?" The teasing in his voice didn't quite cover what she thought sounded like hurt feelings.

"I'm sorry, Gabe. Really, I am."

"Not good enough. I had groveling in mind. You, groveling. Or if you want, I'll settle for a night of bliss. A real long night, the longer the better." He was teasing about the groveling, she thought, but not the bliss.

God help her, she wanted a night with him, too. Her entire body ached with a need that seemed to grow stronger every moment she was near him. Telling him that the bliss would never happen was getting more difficult by the moment. There was no easy way, but she tried to keep the tone light, following his lead. "Now that the custody crisis is out of the picture, Gabe, you know as well as I do that anything personal between us is contraindicated."

"Contra-what? Would you stop with the big words already? You do that when you're trying to keep your distance, and it won't do you any good with me. There's a whole lot indicated between us, and most of it's going to be real personal, if I have anything to say about it."

She felt her heart sink through her chest and land somewhere below, on the boards of the deck. "But you don't, Gabe. Neither of us can have anything more to say. It's over. As of tonight, it's all over between us."

"No, Laurie. I won't let you decide that. Not when I know you don't want it that way any more than I do." His voice dipped to a low, seductive pitch that put every erogenous zone in her body on red alert.

She wanted more time with him. She wanted his arms around her, wanted him to go on insisting that she couldn't let what was between them die away. Turning in the lounge chair, she faced his direction. As Gabe turned toward her, reached toward her, the few cactus prickles she had left sloughed right off of her melting heart. For once, she forgot about caution and did what came naturally. She leaned his way. He leaned hers.

Their lounge chairs tipped inward and dumped both of them onto the redwood deck. They tumbled together, arms reaching, legs clinging, wrapping around each other as the flimsy chairs fell on top of them. A rumble started deep in Gabe's chest and ended in laughter. Lauren snickered at the ludicrousness of their tangled limbs, and then she was laughing, too. They pushed aside the aluminum frames, but the more they tried to catch their breath and get serious, the more they laughed.

When Lauren hiccupped to a stop, she realized one of Gabe's legs was sandwiched between hers, his thigh pressed high and hard against her. He wasn't laughing anymore. He caressed the side of her face and kissed her, starting out soft and tender. But when she held on to him as if her life depended on keeping him near, his mouth became hard and hungry, devouring, demanding.

Never before had desire taken over her entire heart and soul. She'd always held back at least a little of herself, maintained at least some control. But then, she'd never felt as close to anyone as she did to Gabe. He knew the old, dream-filled Laurie, the one she never allowed to surface anymore.

Since she couldn't hide her inner thoughts or inner weaknesses from him, she experienced that same unique freedom she'd found with him in the canyon. She felt as if she could soar with him all the way to the stars. She imagined that a pair of cloud lovers, hidden in sensual splendor in the darkened sky, had likewise embraced from head to toe.

He touched her breasts, her hips, her thighs. Her hands were all over him, too, under his shirt, exploring his chest, memorizing his nipples, the hardness of muscle and bone and sinew, the pattern of hair, broader up high, a thin line down low. She followed it low and lower, to his navel, to the waist of his jeans.

He was already unbuttoning her shirt, unfastening her bra, filling his palm with her breast.

Oh, God. She felt a kind of panic along with the searing heat of desire. What was she doing here with Gabe? Had she forgotten everything, all she stood for, all her life had meant so far? She must have lost her mind, because nothing that was supposed to matter meant as much as staying here and being with him for an hour or a night or . . .

She wanted, wanted. . . .

And couldn't have. She knew that, had known it all along. She didn't allow herself to unfasten his jeans. Instead she trailed her hands to his back and held on so she wouldn't be tempted to touch anywhere else. Regret brought tears to her eyes.

He kissed her breasts, her neck, returning to her face. He must have felt the dampness on her cheeks, because he stopped and brushed his thumb tenderly across her cheekbones.

"Gabe." Her voice quavered on his name, but she cleared her throat and continued. "I . . . can't. We can't." Her belief in logic came back to haunt her. She couldn't love Gabe.

"I know our being together is right, Laurie. It's just that everything else is wrong." He wrapped his arms around her, inside her unbuttoned shirt, and buried his face in her hair. "Don't give up on us, darlin'."

Right now, in the heat of lust, she thought she wanted Gabe. But was she willing to give up her job, her career? Could he matter to her more than that? And if he started boring holes in Red Rock Canyon, could she ever forgive him?

"There's something . . . new," she said. "Something I didn't know until yesterday. I thought I'd be going back to Colorado soon, but as it turns out, I'll be here. If it comes to legal action, we'll be pitted directly against each other."

Sighing, he lifted his head and met her gaze. "We don't have to let what's going on with Great Basin matter, Laurie.

We only have to think about you and me. As far as the outside world goes, and as far as this town will ever know, we can be discreet as easily as we've been blatant."

"We could never be discreet enough. If my boss should find out I've become involved with you, she'd have a conniption fit." Lauren suspected Eve Worthy would spout a stream of Latin nasty enough to send a gladiator leaping into a lion's mouth. And from the CPWA viewpoint, she'd be right.

"Let's think about this," he said. "Don't be too quick to—"

"No, Gabe. I should have said something as soon as I came over here, but we started talking, and . . ." She hadn't expected to end up on the redwood boards of his deck, behaving with no discretion whatsoever. "Surely you can see that tonight has to be the end for us. We have to make a clean break, before this gets more complicated."

"Laurie, darlin', it's already way too complicated." He leaned toward her for one more kiss.

She wanted his kiss, but couldn't accept it. If she did, she'd be lost.

Lauren Van Horn, paragon of self-control, put the armor on her heart and picked herself up from the redwood deck. She reached deep within herself and found the willpower and determination to walk away.

For the first time in her life, she cursed what she'd long considered her greatest strengths.

Gabe figured Lauren had too damn much willpower for her own good. For sure, she had too much willpower for *his* good, and he meant to do something about it. In not quite two weeks, he'd started to care more for her than he'd ever cared for a woman. What did she think, that he was just going to give up?

Not Gabe Randolph, by God.

He went inside, intending to call her on the phone. He'd heard that the prank calls had stopped, so he ought to make it past the answering machine. Then he realized Becca would probably answer, and he didn't want to explain what was going on to her. In case she still harbored some deep affection for him, he didn't want to hurt her feelings unless he had to.

Besides, he didn't know what he'd say to Lauren if she did come to the phone. Butting heads and wills with her wasn't going to win this. She'd resist even more. He'd have to find his way under her prickles, down to her soft underbelly, if he wanted to get through to her.

So he decided to be imaginative about his approach. He'd romance Lauren somehow, really grab her attention. But when he started to think about it, he found that originality was more difficult than it seemed, especially since his whole heart was wrapped up in the outcome. He thought all the next day, while he was at work. He almost got himself slammed in the face with a steel pipe while he was on the rig supposedly supervising a drill bit change.

After that he went home early, only to find that Lauren had gone to Cedar City and wouldn't be back until late.

He'd see her then, he vowed. He'd warm her heart until she was as soft and flexible as Play-Doh. Stealthily he made his preparations, taking off the screen to her window and making sure the sash was partway open. Then he laid his plans. Sitting on his desk and talking out loud to Bullwinkle like some kind of lunatic, he designed one paper airplane after another, trying to get one that would fly halfway decently and look just right.

When she finally came home, he watched the lights, watched her go into her room, saw her sit down in front of her laptop, just as Missy had said she did every night. Shamelessly, he'd pumped the unwitting child for information. He tried not to think about how deep he was reaching to find a way to Lauren's heart.

He slunk across the dark lawn and sailed his best paper airplane in through the window of her room. It glided right over her fingers at the keyboard. She looked up. He ducked. Though he'd thought about climbing in through the window straightaway, he figured she'd slam it down on him if he tried to enter without an invitation. Lauren could play rough, he had no doubt.

He peeked over the sill in time to see her pick up the airplane and look it over. *Starship* Enterprise, he'd printed on the side. *Let me take you to the stars.* She read it, smiled a little sadly, and glanced in his direction.

"No, Gabe," she said. "I can't." And then she began pecking away at the keys, paying no heed, not even when he softly called her name.

Damn. Foiled from the get-go.

The next evening he used the dog. After all, who could resist Winky's big brown eyes? Gabe sent him in through the house to Lauren's room, with Missy's help. The dog wore a made-by-Gabe braided friendship bracelet hooked onto the pink-and-purple neckerchief. There was a note twisted around the bracelet, declaring Gabe's undying love in badly rhymed couplets. Maybe she'd think his love was only lust. Whatever. He just wanted her to speak to him again.

He was right outside watching when she untied the bracelet, put it beside the keyboard, and threw the note away.

Hell. Foiled again.

The following morning, before he went to work, he talked Missy into putting a cloud mousepad he'd found at a shop in Fairfield on Lauren's desk while she was in the kitchen eating breakfast. He'd taped another note, with his own inexpert drawing of the cloud lovers, on the bottom of the pad.

He was on his deck, spying through her bedroom window

with his telescope, when she went into her room. The new note became more fodder for the trash can.

Double damn.

By the fourth evening she'd locked the window, and she'd had a little talk with Missy, so the child wouldn't deliver his gifts. When he returned from the rigs to learn the newest bad news, he resorted to tapping on Lauren's window glass and pressing his nose to it, much as he used to do when they were kids. Whenever Hannah had put her foot down and wouldn't let the girls go out to play, he'd be at the window. Even when Becca was mad at him—he was almost always the one who'd gotten them into trouble in the first place—Lauren would let him in.

Not this time.

He tried one more approach, as direct as he could get without involving Becca, which he was still trying to avoid. He knocked on the back door.

Missy answered. "Aunt Lauren doesn't want me to let you in the house, Gabe," the child said with a sorrowful shake of her head. "She said to tell you she's real busy."

After Missy shut him out, Gabe stood there on the stoop, hands in pockets, feeling lost and lonely. He trudged back to his house and remained there. He had to stay off the streets, because Cynthia Biggs, home for her vacation and diligent in her man-hunting patrol, had already blindsided him in his front yard once this week. Cynthia was quick. She'd been leaning on him and fiddling with his shirt buttons before he could get out three words. "Leave me alone," were the only ones he'd been able to think of. He suspected Cyn, as she called herself, was only temporarily deterred.

Missy, bless her little heart, must have sensed Gabe was having a bad day, because later that evening she showed up at his door with her pillowcase full of rocks.

Gabe was out of ideas on how to get Lauren's attention, but he wasn't quitting, not by a long shot. He'd send mail.

He'd call, if she'd only answer the phone. He'd try Mr. Rogers nice, candy-coated sweet, and . . . black lace erotic might be worth a shot. Hell, he'd try anything. And if none of that worked . . .

Next step: bring in the special forces.

Inside her locked room, curtains drawn, window latched, Lauren carefully reached into the back of her desk drawer and found her collection of Gabe's notes. She'd thrown the first ones in the trash can because she'd known he was spying on her, but she'd retrieved those and saved all the others, one for each of the six days of his campaign. The last ones had been in the mailbox, since she'd frustrated his most recent attempts to get into the house.

She felt a little guilty about sneaking around, hiding the letters from Becca, but this was something she couldn't share with her sister. Better to let Becca think, as she did now, that no love had ever been lost or found between Lauren and Gabe.

Each time she reread the notes, as she'd done every night since she'd begun accumulating them, her defenses grew weaker. If he came to her now, right now, she was afraid she'd fall into his arms and beg him to take her home with him, to let her stay, to never, ever let her go.

He'd decorated the mailbox letters with pasted-on Valentine hearts and flowers and kittens, but what he'd written inside were their memories. The first time he'd seen her in Smurfies. The day they'd released his goshawk. A silly argument they'd once had over the answer to a Trivial Pursuit question. And the clouds they'd wished upon. Her tears marked every page.

She touched the cloud mousepad that lay on her desk. It was so thoughtful, so sweet, so . . . well, so Gabe. And the drawing he'd made of their own special clouds, though lacking in artistic talent, was wonderfully romantic.

The erotic note, the last one she'd received, was in extremely bad taste, so bad it made her laugh at the same time that her breasts flushed with heat. But that, too, was Gabe, the inventive, lusty lover that she knew he'd be.

The starship *Enterprise* airplane reminded her of how well he knew her. She picked up the friendship bracelet and held it to her cheek, imagining him bent over a tangle of colored threads, braiding it for her. She wrapped it around her wrist, deciding to wear it. Just for tonight. Just while she slept.

She smiled at the bad art and the ragged threads on the bracelet, and ended with her throat swollen from a longing to crawl through her window and go running straight to his house.

She'd been lost since day four, when seeing his nose pressed to the window glass had broken some invisible barrier deep inside her.

He'd invaded her heart.

And now that he was there, she had no idea how to get him out.

Chapter Sixteen

A week after Lauren and Gabe's star party, on a Wednesday, Becca arrived at the BLM office to find a milling group of protesters obstructing the path to the door. A television van was parked across the street, and a newswoman trailed Becca, calling to her as she started through the mass of hot bodies. The crowd jostled, pushed, and shoved, and all Becca wanted to do was reach her office door and barricade herself inside.

A homemade sign banged her sore shoulder. She was frightened by the shouts, the ugly mood. The townspeople she'd known all her life had turned into strangers with a mob mentality. The air smelled stale, like unbrushed teeth, with a hint of garlic.

"Don't go in there," shouted a voice—Becca thought it was Elly Montrose, who ought to be working the day shift at the Top Chop Grocery. "If you don't stand with us, we'll know whose side you're on."

"Quit the BLM," someone else yelled. "That'll show 'em."

Show them what? Becca wanted to ask. *A woman filing for unemployment?* How could she buy groceries and clothe her child without a paycheck? But stating her case to this crowd wasn't going to do any good. Many in the town felt threatened by the latest BLM rulings. Some probably feared they'd lose their livelihoods as a result.

Arch McFarlane had called her house last night to warn her that, by this morning, the media and all associated groups would have an official copy of the canyon management plan. Becca had been grateful for the warning, but she'd never expected the big protester turnout. She'd never expected the anger directed at her.

The reporter was still on her heels when she reached the office door. At the woman's insistence, Becca paused for the inevitable interview. A camera lens panned her face, and she flashed her best smile. She hadn't had much occasion to speak in front of cameras. Not that she minded being in the spotlight, but she felt rattled right now, what with much of the town looking on. She heard shushing sounds. The crowd was waiting for her to speak, wondering what she'd have to say.

The reporter spoke into the mike in a low, breathy voice. "Locals here in San Rafael, Utah, are angry about having use and access limitations placed on their beloved Red Rock Canyon," she stated for the network camera. "The crowd around us consists mostly of antiwilderness protesters, but environmental groups are also unhappy with the BLM's decisions. The CPWA is demanding further study. Their spokesman said that the Environmental Assessment that led to this plan was rife with inaccuracies."

Turning toward Becca, the reporter asked, "Mrs. Hewitt, can you shed any light on why the canyon management decisions are being criticized by both sides?"

Since she worried about the scar from the accident showing through her bangs, Becca tried to provide the camera with the best possible angle. Unfortunately her tan uniform blouse made her look fat, and her dark brown slacks were definitely tighter than they used to be. All those mint truffles had had an effect.

"We tried to compromise," Becca said with what she hoped was a dazzling smile. "As a result, no one is completely satisfied. But I assure you, the BLM is keeping everyone's complaints in mind. I'm confident that we can work this out." She hoped she came across as poised and prudent and methodical. Maybe if she lost her BLM job, she could find employment as an actress.

"Confident, my left foot!" someone shouted. "When hogs take up flying, that's when we'll let the government tell us how to handle our canyons!"

Her self-assurance crashed and burned. She'd be the town pariah after this. Now she knew how Lauren felt, being on the black side of public opinion.

The questions continued, and Becca answered as patiently as possible, keeping her tone reasonable and light. "Sorry, I can't give you a time frame for implementation. Sure wish I could, but, as you've said, our management plan faces challenges from several directions. There'll be some discussion before we're through."

"Damn right!" "We'll stick it to 'em!" came the catcalls.

Becca strained to hear the reporter's next question and answered, "No, there's no connection between my recent accident and the community's wilderness protests."

Finally the newswoman asked about Lauren, making it clear that the media had the word on the sibling link.

"I can't comment on Miss Van Horn's position." Becca turned away, waving off the camera. "Sorry, no more questions. I have an office to run." The television station wanted to beef up their ratings with a human-interest side to the story, but Becca wasn't going to put her family ties in the limelight. She felt protective of Lauren all of a sudden, which was strange, because it had usually been the other way around.

The phone rang as soon as she'd entered the building. She lowered and shuttered the blinds, even the ones over the glass door, and dead-bolted herself in. "Hello," she said as she snatched up the receiver on the desk.

"It's Lauren," came from the phone. "You okay in there?"

"So far." Becca stretched the cord to the windows and lifted a single louver to peek outside. "You should see the inflammatory signs out front. Chester has one that says, 'Save the canyons for *us,* not *them.*' Trish is waving a banner labeled, 'Down with BLM tyranny.' Of course, tyranny is spelled T-I-R-N-E-Y, but what else would you expect from Trish? That girl never could spell. Even Buddy skipped school to join the militant masses. His sign's written on a piece of cardboard with purple marker. 'The BLM's busting my daddy's bizness.' Geez, Lauren, you'd think I was a murderer. All I've ever tried to do is get along."

"I know," Lauren said. "It seems going for community approval doesn't always work."

It hadn't worked for her, that was true. She scanned the milling protesters. "I don't see Don Ray."

"He's here in the restaurant. So is Joe. I think they're the afternoon shift. Riot-for-Hire has installed himself by a window. Half the time he's on his cell phone; from what I overhear, he has demonstrations going in several towns at once."

"You're in the Mad House, too? Again?"

"Kayleen called in sick for the second time this week. Funny how Mom forgets to complain about having an environmentalist in the place when she needs my help." Lauren sounded amazingly cheery, considering. "Besides, I think she's decided this whole thing's good for business. She pulled out the old fifty-cup coffeemaker this morning for the first time since Gabe led the Raptors to a state championship."

Becca noticed a Suburban—the occupants looked like tourists—beeping its horn in an attempt to pass through the crowd. Chester and one of Al Hewitt's boys shouted invectives and stood in the way. "How long can this go on?" she asked.

"Too long. The CPWA organizer isn't as on the ball as Riot-for-Hire, but our members will be out in force starting tomorrow. I expect other environmental groups will join in. Let's just hope everyone stays peaceful."

"If I see Chester wielding a knife, I'll worry," Becca said. "But that's not going to happen because the sheriff's wide awake for once, patrolling Main Street like we're in a war zone."

"The comparison is easy to make," Lauren observed. "Be careful."

Becca promised to do so before she hung up and returned to her one-slat lookout post.

Mayor Al Hewitt made a pass through the crowd, shaking hands and patting backs all around. The demonstrators and signs had multiplied in the last few moments. THE BLM DE-STROYS FAMILIES and WILDERNESS IS A CROCK were new ones. Some of the sign wavers were people Becca had never seen before. Riot-for-Hire must have brought in outsiders to swell the protest numbers.

A camera flashed from across the street. Another TV van had just pulled up. Local demonstrators welcomed the media, since they hoped national—or at least statewide—notice would aid their cause and force the BLM to respond to their needs over national ones.

Becca hated having the community angry with her. She hated them blaming her, accusing her, just because she worked for the agency charged with handling this mess. Sick at heart, she left the window and tried to work, but the shouting in the street was distracting.

Arch McFarlane phoned to wish her luck in dealing with the protesters and media. He hinted that he could come over and help out; she said that wouldn't be necessary. Arch was a good man, but he'd been calling the office way more often than necessary, and she just didn't have time to chat. Maybe someday she'd welcome his awkward overtures of friendship, but not now. Not in the middle of a San Rafael insurrection.

A few moments later, someone from the Salt Lake City office called for an update. Next, a deejay from a radio station in Fairfield wanted a word. After an hour of solid calls, Becca turned off the ringer and quit answering the phone.

As noon approached she picked up the receiver, planning to see if Lauren could bring over some lunch from the restaurant. Also, Becca wanted to make arrangements for her mother or sister to pick Missy up after school. She did not want her little girl walking home through all the traffic and crowds and rowdy demonstrators.

She waited for a dial tone, but there wasn't one. "Becca?" a voice said. She knew who it was immediately.

"Joe? Why are you calling here?"

"I was thinking maybe we could meet up for coffee one day this week. We need to talk over . . . the, uh, child support. I don't have it again."

Becca sighed. "Good thing I wasn't counting on it. Missy and I will be okay. Pay me when you can, Joe. There's no reason to talk."

"But there is, Becca. There's a lot you don't know. My head's been upside down here lately."

That wasn't news. "Look, Joe, I'll catch you at the restaurant one evening, okay? I really don't have time for coffee breaks this week."

"Wait, Becca, there's more. We need to talk about—"

"Later, Joe. We'll talk later."

She hung up. Her head was starting to hurt, and she didn't want to hear Joe's bullshit. Why couldn't he ever get it together? What did he want from her?

A horn beeped out front. Giving up on her cluttered desk, she returned to her blind's-eye view. A black sedan crept to the edge of the crowd and parked in front of the sheriff's office. Rio got out carrying a small green-and-white cooler. Lunch, she assumed, touched by his thoughtfulness. She didn't need to call Lauren after all.

Even without food, Rio was a mood lifter if ever she saw one. He'd been to the house three times in the last week, and had finally talked her into letting him take a painting to his shop. She wouldn't let just anybody take one of her paintings. Rio was special—he was the first person who'd shown an interest in her work. Maybe he was becoming special to her for other reasons, too, but she didn't dwell on those.

Shouldering a path through the crowd, he shouted something while holding up the cooler. Sheriff Purdy cleared the way. Grinning, Becca unlocked the door and let Rio in.

"Turkey on wheat, dear one. I give it freely, in exchange for your everlasting love, and a passport to your tender heart."

"Rio, you're the best." Accepting the thick sandwich he offered, she peeled off the plastic wrap. "You are the most considerate man I've ever run across."

"You don't know me well enough to say that." He lounged in a chair, wearing a crisp white dress shirt and green tie, hands resting on his flat stomach, long legs stretched out in front of him. He had perfectly lovely brown eyes. All that, and a nice guy, too.

"I know what I see." She sat in a chair next to him and took her first bite of the sandwich.

"Rebecca, I am not here to be kind. All morning I tried to think of some reason to come to town and see you. When I heard of the demonstrators, I thought you might not want to leave the office, so . . . I had my excuse."

Becca felt a flush on her cheeks. To hide it, she bent over the sandwich, taking another bite.

"I never expected so many people out front," he said.

She wiped her mouth with a napkin from the cooler. "It'll

be worse when the enviro groups arrive. The standoff could last weeks."

Rio glanced at the jumbled stacks of paper on her desk. "Are you getting your work done?"

"Sort of. I'm really tired of paperwork."

He sat forward in his chair, mesmerizing her with his dark eyes. "When will you come to my shop, Rebecca? I've finished setting up my collection of Native American pottery. I'd like you to see it."

She did want to go to his shop sometime soon, but she was still wary of Rio, of her attraction to him. He was smooth. Maybe too smooth. "I'll have to wait until things settle down around here. Since we're on the subject of the shop, has anyone noticed my painting?" Asking about it had been on her mind from the moment Rio drove up outside.

An amused gleam in his eyes told her that he'd been waiting for her to ask. "A tourist from Los Angeles wandered in this morning. He paid the one-hundred-fifty-dollar price tag without question. We'll have to raise our prices on your work. Otherwise you will not be able to paint fast enough."

She jumped up, dropped the sandwich on the desk, and shouted, "Wow! I can't believe it!"

"And I can't believe no one has seen your talent before now." He glanced around the office walls. "That watercolor is undeniably yours. The sand painting, too. The simple lines convey the independent Western spirit to perfection. The vitality captures the eye." He gazed into Becca's eyes as if he saw that same vitality in her.

She turned away from him, embarrassed by his hungry look, afraid that she would look at him the same way.

He came up behind her. "I think you returned to this office too soon after your accident, Rebecca. You should not have to do paperwork during lunch. You must take some time for yourself." He put his hands on either side of her neck, thumbs caressing beneath her hair. He avoided the collarbone, which was still tender. The effect was all pleasure, and her knees felt weak; her lungs labored to keep up with the air she was breathing too quickly. Her appetite quickened, too. She was hungry, starving, and not for food.

"I could offer a full-body massage." He sounded both seductive and a little amused. "It would be my gift and my pleasure."

Becca let her chin fall to her chest and considered giving in. The blinds were closed; the door was locked. She could let him have at it on top of her deskful of papers.

"When you are ready," he whispered. "Only then. Be at ease, *querida.*"

Querida. She loved the sound of the word on his tongue. Soothing, tender, sweet. He seemed too good to be true, which ought to warn her, in big red letters, not to trust him *or* his velvety Spanish words.

She reached to her nape and patted his hand before taking two steps away, putting herself safely out of touching distance. "I'm not in the market for a full-service treatment, Rio." She might have given in, except that she hadn't been with anyone since Joe, and Joe had left scars all over her heart. She didn't want to risk that kind of pain again. Living all those years in a disintegrating marriage had taught her some caution.

Or maybe the knocking was what saved her. Someone was rattling and banging on the door frame. She realized the noisy crowd must have taken a break. She didn't hear them anymore, but whoever was outside wasn't about to be ignored.

With a glance of apology at Rio, she crossed the room and undid the lock.

"Hi." Gabe stood with hand upraised, prepared to knock again. "I wondered if everything was okay in here." He moved past her and stopped when he saw Rio.

The two men stared, taking each other's measure.

Becca did the introductions. "Rio brought lunch," she said. "Very thoughtful of him, don't you think?"

"No more than you deserve, Rebecca," Rio supplied.

"Very thoughtful," Gabe parroted, but only because Becca poked him in the ribs. He didn't like the way this Rio guy looked at her. On the other hand, she didn't seem to mind. She smiled at the man with a dopey expression, as though someone had hit her over the head with a two-by-four and she was seeing stars.

Rio expressed patently false pleasure at meeting Gabe, and kissed Becca on the cheek before he left them.

"What the hell was that all about?" Gabe demanded.

"Nothing," she said, an obvious lie.

Gabe raised an eyebrow. He didn't want to see her make a hasty decision and end up in a second disastrous relationship. "Unless I'm wrong about who Rio is, you can't know him very well. You're getting ahead of yourself, honey. You need to step back and be careful."

She set her mouth in a stubborn line that reminded Gabe of Lauren.

"You worry about your love affairs, I'll worry about mine," Becca said. "Why are you here, anyway?"

"First, to make sure you're alive and kicking. I see we're fine there, especially in the kicking department. You're almost as much of a mule as your little sister."

Becca ignored the goading. "Is there something else? Because unless you're going to be nice to me, you may as well leave and let me get some work done."

He hesitated, unsure how to bring up the subject that had been eating at him. "I, uh . . . Damn, I might as well blurt it out. I miss Laurie taking cheap shots at my oil wells and insulting me right and left. Life's a bore without her. Since we don't have to impress the gossips anymore, she's deserted me. I've tried everything to get her attention. The way she ignores me, you'd think I was a psychotic with a fatal attraction."

Becca smiled for the first time since he'd come in the door. "Are you saying you actually *like* Lauren?"

"I . . . Yes. Yes, that's what I'm saying. And she likes me."

"*Lauren* likes *you?*" Becca looked at him as if he'd lost his frigging mind.

"Yeah, I'm pretty sure that's correct," he admitted cautiously. So now he was sure Lauren hadn't told Becca anything about his efforts over the last week. Whether that weighed in as a plus or a minus, he couldn't guess.

Becca shook her head, still disbelieving. "I'm flabbergasted, Gabe, but . . ." Her lips curved upward. "Well, maybe I should have known. I think Lauren had a thing for you way back when. I never would have guessed it carried over all this time."

Gabe was glad Becca was taking it well. He'd been a little worried about spilling his problem to her.

But hell, he needed advice from somebody, and Becca seemed his best bet. Besides, once she knew what was going on, he doubted she'd want to miss out on a matchmaking scheme, especially one that involved her own sister.

"Keep in mind, we're talking about Laurie," he warned. "It's nearly impossible to predict what she thinks. All I'm saying is, I'm pretty sure I know what she *feels*. What I have to do—and it's not going to be easy—is convince her that spending time with me, and maybe caring about me, isn't a crime against nature."

"And you're here because . . . ?" She drew it out, waiting for him to jump in.

"I'm desperate, Becca. I need guidance."

"Wait. Weren't you telling little ol' me, just a few secs ago, that I didn't know shit from sherry about handling my own love life? And, really, you're right. If you want a dating counselor, put in a call to that love doc on the radio. I'm the last person you should—"

"Becca, honey, I only told you to be careful with this Rio dude because I don't want you to get hurt. Nobody blames you for Joe. You made a mistake, and you had the courage to live with it all these years."

Becca's glare softened a little. "Why, thank you, Gabe. That's nice of you to say."

"You may be rushing things, that's all, so take it easy, will you?" He cleared his throat. "Now, before the barracuda crowd gets back from lunch . . ." He hesitated, not quite knowing how to ask.

"Yes? What do you want me to do?" She acted as if she didn't know, but the gleam in her eyes said she'd guessed.

"You're good at coming up with audacious plans, Becca. And, damn, I sure as hell need one."

At ten o'clock the next Saturday morning, Lauren was hard at work on her laptop. In a search on an environmental law Web site, she'd just found an interesting prior case on blocking oil lease development on federal lands. She smiled, thinking that under other circumstances she'd love to discuss it with Gabe. But since she was avoiding him with all her dwindling resolve, and since she meant to use the information against Great Basin . . .

The phone rang.

"Where are you?" Hannah said. From the noise in the background, she was calling from the Mad House kitchen. "I thought you'd be over here by now."

"Was I supposed to be? I talked to Trish earlier, and she said she saw Kayleen walking over that way in her waitress uniform." Lauren had helped out at the Mad House on several shifts since the demonstrations started on Wednesday, but today she'd hoped to complete her official response to the BLM canyon management plan.

"Come over anyway," Hannah insisted. "You know Kayleen sashays more than she works, so when it gets busy I want you here. We'll just visit awhile until then. No excuses, baby. Don't let your poor old mother down."

Hannah was neither poor nor old, but Lauren agreed to do her bidding. She'd felt closer to her mother in the last few days than ever before, working with her, getting to know her routine, sharing the occasional chuckle over a customer's odd requests or cranky complaints. She didn't want to mess with success, such as it was.

Becca and Missy had gone on a shopping excursion. Before leaving, Becca had urged Lauren to go over to the Mad House and help out, even if Kayleen did happen to show up.

Lauren shrugged off what seemed to be Becca's ability to predict the future. Her sister had always understood Hannah much better than Lauren had, so perhaps it wasn't surprising.

Leaving a note under a refrigerator magnet on her way out of the house, she set off on the three-block walk. The day was clear and bright, pleasant and peaceful. Since it was Saturday, the BLM office was closed and no one was parading with signs on the sidewalk. Even the reporters had left town for the weekend.

As she entered the restaurant, she almost ran into Kayleen, who was swaying toward the alcove with a tray full of dirty dishes mounted on her shoulder. She wore a tight, ultra-short uniform and her usual assortment of facial rings. Without looking to see whom she'd narrowly missed, Kayleen cursed and kept going.

Lauren paused to size up the clientele. She noted several tables of environmentalists who'd been in town since midweek, carrying signs for the CPWA. The back of Riot-for-Hire's bald head shone in its usual booth, with Don Ray and Chester sitting across from him. Chester gave her the evil eye but made no comment.

The only real uproar had occurred on Thursday, when the

owners of the local motel and gas station had "come out" for Red Rock Wilderness. They'd been talking it over with Ezra in the restaurant alcove when one of the Lomax loggers, taking a break from protesting, had overheard. The word had spread like a brushfire with a tailwind. When the rest of the crowd had learned that two of San Rafael's own had gone astray, a shouting match started. Gossip and allegations flew for a good twenty-four hours before dying down. Since then, by tacit agreement, the restaurant had become a sort of limited sanctuary.

Lauren spotted Hannah behind the lunch counter, fiddling and shuffling as if she expected some new incident to rock the Mad House foundations. When Hannah's greeting for her younger daughter included a rush forward for an awkward hug, Lauren became concerned. "What is it, Mom?"

"I'm thinking you and I need to have ourselves a nice chat, Lauren. One of those heart-to-hearts the magazine articles talk about."

"You and me?" Emotional exposure wasn't in Hannah's nature any more than it was in Lauren's. In the three weeks Lauren had been in town, they hadn't yet said anything that mattered.

"What's wrong with a heart-to-heart?" Hannah asked. "I'm not getting any younger, you know. I hope you've forgiven me for being so snippy when you first came home. Truth to tell, I don't know what I'd have done without you this week."

"Without me, you might have had business as usual," Lauren reminded her as she took a seat on a lunch counter stool.

Hannah nodded. "Your being here has stirred things up, but I guess that's not necessarily bad. Not if we needed stirring."

Lauren was flabbergasted at hearing such a statement from her mother. "Aren't you unhappy about my radical friends hanging out in here?" She kept her voice down, because a trio of enviro activists occupied the nearest table.

Locals whispered that the two men with long gray hair in ponytails were hippie communist pinko Nazis, but Lauren and others in enviro circles knew them as the Brothers K, retired engineers from the Wasatch front. The third, a younger man who went by Hayduke, wasn't with the CPWA or previously known to Lauren, but since he was willing to carry a sign, she welcomed him. Hayduke was a huge, burly fellow, the nervous type, always tapping or shaking something, and his head of wild black hair looked as if it hadn't been brushed in weeks. All three men were eating a big breakfast for the fourth morning in a row.

Hannah leaned forward to whisper, "I'm getting used to the crowds." And the tips, Lauren figured. The Brothers K were particularly good tippers.

Through the window she spied Gabe mounting the porch steps with Ezra beside him. The two of them sat down outside on adjoining wooden chairs. Their heads, one gray and one red-gold, were bent close together, as if they were co-conspirators in some devious plot, though Lauren couldn't imagine what that plot might be.

For the last few days Gabe seemed to have given up his silly-sweet courting campaign. She told herself that was a good thing, because she'd been weakening, and she couldn't have held out much longer.

Knowing she'd come through with her principles intact didn't help. She wanted to run out there and talk to Gabe, see how he was doing. She wanted to run her fingers through his curly hair. She wanted to kiss him and feel him against her and tell him how much she . . .

Her throat clogged just thinking about his dear, lovesick-sounding notes and his noseprint on her bedroom window glass. She missed him terribly.

But she wasn't anybody's pushover. She congratulated

herself on keeping her distance, as was surely a tribute to faultless logic and flawless ethics. She was right, blast it, and she was sticking with her decision.

She started to rise from her bar stool. "I can't stay, Mom." She'd sneak out the back way before Gabe saw her.

"Sit down," Hannah ordered sharply.

Startled, Lauren did.

"I'm wondering about the menu for next week," Hannah said in a conciliatory tone as she moved up and down the business side of the counter, spraying it with something that smelled like lemon juice. "I thought I'd serve Ezra's barbecued pork recipe for the lunch special one day, but I don't know how much meat to order. What do you think?"

Lauren narrowed her eyes. "Since when do you ask my opinion on recipes or menus? I know nothing about food."

"You could learn," Hannah said. "I used to consult your daddy on menus. He didn't know anything at first, either."

Lauren glanced outside, where Gabe and Ezra still sat talking. Maybe Gabe wouldn't even come inside. At any rate, running from him in a town this small wasn't exactly practical. She rested her forearms on the glass counter. If Hannah wanted to call this a heart-to-heart, Lauren might as well learn something personal. "Mom . . . tell me about you and Dad. How you met, and where. The love story."

"Don't you know?" Hannah asked, looking surprised.

"Only the basics." She knew Hannah had grown up in foster homes on the East Coast, while Lauren's father had come from a wealthy Southern family. She knew her parents had met in Atlanta, but, to her recollection, Hannah had never elaborated. Now that Lauren's own heart had sparked at the wrong time, for the wrong man, she needed all the insights she could get.

Hannah propped her elbows on the glass, smiling a little, gazing into empty space. "I first saw him when I was on one of those peace, love, and racial-equality marches down South."

"You, Mother? You were an activist?"

Hannah looked almost chagrined. "Not much of one, not at first. I was along for the ride and the party, until I met Chloe."

"Ezra's Chloe? I didn't know you knew her before they moved to San Rafael."

"I knew her before she knew Ezra. She introduced me to your father," Hannah confided. "That was all it took. Daniel Van Horn made a person want to open up and talk. He made me feel good just being around him. Most people don't care much about anything outside themselves, but he wasn't like that. He was fresh out of law school, brimming with ideals about truth and justice. He wanted to save the world, and I believed he could do it, if anyone could. Best of all, he found something in me worth loving.

"His family hated me on sight, because I wasn't their kind. I ran a cheap little coffee shop. I'd never been to college. Didn't know the Junior League from the Daughters of the American Revolution, and that was important to those folks, believe you me. They forced him to choose, and he, rest his soul, said there was no contest. He picked me. I hope he was never sorry."

Lauren flattened her palms on the damp, lemon-scented counter. Her parents had always seemed direct opposites to her. She wondered what kind of love they'd shared, what strange attraction had brought them together. "How long before you married?"

"Two months." Hannah laughed. "I was young, and so sure of myself."

Lauren had trouble picturing her mother full of youthful passion. "You were happy with him, weren't you?"

"Yes, I was happy." Hannah bowed her head. "Right up to the day he got himself killed."

Lauren wondered why she'd never felt her mother's anguish before, never realized that her love ran so deep. She wanted to rush around the counter and hug her mother tight, but she didn't want to embarrass her. Neither of them was good at showing emotions. Instead Lauren just patted her hand. "Thanks, Mom. I'm glad you told me."

"Becca's already heard the story plenty of times. All you had to do was ask."

Lauren felt a sting of the old rejection because Becca had known and she hadn't. Her heart ached because she and Hannah had bypassed so much sharing, so many years when they might have been close. "What else did I miss, Mom? And why? Why couldn't we ever talk?"

"We both missed a lot, baby; I can see that now," Hannah said. "And I don't know why it was. Even when you were tiny you went to your father, not me. I thought you chose him because he was smarter. Now I wonder if you did it because I was too overbearing. I tried to make you into the sweet, docile little girl I thought you should be, but you were too stubborn and willful to bend. When all is said and done, I'm thankful you're so strong."

Lauren was shocked. "You're saying that's good? Me, being me, is good?"

Hannah nodded, rubbing the counter in small, jerky swipes. "I thought a child had to be molded. Daniel, though, he just loved you and let you grow. I wish I'd done better by you." She stopped cleaning and looked up, her hazel eyes glistening with tears. "Maybe I can make up for it, now that I've figured out where I went wrong."

The tears made Lauren angry. So many times she'd wanted to cry, but she hadn't had a mother who'd dry those tears, or encourage her to let them flow in the first place. "I was hurting, Mom. Even when I had Dad, I was hurting because I didn't think *you* could love me." She shook her head.

"At least I understand a little better now, but I don't know if I can . . . forgive. Not right away."

Hannah reached out and touched her daughter's hand. "I know, and I don't expect it. But let's try, okay? Let's both of us try, that's all I ask." She sniffed self-consciously.

As bells jingled, Lauren looked toward the door, hastily brushing a speck of moisture from her own cheek.

Gabe and Ezra came in, arms linked. The two men were grinning like cream-fed Cheshire cats. Ezra went on into the alcove archway, feeling his way with his cane and humming "Moon River," a longtime favorite of Chloe's. When Gabe ambled toward her, Lauren had the distinct feeling that something was afoot. She wished she'd escaped earlier.

Hannah touched Lauren's cheek gently, almost shyly. "Do me a favor, baby. For once in your life just go along to get along."

Before Lauren could determine what that meant, Gabe was beside her asking, "How's it going?"

"Fair to partly cloudy," she answered, still puzzling over Hannah's advice. She glanced at Gabe, whose expression had turned serious all of a sudden, which further increased her apprehension.

He sat on the stool next to hers. "Remember how you said you wanted to see my drilling sites? Well, today's the day. For your own hardheaded edification, I'm going to show you what I do, and how I do it. The lesson'll be good for you, and good for community relations." His voice carried clear across the room and bounced off the rear wall.

The hum of conversation ended as if someone had hit a mute button. Since the subject of their possible romance had been a recent blip on the gossip radar screen, the mostly male clientele in the restaurant would risk expulsion from their wives' beds if they failed to pick up on the latest tidbit.

Gabe and Lauren hadn't been seen together in over a week, so Lauren supposed the word was out that she was too snooty and mean-spirited to give an oil man a chance. He, of course, remained God's gift to San Rafael, and fair game for the likes of Cyn Biggs.

Lauren had met Cyn. She didn't for a moment believe that Gabe would go for a woman so obviously gunning for him, but she didn't want to leave him open to the assault. She wanted—oh, so badly wanted—to have him all to herself.

If she went with him today, the town would probably assume she was doing it for business reasons, that she was being obliging and gracious, willing to give the opposition a listen. Not going would make her seem even more closed-minded than the San Rafaelites already believed she was. Of course, there was also the third option, that people would think she was being coerced in some way, bought out.

Hannah looked worried. *Go along,* she mouthed. So she'd known Gabe was going to ask. Apparently she approved, which surprised Lauren. She'd thought Hannah was still determined to fix Becca up with Gabe, but maybe their mother had decided that was hopeless and was going for the next best thing. Lauren felt deflated. The only heart-to-heart she'd ever had with her mom had turned out to be a setup.

Scanning the room, she saw people at tables and booths craning their heads toward the counter. She found she didn't care what any of them thought. She knew what she wanted to do, what she had to do. Her heart was fresh out of barriers, at least when it came to Gabe. He'd worn away the last shred of her resistance.

She looked at him, trying not to smile too widely, trying not to give away how very glad she was. He'd given her a perfectly good excuse to steal one more day with him, and no way was she going to pass it up.

"Oh, all right," she snapped. "I give."

The blue in Gabe's eyes sparkled. The sun coming through the windows seemed to catch in his bright hair. He bounded off the padded stool, pulling Lauren upright, too.

With a hand on the small of her back, he urged her toward the front door.

Outside, the Jeep was waiting. The open back was packed with colorful quilts Lauren recognized as belonging to her mother, a big picnic basket and cooler, plus Bullwinkle, who began panting and wagging his tail as soon as they appeared. This was more than a tour of Gabe's oil wells, Lauren realized. She stopped in her tracks. "What's—"

"I thought we'd finish up our rounds with food. You don't mind a little social interaction over dinner, do you?"

She should mind. He'd tricked her, and she didn't like being tricked. She also noticed Ezra lumbering behind her onto the Mad House porch. He looked inordinately pleased with himself, which made her wonder how much he'd known about all this.

But when Gabe resumed hustling her toward the Jeep, she didn't oppose him. In fact, she wanted to grab his hands and pull him along. To keep from making a fool of herself, she put on her arctic royalty act, since it was what he expected, what everyone expected. She reminded herself to frown.

Bullwinkle raised his snout to the sky and sent up a howl full of impatience and longing.

Lauren's own spirits soared like an eagle on the canyon's summer wind. She, too, was eager to experience the adventure, fraught with hazard and potential heartache though it might be.

Chapter Seventeen

The Rolling Stones blasted from the speakers as Gabe tooled along the highway. "I can't get no . . . satisfaction." The tune seemed appropriate. He'd resigned himself to spending a frustrating afternoon, being close to Lauren, wanting her. After the last ten days since she'd walked out on him without looking back, he didn't know how much longer he could play this goddamn courting game. Hell, he'd never had so much trouble capturing a woman's attention. Why did his charm have to fail the one time he'd really tried to use it?

He glanced over at Lauren, sitting beside him, dark hair whipping out behind her as the wind blew through the open Jeep. Sunglasses hid her eyes, but he thought he saw a smile playing on her tempting lips. Maybe he'd gotten through to her after all. Maybe she was just making him suffer. He wanted to pull the Jeep over and kiss her. Now, before she stiffened up and turned tough and businesslike again.

"Why?" Lauren finally shouted above the road noise, wind and Mick Jagger. "Why did you coerce me in front of my mother and the whole town?"

"Because I'd tried everything else. You'd slammed all the doors, locked the windows, and even told little Missy not to let me in," Gabe shouted back. "I'm not going to let you condemn me to never seeing you again until you've at least given me a fair trial."

She reached over to click off the radio. "All right, Gabe. You've got it. One afternoon." But since her trace of a smile had vanished, he figured their continued relationship could be a hard sell.

The chain he kept behind the rear seat for emergency towing rattled fiercely as they jounced over a bump in the road. Lauren turned to see what was making all the racket, and Bullwinkle, ever alert, took the opportunity to work her over with a sliming.

"Yuck." She hastily faced front and wiped her cheeks with the hem of her eyelet blouse. The holes in the material showed just enough skin to keep him wondering what, if anything, she wore underneath.

When she'd retucked the blouse into her jeans, she asked, "Whose idea was this, anyway?"

He hesitated for a couple of seconds. "Mine."

"Come on, Gabe, I know better. Good grief, what an embarrassment. Becca was in on it, wasn't she?"

"Laurie, if you needed a wild scheme, who would *you* go to? Your sister has more creativity in that direction than anybody I've ever met. She left Missy over at Trish's house, then met me and my Jeep behind the restaurant. She packed up the supplies while Hannah kept you busy inside. Ezra and I guarded the porch to make sure you didn't leave that way. Believe me, Becca had more fun being in on this than she's had in months."

"She wasn't . . . upset?"

"About us? Maybe for a couple of nanoseconds. Then she was rooting for us all the way."

"I'm glad to hear that. But have you forgotten that Becca's plans always go wrong somehow?" she asked, too sweetly.

Gabe scowled. He had put Becca's success record out of his mind, mostly because Becca's and Hannah's involvement

282 Mary Jane Meier

had seemed the most expeditious way to get Lauren alone. Wondering what *could* go wrong, he wheeled off the pavement onto a gravel road.

The force of the turn slid Lauren in his direction, but the seat belt kept her from coming all the way over. She straightened and shifted to face him. He wished he could read her eyes through the sunglasses, but he was heartened to see that her mouth was verging on a grin.

"If you think you're going to get me out here alone and have your way with me, think again," she said. "I'm not that easy."

"You, easy? Getting a two-ton gorilla in a wrestling hold would be easier." He studied her cautiously. "If you don't mind my asking, is there anything that *would* soften you up?"

She smiled—full-out, plain as day. "If there were, do you think I'd tell you?"

"No," he said. "And, come to think of it, I don't want your advice anyway. Trying to guess what's in your head is part of what makes being around you so damn entertaining."

"You made points with the paper spaceship." She was giving hints after all, it seemed. "But the poetry? Really, Gabe. Much too gushy. And that friendship bracelet, although it was about the sweetest thing anybody's ever made for me, was not the height of fine craftsmanship. You need lessons."

He laughed. "If you want to give me some, that's fine with me."

She smiled wider. "No, no, you need professional help. Your level of ineptness is beyond my abilities."

"Laurie, darlin', I doubt that. For any problem I have, you've got the cure." He recalled saying something like that in his attempt at an erotic note.

He thought she might be blushing, but he wasn't sure. She opened her mouth for a comeback, then seemed to think better of it. Instead she looked around. "Where are we going?"

"We're headed for a spot where I hope I can heighten your

goodwill toward men, especially me." While she frowned and looked puzzled, he grinned and kept driving. A few miles down the road, he pulled over and parked.

Baffled, Lauren took in the view, wondering what was up. They were well north of the canyon, on a high, broad plateau. No oil derricks. Nothing manmade. "Why did you bring me here?"

"This is the site of that August EPA violation, Laurie."

She took off her seat belt, stood up in the Jeep, and did a three-hundred-sixty-degree survey. "Are you sure?" She didn't see any sign of the devastation described in the report she'd read.

"I'm positive." Gabe hopped out of the Jeep, gesturing and explaining. "We hauled out the concrete rig platform, got rid of the metal, buried the nontoxic materials, and disposed of the rest. Then we replanted natural vegetation over the scars."

When she joined him, he took her hand and walked with her away from the truck as they viewed the wide expanse of open land. "What do you think?"

The ground was a little uneven in places, but coral-colored globemallows and tall, elegant golden prince's plumes bloomed in all but a football field–sized area, and even that had a sparse covering of native grasses, small sage, and young pinyon and juniper.

"It's . . . amazing," Lauren said. "I wouldn't have thought, after such a short time . . ."

He pointed out where the rig platform had been, but the only remaining evidence was a few crumbs of concrete. Bullwinkle romped in front of them and managed to scare up a jackrabbit for a playful chase.

"We hand-planted a lot of this, Laurie. I could do the same thing in the canyon. I wouldn't destroy—"

"Sorry," Lauren said. "There is no comparison, as you well know. The terrain here is vastly different. Even temporary roads down there could cause irreparable damage to wildlife, to stream integrity, to—"

"I get the picture." He raised an eyebrow. "But you have to admit that Great Basin did a good job up here, don't you?"

"Well, yes."

"And you don't really want to argue about the rest now, do you?" He looked happy and hopeful, and the way he asked his leading questions made Lauren feel as if she were being hypnotized.

She shook her head. "No, Gabe. We'll leave the arguing for another day." She certainly didn't want to spend this precious time in conflict.

"That's as good a deal as I could hope for." He grinned at her. "I know it's going to be hard on you, and I hate to cramp your style. So if you change your mind and *need* to argue, let me know. Maybe we could do some . . . negotiating."

She thought negotiations with Gabe might keep her mind off controversy for a long, long time.

"Meanwhile, just to test your resolve to stay agreeable, I'll take you by a rig site. That is . . . if you want to go."

She did. She wanted to know more about Gabe, about his work. All about him. And this might be her only chance.

With the two of them plus Bullwinkle back in the Jeep, they sped more than thirty miles south to a metal skeleton that dominated the landscape. The rig platform was noisy with activity. Gabe ordered the dog to stay put while he outfitted Lauren in a hard hat like the ones he and the crew wore, and took her up onto the steel mesh so he could show her where the drilling pipe disappeared into the earth, and, more significantly for her environmental concern, how the mechanism was designed to prevent blowouts.

The tool pusher seemed to be the man in charge. Lauren knew him as one of the Rigsby boys, a few years older than Gabe. Of the remainder of the crew, she recognized the family names of three of them. Gabe explained about mud log-

ging, wirelines, and core samples, all ways of figuring out
the qualities of the formations and the likelihood of finding
extractable oil.

In a nearby dented aluminum trailer, she met the mud logger, who turned out to be a woman who'd been in Becca's
class through school. The crew was a living testament that
Great Basin could help the town and had already done so.

A sentimental warmth settled in Lauren's chest. In the
ways that counted, Gabe hadn't really changed from the boy
she'd grown up with. He worked hard, knew how to succeed,
and was able to accomplish his goals through teamwork. He
balanced generosity with ambition, love of land with love of
people.

Deciding that she might as well make this trip a meaningful goodwill gesture of her own, she asked Gabe to come
with her to the Jeep, where she checked the contents of the
picnic basket. "Just as I thought," she announced. "Mom put
enough food in here for a dozen day laborers. Why not pass
out some to the crew?"

Gabe frowned at her. "You're kidding, right? I thought
we'd . . ."

Obviously he was eager to move on to the next stage of
his plan, but Lauren wheedled. Okay, maybe she even argued
a little—just until he gave in.

"Laurie, honey, I— Shit. It's not what I had in mind, but
go ahead, if it makes you happy."

She smiled to herself, knowing exactly how he felt. She
wanted to be alone with him, too, but she really did want to
offer something to the crew. And since Gabe had used a certain amount of deception to get her here, she didn't think a
little payback was out of order. He tended to be overconfi-
dent, teasing her without mercy. He'd wooed her without
mercy, too. She intended to give him a taste of what she'd
been suffering for days.

On the steps in front of the aluminum trailer, they shared

lunch with the crew. While the workers ate and joked with each other, Lauren sat next to Gabe and stole glances at him.

He wasn't trying very hard to hide his impatience. He spent most of his time scowling, not even bothering to join in the conversation. Lauren didn't say a word to him, but she did talk to everyone else. In between, she added to Gabe's frustration by reaching over with barely-there touches on his shoulder, his knee, his hand.

He soon seemed to realize what she was up to and began his own onslaught, driving her to distraction with the occasional whisper in her ear, brush against her breast, hand on her thigh, caress on her hips. She never would have started the game if she'd realized she was dealing with a master of the art. In minutes she was practically squirming where she sat on the trailer steps.

She ran out of patience before he did. She feared she'd jump on him and start tearing his clothes off right in front of the rig crew. Abruptly she stood, brushed the crumbs off her lap, and suggested they leave.

Gabe offered her a slow "gotcha" grin before ambling off to the rig platform to check some numbers before they left. Sammie, the mud logger, drew Lauren aside. From the surreptitious glances between her and her coworkers, Lauren assumed she was speaking for all of them. "If it makes any difference, we're all hoping you'll take our jobs into account next time you make a move for your environmental group, Ms. Van Horn. It would be bad news for us, and for the company, if Great Basin ends up being shut out of those Red Rock leases."

Leave us alone, Sammie was saying. *Give us a chance to work and live.* Lauren wished she knew how to reply, or had a good compromise, a good something, to offer, but she didn't know what to say. She was still trying to come up with a meaningful reply when Gabe's return saved her. Sammie wished Lauren a nice day and got back to her work.

Lauren was quiet as she and Gabe drove away, toward the canyon and then along the craggy bluffs of a formation known as Devil's Castle.

"I liked your crew," Lauren said finally. "And it's obvious they like you and want to keep working for you."

Gabe glanced her way. "They'd like anybody who pays them three times what they'd make otherwise. I didn't know how they'd feel about you, whether there'd be friction, but it went pretty well. That was nice of you, sharing the food. A good move. Won't make card-carrying CPWA members out of any of them, but I think you smoothed over the hostility."

Lauren didn't think she'd made a lot of progress, but she'd put forth the effort. And she did understand Gabe and those who worked for him better, as a result.

He pulled off the road at a high point on the rim, a place they both knew.

"We're stopping here?"

"What does it look like?" he asked, setting the parking brake.

"But this is . . ."

"The San Rafael version of Lovers' Lane." He smiled warily. "I figure a little atmosphere can't hurt. If you hadn't been so damn nice to my employees, we'd have had our picnic up here, too."

"Sorry," she said, the picture of innocence. "I thought you were fine with sharing."

He turned toward her, knowing full well that she knew how much he'd wanted her all to himself. "Did you have to pass out the pink-iced cupcakes, the very last of the fruit tarts, and even pour all of the iced tea? I'd say you carried generosity a little far."

She raised her stubborn chin, hiding a smile. "Then we're even, because your asking me for a date in the middle of a Mad House crowd was way over the line."

He got out of the Jeep and went around to her side, taking

her hand and pulling her up beside him. "Look, woman, what do you want? I've done all the romancing I can stand. And I'm not willing to let you throw us away just because we don't fit into some cramped little pigeonhole where you think love belongs."

"What pigeonhole?"

"The one Dr. Whoever and Tom fit in."

"Tim," she corrected. "And they are none of your business."

"I think they are, because you must have thought they were right for you. Why, Laurie?"

"We . . . uhm, we had the same values. At least . . . I thought we did. Besides being reasonably attractive, they supported the CPWA, seemed gung-ho environment, were dedicated to worthwhile careers. They were . . ."

"Were they fun?"

"Well, I *could* carry on a conversation with either of them without arguing. We—"

"Wait. No arguing? Darlin', you *love* to argue. Those guys sound about as exciting as solitary confinement. No wonder they didn't last." He bent down to give her a quick kiss on her mouth. So brief all it did was sensitize and tantalize. She wanted more.

He shook his head with a one-sided smile that said he knew what she wanted, and he wasn't going to give it to her . . . yet. Lord in heaven, why had she ever started with the frustration game?

"C'mon, let's go see the sunset," he urged.

Lauren went along because, frustrating or not, there was no place she'd rather be, no one she'd rather be with.

Bullwinkle jumped from the Jeep's open back and began bounding around like an oversize kangaroo. Afternoon sun hazed over the canyon country. Ancient, twisted juniper and pinyon cast isolated patches of shade. A lone ponderosa pine inclined over the rim at an angle that defied gravity.

Together, Gabe and Lauren strolled across the sandstone to the edge of Red Rock Canyon, and looked down into the yawning abyss. He draped his arm around her and pulled her close to his side. Lauren leaned against him, feeling content, at peace. They gazed at each other, minus the sunglasses they'd left in the Jeep.

"Too bad we can't just let the wind blow us together like cloud lovers up in the sky," she said. "I've been thinking about that a lot. I wish . . ."

He brushed a kiss onto her forehead. "I'm thinking that if you don't let me stay in your life, Laurie, I'm going to take up meteorology. I'll figure out a way to make my own damn air currents."

She laughed. "If you put your mind to it, I think maybe you could."

Holding hands, they strolled along the rim as the red ball of the sun descended toward the horizon.

"I've always loved a canyon sunset," he said. "As the sun goes down, the shadows rise layer by sandstone layer. It's like watching a march of time through the eons."

She leaned her head on his shoulder. "The canyon is Earth's history," she said. "It cuts right through all the modernization, all the changes man has wrought, and goes back to basics."

"Today versus yesterday. And everything in between," he mused. "The rocks hold the secrets, because they've outlasted everything else."

She glanced up at him, grateful to be sharing this moment in time with him and the rocks and the sun. "I like hearing your thoughts, Gabe. I always have." She liked so many things about him.

In quiet companionship, they sat on the sandstone near the canyon rim, his arm over her shoulders, her arm around his waist, and watched the colors on the cliff walls change from hazy gold to deep russet. The sky melted through shades of pink, rose, and purple.

Bullwinkle had finished checking out new scents. He circled them and then settled himself on the sun-warm rock right beside Lauren, plopping his big head in her lap. His muzzle pressed on her thigh, drool making a wet spot on her jeans. She scratched his ears, accepting the dog as part of the scene, part of Gabe.

As the light faded they began to talk of little things. Gabe told how he'd started up Randolph Drilling, choosing the right leases, making good on them. She responded by telling stories about her more eccentric law professors. And about her work for the Sierra Club during the summers.

"You chose environmental law because of your father, didn't you, Laurie?"

Since she'd been thinking about her dad, she wasn't surprised Gabe had asked. Finally she was able to talk about him. And Gabe listened. He seemed to know what she needed to say, seemed to ask the right questions to draw out all the memories and pain that had, at times, festered and ached inside her. "I admired him so much, Gabe. I've tried to follow in his footsteps. I've tried, but . . ."

"But the footsteps seem too big? I know what you mean. I've felt like that with my own dad, lots of times. Except I still have him around, so I can see his faults, too. He's not perfect. I doubt your dad was either." Gabe rubbed his hand along her arm, soothing and gentle. "He did love you, though. I can remember seeing you with him, usually with the two of you bent over one book or another."

Lauren's eyes burned with tears as Gabe drew her close and kissed her cheek.

"I don't think he'd have cared whether you followed his path or your own," Gabe said. "Either way, he'd have loved you for who you are."

They sat in silence for a moment or two, watching the sky

darken to a deep midnight blue, listening to the sounds of the night. The dog rose, stretched, and left them for a romp in the darkness. Moments later they heard his mournful bay as he found something to hunt.

The first bats swooped low; crickets began to chirp. A great horned owl, far down in the canyon, sent up its eerie cry. She leaned against Gabe, feeling closer to him than ever. The night seemed to encircle them, whispering, urging, nudging them into their own private niche of time and space.

As Venus appeared and shone like a lighthouse perched above the desert floor, Gabe touched the side of her face and turned her toward him. He kissed her mouth, soft and slow. Lauren had never felt such tenderness. She wanted the moment to last forever.

When he lifted his head, his eyes were clear, pale blue in the impending night. Beneath her hands, his arms were muscle and sinew and heat. Lots of heat.

His gaze roamed over her face, settling on her mouth. "I love your lips, Laurie. Did you know they get redder and fuller when you're in the middle of an argument? Same as when you feel passion, desire, need. It's a dead giveaway. Makes me want to kiss you senseless."

"Not senseless. Nothing you could do would—"

He grinned. "Don't bait me, or I just might have to prove you wrong. And I'm trying to hold off, because there's a tradition to follow here. We're supposed to have a campfire, and marshmallows, and all the hand-holding and hip-bumping and secret-telling that goes with courting in San Rafael. Once we've made it through the fundamentals, I'll see about kissing you till your brain malfunctions."

As they returned to the Jeep, she bumped her hip toward his at the same time he tried it, with the result being a little more oomph than they had counted on. "Ow," she cried. He laughed, pulled her closer, and offered to kiss it better.

"Maybe . . . later," she said, giving him a look that was as close to flirtation as she'd ever attempted before. From Gabe's self-satisfied expression, he was confident that he'd get his chance.

She spread Hannah's quilt a few feet in front of the fire ring, in a sandy area where teenage passions had raged during their high school era.

"Ever heard the rumor that Trish and Don Ray's firstborn was conceived right here?" he asked as he made a neat teepee of branches and twigs.

"That's not a rumor," Lauren informed him. "Trish swears it's true." She sat back on her heels in the middle of the starburst pattern that she remembered her mother stitching during a quilting party at their house one summer evening long ago. She felt at home here with him, more than she had in any other place in her memory.

He lit the fire, blowing on it to ignite the smoke into flame. She smelled the sharp scent of burning pinyon. The wood popped and sparked in the otherwise still air. When it was crackling through the twigs, already catching the first of the branches, he left it and came to her. He knelt on the quilt and outlined her cheekbone in a gentle, romantic gesture that made her insides flutter.

And then he settled in beside her, pulling her close.

"Familiar, isn't it?" he said, referring to another night when they'd enjoyed a campfire together in this exact same spot.

The night of Gabe's and Becca's graduation, there had been a party here. Since the school was small, everyone was invited. Lauren hadn't had a date, but Becca had urged her to go anyway. Almost as soon as they arrived, Gabe and Becca had had a heated argument. Becca had flounced off with her cheerleader friends for the rest of the evening. Her pique had stemmed from Gabe's choosing a Texas college over a Utah one, even though it was obvious to Lauren that a better scholarship warranted the decision.

It had been Lauren who had stayed with Gabe, ostensibly to soothe his ruffled feelings, but secretly she was pleased to have him to herself, with no Becca to divert his interest. The entire evening had seemed almost magical to her. She'd felt the first stirrings of real desire as they'd sat side by side, staring into the fire. She'd longed to touch him, but hadn't had the courage. She'd yearned for him to touch her, to kiss her, but he hadn't seemed to notice.

Then they'd been friends. Now "friends" didn't seem to be enough. Not close enough. Not deep enough. Not enough in any way.

He touched her throat, idly caressing along the V-neckline of her eyelet blouse. "I wish you'd been older, Laurie."

"I wanted you to kiss me that night," she admitted. "I was fifteen, you know. I wanted you to notice me as a woman."

He smiled. "I wanted to put my arm around you, but I didn't want to make you mad. Damn, even then you were prickly."

She made up for it by putting her arms around him now. "I was prickly because . . . the truth is, I'd had a huge crush on you for years, and I didn't want you to know it. And even though you talked to me like an equal, I felt gauche and childish. While you were"—she exaggerated a sigh—"*so* strong and manly."

He grinned. "I'm better now, woman. And you're all grown up, beautiful and sexy. You're driving me crazy, playing hard to get."

"You should talk," she said. "You have no idea how crazy you've made me with all your little letters over the last week. This is your comeuppance."

He leaned close to her ear and whispered a few lines of his naughtiest note. She felt an all-over flush, even more than when she'd read those words alone. She tried to turn her head so he wouldn't guess, but from his soft laugh she knew he knew. She laughed, too, relaxing against him, because it didn't matter. She couldn't hide anything she was feeling from him, and the beauty of it was that she didn't have to.

It was pitch dark by then, and quiet, a good time for sharing. "Tell me about all the women in your life," she said. "Because if I'm going to be one of them, I want to know the competition."

He brushed his fingers through her hair and urged her to lay her head on his shoulder. "Not one compared to you, Laurie. Sure you want to talk about them?"

"Just hit the high points," she instructed.

And so he did. A sorority girl. A cowgirl who rode saddle broncs in rodeos. "I fell hard for a woman geologist the first summer I worked as an oil field roughneck. She took me to her bed for a while, which was . . . a real learning experience. It turned painful when I figured out that she liked variety, and there were plenty of young bucks ready to oblige. I got in a fistfight with one of them. Broke my nose, and the lady had no sympathy. She told me to get lost."

Lauren tested his nose and found a bump on it. She felt sad for him, for the time when he'd been with someone else, someone who had treated him badly. "Was your heart broken?" She very much wanted to love away the hurt.

"Cracked clean in two." He held her hand over the injured organ. "I recovered. Later there was Fran."

"What happened with her?"

"We had some good times, Fran and I. She liked designer clothes and champagne parties more than going outside to look at the stars, but I was pushing thirty, tired of hunting for perfection, and ready to settle down with one good woman."

"Why didn't you?

"Because once we started talking marriage, I realized her whole life revolved around Austin society functions. One Saturday night I found myself at a black-tie affair, bound up in a cummerbund and feeling like a painted monkey on a short leash. I'd been to those events before with Fran, but if

I married her, it would be a life sentence. Both of us were going to end up miserable. So we split. She's engaged now—to somebody who's better suited to her than I ever was. I call her once in a while to see how she's doing. I'm happy that she's happy."

"Do you miss her?"

"I miss not having someone I can share everyday joys and sorrows with, but she wasn't the right one. My dad has told me how he felt about my mother. I always hoped I'd have something like they had. I want a woman who makes me complete."

Lauren wanted the same in a man, but she couldn't define or judge such a thing. "How? How does that happen between two people? How can you tell?"

"I don't know how, but I think I know who. In spite of all the ways we disagree, talking to you, tonight, is just like I knew it would be. As natural as breathing."

Lauren smiled. "I know. I want to tell you things, Gabe, even things you're not supposed to know. I was researching an angle to use against Great Basin, and all of a sudden I found myself wondering what you'd think about the case law I'd dredged up. It didn't make sense, but—"

"But *we* make sense, Laurie. We do, and don't you forget it."

Bullwinkle came galloping up to the fire, sniffing around until he found the bag of marshmallows Gabe had forgotten was part of the San Rafael tradition.

"You hungry?" he asked her.

"I am. But I'm not sure marshmallows are exactly what I want."

He grinned. "It's the appetizer, darlin'. We're working up to the main course." Already he'd taken out his knife to sharpen a stick. After blowing off the wood shavings and testing the point he'd made, he held it out to Lauren. Obligingly, she stuck on two marshmallows.

"You're gonna love it," he said with enthusiasm, holding the stick out over the campfire. "If I do say so myself, nobody roasts a better marshmallow." He drew her to his side and took his time about getting her settled in just the right spot, her head on his shoulder, turned just enough so he could lean down and . . .

"They're on fire!" Lauren giggled.

"Damn." He jerked the blazing stick out of the flames and blew until the sparks were out. Making a rueful face, he held the blackened blobs on the end of the stick out to Lauren. "Want a taste?"

She grimaced. "I haven't had burned marshmallows in years. What a treat," she said, half-sarcastic, half-teasing. "Actually, I think the last one I had that was roasted this 'perfectly' was a Gabe Randolph special." She giggled again when she bit into the charcoal-hued crust and came away trailing warm, sticky, sugary marshmallow insides all over her face and down the front of her blouse. "Look what you've done to me! I'm a mess."

"I'm the cleanup crew," he said, after finishing off what was left on the stick. He leaned closer, catching the sweet goo in his mouth, licking her eyelet blouse, her neck, her lips. She laughed, because he wasn't curing the problem. His mouth was even stickier than hers. But it didn't matter.

So what if his hands stuck to her arms. So what if her lips stayed on his neck a little longer than she'd planned. They couldn't keep their hands and mouths off each other anyway. They might as well let the marshmallows help them along.

"You'll have to try again," she said, breathless from laughing and wanting at the same time. "If I'm going to be your woman tonight, you'll have to prove you can feed me."

"I'll roast like a pro this time, I swear." His brows drew together in a determined, boyish scowl as he stuck two more on the stick and held them over the fire.

Lauren laughed at him, cuddling up close to his side. She

hadn't felt so young in . . . ever. She'd skipped this part of being a teenager, the giggly, touchy-feely phase. And it seemed to fit right into being in love with Gabe. In love. Yes, she really, really was. . . .

Gabe settled back with one arm still holding his marshmallow stick, and kissed her again. The residual stickiness seemed perfect, binding them slightly, making it hard to part.

Remembering just in time, he glanced over at the toasting marshmallows, catching them when they'd reached a rich brown. "See, I told you I could do it right. You didn't believe me, did you?"

She laughed as she ate. He followed up by kissing her long and deep, sharing the sticky sugar on lips and tongue. He held her, swearing he'd never let her go, while she avowed that he probably couldn't, not with all the marshmallow goo holding them together. They laughed, and ate, and licked each other almost clean, and laughed some more.

The fire had burned down to embers. Gabe paused in their play just long enough to stir the ashes and add a branch of pinyon. Sparks flew, rising high into the night sky, red specks against the backdrop of stars.

His gaze sought hers in the flare of light. "We have some things to work out, but we'll manage, you and I. We're good for each other. We're a good balance, and we can make each other happy. Together." He took her hand and kissed her sticky fingers one by one. "Whenever I'm with you, especially when I'm kissing you, touching you, I want . . ."

"I know." Her hand rested on his thigh, trying to make a subtle move higher, but sticking to the denim too much to quite succeed. "It's time, Gabe. It's our time."

"Ah, Laurie." He turned her, lowered her to the quilt. Slowly he outlined her mouth with his tongue.

When he raised his head, the way he looked at her made her burn almost as hot as the pinyon coals. Her heart beat faster; her gaze drifted from the fire reflected in his eyes, to his once-broken nose, to his mouth. She sighed, and he touched his lips to hers again. His kisses were tender at first, skin barely brushing skin. He caressed her breast through her clothes, circling the nipple, and neither of them noticed the stickiness anymore. She pushed her body up, her taut, tight nerve endings meeting his hand.

He covered her flesh with his palm, brushing across the nipple with only the slightest hint of pressure. Not enough. Oh, not nearly enough. His caress roamed to her waist, her hips, her belly, her woman's mound. Her desire grew and grew, more and more out of control. And for once in her life, she knew it was all right—no, it was good, great, exquisitely wonderful—to let herself feel.

"I want you." She tore at the buttons of his shirt. "I've wanted you forever."

"Sweet Laurie." Between kisses, he opened her eyelet blouse, whispering how he'd wanted to know what was under it all day. Hell, he'd wanted to take off whatever she was wearing for weeks. Once he'd pulled off the blouse, he kissed her through the flesh-colored bra, and settled his hips in the cradle of her thighs.

He held his weight off of her with his elbows while he reached into his back pocket, pulling out his wallet. His muttered curse brought her out of her sensual daze for a moment.

After fumbling through the fives and tens, he came up with a condom. "Thank God. I brought one."

"Only one?" she asked.

He grinned. "I didn't think I'd get the chance to use even one. You haven't given me a whole lot of encouragement."

"I didn't think you needed any. But don't worry, I plan on giving you full satisfaction tonight."

He wiped his forehead with the back of his hand. "I feel like I fell into the fire. I'm burning up."

"Me, too," she said. "I like it."

She liked him between her thighs even more. They helped

each other peel off their clothes, both eager, both starving for the ultimate contact. When he lay with her again, skin to bare skin, she moved her hips against his, letting him know how much she wanted him.

Gabe seemed to know what she wanted and how to give it to her. He tasted her mouth, her breasts, her belly. She tasted him, and thought she'd never tire of his tang, his scent, his flavor. He was the man she'd wanted her whole life, and he was every bit as wonderful as she'd hoped. When they joined, thrusting together in passion and heat, they were one in body and spirit. Together they were more than flesh.

He rocked within her slowly, then faster, higher. Harder, she urged him with her hips and body and all the passion in her soul. *Faster, move faster, higher, stroke longer, delve deeper.* She bucked and stroked and arched, the desire so strong she couldn't stop, wouldn't stop, no power on earth could make her stop. She wasn't on earth. She flew, higher and higher like the sparks, except the heat didn't fade, nothing about this could fade. Too intense. Too high. Too forever.

Her breath caught. She cried out. And then she was falling as he thrust into her again and again until he, too, fell with her, flowed into her.

Lay with her. On her. In her.

A contentment, a peace, pervaded Lauren. She felt Gabe's heartbeat, heard his breathing, was warmed by his skin. Her own heart was bursting with love for him, with gladness. In that moment she truly felt complete.

He lifted his head and gazed down into her eyes. To her, he shone with more beauty and light than all the constellations of the night sky above.

She smiled, brushing a curl off his forehead. "I knew what you were thinking this afternoon when that Rolling Stones song came on the radio. No satisfaction, and you were hoping to remedy the situation."

He nuzzled her neck. "How'd you know?"

"I read your mind. Believe me, it wasn't difficult."

"Because you had the exact same thought?" he teased, moving up to nibble her ear.

"Maybe. So how are we doing on that score?"

He kissed her mouth, softly, gently. "Darlin', I think we've got the problem cured. I'm satisfied. Are you?"

"Oh, yes." She kissed him back, long and slow, tasting just the faintest hint of just-right toasted marshmallow. "So asking for more would be . . . greedy, on my part?" She rubbed her thigh against his, an invitation no man could miss. "Because if you're already satisfied . . ."

"Mmm," he said, rolling over so she could move on top of him. "It's temporary, sweetheart. Only temporary."

Already the need was growing. Already he had to touch her. She had to touch him.

Once again, both of them were thinking the same thing.

Chapter Eighteen

Near midnight, Lauren and Gabe rented a motel room some ten miles outside of San Rafael. Along the highway, they'd stopped by a convenience store and stocked up on protection, because sleep was not what they had in mind. They made love in the shower, on the bed, on the floor. Never before had Lauren abandoned herself to desire so thoroughly. Never could she imagine doing anything so wild and wanton except with Gabe. The night was perfect, she thought. Absolutely perfect.

Until the next morning, when they were leaving their room and ran into the Brothers K and Hayduke in the motel parking lot. Lauren had heard the brothers were staying at a motel on the highway, but she hadn't made the connection, hadn't even considered that she might see them there. From the disgusted looks the three activists sent her, she surmised they would be calling Eve to fill the CPWA boss in on the latest development.

Lauren knew she should be upset about that, but she was still too passion-sated to care. She'd deal with Eve . . . later. She'd think of something.

Even now, as they drove into town, she still felt incredibly happy, dazed by the wonder of being with Gabe, of feeling him, tasting him, becoming one with him. She hadn't

wanted the night to end. She stayed close for as long as possible, straddling the gearshift in the Jeep, forcing Bullwinkle
out of his usual drooling space on the console. Only as they
entered town did she reluctantly scoot over.

A pickup passed going the opposite way. It was exceeding
the speed limit, with its horn blaring as it went by. Lauren
turned in the Jeep's front seat and stared. The truck was a
faded green, covered with dust. A chain clattered in its wake,
dragging a small yellow bumper with colorful stickers spotted and stained with the remains of red paint. As she glanced
up from the wildy bouncing bumper to the rear window of
the truck, trying to catch a glimpse of the driver, she had a
clear view of a double set of naked buns pressed up against
the cab's back glass.

"Did you see that?" she demanded of Gabe, who had
slowed the Jeep as they entered the six-block length of San
Rafael's Main Street. "Not only are they dragging a piece of
my car, but the sons of bitches are mooning me!"

Even Bullwinkle seemed to notice something was amiss.
He stood on the backseat and bayed at the serpentine path of
clanking chain and attachment.

Gabe glanced into the rearview mirror. "Damn. Maybe we
should turn Winky loose on them."

"Fat lot of good that would do," Lauren scoffed.

"Wanna go on a chase?" he proposed.

"No." She glanced over to see if he meant it, but from his
sly sidelong glance, he wasn't inclined to chase after anyone
except her. After the night they'd had, she couldn't have run
far. She frowned to discourage him. "Stop at the sheriff's office. I'm going to report this outrage."

"Don't expect much help from LaDell Purdy," Gabe
warned. "That pickup looks like a dozen others I can think
of. The license plate is too muddy to read, and it's hard to
identify a bare ass."

Lauren had no intention of taking her bumper's loss

lightly. When she didn't see the sheriff sleeping in front of his office, she asked Gabe to stop at the Mad House, where she spied LaDell through the window, loitering with Hannah.

"No wonder there's no law and order in this town," Lauren complained as she and Gabe exited the Jeep and bounded up the restaurant steps, leaving Bullwinkle behind.

Inside, the scene that greeted Lauren gave her momentary pause. Hannah gazed at LaDell while his hand covered hers on the tabletop. The sheriff was reading from an open book in front of him. A smile played on Hannah's lips.

"Mom," Lauren said.

Hannah snatched her fingers from LaDell's as if she'd been caught in some shocking act. She stood abruptly, smoothing her white apron. "Hello, baby." Her gaze slipped to Gabe, who had followed close on Lauren's heels. "You two sure took your time getting back here. I was worried."

"We . . ." Lauren couldn't think how to finish the sentence.

"Hannah, honey, you knew I'd take care of her," Gabe said.

When neither Gabe nor Lauren volunteered where they'd been, Hannah shook her head and pointed to the first booth. "Take a seat, and I'll fetch coffee and pie. I have—"

"Not now," Gabe said. "We'd like a word with LaDell. That is, if we're not interrupting." He raised a speculative eyebrow.

LaDell's ears tinted red. He covered what had to be his Shakespearean sonnets with one of his broad hands. "I, uh, was just about to head back to the office."

To snooze and dream of Hannah, perhaps? Lauren wondered what was going on between them. She wondered if her mother was finally getting lonely enough to consider keeping company with a man.

Hannah retreated toward the kitchen. Before LaDell could escape, Lauren plopped into the chair her mother had vacated. Gabe sat across from her. LaDell slid his book out of sight.

"Did you hear someone leaning on a horn a few moments ago?" Lauren asked the sheriff. She described the truck, the drivers—what she'd seen of them—and the chained bumper.

LaDell claimed he hadn't noticed a thing, which Lauren knew wasn't true. He'd noticed Hannah, to the exclusion of everything else.

"Al Hewitt's boy Andy drives a truck like that," he admitted cautiously. "He was in here earlier, talking to the Lands West organizer." He jerked his head in the direction of the rear booths. "Young Andy's running wild as a cougar these days, and some of his friends are just as bad. I'll have a word with him. If he took the bumper, I'll make him put it back."

"Put it back? That's not good enough. I want the responsible party arrested," Lauren said.

"Want me to get myself fired? I can't put Al's boy in jail for a prank. Nobody's hurt, and I'll see he fixes up your car good as new. He'll pay damages, if need be."

Lauren glanced toward the booths at a hint of movement. Riot-for-Hire was there, alone, ensconced in his usual seat, and must have overheard. He turned to grin at Lauren. She had a huge urge to stick out her tongue. Instead she merely shot him a glare before concentrating on the sheriff again.

"Thing is, Lauren, we heard just this morning that more environmentalists are coming in for a rally next week. That really got young Andy's goat."

"I don't care whose goat it got. You'll do your job, LaDell, or I'll call in reinforcements. I won't put up with—"

The bells on the front door jangled as Don Ray walked in. "Gabe! I've been looking all over for you. One of the crew called me this morning about the diesel engine on your southside rig. Somebody monkey-wrenched it last night, looks like. I'll need some expensive parts to get it going."

"It's the environmentalists," came Riot-for-Hire's whispery voice from the booth. "Stirring up trouble."

Gabe didn't say anything, and Don Ray looked embarrassed. Lauren was worried. The town had been simmering for weeks, but it seemed as if the broth had suddenly reached boiling point. Her bumper was bad enough. With Gabe's rig sabotaged, the sides were lined up, mutually accused, mutually guilty.

The sheriff stood, stuffing the telltale poetry book discreetly into a hip pocket. "Seems like things're getting lively around here. I'd better hightail it over to the office."

Lauren hoped he wasn't going over there to take a nap. While the sheriff strolled out the door, Gabe drew Don Ray a few steps distant from Lauren's seat, which seemed like a reproach. She felt cold, shut out. It had been easy to forget their differences during their passionate interlude, but it wasn't so easy now.

She listened in on the conference about the engine.

"I usually keep an extra diesel on hand, but I'm overextended these days," Gabe confided to Don Ray. "Give me a list of what we need. I'll make some calls."

Don Ray agreed and hurried away, presumably back to the oil rig. Lauren migrated to Gabe's side. He raked a hand through his hair and was about to say something when both of them saw an arm motioning from the back booth.

"Mr. Randolph?" Riot-for-Hire scooted to his feet. Short and stout, he bore a truly striking resemblance to a comic strip Charlie Brown. "I have something here you should see."

Lauren had a sinking feeling. She'd never known Riot-for-Hire to make the first move. The fact that he had taken the initiative with Gabe was a bad omen.

With a shrug in Lauren's direction, Gabe strode over to the booth. The Lands West organizer pointed to the newspaper lying open on the table. Gabe looked down. After a moment both of the men sank onto cushioned seats across from each other. Gabe picked up the paper and started reading.

The incredulous look on his face kept Lauren from going to him. She thought about taking a walk out front to see if there was another paper in the glass case, but decided she should wait. Still, she knew something was terribly wrong. The tension was almost too much to bear.

Finally he stood, newspaper in hand, and approached Lauren. He laid that morning's copy of the *Salt Lake Tribune* open on the nearest table and indicated a full-page article. OIL COMPANY FLAUNTS HISTORY OF POLLUTION was the headline.

Lauren read the first paragraph.

> *Gabe Randolph, wildcatter, hopes to strike it rich on federal leases near San Rafael. The EPA has fined Great Basin Petroleum, Randolph's company, more often than any other in Utah for shoddy reclamation practices. Mr. Randolph's bid to drill half a dozen wells in pristine Red Rock Canyon strikes fear in the hearts of environmentalists.*

The article quoted Lauren at length. In fact, the information had been taken verbatim from the first report Lauren had sent to Eve Worthy.

"You said all this?" Gabe asked.

"I wrote it, but that was before—"

"You sliced and diced me in there, Laurie. You know better."

"But all I knew then was Great Basin's reputation, and you didn't tell me enough to defend yourself."

"You didn't let me, if you'll recall."

She winced, because it was true. "I didn't know all the good things you'd done. When I found out, I—"

"Yeah." A hard nod. "You must've thought I was easy prey. Hell, I showed you my entire operation, never once guessing that you'd backstab me. And I haven't even hit oil on the rim yet. Once I do, you'll really be busy spewing propaganda to the media." He slapped the back of his hand onto the open newspaper. "Why didn't you just go ahead and cut my balls off last night and be done with it?" Muttering something about the "damn diesel engine," he stalked out the door.

Lauren was left standing there, staring at the paper through the tears pooling in her eyes.

Riot-for-Hire kept his bald head turned away, not that Lauren would have spoken to him. With Gabe gone, she felt lost. Last night she'd thought they'd been mind- and body-melded for life. The closeness had seemed so deep and profound, she couldn't imagine it coming to an end.

One swift blow was all it had taken to sever the connection, leaving her raw. And from his last bitter words, she knew Gabe felt the same way.

Wandering into the alcove, she was relieved to find Ezra. She desperately needed the company of someone she could trust, someone who loved her without question.

"How's my Laurie?" he asked as soon as she passed under the arch.

"Not so great." She slumped into a chair beside him at his customary table. "Did you hear?"

"I did," he said. "About Gabe's engine and the newspaper. He's mighty unhappy right now, I reckon."

That was a bit of an understatement.

"Don't you worry, child. Gabe's about as reasonable as any man I know. He'll come round."

"Ezra . . . the truth is that I wrote everything the article attributes to me, word for word. I'd state it otherwise now, but that won't change what's there. I roasted Gabe, telling none of the good. How can he forgive that?"

"Would the CPWA have put the good things in the paper?"

She shook her head. "Apparently not. I sent further information, but my boss didn't pass it on."

"See what I mean? Gabe'll know the article wasn't up to you, once he thinks about it. That boss of yours . . . Huh. I was supposed to tell you something if you stopped in, and my weary brain clean forgot. Becca's gone off to that Rio man's shop, but she wanted you to know your boss called two times last night."

With the article due to hit the press, Eve must have wanted to notify her. But by now Eve would know all about last night and Gabe. Lauren would be lucky if she still had a job when next she spoke to her boss.

Everything was coming down on her head at once. The war had started, and she was Benedict Arnold—to Gabe, to San Rafael, and even to the CPWA.

She clicked on a radio that Hannah kept on Ezra's table, thinking music would distract her from the quandary she'd created for herself. When she heard the confident, upbeat voice of Dr. Susan Farnsworth, she grimaced and turned the dial to a classical station.

"Don't you like Doc Susan, child?"

"Ha," Lauren said. "What does *she* know about how I should live, or whom I should love? I'd much sooner believe you, Ezra. Why don't you tell me how I'll know . . . when I've found the man who's perfect for me?"

"No need for ol' Ezra to be telling you that, Laurie-girl. You can listen to your own heart better than I could."

Lauren rested her elbows on the tabletop and put her head in her hands, her fingers digging into her hair. "What am I supposed to hear?"

"When you find the one who's just right for you, he'll make your heart boomp, honey. That's how you'll know."

Lauren raised her head and put her hand over her heart, thinking of Gabe. "When I'm with him, there is definitely something. A thump, a bump, maybe a boomp." No, it was more than that. He rocked her like an earthquake.

Ezra grinned. "Sounds the same as it was with my Chloe." He pooched his lips thoughtfully. "I'd say your heart's about to jump out on the floor and start doing the hokey-pokey, child. And I'd bet my last dime that Gabe's raring to jive with you."

Lauren rubbed her hands over her face. Last night he'd been raring. Not anymore. "We have our differences, Ezra. Right now, they seem too vast to overcome."

"If you really love somebody, 'different' doesn't matter as much as you think."

"Yes, but with Gabe—"

"Sweet Laurie, you don't know what different is. Look at me and Chloe. Thirty years ago a black man didn't hitch up with a white woman. Now that," he said, "was different."

"I know there must have been plenty of difficulties with prejudice, but at least the differences between you and Chloe ended with skin color. For me and Gabe, it goes deeper."

"That's where you're wrong." Ezra gazed toward the front window, as if he saw something there that gave all the answers.

"What do you mean?" Lauren hoped he was gifted with second sight, or knew something she didn't.

"The outside, the whichever side you're on about the canyon leases, that's the skin. Go deeper yet, child, and you'll see." He tapped the center of his chest. "What counts is here. Right here in your hearts."

When Becca opened the door to Through the Ages, Rio's shop, she felt as if she'd actually stepped into another century.

The scent of old wood mixed with furniture polish. The wallpaper in the entryway, stripes and flowers in muted hues, had a flavor of the past. Becca liked the place instantly. The ceilings were high, the doors big and heavy and solid. An oval mirror in a beautifully carved frame adorned the hall, above a foyer table, also exquisitely carved.

"Rebecca," Rio said, coming to her from another room. He held out his hand, and she took it in a greeting that seemed too formal but was somehow what she'd expected from him. He raised her hand and kissed her knuckles, watching her with his dark eyes as he did so. He looked refined, cosmopolitan, and well dressed, as always.

She felt young and pretty in her new Western-print wrap skirt, with a low-cut blouse that showed off her curves. "I know I'm late. I had to take Missy over to her friend's house before I could get away. She wanted to come with me, but I thought—"

"Next time, *querida*," he said softly. "This is special for you, seeing your work here, in a place where others can admire all you've done." He'd transported four of her paintings to his shop over the last two days, and he'd pleaded with her to come see them before they were sold.

He steered her into the main room, where one of her larger watercolors dominated a wall. Becca's gaze locked on it. For a full minute she couldn't look away. Her painting in a classy place like this was a dream come true. She couldn't stop smiling. "Oh, Rio," was all she could say.

"I am not your only admirer." He took her hand and held it in both of his. "Only this morning a woman came in who was fascinated with that very landscape. She said she'd be back for it, but if not her, *someone* will take it home. There's so much"—he drew a breath—"feeling. The beauty comes from pure emotion."

She didn't know about that. She only knew she loved to paint. She took in the rest of the room, cherishing all of it. There was a large, old-fashioned desk that held canyon postcards. On a bookcase next to it, touristy souvenirs were arranged in a tasteful display. The rest of the room was set up much like a parlor, quaint and homespun.

The long, curved staircase caught her eye.

"Yes," he said. "We must go up. I've hung the rest of your work on the landing."

He seemed almost as excited as she was as they climbed the stairs. One oil and two sand paintings were bathed in natural window light that lent the earth tones a rustic glow. She couldn't have chosen a better location herself.

As Rio continued the tour, she admired the extraordinary woodwork, the beautiful embossed wallpaper, the flawless good taste. The house itself was an antique, dating from the 1860s.

"I had no idea you'd done so much restoration." She knew the house had been on the market for years. She'd heard it went cheap. Locals had figured the old structure would be torn down, but seeing the beauty of its basic design, she was so glad someone had saved it. Even gladder that the someone was Rio. "What made you decide to do all this? Why relocate from California?"

"My three sisters have married; my parents are busy doting on their grandchildren. I wasn't needed in San Diego any longer. I wanted something new, and I enjoy the high desert climate, the canyon views." He looked at Becca as if she were part of the attraction. "I hadn't bought the property yet when I met you the first time. I didn't know you, but you were friendly and interested and kind. I believe that played a part in my decision."

She brushed her fingers over the smooth wood of an antique dresser. Though bearing the scars of age, it was otherwise in perfect condition. She loved the piece.

"Is it too warm for you, dear one?"

She'd thought she was warm from sheer happiness, but she supposed it might be the room temperature.

Rio was already apologizing as he searched through a

drawer and came up with a Japanese-style folded fan. Sweeping it open with a flourish, he presented it to Becca.

"I have something more to show you." With a charming smile, he led her down the hall to a back room where a gentle breeze blew through an open window. "I collect Native American art from all over the West, and I thought you'd like to see it." He had Navaho turquoise jewelry, Hopi baskets, Ute, Cheyenne, and Sioux ceremonial clothing, and a variety of pottery.

"Is all of this for sale?" she asked.

"To the right buyer, for the right price, I would part with them. But I've had some of the pieces for a long time. I'd prefer to keep them."

"Sentimental?" Becca thought he would be.

"When I like something, or care for someone, I don't change my mind. For instance, I care for you, Rebecca Hewitt. And I will keep on caring."

Becca put down the fan, feeling warmer than ever. As Rio came forward, she moved back, as if they'd planned a march or a dance. Each succeeding step, his longer than hers, brought them closer. Three steps along, their bodies touched. Becca felt the wainscoted wall behind her, and a smidgen of panic. She shouldn't be here. She didn't want to get involved with any man right now. She was just starting to enjoy her freedom.

She meant to push away, to run downstairs and escape, but Rio leaned near to kiss her. One chaste kiss. He did not paw her body, but merely held her hand, which reassured her. He reached onto a shelf above them and turned on a sound system. Soft music filled the room. Slow-dancing music.

His hands settled on her hips, and the two of them began to sway. Becca forgot her reservations, her doubts, her better judgment. She looked into his eyes as she embraced his shoulders. The crisp coolness of his starched shirt felt good under her fingertips. He dressed with class and treated her with respect. She liked that.

The gentle rhythm of the music coursed through her. She moved with the sound, with him. She hadn't done anything this romantic in many years. Dancing, gazing into a lover's eyes. A wanna-be lover. A gonna-be lover, if she continued on this way. She stroked his close-shaved face, traced his full, firm lips.

He kissed the new scar on her forehead, and then slowly grazed her skin as he moved down the side of her face to kiss her neck. His hot mouth aroused her, brought all her needs to the surface, nerve endings bare and open and hungry. She moaned as he murmured honeyed Spanish words she couldn't understand, and then he kissed her mouth again, this time with passion.

The music faded from Becca's ears. As she kissed him back, wanting him, a new rhythm came from inside, from the pulse of her body, the force of her need.

"Rio," she whispered. "Oh, Rio." She so, so wanted to feel womanly and wanted. She'd forgotten how much she needed that. He caressed her breast, cupping, chafing his fingers over the nipple through her thin blouse and bra. She wanted him. She didn't know when she'd wanted so much. She wanted to let him take her, right up against the wall. She wanted . . .

He was kissing the upper curve of her breast, so passionate, so intense, and it felt so good, but she . . . couldn't. . . .

She had responsibilities. She had Missy. She wasn't going to do anything impulsive, not ever again. "No," she forced herself to say. "Rio, no. We're going too fast. I can't—"

He raised his head, gazing at her with his hot, dark eyes, and she wanted to give him what they both wanted. She might have given in if he'd insisted. If he'd asked. If he'd even looked at her for half a second longer. But he embraced her, cheek to cheek, breathing hard. "You're right, *querida*. Too much, too soon. I will wait for you."

She put her arms around him and held him for a second before letting go. Silently she thanked him for understanding, for agreeing with her, for not trying to talk her into going on, because he could have. She knew good and well he could have.

Instead of touching, which would have inflamed them both more than they could stand, he braced his hands against the wall and whispered to her in Spanish, musical and sweet, in a silken stream of words she felt to the depths of her soul, though she didn't understand a single syllable.

He was smooth. Too smooth. Hot. Way too hot. She shouldn't let him near her. Instincts had failed her before when it came to men, and . . .

With a start, Becca recognized an unfamiliar thought process running through her overtaxed brain. Logic, for goodness' sake. Any form of logic was definitely un-Becca. If she didn't watch out, she'd turn into her analytic little sister.

Maybe it was a sign she was changing, becoming more mature, because the prospect of being like Lauren, of taking control of her life choices and her relationships *before* disaster struck, didn't seem all bad.

Chapter Nineteen

"**B**eing you wouldn't be all bad," Lauren told her sister as the two of them set up a couple of low-slung beach chairs under the shade of cottonwood trees.

"Yeah? What's good?" Becca asked, flinging her wind-loosened braid over her shoulder.

"You have a sense of place," Lauren said. "You know exactly where you belong. When the wilderness controversy began causing hard feelings against the BLM, you weathered it better than anyone else could have because people around here know and like you."

"For better or worse." Becca sounded as if the bad were on top. "I'm afraid I've let the town make decisions for me. When no one here wanted wilderness, I was willing to brand it as a crock. When no one here noticed my paintings, I figured I had no talent. When no one here thought Joe had a problem, I figured the problem was me. I'm only now learning to think for myself."

"Maybe, but you've always been good at respecting other people's thoughts and feelings, which is something I need to learn," Lauren admitted.

Becca grinned. "That's not such a bad deal, learning from each other."

They settled into the beach chairs. Lauren felt accepted

and accepting, glad to be where she was. She'd put aside yesterday's disaster with Gabe. Since he'd learned of the damaged engine, Becca reported that he'd been busy calling around to find spare diesel parts. He hadn't sought Lauren out, and she thought it best to wait until he'd solved that crisis before trying to explain the newspaper article.

Today she'd enjoy the time with her family, and let the rest of her life sort itself out as it would. Missy and Buddy Lomax were with them. It was Memorial Day, the beginning of summer vacation.

Lauren immersed herself in the cool breeze, the sound of cottonwood leaves rustling, the smell of moss and dirt and the rich life of a stream bed. They were on the banks of Rafael Creek, only a few miles from town, a place from their childhood.

A few feet away, Buddy pushed up his glasses as he held a wiggling worm under Missy's nose. "You're *supposed* to use it for bait," he insisted. "Want me to put it on the hook for you?"

"No." Missy whipped the worm out of Buddy's hand. She deposited the squirmy creature in soft dirt at the edge of the stream. "His name is Jeremiah, and he is *not* bait." She scooped damp sand over her slithery friend before brushing off her hands.

"You're not supposed to name worms," Buddy scoffed.

"I can name him if I want to."

Buddy ended up baiting both their hooks with plastic worms from Becca's fishing box. He didn't seem to mind giving in.

"Buddy's a likable kid," Lauren said, as she and Becca lounged in the shade, out of range of flying hooks. Within seconds of the first cast, the boy was busy disentangling Missy's line from the branches of a box elder overhanging the bank.

"He's bighearted," Becca said. "Reminds me of Trish."

"Good old Trish. I never thought I'd say it, but she's been lucky. She's had a storybook romance with Don Ray."

"Not quite." Becca craned her neck, watching as Missy finally managed to fling her hook in the water. Satisfied, Becca settled back in her chair. "Trish has a man who adores her and a houseful of kids, but a real money shortage. She might be sending them out with a bag of breadcrumbs before she's done."

Lauren wondered what it would be like to be Trish, to have a man who loved her through everything, good and bad, for a lifetime. With all the inevitable conflicts between her and Gabe, she doubted she'd ever have that with him.

Her heart had boomped for the wrong man. She wondered if there were some magic cure, if somehow she could say the word, or take a pill, and make it stop boomping.

Missy squealed. Her cork was bobbing, and her line quivered. "I've got one! What do I do next?"

Becca jumped to her feet, but Buddy was quicker. He dropped his pole and ran over to help. As it turned out, Missy waved everyone off and proceeded to haul in a twelve-inch trout all by herself.

After they'd admired the catch, Lauren tugged Becca back to their vacated chairs. "Relax. Missy is more capable than you think. After seeing the way she picked up chess from me in a few lessons, I'm convinced she's one independent-minded kid. If she becomes a world champion someday, I want all the credit."

Becca's smile brimmed with motherly love. "Missy will do something wonderful with her life, I'm sure. Even Joe is proud of her."

Lauren snorted.

"No, really. Joe loves Missy. He always has; he just didn't know how to show it. Did I tell you he's going to Alcoholics Anonymous twice a week?"

"Since when?" Lauren had heavy doubts that Joe was capable of improvement.

"Well, he did only start last week, but I think—"

"Becca, don't get your hopes up." Realizing she sounded harsh, Lauren tried again. "I guess Joe must have *something* going for him. He did provide half of Missy's gene pool."

Becca rearranged her lawn chair, taking her time as if she couldn't quite get it on an even keel. "I wish you'd try to understand him, Lauren."

"Understand what? That you could have ever loved a guy like Joe?"

Becca leaned back in her chair, which seemed to tilt more than before. "He was handsome, strong, sexy. Sometimes he could be tender. And . . . he was a wild adventure that I could have without leaving home. He had such big plans. I guess they turned out to be too big. He never lived up to them."

They heard another squeal from the creek bank. Both of them stood, only to see Missy hauling in her second fish.

"She's good," Lauren commented, after they'd waved and congratulated. "Like you, Becca. You were always good at the outdoorsy stuff. Dad loved taking you fishing. I'm sure he dreaded taking me."

"You made up for it by being the perfect intellectual. He'd talk about the life cycle of the stream with you, while he'd just give me a pole and let me go. If you ask me, I'm the one he dreaded. He was stuck cleaning all the fish I caught."

Lauren leaned back in the chair and looked up at the sky. No clouds today. She had nothing to wish upon. In any case, wishes wouldn't bring her father back, no matter how much she missed him. "He always bragged on those fish. I never caught a one."

Becca swatted her sister's shoulder. "As if he cared. I could have caught a whale, and he'd have nodded and said it was nice. While you . . . Lauren, he crowed about your brains all the time."

Lauren laughed. "A kid's perceptions must be awfully skewed. We both thought he loved the other best."

"No doubt he loved us in different ways," Becca ventured. "With Mom, though, it was harder to be sure."

Lauren hadn't expected her sister to bring up the subject so directly. Maybe her efforts to keep the pain hidden hadn't been successful after all. "I never questioned which of us she loved best. I knew. So did you."

Becca shrugged. "I don't think she planned it that way. Lord knows, *I* didn't. Mom's been on my case my whole life, dressing me up like Shirley goddamn Temple, pushing me to be popular, to be head cheerleader. After high school she pushed me to marry, to have kids, to be the perfect wife. I've had to battle with her over everything I've done. She wanted me working in the restaurant, not for the BLM."

"What, she didn't like the uniforms?" Lauren teased.

"Too bland. No frills, ugly color. Not enough money, either, and there she was right. The divorce was another skirmish. She fought it harder than you know."

"I never would have guessed," Lauren said. "To me, Mom constantly sings your praises."

"She won't admit I'm less than perfect to anyone else, especially you, because that would mean she picked the wrong racehorse." Becca brushed her bangs off her forehead, momentarily revealing the pink scar. "Mom doesn't like the fact that you've left us, but she respects you. She knew you'd find your way without her pushing."

"I could have used a *little* encouragement." After the "heart-to-heart" of Saturday morning, Lauren felt less resentful about the lack. She was beginning to understand Hannah, but she was still angry and hurt, deep inside. "All I wanted was what every kid wants. Unconditional love."

Becca nodded. "I know that's what Missy wants, and she craves it from both her parents."

Lauren looked out across the creek, thinking about the

good times she and her sister had shared. "What happened with Gabe, Becca? Would it have worked out between you if I hadn't come home? I feel guilty about—"

"Oh, no." Becca reached over to touch Lauren's hand, reassuring her. "It wasn't you. It should have been obvious that we weren't meant for each other, even in high school. He liked to talk about books and ideas, and . . . well, I could never pay attention for long. Then he'd get mad because I wasn't listening, and I'd feel dumb because I didn't understand what he was talking about. When he came back all these years later, I thought maybe . . . But we're better off as friends. Mom was pushing me at him at first, but she's given up. Now she's working on you."

Lauren forced a smile. "If she thinks I'll end up with him, I'm afraid she's going to be disappointed."

"Geez Louise, what do you want?" Becca protested. "I've seen the way he looks at you. Most women would kill for that. It reminds me of . . . well, Rio has those smoldering Spanish eyes that make a girl all hot and shivery."

"Now, now," Lauren said. "Calm yourself. Are you head over heels, or is it just that he sold one of your paintings?"

"Make that two paintings." Becca grinned. "He's . . . wildly romantic, and you know I'm crazy for wild and romantic. But I am trying to be cautious in my old age."

"Good," Lauren said. "Just don't be too cautious—not that there's any worry. You don't *need* a man. However, *if* the right one comes along, you'd be a fool to walk away."

Becca's eyes rounded. "Lauren, aren't you a fine one to talk! You know you're in love with Gabe, but you've been running as hard as you can in the opposite direction, scared to death he'll somehow control you, or change your beliefs, or take over your life."

"That's not it. I'm worried about the basic conflicts."

"There are always conflicts," Becca said. "Why don't you

tell me about Saturday night? I promise I won't blab to Mom."

Lauren shot her an accusing look. "I figured out you were in on that right away, so don't bother acting innocent. The plan itself, pitting me against public opinion, had your fingerprints all over it."

"But it worked, didn't it?"

Lauren rolled her eyes. "Temporarily, maybe. The rest depends on whether Gabe ever speaks to me again. If we're going to talk about wild attractions, how about describing one of his searing looks in my direction?"

Becca laughed. "He looks like he wants to take you straight to his bed, without passing go, without collecting a single thing except maybe a condom."

Lauren felt a flush go from her chest to her forehead, partly from the memory of Gabe's eyes on her, partly from embarrassment that her sister had seen. She lifted her hair off her neck and held it up to let the breeze reach her skin.

"If you're going to start taking chances with your heart all of a sudden, Gabe's a good risk," Becca said. "Make up with him. He's worth it."

"I don't know if we'll get past the newspaper article, and that's just the first of many hurdles. I hate to hear what the various pro-wilderness groups will say if it gets out that Gabe and I—"

"Don't listen," Becca advised. "You know your own mind. If you love Gabe, go for it. Be happy with him, if you can. Want me to help you think up a plan?" Becca looked so eager, so sincere.

Lauren laughed. "Maybe later."

"Thinking back on it, you and Gabe argued a lot when we were kids, but you were always close," Becca said. "I can remember envying you sometimes, because you two would go off on your intellectual tangents. You understood him, and I never did."

Lauren had thought she understood a lot of things. Her sister. Her mother. Gabe. The land and what was best for it, as well as for everyone else involved.

Now she saw that she understood very little. She could study and attempt to protect the land, because it changed slowly. Humankind was much more difficult. Everyone's needs had shadings she had only begun to see. People changed from moment to moment, day to day. The wind of life could blow in many directions. It could erode or polish, punish or reward, pollinate or eradicate.

Her own heart was uncharted territory. And exploring her capacity for love was perhaps the most difficult task of all.

She looked up at the sky again. Clouds were forming. She thought of cloud lovers, blown by the summer breeze, and wondered.

Together, or apart?

Becca, Lauren, Missy, Buddy and a pair of footlong trout all tumbled in the kitchen door at once. The lock had stuck. They'd been united in a group heave-ho when the door suddenly burst open.

The phone was ringing. Lauren started to grab the one on the wall, but Becca yelled, "Leave it."

Lauren turned, frowning. "Why?" She thought of Eve Worthy, and decided she didn't want to answer the phone anyway. But that didn't explain her sister's reluctance.

Becca had stooped to take off her tennis shoes. She concentrated on the laces instead of looking up. Something was wrong; Lauren knew it.

The phone quit ringing. "Tell me what's going on," Lauren said.

Becca jerked her chin toward Buddy and Missy, who had turned on the sink faucet and begun washing their catch.

"Can we go over to Gabe's and show him the fish,

Mama?" Missy asked. "His Jeep's there, and I know he'll want to see."

Becca gave permission and sent kids and fish outside before again meeting Lauren's questioning eyes. "The answering machine's taking the calls again."

"Has Joe been pestering you?" Lauren asked. "Because I'd have no problem telling him to go to hell on a Harley."

"No, don't. I called *him* last night and told him how much Missy wants to see a circus. He'd forgotten all about his promise of a few months ago, and he swore he'd hunt down some tickets. I think he might really do it, so don't rock the boat."

"Then it must be the antiwilderness threats." Those calls had stopped over the last week, but Lauren should have known the worst wasn't over.

"Yesterday, after you and Gabe left, we had at least a dozen calls with disguised voices. The nastiest ones mentioned your name, Lauren. They threatened to remove body parts if you didn't leave town, and soon."

"I suppose my bumper was exhibit A," Lauren said as lightly as possible. "It's still missing. I'll have to speak to LaDell again."

"I've never had hate calls before this Red Rock issue." Becca sounded worried.

"Well, I have," Lauren admitted. "An unlisted number helps for a while, but eventually it's found out. When I'm living alone, I don't let the calls bother me. But here . . . Did I ever tell you about the drunk who shot through my motel room window once? I think it was in Durango, or maybe it was Silverton." She hesitated. "The point is, it could happen here. I don't want my activism putting you or Missy in danger."

"Working for the BLM isn't the most coveted occupation these days, either. Don't worry about us. Just make sure you talk to Gabe and settle your latest disagreement," Becca advised. "Oh, and please call your boss. She sounds furious in her messages. I think she's cussing in some foreign language."

"She probably is." Lauren didn't particularly want to hear Eve ranting in any language.

Lauren could no longer deny that Gabe had affected her commitment to her job. He'd created a whole new variety of passion in her. She'd had errant thoughts about bearing his children, for heaven's sake. He might as well have dropped a stick of dynamite in the middle of her previously well-ordered life.

Or maybe it hadn't been so well-ordered. She'd known phone threats to escalate into violence all too often. She'd heard of houses being set on fire, cars bombed, people attacked or even killed over land-designation battles similar to the one raging over Red Rock Canyon.

Lauren decided then and there that she'd take a room at the Sandman Motel. Becca didn't need an environmentalist living in her house just now. As soon as her sister retreated to the bathroom for a shower, Lauren grabbed the phone book. She'd call and make sure a room was available before breaking the news to Becca and packing her things.

She had just found the number when the phone rang. Without thinking she picked up the receiver.

"Lauren Van Horn? *Gloria in excelsis Deo!*"

Oh, shit. Lauren took a deep breath. "Hello, Eve. No, I haven't dropped off the face of the earth." She winced while Eve yelled at her for not answering her phone messages.

"I saw the article in the *Tribune*," Lauren said. "Didn't you receive my updated report? You were totally out of line to submit—"

A growling sound came over the wire. "I don't care if Great Basin's run like a freaking granola factory," Eve said. "We're not trying to get the company voted Most Popular

Polluter. We want the oil industry to stay out of Red Rock Canyon. Don't we?"

"Yes, Eve, but character assassination isn't the way to go. We need to be fair."

"Fair?" Eve screeched. "Big industry plays dirty all the time. You know that. To the devil with fair!"

Lauren held the phone away from her ear as a spate of Latin came out.

After a thorough litany, Eve said, "I heard a Great Basin truck almost killed your sister. That alone should make you happy to expose our Mr. Randolph."

Lauren blinked. In light of the recent monkey-wrenching, she wondered if Becca's wreck could really have been an environmentalist attempt to vilify Great Basin. She hoped and prayed that the CPWA was not guilty of something that heinous. By association, Lauren would be guilty, too.

"There's also a rumor running around that you and the owner of Great Basin were seen checking out of a motel room together," Eve said in sarcastic tones. "I thought that had to be a lie, but now I'm not so sure."

Lauren had been dreading this and wondering how to explain the inexplicable. "My personal relationships don't affect my work."

"What? A personal relationship with the guy you're slated to sue *is* a conflict of interest."

"Yes, I . . . Don't worry; if Great Basin makes a move into Red Rock, if it comes down to legal maneuvers, I'll zap the company as quickly as any attorney you could hire."

"You'd *better* be quick," Eve warned.

"Stop worrying about me, and start worrying about the destruction of an oil company's property that occurred yesterday," Lauren parried. "If any of our people are involved, I suggest you call them off. Now."

"We can't be held responsible for the individual acts of

our members," Eve said. "If the Brothers K or some of the others enjoy thwarting the foe, that's their choice."

Lauren hated to acknowledge that enviros had been, at times, every bit as malicious as the other side. And Hayduke, the nervous, edgy activist who'd been hanging around town, made her nervous, too. Especially since his pseudonym—she presumed it wasn't his from birth—came from a character in *The Monkey Wrench Gang* whose mission in life was causing mayhem.

"At least we should formally protest," Lauren insisted.

"What's happened to your priorities?" Eve asked. "Get your act together, or I'll find a replacement. CPWA needs someone loyal to the cause. I won't have anyone in our camp sleeping with the enemy."

Not sleeping. Loving. She loved the enemy. And that, it seemed, was the worst mistake of all.

Chapter Twenty

"Harriet loves fish guts!" Missy exclaimed as she rushed in the door, crashed into Lauren, and grabbed onto her with fishy hands.

After a second's thought, Lauren recalled that Harriet was the golden eagle.

"Gabe helped me and Buddy clean the fish, and I said maybe Harriet would want the insides." Missy looked up at Lauren with eyes shining, mouth smiling. "He says I was smart to think of it. He says she'll love me forever for bringing her a treat."

"I'm sure Gabe is correct." Lauren gave Missy, fish slime and all, a quick hug. Missy returned it, locking her hands around Lauren's neck and planting a big wet smack on her cheek. Lauren held on an extra moment until the child escaped to dance around the room.

Lauren felt like dancing, too. Her chest ached, and her throat and eyes burned with all the love she had for Missy, all the hugs she wanted to give. She'd keep this closeness now, she knew she would. She'd visit often enough to keep it, because nothing could be more important. No legal victory, no career ladder, none of that mattered more than the simple beauty of earning this child's love.

"Can I eat now?" Missy asked. "And then can Buddy come over to play chess? I'm teaching him."

Poor Buddy, Lauren thought. He wouldn't have a prayer. "Wash your hands, and help yourself to a couple of cookies from the cookie jar. You'll have to ask your mom about Buddy."

She wished she'd accompanied Missy to Gabe's house, because she had some love to give there also, though she wasn't sure how it would be welcomed. Only a day had passed since she'd seen him, but it seemed like forever and a winter. She wished she knew how to approach him, how to resolve their differences. She wondered if it was even possible.

"Harriet likes you, Aunt Lauren," Missy said after munching down her first cookie.

"What makes you say that?"

"Gabe said so. He said he likes you, too."

Lauren assumed Missy's statement must be true. Didn't children always repeat exactly what they'd heard?

Later, after she'd washed off the fish smell and obsessed for thirty minutes over which T-shirt to wear, she traversed the short distance to Gabe's front door. Bullwinkle greeted her with a joyous howl. She only hoped she'd be so lucky with the man of the house.

When he answered her knock, Gabe was barefoot, shirtless, wearing a pair of denim shorts that hung low on his hips. His hair was damp and tousled, as if he'd just come out of the shower. Seeing the expanse of his bare chest reminded her of holding him, lying with him, loving him, and she almost couldn't stand to look at what she couldn't have. As always, his blue eyes made her heart race, but the set of his mouth was anything but friendly. She hoped she could erase the suspicion, if only he'd let her in and listen to . . .

"What are you doing here?" His greeting, or lack of it, made her forget what she'd planned to say.

Finally she came out with, "The eagle. I thought I'd, uh . . . see how she's doing."

He raised an eyebrow. "I didn't know you two had formed an attachment."

Since it was too late to think of another excuse for being there, Lauren resorted to the simple truth. "I had to see you." *Had to. Had to.* The words seemed to reverberate between them.

He smiled. Not a full, teasing grin, but an uncertain, crooked smile that touched her as nothing he could have said. "Missy told me you took her and Buddy fishing. That explains why you weren't at the house when I stopped by."

"You stopped by? To see me?" Lauren's throat was so tight, her voice squeaked.

He nodded, offering no more, leaving her to grope for her next move.

"I knew you'd been busy with the engine, and I . . ." Since the engine was bound to be a sticking point, she gave up pussyfooting and asked what she wanted to know. "Why did you stop by? What do you want with me?"

He scowled at her. "That's a dumb question, but I'll answer, just for the hell of it. Three reasons. One, to ream you out about the article in the *Tribune*. I didn't expect that from you. I know I've been saying I could handle your criticisms, your injunctions, even a lawsuit aimed at me, but seeing your name condemning my name in print was harder to take than I'd thought."

"I'm sorry, Gabe." She explained what had happened. The timing. What *hadn't* been included, at Eve's discretion.

"I have to admit that Great Basin deserved a public rebuke for past performance," he said. "Maybe I deserved it, too, by association. Since I know you were only doing your job, I . . . well, I'm going to try my damnedest to be understanding."

She smiled, or made the attempt, but her heart was in her

throat, choking her. "What were your other reasons for stopping by?"

"I needed to vent my frustration about the dead engine. You and I both know it was one of your environmentalist friends who did the damage. I called every parts house in a dozen states before I found what Don Ray needs to fix it. By the time I'd finished, I wanted to wring the skinny neck of anyone who ever tried to save a tree. I can't afford this shit."

He was still upset, and Lauren couldn't blame him. "I had no idea my side would stoop to sabotage," she said.

"You think that excuses you? I'll bet the CPWA condones what happened on my well site."

"N-not condones, exactly." *But close.* Eve Worthy wouldn't be voicing any complaints.

"The irony is, I want to protect the land as much as you do," he said. "I just don't want to see the people of this town go down instead."

She rubbed at a sun freckle on the back of her hand, like Lady Macbeth trying to erase the stain of blood and guilt. "You think I want that? I thought my role was simple and direct. Save the canyon. That's a good, right? But it seems there are other 'goods,' and other ways to be wrong. Nothing is clear anymore. Except one thing."

"What's that?" he asked.

She hesitated. "What was your third reason for wanting to see me?"

He shoved his hands in his rear denim pockets. His broad chest, sprinkled with swirls of red-gold hair, was both intimidating and gloriously male. "I think you know, darlin'."

She moved half a step forward. "I think I do, too."

He drew her into the house. As soon as she passed the doorway, he held her face in his hands. He tasted her lips and licked inside her mouth. "I can't stand this," he whispered, breathing into her, through her. "Being away from you is driving me crazy. I don't care whose side you're on, or whose side I'm on. Let's get amnesia for a few days."

"Bad idea," she said, between bone-dissolving kisses. "Eve Worthy, my boss, called a few minutes ago. She already knows about our night together, and she's irate. She warned me to shape up and live right. How could I explain disappearing with you again when . . ." Another kiss sucked the objections right out of her. His hand was under her T-shirt, pushing past her bra, stroking her. She moaned. "What did you have in mind?"

He lifted her against the door frame and applied his mouth to her breast. When her nipples were hard and thoroughly aroused and her thighs were trembling, he lowered her feet back to earth. He brushed the hair from her hot face and smiled, both suggestively and tenderly. "There are things you need to know . . . about the canyon. I'll take you. Show you."

She knew one thing for certain: she ought to protest. Really, she should. Instead she said, "Where to?"

His mouth quirked up on one side. "Ever see the mating ritual of the spadefoot toad?"

She laughed.

"What's so funny? Haven't you ever been invited to watch toads do their thing before?"

"The toads are a new one," she said. "Luring a girl with empty promises isn't. My plastic surgeon—Dr. Frankenstein, as you call him—lured me to his town house by offering to show me a paper he was writing on the true meaning of beauty."

"Did you ever see the paper?" Gabe asked.

"No. I don't think it existed."

"Damn, I don't like other men tricking you."

"But it's okay if you do it?"

"The toads aren't a trick."

"I don't believe you," she said. "Not with that mischievous grin lighting up your face."

"Who else promised to show you things?" he asked.

"There was a guy in law school who said he had a CD collection I just had to see. Really, though, he was only interested in showing me one thing, which he accomplished way too fast for me to be appreciative. Then there was Tim. He claimed he had etchings in his bedroom. No imagination, that one. And now toads, of all things." She stood on her toes and kissed him. Once, quickly, so as not to get carried away. "You're an original, Gabe."

"I promise to keep you interested, darlin'."

On that one point, she believed him without question.

Late that afternoon, they made their way down a slippery game trail, gradually descending about a thousand feet into the canyon. Lauren heard voices, sheeplike voices, a repetitive *maa* sound, all the way down. She kept asking Gabe if he knew of any sheep or goats in the area. He chuckled and said, "You'll see."

Just before the sun dipped below the canyon rim, he announced they'd reached their destination. The *maa*ing was louder than ever. Gabe drew her next to him and pointed to a sandstone water pocket, filled as a result of a rainstorm earlier in the week. The water appeared shallow, but extended over the area of a small room.

Lauren saw toads. Hundreds of two-inch toads. They were the "sheep," still making sheeplike sounds that echoed off the canyon walls. The creatures were poised around the periphery of the water, as if preparing for some sort of toad convention.

As dusk descended, the calling suddenly stopped. For a full sixty seconds the silence was profound. Lauren's senses went on alert. The hair rose on the back of her neck. And then she heard plops and saw ripples as the toads leaped into the water, driven by instinct, perhaps triggered by a change in temperature or light.

The toads went wild, swimming madly, swirling the water as they sorted themselves out. Half of them swam to the sides of the water pockets and hung on to the sandstone edge with their front legs. The other half leaped on the anchored ones' backs. Their sounds resumed, but with a difference. Instead of the mournful *maa*s, their song burgeoned to a higher, faster, fevered pitch, to what could easily be interpreted as orgasmic ecstasy.

With open mouth and wide eyes, Lauren watched them, so astonished she was temporarily mute. Gabe ushered her to a boulder, where they sat side by side. Her eyes remained fixated on the mating frogs for several minutes. Then she glanced up at Gabe. "I thought you were kidding. I had no idea. . . ."

"Erotic, isn't it?"

She smiled. "I don't know if I'd characterize it that way, exactly."

He pulled her close to him, encircling her waist. "You're going to think I'm weird, but watching the toads do their thing makes me want to jump my own female."

"I'm shocked. I'm insulted, too. *I* wouldn't put up with a male toad jumping on me. They have no finesse. I've also heard they have no . . ."

"Penis? Yeah, so they say. But some of us have finesse *and* a penis. I could show you," he offered.

"Not here." She pretended to concentrate on the frantic mating still going on, but she was more interested in Gabe. He could drag her off by the hair and show her anything he wanted, anytime he took a notion to.

She couldn't wait for him to make his move. She couldn't wait to respond. Thinking about the sheer joy of being with him, she laughed aloud.

She realized how rarely she'd laughed with a man. In the past she'd favored the serious, humorless type. Shared values had seemed of prime importance at the time. But as it turned out, she hadn't shared her heart with them. She hadn't laughed with any of them. With Gabe, though, she'd learned a great deal about laughter, and she hoped to keep on learning.

He was fun. Not that he couldn't be serious when he needed to be. He ran a company, organized and ordered other men, made things happen according to his vision and his will. But he also knew how to laugh, and she needed that. He knew how to touch her skin, her mind, her soul. She needed everything he had to offer. She needed him.

He took her hand and led her a few hundred yards down a side creek, to the main part of Red Rock Canyon. A waterfall cascaded twenty feet down the slickrock. The spray had turned the rock surrounding the water into a rich green of new life. The water spilled into a clear pool that reflected the moonlight. Surrounding the water, the growth was almost tropical, lush with moss and fern.

With typical foresight, Gabe had brought a pack with food, drinking water, and a quilt, which he spread where the grass grew thick and green. Standing beside the nest he'd prepared for them, in the light of the evening's full moon, he kissed her mouth more thoroughly than she'd ever been kissed before. She wanted to sink onto the ground, but he held her upright while he kissed her neck and gradually worked her T-shirt up and off. The sensation of his caresses, through her clothes and under them, filled her with desire.

Her shorts went the way of the shirt. She stood quivering with need in her matching pink panties and bra, feeling more naked than if she'd been bare. When his gaze drifted over her, she held her arms out to him, inviting him in.

He smiled, standing just out of reach. "Not yet. I want to look at you. I want to see how you want me."

"I'm not going anywhere," she said, letting her arms fall to her sides as she waited for him to look as long as he liked. His gaze, slow-moving and appreciative, made her feel desirable, needed, wanted. He touched her then, a soft, gentle caress. Face. Throat. Breasts. A moan came from deep inside her. Her legs seemed to dissolve in a rush of heat and hunger.

He moved closer to touch her with his mouth. His kisses began with her lips and moved lower and lower. He exposed her nipples one at a time, and took them, naked and chilled, into his hot, wet mouth. He knelt on the ground in front of her and continued his downward path. Along the underside of her breasts, to her stomach, lower abdomen, and . . . so on. *Oh, God.* The "and so on" felt good. He made her feel more beautiful than she was, or had ever been.

His mouth covered her, lathed her, licked her. He tenderly removed her bra and panties, kissing and claiming the territory he discovered.

When she couldn't wait any longer, she tugged off his shirt and knelt on the soft streamside moss to remove his hip-riding denim shorts, peeling away his underwear at the same time. She stroked his body with a boldness that seemed to match the earthy, unpretentious man that he was. She saw his beauty, inner and outer, through the eyes of a lover.

He lay with her on the blanket. There, in full view of moon and stars, over sand formed by thousands of years of wind and water washed from the cliffs above, they made fervent, uninhibited love. The climax was agony prolonged, ecstasy enhanced, a violent, earth-shattering release that made both of them cry out with joy. There was no one to hear. No one at all but each other, and the rocks and water, desert plants and animals, and the eons and eons of time that created their solitude.

As she breathed in the warm, dry air, sated and satisfied, she realized she'd lost all hold, all control, on her passions. And she didn't care. With Gabe it felt right.

When they'd rested awhile, they swam in the pool beneath the waterfall, in water still warm from the day's sun. Refreshed, they lazed in the shallows.

"It's late," she said. "We should go." She didn't want to go. The night had been a taste of paradise, a break from the madness of the outside world, a desert mirage.

He pulled her against him, naked skin to naked skin. "Do you think I brought you here to ravage you only one time?"

"I confess I hadn't thought . . . How many times did you have in mind?"

"I brought enough protection for a three day orgy, sweet darlin'. My, uh, male pride—how's that for a euphemism?— is a renewable resource, in case you forgot."

She looked through the clear water to that euphemistic part of him. Already he was renewed. And so was she.

More lovemaking followed, with languorous "and so ons" leading up to a climax that surpassed good, great, or even sublime. They outlasted the frogs, the insects, and whatever other beings made love that night.

Sometime before dawn they slept, curled together on their blanket. They awoke to full sun, the trickle of water on sandstone, and the graceful notes of the canyon wren's descending musical scale. Lauren lay sprawled half on top of Gabe. Neither of them wore a stitch of clothing. With any other man she might have been embarrassed to be naked outside in the daylight. But not with Gabe. He was so much at home in the natural world that she felt natural, too.

"Laurie, my love." He stroked her hair and on down the bumps of her spine. "Think we could hide out here forever? No drilling rigs. No wilderness plan. Nothing but you and me."

"I wish," she said. "Once the diesel engine is fixed, how long before you know if the rim well is productive?"

"A few hundred feet to total depth. Then, if everything looks promising, we run pipe and perforate. A month ago I was certain we'd hit. Now I'm not even sure I want oil. I'd rather have you."

She wanted him, too.

If his rim well struck oil, if she had to start filing motions for injunctions and thinking lawsuits, the dynamics of time and place would shift drastically. One article in the newspaper would be nothing compared to the uproar they'd face. Their love affair, which had begun as a farce and turned alarmingly, wonderfully real, would become an even more shocking breach of ethics than it already was. If Lauren cared anything about her job, or her standing in the environmental community, all ties between them would have to end.

Lauren developed situational amnesia. She did move into the motel, but so did Gabe. His diesel parts arrived; his drilling began again. They slept together every night, even though his days were spent on his rig sites, and hers in reviewing various defenses for the environment that she could ultimately use against Great Basin.

She received messages through Becca, and from her colleagues at CPWA. Several reporters sought her out in the motel and begged for the story of her private romance—which, of course, was no longer private—with her public enemy. She communicated solely by e-mail, tuning out her boss's ire. She didn't give interviews or answer calls.

Gabe didn't answer the phone either.

They avoided Main Street and demonstrators from both sides. When they were alone, they were an island unto themselves.

On the following Saturday, in silent agreement that they were running out of time and should make the most of the little that remained, they drove to the highest reaches of Red Rock Canyon accessible by road, then hiked three miles into the canyon's very heart.

Early June was still flowering season in the high desert. Cliff-rose bloomed all around them. Bees buzzed. Indian paintbrush, yellow primrose, and blue lupine were everywhere. The cactus showed off waxen blooms of pink, yellow, and red. The scents, sounds, and textures of the canyon surrounded them. Their destination was a desert spring, replete with huge cottonwoods, far from trails and prying eyes. The water was a rare treasure, giving life to the land, and to them.

They drank from it, bathed in it, made love in it. As they prepared to leave, to make the long hike back to the Jeep, Lauren looked up at the hundreds of feet of sheer rock canyon wall surrounding them and was overwhelmed by the magnificence. She felt as if she was seeing Red Rock Canyon's true splendor for the very first time.

"Before I came to town a few weeks ago, I would have fought for Red Rock Wilderness," she said, "but I wouldn't have known what I was fighting for. Now I've learned all the lovely nuances. I've learned passion for . . . the land. I've developed empathy, too, for the people who live here. And most of the changes in me came from you. From being with you."

"Sounds like I've complicated your life considerably," Gabe told her, taking both her hands in his. "Maybe I should apologize."

"No need. You've opened my mind." *And heart and soul and body.*

"I've learned, too, Laurie. I'd forgotten . . . a lot. How beautiful this land is, and how beautiful you are." Gabe closed his eyes, sick with wondering how he could get around drilling in the canyon. What could he do about the investors? How could he keep Great Basin alive without using the canyon leases? He didn't have an answer. He kissed her once more, cherishing the moment, and then he led the way onto a narrow game trail that headed uphill.

Halfway up, Lauren stopped him. "It's been five days since the drilling started again. When will you know?"

"Any day. Any hour, really. The crew is perforating the casing today. After that, we either have reasonable flow and pressure, or we don't."

After that, Lauren would learn whether Gabe would become the biggest conflict of interest in her professional career. And he'd know just how impossible their love was going to get.

In the late afternoon they drove along the canyon rim road to the rig site. From a mile away Gabe noticed a difference. No clanging of pipes, no diesel churning. As they drew closer, he heard shouts, saw men throwing hard hats into the air and laughing like kids just let out of school. Petroleum was flowing. The well was good.

The crew ran to greet them, cheering, overwhelming the car, grinning and slapping each other on the back. To Gabe, the oil was a catch-22. Wealth. Success. And loss. All rolled into one.

Reaching across the Jeep console, he grasped Lauren's hand. He felt like the *Titanic,* listing lower and lower before that inevitable journey to the bottom of the ocean. Except in this case, the canyon was where he was headed, with drilling rigs and noise and a certain amount of unavoidable destruction.

He looked at Lauren, wondering if she could accept that.

From the desolation in her cloud-gray eyes, he knew that the vast chasm of Red Rock would loom between them for a long, long time. Maybe forever.

Chapter Twenty-one

"I'm not going to the circus," Missy told Buddy on that next Friday afternoon. She was disgusted with her daddy because he hadn't met her after her piano lesson like he'd promised. She was angry, and convinced he didn't care. "Tonight was supposed to be special, just for us. He knew I wanted to see the trapeze."

"Maybe your mama would take you." Buddy pushed up the glasses that were always sliding down his nose.

"No, she has too much paperwork. Gabe's busy with oil troubles. Aunt Lauren is worried about her job. Nobody has time for me." Missy scuffed the toes of the new cowboy boots Gabe had bought her, dragging them across the cracked sidewalk. Even the boots didn't make her feel better. "I might as well run away."

"Okay," Buddy said. "I'm not doing anything this afternoon."

"You'll run away with me?"

"Why not? Somebody'll find us. Then they'll be glad to see us, like when my cousin Sal ran away. Her dad grounded her for a while, but her friends sent flowers and candy and books and stuff, so it wasn't too bad. Let's do it. Let's run away today."

Missy shrugged. She hadn't expected Buddy to agree, and

she wasn't sure it was a great idea. "How? My bicycle's chain falls off when I hit a big bump. Yours gets flat tires all the time."

He grinned. "I could sneak my mom's car out of the garage. As long as I don't run into those old pickups with flowers in 'em that're parked at the end of our driveway, she won't notice. Dad lets me sit in his lap and drive his truck sometimes. I know how to do it. Course, I'd have to slouch way down to reach the pedals, so it'd be hard to see much."

"No way, Buddy. We'd crash into something, and then we'd be in big, big trouble." She breathed easier, thinking they couldn't run away after all.

Buddy looked around at the protesters' cars parked along Main Street and spotted Kayleen's ice-cream truck in front of the Mad House. "I heard Kayleen tell Uncle Chester that she had to go somewhere tonight. Can't remember where, but it sounded far away. If we climbed in the back, we could hitch a ride."

"I don't think . . ."

Instead of listening to Missy's objections, Buddy was already headed for the back of the truck. He opened one of the double rear doors and peered inside. "Dude, it's dark in there." Leaving the door partially open, he went around to the front to check out the glove compartment. After rattling through papers, he came up with a flashlight. He shined it on the ground, making a weak circle on the pavement. "The batteries aren't too good, but at least we'll have something." He grabbed Missy's hand and pulled her around back again.

She crouched low to avoid being seen. "I don't want to be in trouble, Buddy. We're going to get in bad trouble, I just know it."

"I thought this was your idea." He stealthily climbed in through the open door. When he noticed Missy wasn't following, he said, "If you don't wanna come, that's fine by me."

She bit down on her lip hard and told herself not to be a baby. "I'm getting in." She clambered up, with Buddy's help.

He started to close the door.

"Wait!" she hollered. Scrounging on the floor, she came up with a piece of cardboard about the size of a notepad. She wedged it between the two door panels as Buddy shut the back, so the door didn't close all the way. A sliver of light came through.

"That's so we can get air," Missy said. "You can die in old freezers, and an ice-cream truck's the same as a freezer. I saw a show on CNN about little kids suffocating in places like this."

Buddy nodded. "You're smart, Missy. It's a good thing I'm with you, or I'd've likely suffocated right off."

She backed away from the door to find a seat. She tripped. Her bottom smacked on something hard that turned over and clattered. "Ouch! Bring the flashlight, Buddy."

He flicked on the light.

Missy had stumbled over a long yellow piece of what seemed to be plastic, with reddish paint and rectangles of paper with writing on it. "Look! It's Aunt Lauren's bumper!"

"How'd it get in here?" Buddy wondered. "Dad said some men in a pickup truck stole it."

Missy sighed, exasperated. *Exasperated* was her word for the day, because she'd heard Gabe say that Aunt Lauren made him exasperated sometimes. Same as Buddy did to her. "They just put the bumper in here to hide it, that's all. I'll bet Chester and his friend Andy Hewitt dragged it off with a chain, and then they had to hide it somewhere."

"Probably Uncle Chester and Kayleen are gonna drive off and dump it before they're caught."

"Aunt Lauren's sure going to be mad when we tell her about this. The sheriff might have to put Chester in jail." Missy shook her head. "It's wrong to steal a bumper."

"I don't think we should tell. My daddy looks out for

Uncle Chester, so I can't go snitching on him. Besides, if we get out now to hunt down the sheriff, we'll lose our ride."

She decided the telling could wait.

Exploring the inside of their hideout, Buddy flashed the light on a big cardboard box. The top flaps weren't sealed, so Buddy pulled them down. Together he and Missy peered inside.

Missy stuck her arm in and felt around. She came across something hard and slippery and heavy.

Buddy helped her pull it out. The dim flashlight shone on black metal that looked like it came from an engine. "Wow," Buddy said. "It's, like, just the same as that new part my dad had to order for Gabe's diesel engine." He looked up, his eyes white-rimmed. "You think Chester stole it?"

Missy frowned, then shook her head. "I don't think so. He likes Gabe. But maybe Miss Kayleen . . . Aunt Lauren told Mama that Mrs. Throckmorton said Miss Kayleen is an environmentalist. Aunt Lauren didn't believe it, but that would make Miss Kayleen want to steal Gabe's engine parts. Wouldn't it?" She hoped her daddy didn't like Kayleen anymore, because she wasn't a nice lady. Not nice at all.

Buddy shrugged. "I don't know why she'd want these old parts, but she'd be in big trouble if we told on her, worse trouble than for the bumper. She's not gonna like it if she finds us in here."

Buddy and Missy inched toward the doors, hunched over and tip-toeing as if someone might catch them any second. All of a sudden the engine started up and the whole truck vibrated. Buddy turned to Missy. His eyes behind his glasses were big and round. They heard a voice shout something from outside the truck's back panels.

"Hide!" Buddy yelled, diving behind the box.

Missy was right behind him, her heart pitter-pattering, her stomach queasy. She thought she might throw up, she was so scared. "Turn off the flashlight," she hissed.

"Freakin' A," said the voice outside. "Chester, did you leave this door unlocked again? It's not even shut tight. I told you to . . ." The back door opened a fraction before slamming closed again.

"Uh-oh," Missy said, still whispering. "No more light. The cardboard must've fallen out."

"Damn," Buddy said. "Double damn. Why didn't you run?"

"I was scared. And you said to hide."

The inside of the ice-cream truck vibrated with engine noise. Outside sounds seemed muffled, so they couldn't hear what was going on.

"The flashlight's broken." Buddy sounded even more scared than Missy felt. "Are we gonna suffocate?"

She nodded, knowing Buddy wasn't going to see. It was black. Blacker than night.

The truck started to move.

"We're in big trouble now." Buddy banged on the side wall. He yelled. Missy stood beside him, banging and yelling. The truck bounced, knocking both of them down.

Buddy made a choking sound. Missy thought he was crying.

She scrunched beside him. Her ribs felt stiff, and it hurt to breathe. She wondered if she'd broken something inside. She wondered if she'd ever see Mama again. Hot tears filled her eyes and began to stream down her cheeks.

She reached over and felt along Buddy's arm until she found his hand. It was hard to tell who held on the tightest.

Becca was still in her office at a quarter past six. With Lands West and CPWA protesters taunting each other outside all day, she found it hard to concentrate during regular working hours. Her paper backlog was starting to look like Mount Everest. Since Missy wouldn't be home tonight, she intended to play catch-up for at least the next hour.

Twirling her pen between her fingers, Becca stared down at the paperwork. After another fizzle last Saturday, Joe had finally come up with circus tickets. He and Missy would be on their way to Fairfield by now. Becca smiled, thinking about Missy's excitement. Once in a while Joe showed basic human decency. Maybe there was hope for him yet.

All was quiet now that the protesters had packed it in for the day. The din of their departure had seemed greater than usual, horns blaring and doors slamming, but Becca hadn't bothered to peek through the blinds to see what was going on. With so much work to do, she couldn't afford to be curious. She'd kept right on sorting and authorizing camping permits, determined to get through the stack before she went home.

She would have thought the Red Rock hoopla would die down after more than two weeks of protests and sign carrying, but with the oil discovery last weekend, everything had heated to fever pitch again. The enviros were desperate to prevent drilling. The townsfolk were desperate to keep jobs. Nothing had changed, except folks were even more inflamed, now that they knew drilling in the canyon was almost certain to be profitable.

Lauren and Gabe had suffered the worst of it. They were both miserable. He'd moved back to his house; she'd stayed in the motel. Becca hoped they'd work out their problems, but right now their future didn't look all that promising.

When she heard a faint knock at the door, she threw down her pen. She prayed she wouldn't have to face another obnoxious newsman, since she'd already had it up to her eyeballs with those guys. She hadn't locked the door, but now she wished she could zap on a dead bolt in a hurry.

The door opened. "Hi, Becca."

"Joe! What are you doing here? Where's Missy? You were supposed to pick her up from Mrs. Throckmorton's."

Joe halted just inside in the door. "After piano? Today?"

"How could you forget?" Becca was alarmed at first, and then bitterness took over. She was the one who should have remembered—that good old Joe didn't keep promises. After all the talk of shaping up, he still hadn't come through.

He didn't look so good, now that she took note. His hair was messy; his rumpled clothes had probably been slept in. From his rounded shoulders, she guessed he was depressed. He'd had a bad day. A bad week. Maybe a couple of bad months. She might have felt sorry for him if he hadn't made a habit of disappointing their daughter.

"Didn't Missy come to you when I didn't show?" he asked.

"No," Becca said, worry nibbling at her stomach lining. "She always has before, so I don't understand. . . ." But maybe she did. Missy would have been even more disappointed with her daddy than usual this time, and she didn't like to cry in front of anyone. The poor little kid didn't like anyone to see her pain.

Becca felt like crying herself. She wanted to punch Joe for being a jerk, because Missy was sure to be heartbroken. She reached for the phone and dialed the Lomax number. "Missy likes to play with Buddy while I'm working, so I have an arrangement with Trish. If she isn't home, Sal Lomax babysits. That's probably where Missy . . ." The line was busy. Becca hung up.

Joe sprawled in the chair across from her. "I think Buddy's a bad influence. Our kid's getting too big to run around with boys all the time."

"There's nothing bad about Buddy," Becca said. "He's Missy's friend, and she needs one. She certainly doesn't have much of a daddy."

Joe's hazel eyes flared. "Maybe she doesn't have much of a mama, either. You should be with her when she meets me."

"I do have to work for a living, Joe. Someone has to provide financial support for the child."

Joe slumped. "More bad news on the money, Becca. The bank repossessed half my ATVs this morning, and the rest are likely to be next."

"I am sorry, Joe. I really am." She wished he'd asked her opinion before buying double the amount of equipment he needed, but he'd always thought he knew best. "It's Missy I'm worried about, not the money. If you'd just spend more time with her, more good, honest time . . . Why are you here?"

He rapped his knuckles on the table, avoiding her eyes. "It's, uh, about your accident."

Becca put her fingertips to her temples. Every time she talked to Joe, heard his excuses, his complaints, her head throbbed. The pain was worse this time, and a dark foreboding pulsed through her. "I don't want to hear any more theories on how I managed to trash a BLM truck. I've heard enough from the sheriff and investigators and insurance people. We'll never know what happened."

"But I . . . I know," Joe said quietly.

"Oh." Becca leaned back in her chair. She felt as if her chest had collapsed, driving out all the air. She'd refused to believe he was involved. His voice, though. She'd heard his voice in the hospital. His voice the way it used to be, soft, caring, heartfelt. She knew that. Maybe she'd known it all along. She forced herself to breathe. "Go on; tell me what happened. I'm listening."

"After Gabe came to town, I was sick about you and him, Becca. When I'd hear people talk, it just made me want to puke. I was lonely, dying from it, and he had you. It didn't seem right. Not fair. So when Kayleen moved here from Vegas, I wanted companionship so bad I didn't care that she was a little strange. Turns out she belongs to one of those underground greenie operations. An enviro *bandita,* you might say. Out to stop big industry. Like oil, for one.

"So we got to talking one night, got to figuring we were

on the same side when it came to Great Basin and Gabe: We
wanted 'em gone. She said we ought to do something, and I
said yeah. I went with her while she put sand in a gas tank
once. Another time she started a fire out by one of the rigs. I
was worried somebody'd get hurt or go to jail, so I quit going
around with her at night. Then one day we were out joyrid-
ing in my old Dodge pickup, me drinking, her thinking how
to get us into trouble. We went out that road to Gabe's
drilling rig, and there was the . . . uh, the Great Basin winch
truck."

"Oh, no." Becca could see it, though. She could imagine.

"I wasn't thinking too clear by then. Kayleen wanted to
block the road with the Great Basin truck. She said it'd be
good to raise a little ruckus, give Gabe and his company a bad
name, make it look like Great Basin was getting uppity and
taking over the whole dang road. It didn't sound like a bad idea
at the time. I thought, what the hell." Joe shrugged, and then
his shoulders hunched again. He looked defeated.

"I'm sorry," he said. "You don't know how sorry. I never
thought you'd get hurt. I just hoped maybe it'd cause trouble
for Gabe. I never thought . . . Kayleen backed the truck out,
and you were right there. You had nowhere to go."

"How did you get me to the hospital?"

"Kayleen drove my pickup, you and me in back. I sobered
up, seeing you that way. Couldn't stand it. Can't even say
how bad I felt. I put on a doctor's white coat and went into
your room so I could stay as long as . . . Your sister almost
caught me when I left. I've felt like shit ever since."

She knew now why the voice had seemed a sort of déjà
vu. He was guilty and sorry, just as he'd been after the last
accident he'd gotten her in. Joe had whispered to her, en-
couraged her. And then he'd deserted her, alone and afraid, in
a sterile environment, and never breathed a word of explanation until now.

The son of a bitch.

She bit her lower lip so hard she tasted blood. "We'd better go find the sheriff, Joe. You have some explaining to do."

The bells on the Mad House door jangled wildly as Becca burst in, Joe lagging behind her. The main room appeared empty, which was unusual for a Friday evening. Since the sheriff hadn't been at his office, she'd expected to find him in the restaurant, but he was nowhere in sight. She hurried toward the back to check the booths and almost ran into Rio.

"Rebecca! I waited here, thinking I'd take you out after—"

"Rio, I can't talk about that right now. Check the alcove and kitchens, would you? See if the sheriff's around. And ask my mother if she's seen Missy."

Alone with Joe again, Becca asked, "What else? I don't need any more surprises, so tell me now. Have you been in on the rest of the sabotage out at the Great Basin rigs?"

"I, uh . . . I helped Kayleen one other time, right after you got hurt. Only because if I didn't, she said she'd tell Chester. And he . . . would've told somebody, and then everybody would've known. Chester and Don Ray both think real highly of Gabe, and . . ." He sighed. "Everybody's gonna know now anyway. But it hasn't been me lately. Somebody else is helping her."

"Chester's involved?" Becca knew Kayleen spent a lot of time with Chester.

"Naw, he's just a cover. It's one of those enviro guys. Hey-Luke, or whatever his name is. You know the one I'm talking about."

"Hayduke. We'll tell the sheriff. Meanwhile, we'd better figure out where our daughter is. I should call the Lomax house again." Becca glanced around the empty room. "Where is everyone?"

Joe shrugged. "I thought you'd be the first to know. They've all gone—"

A crowd of three came through the alcove arch at once. Lauren was talking on a cell phone, gesturing with one hand as she spoke. Rio had taken off his tie and loosened his collar. He looked worried. Ezra clumped along with his cane, continuing forward when the others stopped.

He sniffed. "Mmm-mmm, Becca's mint truffles. Evenin', honey. Mighty interesting happenings around here today."

Lauren clicked off her cell phone. "Sheriff Purdy's on his way out of town to stop them. He'll try to hold them off until reinforcements arrive. Meanwhile, he needs our help."

"What's going on?" Becca thought maybe the sheriff had gone after Kayleen already, but how would he know? "Joe, did you tell them before—"

"He didn't have to tell us." Lauren looked puzzled by Becca's confusion. "Are we talking about the same thing? Don't you know there's a parade of cars and trucks going down the highway? An industrial-size bulldozer is leading the charge, with our esteemed mayor driving and Riot-for-Hire perched right beside him like a Mardi Gras king on a float. Something tells me they plan to blade that old two-track around south and on down into Red Rock Canyon. They'll try to claim the track has been a county-maintained dirt road all along, when we know nobody's touched it in thirty years."

"Criminy," Becca said. "We won't have a wilderness study area to worry about if it suddenly sprouts roads."

"That's why we're going to stop them." Lauren dug in her purse and pulled out keys. "I called your house and didn't get an answer, so I'm glad you showed up. My car's out front. We can—"

"Wait," Becca said. "Have you seen Missy?"

Lauren looked over at Joe. "I thought she was with—"

"No. I bailed on her," he said.

Lauren blew a huff of disgust. "Should have known."

Hannah came from the alcove, looking flushed from the

ovens, flour graying her hair. "The kids must have hitched a ride with the road-blading folks. Little Sal Lomax just called over here. Says she's looked everywhere and Buddy's gone, too. It's past suppertime. If they were around, I'd sure expect those kids to be here or at the Lomax place hunting for something to eat."

"Missy and Buddy were out front, right by Kayleen's old ice-cream truck, about the time the engines started and the parade cut loose," Ezra volunteered. He knew every local vehicle by sound, by bounces and rattles and horsepower, just as he knew every San Rafaelite by voice and scent. "I didn't hear 'em after that. Didn't think much of it then, but seeing as how they're gone, I reckon they might've climbed aboard with Kayleen."

Becca exchanged a glance with Joe. After what she'd just learned, she was alarmed that the children might be with Kayleen. She couldn't imagine why they would have chosen the ice-cream truck for transportation. But whatever the means, Missy was going to be in big trouble for going anywhere without letting her mom, or at least someone in the family, know.

The bells on the front door jangled. Gabe came in wearing his usual jeans and workshirt. He brushed the dust out of his hair and grinned when he saw the gathering. As he caught their expressions, his smile faded.

Lauren quickly explained what was going on. "Souped-up rallies like this can escalate," she said. "The sheriff's already called in the Cedar City riot squad. With tempers as hot as they're bound to be, we could have a demolition derby with shotgun fireworks before we're through. It's no place for the kids."

Gabe narrowed his eyes. "Before imported troops get here and rile everybody past the flame-out point, we'd better take action on our own." He was already halfway to the door. "We'll stop them. If we don't find Missy and Buddy right

away, the good news is that the whole town'll be on hand to
help us search."

As Gabe started his Jeep, Lauren climbed in beside him,
shooing Bullwinkle's slobbering jowls into the backseat.
The dog barked and sniffed the rushing air as they sped out
of town.

In his rearview mirror, Gabe noted Becca and Joe riding
with Rio in a black sedan, which followed close behind them.
Hannah had stayed at the Mad House in case the kids showed
up in town, but he didn't think that was going to happen.

They were driving down the main highway, past the motel
where the Brothers K were staying, when Gabe noticed the
brothers outside talking with the motel manager. He stopped
long enough to fill them in on the road blading. The pair
looked surprised that Gabe would ask them for help, but they
readily hopped into their own Chevy Blazer and joined the
crowd.

Gabe was worried about Missy. He'd heard this morning
that the bank had sent somebody to repossess Joe's equipment. He should have guessed that the circus trip was off,
should have called Becca, should have made sure that she or
Lauren could meet Missy after her piano lesson, in case Joe
didn't show. If the kid was in trouble now, he blamed himself. He accelerated, determined to find both missing children as quickly as possible.

Within fifteen minutes they'd caught up with the sheriff.
In his blue-and-white squad car, LaDell poked along at the
back of the line of demonstrators. The group of cars and
trucks had already left the highway and started along a dirt
road leading toward Red Rock Canyon.

Never one to eat dust, Gabe wheeled past the sheriff.
LaDell Purdy raised his hands from the steering wheel as
Gabe went by. If looks could kill, the sheriff would have shot

him dead. Since a glare didn't work, LaDell hunkered down, mouth grim, and followed.

Blading a road on restricted land would cost the town big money in federal fines that they couldn't afford to pay. For that reason alone Gabe knew it was a lousy plan. In addition, he was mad as hell that they were out to ruin Red Rock's chance for wilderness designation just when he himself had decided he wanted to save the canyon, if he could. He hadn't even told Lauren his good intentions yet, and here these ingrates, whom he'd come here to help, were about to thwart him.

The dirt road was narrow and winding in places. Gabe passed the entire line of cars and trucks, one by one, until he whipped around the huge bulldozer at the front of the line. The dozer had reached the old two-track that the San Rafaelites meant to illegally "improve." The surrounding land had flattened at that point, making a total blockade impossible.

Gabe stopped broadside across the two-track. The sheriff followed suit, coming to a halt right behind the Jeep. Rio likewise positioned his car to obstruct the heavy machinery's path. Still, there was enough room for the bulldozer to go around them. For that matter, the machine had enough power to drive right over another vehicle, if Mayor Al Hewitt took a notion to bull his way through.

With heedless courage, Lauren jumped out of the Jeep only a few yards from the monster steel blade that extended across the front of the machine. As Gabe joined her, the dozer slowed to a crawl. Rio, Joe, Becca, and the sheriff popped their doors and also blocked the path with their bodies, waving their arms and shouting. Yielding that route, Al shifted into reverse. He was going to go around them.

Lauren ran to the side of the dozer and started climbing up a ladder toward the bench seat occupied by Mayor Hewitt and Riot-for-Hire. Becca hopped on from the opposite direction.

Seeing the sisters' rash move, afraid they'd get hurt in a real struggle, Gabe jumped on top of the front blade and climbed over the engine hood to lunge for Al. While Lauren and Becca planted themselves on either side of Riot-for-Hire, Gabe put Al in a headlock to persuade him to turn off the engine. As he made his move, he caught a flash of Lauren's hand nimbly snatching the keys. She'd beat him to the rescue once again. *Damn.* Being John Wayne to a woman like Lauren was no easy mission.

Joe jumped up and down in front of the dozer blade, yelling, "Stop, Uncle Al. You're gonna get this whole town in trouble with the feds."

LaDell Purdy ambled alongside the bulldozer until he was even with the driver. "Can't do this, Al. It's against the law."

"And headlocking the mayor isn't?" Al cursed as he rubbed his neck where Gabe had applied his persuasive powers.

"Shut up and listen," Gabe said. "If you want me to pay top dollar for your land leases, you'd better not make me mad. Besides stopping your march of lemmings to Red Rock, we need to find Missy. She's with your group somewhere."

"I haven't seen her," Al grumbled. "You think I'm running a baby-sitting service?"

Riot-for-Hire furrowed his Charlie Brown forehead. "Missy? The cute little elf? Hannah's grandbaby? We'd better find her. Don't want a lost little girl on our conscience." He climbed off the machinery and offered a hand to assist Becca and Lauren down. "You folks go ahead and look for the child. If I can do anything to help, let me know."

That was a switch, Lauren thought. She'd never known Hyrum Riot-for-Hire to actually hurt anyone, but she wouldn't have expected compassion, either. However, if he was going to temporarily put aside their differences, he'd picked a good time.

She followed Becca down the line of cars and trucks, looking for Kayleen's rolling ice-cream freezer, shouting to everyone that they were searching for Missy and Buddy. Dusk was setting in, making it harder to see. Most of the vehicles had turned on their lights. Lauren held a hand over her eyes to screen out some of the blinding glare.

They came across Don Ray, Trish, and Chester only four trucks back, all three of them in the pickup's single seat.

"I saw the kids before we took off," Trish said. "Buddy was supposed to go on home."

"He didn't." Lauren related what they'd heard from the Lomax house. "No one's seen Missy or Buddy in town since the blading party left."

All three Lomaxes climbed out of their truck. "We'll help you look," Don Ray said. Bless him, Don Ray did love kids. No cause in the world could be more important to him than the well-being of a child. Chester looked as worried as any of them, and Lauren was sure he'd let them know if he had any idea where his nephew was. Chester might be half-crazy sometimes, and not all that bright, but he wouldn't hurt little Buddy.

Joe passed by, stopped long enough to find out the Lomaxes didn't know anything, then continued down the line, shouting into vehicle windows loud enough to be heard above the engine noise. "We can't find my little girl! Anybody seen Missy? Or Kayleen? We think Missy's with Kayleen!"

Way down the line, one of the Whalen clan recalled, "That old ice-cream truck was with us for a while. Right as we turned off the highway, it peeled out of the lineup."

"Were the kids riding up front?" Joe asked.

"Didn't see hide nor hair of them."

"Why are you asking that?" Becca demanded, elbowing

Joe as she caught up with him. "What difference does it make?"

"Because if they're in the back . . . A person could suffocate in one of those freezer compartments," Joe said. "I saw a show on CNN."

"Oh, God," Becca moaned.

Lauren felt the same cold fear. Joe was never right about much of anything. How horribly ironic if he turned out to be right about this.

As they neared the very last truck, it became obvious they weren't going to find the kids in this group. Lauren, Becca, and Trish stopped in the red glow of taillights, wondering what to do next. Gabe was leaning in the window of that last truck, talking to one of the men who worked on his regular crew. Gabe argued that the whole blading idea was a bad one, and urged the man to come along on a search for the kids.

Lauren listened, nearly paralyzed by the weight of her guilt. Red Rock's wilderness status had seemed crucial to her, but if something happened to those two children as a result of this opposition protest, no amount of pristine canyon could make up the loss.

The Brothers K and the sheriff walked up together, all three of them looking as if they were headed for a funeral. One of the Ks—Lauren had never gotten their individual names straight—said, "I know where to find them."

Lauren didn't understand how he'd know, but as they jogged back to their vehicles, K clarified. Little Kayleen really was an environmentalist, with Alive!, same as Hayduke. Hayduke had bragged to the brothers about his oil-well-sabotage exploits with the ringed queen, as he called her, and had said he was meeting her tonight, up on the plateau above Red Rock.

Once again Lauren climbed in the Jeep, pushing Bullwinkle into the backseat.

Gabe's focus was entirely on getting the kids back and

making everything better. Since only one well in the area hadn't been sabotaged yet, he had a pretty good idea where to go. Familiar with the roads, he led the way in his Jeep.

They covered the ground at a world-record speed. The vehicle's shocks took a beating as they bounced up and down over rocky terrain. Lauren didn't mind the spine-racking jolts. She'd take any amount of pain to get those kids back safe and sound. Bullwinkle whined as a vicious bump jostled him off his perch between seats. The tow chains and assortment of tools Gabe carried rattled in the rear compartment.

Lauren tightened her seat belt and wrapped an arm around the dog to steady him as he balanced his paws on the console again. She was scared half to death that they were making a mistake, headed in the wrong direction when time might be a critical factor.

Had the Brother K told the truth? Had Hayduke given the actual meeting location, or was he cagey enough to lie? Were the kids in the truck as they thought? Were Buddy and Missy okay?

Looking over her shoulder as they steered from the dirt road onto the highway, Lauren saw that all the vehicles had followed them, even the bulldozer, albeit at a caterpillar pace. Al Hewitt must have realized that the kids could be in real trouble. Lauren wondered if the surprisingly grandfatherly Riot-for-Hire had been a determining factor.

The line of headlights had spread out behind them over several miles. Turning down another dirt road, Gabe looked in the rearview mirror and cursed three shades of blue. "Damn it, why don't they turn off the headlights?"

He had shut his off moments earlier. They'd been feeling their way by moonlight, but the rest of the cavalcade presented a moving beacon.

Lauren saw the ice-cream truck up ahead, parked near the canyon rim. Another, smaller vehicle was nearby. Hayduke and Kayleen must have spotted the lights coming at about the same time. They'd been standing outside the truck, but now they jumped in from opposite sides and began driving recklessly across open ground. Gabe flicked on his lights and chased them in the Jeep, well ahead of the sheriff and the rest of the entourage, who followed more slowly over the rocks and the biggest of the sage. Rio, still ferrying Becca and Joe, risked all in his low sedan, not slowing a bit.

The unwieldy ice-cream truck hit something and went airborne. It thumped and teetered, finally landing on hissing tires and coming to an off-balance stop. All Lauren could think about was how the kids had fared. The abrupt halt would have been rough without a seat belt.

Kayleen popped out of the driver's side and started to run. Hayduke raced after her. Sheriff Purdy headed his squad car out over open terrain to chase the pair down, but Becca, Joe, Gabe, and Lauren rushed to the back of the truck and tried to open it. The doors were locked.

Bullwinkle leaped out of the Jeep and began baying wildly, standing on his hind legs and pawing on those rear panels.

"They're in there, I know they are." Becca banged on the metal. No answer. "Oh, God, what if they ran out of air?" She banged harder, sounding hysterical. Rio tried to pull her away, but she fought him off and kept pounding. Joe, too, seemed out of control, trying to pry the door open with his fingernails.

Lauren had already checked the ignition. No keys. She'd seen Kayleen throw something, and figured the keys were out in the sage somewhere. She was about to mount a search with a flashlight when she saw Gabe going for the back of the Jeep. Instantly she knew what he planned to do. He reached in to heft out the big chain, which was finally going to come in handy for something.

Without a word, Lauren helped him pull it out. While he wrapped one end around one of the ice-cream truck door handles, she attached the other end to the tow hook on the rear of the Jeep. They seemed to be thinking faster than the others. Joe caught on and tried to help, but Becca just looked scared. Rio ran to the front of Kayleen's truck, saying he'd put on the parking brake.

"Want me to drive?" Lauren asked.

Gabe nodded, still securing the chain. "Put it in four-wheel low and pull slow and easy."

She hadn't driven a stick shift or a four-wheel drive since high school, but the old skills her father had taught her returned in the heat of panic.

"Stand clear, everybody," Gabe shouted.

The others moved out of the way. Gabe motioned for Lauren to drive forward. With her heart beating like a hummingbird's, she eased on the gas.

She felt a jolt as the chain tightened. Kayleen's truck shook, but didn't move more than a few inches. Slowly Lauren crept forward. With a metallic ripping sound, the door was torn from its frame. Lauren killed the Jeep engine and hurried back to see if the kids were there, praying they were alive and unharmed.

Joe and Becca had already crowded inside the freezer compartment. "They're here!" Joe shouted.

Headlights and Lauren's flashlight showed Missy and Buddy lying side by side, hands clasped. A hunk of black metal rolled at their feet.

To be so still, the children must have been oxygen-deprived, besides being badly jarred by the wild ride. Lauren feared the worst. Apparently Joe and Becca did, too. They seemed afraid to pick up either child. With tender care, they touched their dear faces, felt along the small, fragile bones.

Missy stirred, giving them reason to hope.

Buddy's arm twitched. He slowly sat up and rubbed his head, which must have suffered a few bumps during the truck's careening. He felt around for his glasses, located them, and slipped them on. One lens was cracked. He yawned. "Did we run away yet?"

Missy opened her eyes. After blinking in surprise to find her parents looking down at her, she beamed an elfish, gap-toothed smile. "Looks like we're already found."

Becca reached out, but it was Joe who took the child in his arms and hugged her as if he'd discovered something precious. Lauren hoped that maybe, at last, he'd gained the smarts and maturity to realize what a gem he had in his daughter. With a big sigh and tears streaming down her face, Becca knelt beside Buddy and embraced the boy until he squeaked out that he couldn't breathe.

Gabe wrapped an arm around Lauren's shoulders, holding her close. She felt chilled, a little shaky. Bullwinkle was slobbering on her thigh, but she was too happy to complain. Thank God for Gabe and his quick-thinking practicality. When she'd helped him pull off that door, they'd been of one mind. United. They'd worked well together, as if their purposes had converged in that moment to accomplish the task that mattered.

In the distance, they saw Sheriff Purdy's squad car, its blue and red lights flashing, stop near the canyon rim. Since there was precious little place to hide, other than jumping over a thousand-foot cliff, LaDell had located and caught up with the fleeing couple. LaDell was a big, powerful man, something not generally appreciated when he was lazing around town, and he had no problem subduing even Hayduke's bulk. After a brief struggle, he loaded the wayward couple into the squad car.

The sheriff drove back toward the rest of the group. Drawing even with the ice-cream truck, he stopped to make sure everything was all right. Joe was just coming out of the truck with Missy in his arms.

"Joe, you chicken-livered fart, did you tell on us?" Kayleen's screech came through the open front window of the squad car with startling clarity. She was in the backseat, behind an imprisoning wire screen. All they could see of her was the glint of the gold rings in her face. "Everybody's gonna know you're in on this, Joe Hewitt. Everybody, you freakin' asswipe! If they don't figure it out, I'll tell 'em."

Joe nodded his head slowly. "You do that, Kayleen. You tell 'em whatever you want." Kayleen may not have heard his quiet reply, but Lauren did. She didn't know exactly what he'd done, but at least he seemed ready and willing to take ownership of his mistakes. That alone was a big step for Joe.

The sheriff drove away, taking Kayleen and Hayduke with him.

From the shelter of Gabe's arms, Lauren peered into the ice-cream truck's interior and saw a long piece of metal that she suddenly realized was her bumper.

So, Kayleen the "environmentalist" had been engaging not only in oil-well sabotage, but also in aiding and abetting the good old boys as a way of masking her underground activities.

Trish and Don Ray arrived to envelop Buddy in sequential bear hugs. The rest of the caravan participants gathered around to beam at the children as if they'd performed the rescue themselves. The town seemed to forget, for the moment, the act of civil disobedience that had brought them to this place and time. First and foremost, they cared for their own. Always had, always would.

A sense of community united them, one human being to another. Watching them, seeing their real joy in the children's safety, Lauren felt her throat tighten. For once in her life, she was almost proud to call San Rafael her hometown.

Chapter Twenty-two

The crowd that gathered in the gym was quieter this time, two full months after the last meeting. Tonight the BLM would announce the results of their latest environmental studies and give the agency's final decision on Red Rock Canyon's management for as long as it remained a wilderness study area.

Riot-for-Hire, the Brothers K, and all the other outside agitators from the enviro and the anti-enviro sides were gone. Hayduke and Kayleen had been charged with destruction of property after their arrest on the night of the road blading, some three weeks before. They were out on bail, but they wouldn't be showing their faces tonight.

Joe was present, which demonstrated more courage than Lauren would have given him credit for. Though an accessory to several property crimes, his aid in catching the main perpetrators would save him from jail time.

From a seat near the back of the gym, Lauren watched the people assemble with a sadness she hadn't expected to feel. Joe and Al and the Hewitts, Chester, Don Ray, and the Lomax clan. Mrs. Throckmorton had come, dismayed by her granddaughter's misdeeds, but still holding her head up, chatting with friends about how her son Doug needed to bring all her grandbabies home. Almost everyone who lived in or near San Rafael came through the gymnasium doors.

The CPWA had won this round, but Lauren hated to see the new rules forced down the throats of those whose livelihoods were at stake. She wished she knew how to heal all the differences so no one was hurt. The threatening phone calls had stopped and the bumper was back on her car. As far as she was concerned, all was forgiven. She just hoped her fellow San Rafaelites felt the same way.

When the crowd had settled in their folding chairs, Arch McFarlane began. "As most of you know, our new management regulations will go into effect September first. The good news is, grazing allotments won't change. The ranchers ought to be happy."

A few ranchers did applaud. Most of the assembly had other interests.

"Even though we received a lot of complaints," Arch said, "we're sticking to no logging and no dams. Our studies support that decision. As far as off-highway vehicle use, our second assessment found significant damage. We're closing the entire area to motorized vehicles of any kind. You can run ATVs up on the rim trail, but that's it. And we're firm on no new oil, gas, or mineral leases in the canyon itself."

The crowd buzzed and rumbled. Arch waited a full minute for them to quiet sufficiently so that he could continue.

"All of these rules will remain the same if Red Rock ends up gaining Congress's approval for wilderness status, which could happen within the next year or two."

"What if we don't want it?" Mayor Al Hewitt complained. "Can we send the doggone status back to Washington and tell 'em to stuff it where the sun ain't never gonna shine?"

Guffaws rang through the room, and even Arch chuckled a little. "Afraid not, Mayor. You're just going to have to live with the status and the new rules. One more point: the BLM had hoped to allow the existing oil leases to go forward.

However, as you may know, the CPWA has filed for an injunction to block drilling, and the court's granted a temporary one. Enviro groups still aren't satisfied with our new and complete Environmental Impact Statement." Arch sighed. "It's out of the BLM's hands now. The end result will be decided by the legal system."

Lauren, of course, had already known about the injunction, since she'd filed for it herself.

The packed auditorium was silent, absorbing the latest blow. Becca, who stood beside Arch, leaned in to the microphone to add, "I know this final management plan isn't what most of the town wanted, but I hope we can work together to make the best of it."

Lauren asked to make a statement, and Arch invited her to the front. As she approached the podium, murmurs followed her in a wave. When she began to speak, she thought the crowd might boo her, but all the fight seemed to have gone out of them. The blading attempt had resulted in censure from the state and national press, plus a formal rebuke and pending fines from the federal court system. After all the uproar, no one was interested in pushing his luck. The group seemed in an almost conciliatory mood.

"I know how much all of you love this canyon country," Lauren said. "Our differences lie in how we view it. I suppose you think my side has won." She glanced at Ezra, at Gabe, at Hannah. "And you're correct. However, I've learned to see your side, too. Therefore, I've resigned from the CPWA as of this morning."

A hum started among the rows of chairs. She tapped on the microphone to regain the audience's attention. "I've decided to start an organization of my own, one that will lobby Washington to provide help for small towns affected by wilderness and other restrictive land designations.

"I still believe wilderness is the right way to go, but we must come together, not as adversaries but as friends conscious of each others' needs. As Red Rock Canyon's management plan goes into effect, I intend to negotiate for increased BLM funding directed toward building trails, studying wildlife, and preparing visitor information. You know the canyon best. Those jobs should be yours."

"We don't have the training," one of the Lomax men said. "The BLM's gonna hire city boys."

"Not if you get the training to compete, and I hope to make that option available. In time, probably within only a few years, there will be other opportunities in tourism and associated activities—motels, restaurants, guided river trips, and horseback riding concessions. My goal is to help you obtain federal grants and loans for those businesses. The opportunities will be there, I promise. Red Rock Wilderness can and will be a victory for all of us."

She stepped away from the podium. No applause. She hadn't expected any, but neither had she expected silence. Even Becca said nothing. Her mouth was open, but she couldn't seem to think of what to say. Lauren hadn't breathed a word beforehand, and now she wondered if her speech had been a mistake, if maybe the town didn't want her meddling in their affairs.

Then Hannah, near the front, stood up and clapped. She stuck two fingers in her mouth and whistled, a skill Lauren had never known her mother possessed. Hannah reached down to poke the sheriff in the next seat. He stood up, too, looking meek and henpecked.

Lauren smiled. Her emotions were a jumbled mix of sadness for the years of miscommunication, and gladness that Hannah had, literally, stood up for her daughter at last. Tears flooded her eyes.

Trish popped out of her chair. "Way to lend a hand, Laurie!" Don Ray pulled her back into her seat.

Becca recovered herself and tapped Lauren on the shoulder. "You ought to get an honorary San Rafael Raptor plaque for that speech," she whispered.

Gabe was the only other person to move. He rose from the front row and leaped onto the raised platform. Lauren stepped aside to give him the mike, though she had no idea what he had in mind.

He wasn't smiling, which worried her, and when he spoke it was to the crowd, in the most solemn tones she'd ever heard him utter. "I think you all know how much I admire Ms. Van Horn. In support of her and her efforts, I'm . . ." He glanced at her, his eyes sparkling in the lights. "I'm giving up the leases in the canyon and ending the court battle. I've been in touch with the BLM office in Salt Lake all week. Earlier today we finally reached an agreement."

It was Lauren's turn to withstand shock. She wasn't the only one who'd kept a secret.

Trish bounced out of her chair again. "Way to go, Gabe! Who ever said a redneck can't be romantic?" She clapped. She whistled. Romance, or even the possibility of romance, caught Trish's attention.

Don Ray frowned and tugged on her arm. When she refused to sit down, he stood up beside her with a long-suffering sigh. "I'd be downright mad at Gabe, but he has promised to stay and keep Great Basin operating on private and nonwilderness government land." To Trish, he added, just loudly enough for everyone to hear, "Don't you go thinking about another man being romantic, hon. I'm the only lover you'll ever need."

Snickers came from the crowd. The two of them sat down together, holding hands.

"So you're not running out on us, Gabe?" Al Hewitt shouted.

"No, I'm not. Ready to talk money on your lease, Al?"

That drew some laughs, since everyone knew how eager their mayor was to make a deal. The meeting ended in chaos, everyone chattering at once. The Olympus Petroleum man, whose company still held drilling rights in Red Rock, came forward to speak to Gabe. From snippets of the conversation that Lauren caught, Olympus was afraid they'd look bad if they kept their lease when Gabe had given up his. Olympus would have to go along with Great Basin's example, as Gabe must have anticipated.

He had followed his heart, Lauren thought. He'd get a cash settlement on the leases, but not nearly what he might have made with successful wells. He was far-seeing enough to know the canyon should be protected by law, and generous enough to do something about it. She loved him for that, among other reasons. Their lives had different paths and would probably soon diverge, but her few weeks with him were enough for her to live on for years.

He'd given no indication that he wanted her to stay, or that he'd be willing to travel with her when she left. She didn't count on their having a future together. Nevertheless, she would always love him, the redneck oil man of her dreams.

Becca discreetly increased her distance from Arch Mc-Farlane, who had a habit of standing in her space. Tonight he seemed to be inching even closer than usual.

"The meeting went well, don't you think?" she said brightly. "The town's not thrilled, but we knew—"

"I have tickets to *Romeo and Juliet* Saturday night at Cedar City's Shakespeare festival. I'd be delighted if you'd accompany me." He'd rushed through the sentences as if he'd memorized them, which he probably had. While Becca tried to think of a polite way to put him off, he added, "Or, uh, I could trade for *Hamlet*. I'm just asking as a friend. No expectations."

Becca glanced at Lauren, who must have overheard and had looked over her shoulder to meet Becca's eyes. Lauren had warned her that Arch was romantically interested. Becca had tried to pretend otherwise.

He's safe, Lauren mouthed from an angle only Becca could see.

Becca had told Lauren just last night that though she was attracted to Rio, he was a little too breathtaking, and she didn't need that kind of trouble. *If* she took on another man, she'd order him up dull, plain, and safe.

Arch was exactly what she'd claimed she wanted. Now that she came to it, though, she wasn't so sure *safe* was going to do the trick.

Becca looked squarely into the face of her colleague with the acne scars and steady brown eyes. She did like him; she really did. It was just that he was boring in the extreme. "I'll . . . have to check my calendar, Arch. I'll let you know."

Obviously disappointed, Arch gathered up his papers and left. Meanwhile, Lauren had stepped off the speaker's platform to mingle with the crowd. She exchanged a handshake with Don Ray and was now embracing Trish. Gabe was near the back, talking to a gathering of men.

Becca caught sight of Rio elbowing his way through the townspeople. She hadn't expected him to be there. She'd only seen him a few times since the road-blading debacle, and then only when they'd met in the Mad House to discuss her art sales. She'd tried very hard to keep everything between them strictly business, although it hadn't been easy. His beautiful, musical, accented voice was hard to resist. And his eyes, dark, sexy, knowing . . .

"I have been patient, Rebecca. Now that the meeting is over, I hope you will have more time. I hope you will make time for me."

"Rio, no. I don't think—"

"We could go to dinner. Or somewhere for the weekend would be even better." He had his hands in his pockets, hair neatly combed, bedroom eyes licking over her, eating her heart out. He was smooth. Oh, so smooth. She knew how easily she could fall for him.

"Give me a chance, *querida*. Just a small chance."

Becca had never been good at risk reduction. However, she owed it to Missy to be conservative, take it slow, know what she was getting into. "Not yet, Rio." *When?* she asked herself. *How long and how carefully must a woman guard her heart?* Wasn't it possible to overdo the guarding? Didn't a person have to take some risk?

She cleared her throat, glancing toward the door, thinking about Arch, and safe—and maybe sorry.

If she made the decisions, if she was in control, she ought to be able to handle the risk. No need to bring her life to a screeching halt.

"Maybe . . . a walk down Main Street on Saturday night," she said with sudden inspiration. That ought to be safe enough. "Or, if you like ice-cream cones and don't mind including Missy, I know a place in Fairfield that serves chocolate mint to die for. And if you pass the first date test—I'm warning you, it's a big *if*—then there's a spot on the canyon rim. . . ."

Lauren was gathering her papers and fliers and notes, stuffing them into a briefcase, when she looked up and saw Hyrum Riot-for-Hire Dupont in the flesh.

Startled, she asked, "What are you doing here?"

"I was in the neighborhood. Thought I'd stop by the restaurant and drop off some kid books with Hannah. My grandkids have outgrown them, and I thought Hannah's cute little granddaughter might want them."

"That's nice," Lauren said, going back to overstuffing the briefcase.

"Then I found out everybody was in the gymnasium, so I came, too. I heard your talk tonight."

"That's great, Mr. Dupont. I hope you approve that I'm leaving the CPWA." She wished he'd go away, because she was certainly not going to explain herself to him.

He lingered, shifting his weight from one foot to another.

"I do approve, but what I wanted to say is that I knew your father." His distinctive, whispery voice made Lauren shiver.

She glanced up sharply and looked straight into Hyrum Dupont's eyes. He had nice eyes, she realized. Not small and mean, as she'd always thought, but almost neighborly.

"I admired Daniel Van Horn," Hyrum said. "He was one of the few environmentalists who would talk about issues and recognize that there could be other viewpoints. He was rational, reasonable, and logical, always."

Her father had been adamant about protecting the canyon country, but Lauren did remember his extraordinary efforts to communicate, without rancor, with all the parties involved. However, she'd never realized he'd been respected by the other side.

"First time I heard about you from the folks in town, I thought you were about as opposite from him as you could get." Hyrum's voice gentled the words, which otherwise would have cut Lauren to the marrow.

"But now," he said, "hearing you tonight, I've changed my mind. You have the best of your father in you, Miss Van Horn. He'd be proud."

Those words touched Lauren deeply. She thought maybe she'd been waiting to hear them all her adult life. "That's very kind of you, Hyrum."

He was about to turn away when her voice stopped him. "Do you know . . . Can you tell me anything about his death?"

"You mean, do I know who killed Daniel?" he asked.

Lauren nodded. "I never believed it was an accident. Please tell me. I know we'll never have the evidence to prosecute anyone, but for my own peace of mind . . ."

Hyrum inclined his bald head. "My guess is that one of the high-and-mighties in the coal mine ownership sent a hit man to mess with his car. We'll never know who. The corporation he was fighting was like one of those Chinese dolls, one company hidden inside the other. When the feds ruled against the power plant in this area, the whole Utah operation dissolved. Poof. Everybody gone. I'd have nailed the murdering SOB myself, if I'd known who was responsible."

Lauren's heart ached with an old sorrow, but somehow knowing Hyrum Dupont's view of her father and his version of the truth eased her animosity and her need to find someone to blame. In addition, she saw now that the key to success in her work, perhaps in any work, was in accepting differences, and then using that acceptance to find ways to live together. Her father, she thought, would agree with her. "Thank you, Hyrum. I appreciate your coming here and telling me you cared about him."

"Your father was one good man." Hyrum offered his hand, and Lauren held it for a moment, making peace with the past. Perhaps making strides toward the future, as well.

After most of the crowd had filed out of the meeting, Missy sat with her father on the outside steps of the gym.

"I'm sorry you've been sad, Daddy. Kayleen wasn't a very nice friend for you, was she?" Missy observed. "She was a robber. Mama says Kayleen and Hayduke might have to go to jail."

Her daddy rested his elbow on one knee and propped his chin in his hand. "I didn't do a very good job of choosing my friends, pumpkin. I've done some dumb things, and that's gotten me in trouble with the sheriff. I never meant to hurt your mom, but I did and I'm sorry. From here on out, I'm going to try and be a whole lot smarter."

Missy patted his back. She knew he hadn't hurt Mama on purpose. "People would like you more if you were responsible. It's responsible to take a person to the circus when you say you will."

He turned to look at her. She wondered if she'd said the wrong thing and made him angry. She only wanted to see the elephants and the flying trapeze with her daddy. That didn't seem so bad. "It's okay, though," she said reluctantly. "Even if we don't ever go to a circus, I still love you."

He nodded and smiled a little bit. He had a nice daddy smile. "Maybe I need to pay more attention to who my friends really are. Like you, Missy. My little girl is a good friend. And you know what? I'm working hard on business from now on, so I can help out your mom more and take better care of you. And I sold my big Harley."

"That's good, Daddy," Missy said. "Your big Harley scared me."

"Know what else? I'm working Saturday, but I have my eye on two circus tickets over in Cedar City for Sunday afternoon. How'd you like to go with me, if we can clear it with your mom?"

Missy was wary, but she wanted to believe he'd keep his promise this time. She took a big breath and thought about the flying trapeze. In her head, she let go of the swinging bar. In real life, she zoomed through the air, launching herself into her daddy's arms.

"It was the toads," Gabe told Lauren as they walked down the dark street from the gymnasium toward his house. He'd persuaded her to go home with him tonight. They weren't in legal conflict any longer, which made him feel as happy as a man who'd just finished serving a long prison sentence.

He'd been planning tonight's surprise for weeks, ever since he'd figured out how to accomplish it. He just hoped what he'd say now, and how he'd say it, would convince Lauren that they needed to be in the same bed, the same house, sharing their lives from here on out.

"Toads?" Lauren asked. "What do the toads have to do with your giving up the leases?"

"I read about them." He put on his documentary voice and demeanor. "The mature spadefoot toads dig deep underground at the end of the rainy season, conserving moisture and energy during the dry months. For nearly a year, even longer in droughts, they wait for the right conditions to arise. When they hear thunder and feel the earth vibrate, they become seriously aroused—"

"You're making that up," she accused.

"Only the aroused part." He continued the mock documentary. "Seriously hot to hop, they dig to the surface, knowing the rains have finally come. In small, still desert pools, they mate with exceptional efficiency and speed, since the little toadsters must reach adulthood and follow their parents' lead into the cool underground before the water pockets dry up and the sandstone cliffs roast them to a crisp."

"I knew that," she said. "I read about them, too."

He grinned. "I should have guessed." Again the documentary voice. "But there's a serpent in paradise. Machinery, such as big oil trucks, or even small ATVs, shakes the ground and simulates thunder. The toads dig out at the wrong time. They die instead of . . . well, instead of having a noisy, great time and producing lots of little toads."

"You couldn't let a disaster like that happen," Lauren concluded. "Thus, no drilling in the canyon. Thank goodness you have a conscience and an ecological sense of right."

"Yes. Besides, I'm planning to bring my woman back there year after year, maybe even when we're eighty-something. Good memories do good things. A person needs those renewable resources renewed once in a while."

"Must you always resort to innuendoes?" she asked primly.

He tickled her along her waist, along the top of the skirt she'd worn for the meeting. "You love it, darlin'. Admit you love it."

She laughed. "Okay, I love it."

He stopped walking, turning toward her as she turned toward him. She waited expectantly. He reached in his pocket and took out a ring, which he held on the open palm of his hand. "Want to see if this fits? It belonged to my mother, and I thought—"

"Oh, Gabe, your mother's ring?" He treasured the few yellowed photos he had of her, and Lauren knew the ring would mean much more. "I don't know what to say."

"You don't have to say anything, Laurie. Just put it on." He slipped it onto her ring finger. "You are going to marry me, aren't you?"

Lauren stared down at her hand, amazed that the ring seemed a perfect fit. "Of course," she said, as if she'd never doubted that he would ask. "But where will we live? What about—"

"I thought we'd start out here, if that's okay with you. Both of us have been tumbleweeds long enough. I have a hankering to put down roots, and I think you do, too. Here, we have a head start on growing some. If you don't mind my help, I'd like to work with you on your new organization. I came here hoping to do some good for San Rafael, and I wouldn't mind expanding on the means. I know once you set your mind to it, there'll be good done, or else."

"It won't be easy. Everyone will probably end up hating us," she warned.

"I enjoy a challenge as much as you do, sweetheart. We'll pull this town together all by ourselves, if we have to."

"What happened with the Great Basin investors? Won't they be angry about this deal you made? Not that I care about you being the rich, powerful oil baron, but—"

"Yeah, well, that's good, because I had to sell most of my shares of Randolph Drilling to pull this off. I bought out the Great Basin investors, so now it's my baby. I can run it my own way."

"But selling Randolph Drilling? That must have been a terrible sacrifice," she said, feeling for him, loving him for what he'd done. "Your first company, and I know you were proud of it."

"Not as much of a sacrifice as you'd think. I've realized since I've been here that I don't like administration. I don't like trying to run a company without touching a single piece of machinery, without even looking at the mud logs. That's how it was getting to be with Randolph Drilling. I'd rather work on a smaller scale, where I can be active in every aspect."

She nodded. "If you're happy with the decision, I can be happy. It's good for the canyon."

"Damn right," he said. "Good for us, too. I have some new ideas for finding and extracting oil efficiently, and I mean to put them to work. Hell, Laurie, I've always tried to be environmentally correct. I'll try harder with you helping me. You've lit a fire under my conscience, and I imagine you'll keep it burning."

"Guaranteed." She smiled. "But Gabe, I'm really obnoxious sometimes. And I take everything too seriously."

"Don't I know it. That's why you need me to tease you, Laurie. And I need you to tease. Plus, you'll keep me learning and thinking, just to stay even with you. I love you, darlin', and you love me."

She nodded, not at all surprised that he'd taken it upon himself to speak her mind. "For once, I have better sense than to argue."

"Good." He touched his forehead to hers. "Now that that's settled, what kind of wedding do you want?"

She laughed, because she had thought about it, as he'd probably guessed. "An outdoor ceremony on the canyon rim at sunrise. And could we plan it for the day you set Harriet free? After we've said our vows, I'd love to watch the eagle soar on the canyon breeze."

"Unusual way to set a wedding date, but what the hell." He couldn't wait. He couldn't imagine a more perfect choice. With luck, Harriet would be ready to fly in a week or two, which would give his dad plenty of time to come over from Florida.

They had stopped directly in front of the Mad House. Gabe heard scrabbling behind him and turned to see Bullwinkle and Buddy wiggling out from under the broad wooden porch.

Bullwinkle started his sniffing routine, taking liberties under Lauren's conservative pale green skirt that Gabe was longing to take himself.

Buddy pushed up the glasses that were sliding off his nose. "I could spread the word about your wedding," he offered.

"That'd be fine, Buddy." Gabe winked at Lauren as he reached for his wallet.

"I sure have a lot of expenses right now, Mr. Randolph. I have to pay for new glasses, since I broke 'em when I ran away." Buddy pointed to the cracked lens on his specs. "My dad's still pretty mad. And I need new bike tires. Could you spare two dollars this time?"

"On one condition. I want you to go tell Mrs. Marley about the wedding. Go right up, knock on her door, and tell her everything she wants to know." Gabe gave Buddy a ten-spot. The kid's eyeballs bugged so far out, they almost went through his glasses. He skipped and stumbled across the street, Bullwinkle jumping at his heels.

"Why tell Mrs. Marley?" Lauren asked.

Gabe leaned in close, nibbling her ear as he whispered, "Who else is going to inform the aliens?"

Lauren wanted to shout to the sagebrush and announce their love to outer space. Instead she laughed and kissed his mouth again, very, very slowly, savoring the moment. No holding back, not anymore. Their love was as big and beautiful as all of Red Rock Canyon.

A legacy as enduring as the stars.

Inside the darkened interior of the Mad House, Hannah was attempting to sidestep LaDell Purdy and his infernal poetry reading as she checked the doors and windows and locked up for the night.

" 'Shall I compare thee to a summer's day?' " the sheriff asked, for the umpteen millionth time.

"Not right now, LaDell. I'm busy. And the truth is, I'm getting real tired of sonnets."

"Is it the Shakespeare you don't like?" he asked. "Should I try Byron maybe, or Keats? The love doc says Keats is good."

"If you're wooing a woman, LaDell, you can't ask her what to do. You'll just have to figure it out for yourself." She pointed to the window. "Looks like *they've* sure as heck got it down."

Lauren and Gabe were standing in plain sight at the foot of the porch stairs, kissing as if their lips had been painted with superglue and they couldn't manage to break free.

"We'd better get those two hitched in a hurry, before my girl ruins her reputation entirely," Hannah said. "You can help plan the wedding supper, but no poetry, you hear? Not one word."

In a dark corner of the Mad House porch, Ezra sat in one of the rocking chairs, listening to the crickets, hearing the bat wings swoop, smelling the clean, clear night air. He'd heard Gabe's proposal, and a good bit of the smooching that followed. Ezra wouldn't miss Gabe and Lauren's wedding. If he could get his old legs going, he might even dance with the bride.

"Or maybe I'll just listen, Chloe, honey. I'll listen and re- member how it feels." He patted his vest pocket, where his locket was stored, right over his own still-boomping heart.

ONYX

Mary Jane Meier

"[A] heartwarming story of second
chances and the healing power of love."
—Barbara Freethy

CATCH A
DREAM

When rancher Zack Burkhart finds Meg Delaney
stranded alone in Yellowstone, he offers her a
place to stay. After being dumped by her
ex-fiance, Zack's Idaho ranch seems like a
blessing—and the tall quiet rancher with tough
hands and a soft touch makes Meg's heart sing.

Common sense tells her to return to Chicago
and leave Zack to her fantasies.

But sometimes you have to throw your heart on
a line—to catch a dream...

❏ 0-451-40975-2

To order call: 1-800-788-6262